ON A PALE HORSE

Book One

INCARNATIONS OF IMMORTALITY

On a Pale Horse

PIERS ANTHONY

A DEL REY BOOK
BALLANTINE BOOKS • NEW YORK

A Del Rey Book
Published by Ballantine Books

Manufactured in the United States of America

First Edition: October 1983

Library of Congress Cataloging in Publication Data

Anthony, Piers.
  On a pale horse.

  (Incarnations of immortality; bk. 1)
  "A Del Rey book."
    I. Title.   II. Series: Anthony, Piers.
Incarnations of immortality; bk. 1.
PS3551.N73O5   1983   813'.54   83-6043
ISBN 0-345-30924-3

10 9 8 7 6 5 4 3 2 1

CONTENTS

-1-

TO BUY A STONE

"Death," the proprietor said clearly, showing the stone. It was a bright red ruby, multifaceted, set in a plain gold ring. It was a full carat— large for this quality.

Zane shook his head, experiencing a chill. "I don't want that one!"

The man smiled, an obviously perfunctory and practiced expression reserved for wavering marks. He was well dressed, but somewhat sallow, in the manner of those who remained in the shade too long. "You misunderstand, sir. This fine gem does not bring you death. It does the opposite."

Zane was hardly reassured. "Then why call it—?"

"The Deathstone." Again that annoyingly patronizing shaping of the face, as the proprietor eased the ignorant concern of the balky customer. "It merely advises the wearer of the proximity of termination, by darkening. The speed and intensity of the change notifies you of the potential circumstance of your demise—in plenty of time for you to avoid it."

"But isn't that paradox?" Zane had seen such stones advertised, usually at prohibitive prices, but discounted the claims as marketing hyperbole. "A prophecy isn't valid, if—"

"No paradox," the proprietor said with professional certainty. "Merely adequate warning. You could hardly obtain a better service, sir. After all, what is more precious than life?"

"That presumes a person's life is worth living," Zane said sourly. He was a young man of no particular stature or distinction of feature, with acne scars that neither medication nor spot-spell had been able to eradicate entirely. His hair was dishwater brown and somewhat unkempt, and his teeth were unfashionably irregular. He was obviously a depressive type. "So it darkens, and you change your course, and you don't die. You figure the warning saved you. But it could be a random turning of the stone. Color-spells are a dime a dozen. No way to prove the prophecy was valid. On the other hand, if it fails to darken, and you die, how can you complain? You'll be *dead!*" He scratched distractedly at a scar. "If it's wrong, how do you get a refund?"

"You don't believe?" the proprietor asked, frowning expertly. Apart from his complexion, he was a moderately handsome man of early middle age whose hair was enchanted to carry a permanent chestnut wave. "I run a respectable shop. I assure you, all my spellstones are genuine."

"According to the Apocalypse, Death rides a pale horse," Zane said, warming to his melancholy. He evidently had some education in this area. "I question whether an inanimate object, a chunk of colored corundum, can stay that dread horseman so simply. Given the uncertainties of the situation, such a stone is of no practical use to the owner. He can only test it by seeing it turn, then refusing to change his course. If it is a valid prophecy, he is doomed. If it is not, he has been cheated. It's a no-win game. I have played enough of that type."

"I will provide you a demonstration," the proprietor said, perceiving a morbid streak that could make this customer vulnerable to an aggressive and properly slanted sales pitch. "Skepticism is healthy, sir, and you are obviously too intelligent to be deceived by defective merchandise. The value of the stone can be proved."

Zane shrugged, affecting indifference. "A free demonstration? Can it be worth more than I pay for it?"

The proprietor smiled more genuinely, knowing that his fish, despite evasive maneuverings, was halfway hooked. Truly disinterested persons did not linger to argue cases. He took the stone from the magically theftproofed glass display case and proffered it.

Zane smiled quirkily and accepted the ring, putting it on the tip of his thumb. "Unless there's some immediate and obvious threat for the stone to point out—"

Then he was silent, for already the ring was turning. The bright red deepened to dark red, and then to opaque.

Zane's mind began to numb around the edges. Death—he had a deep guilt there. He looked at his left arm, feeling a spot of blood burning into the skin. He pictured the face of his mother as she died. How could he ever exonerate that memory?

"Death—within hours, suddenly!" the proprietor said, aghast. "The stone is absolutely black! I've never seen it turn so fast!"

Zane shook off his private specter. No, he could not afford to believe in this! "If I am to die within hours, I'll have no need of this stone."

"Buy you *do* need it, sir!" the proprietor insisted. "With the Deathstone you can change your fate. Hold it and decide on a new course, and if the color returns, you know it's right. You can save your life! But you have to have this fine magical ruby to guide you. To steer you away from death. Otherwise you will surely perish before the day is out. That warning is emphatic!"

Zane hesitated. The Deathstone was an impressive item now. It had, as it were, not minced words. But he had been thinking about death while holding the stone, and that could have made the color turn. Emotion-indicator spells were simple and cheap, hardly deserving the name of magic. There could be many things like that to give false readings. Still—

"How much?" he asked.

"How much is life worth?" the proprietor asked in return, with a certain predatory gleam in his eyes.

"About two cents, if this stone is right," Zane said grimly. Yet his heart was beating with nervous power.

"Two cents—per minute," the proprietor said, going into the closing spiel. "But this phenomenal and beautiful stone is available presently at a discount of fifty percent. I will sell it to you for a mere one cent per minute, including principal, interest, servicing, insurance—"

"How much per month?" Zane demanded, seeing himself getting reeled in.

The proprietor brought out a pocket calculator and punched buttons dexterously. "Four hundred and thirty-two dollars."

Zane stiffened. He had anticipated a high price, but this was impossible. A family could buy a good house for a similar figure! "How long?"

"Only fifteen years or less."

"Or less?"

"In case the gem should miscarry, the insurance will pay off the balance owing, of course."

"Of course," Zane agreed with a wry quirk of his mouth. A miscarriage meant death, which meant a bum enchantment. They planned to collect their money regardless of the effectiveness of the Deathstone in protecting its owner. He performed a quick mental calculation and concluded he was being charged a little over seventy-five thousand in total. About two-thirds of that would be interest and other peripherals; still, it was a lot of money. A great lot! More, probably, than his life was worth. Literally.

He handed back the ruby. Its color returned rapidly as the proprietor took it. In moments its special, deep shade of red glowed beautifully in the lighting of the shop. A ruby was indeed a lovely gemstone, even when it wasn't magic.

"What else?" Zane asked. He was shaken, but still wanted to find something that would help him.

"Love," the proprietor said immediately, bringing out a cloudy blue sapphire mounted on another gold ring.

Zane looked at the stone. "Love, as in romance? A woman? Marriage?"

"Or whatever." The proprietor's smile was not quite as warm as it had been, perhaps because of the misstep on the prior stone. He did not enjoy seeing fish slip the hook. This gem was probably less expensive, meaning a smaller profit. "This fine stone brightens at the prospect of romance of any kind. Sapphire, as you know, is chemically the same stone as ruby; both are corundum, but because the colors of sapphire are not as rare as those of ruby, the value is less. This is therefore a bargain. It will tune in to your romance; all you have to do is follow its signal until you score."

Zane remained skeptical. "You can't find romance by zeroing in as if it's a target! There are social aspects, complex nuances of compatibility—"

"The Lovestone takes account of all that, sir. It orients on the right one, taking all factors into consideration. Left to your own devices, you are very likely to make a mistake, and suffer an unfortunate liaison, perhaps one that will become a grief to you. With this stone, that will never happen."

"But there could be many excellent combinations," Zane protested. "Many right women. How can a mere gem select among them?"

"Circumstances alter cases, sir. Some women are ideal for any man, with qualities of beauty, talent, and loyalty that make them highly desirable regardless of the variations in the males. But most of them are already married, as these qualities are readily preceived by the boy next door, lucky fellow. Others may be destined for some devaluing development, like a disfiguring illness or serious problems among their relatives. The Lovestone knows; it orients on the most suitable, most reliable, most available individual. It is unerring. Simply turn it to obtain the brightest glow and follow where it leads. You will not be disappointed." He held forth the blue sapphire. "One demonstration trial, sir."

"I don't know. If it's like the last one—"

"This is romance! How can you lose?"

Zane sighed and took the stone. It was certainly pretty and twice the size of the Deathstone, and its theoretical power intrigued him strongly. A really good romance—what more could a man ask for?

As the ring touched his hand, the stone brightened, turning a lighter blue, becoming translucent. Again his mind faded to memory. Love— it was a second leg of his guilt. There had been a woman, nice enough, pretty enough, and she had wanted to marry him. But she had lacked the one thing he had to have. He had liked her, perhaps loved her, and she had certainly loved him—too much.

On A Pale Horse

"The perfect romance—within the hour!" the proprietor exclaimed, seeming genuinely amazed. His voice snapped Zane out of his reverie. "You are a remarkably fortunate man, sir! I have never seen the Lovestone so bright! So clearly directional!"

The perfect romance. He had, really, had that before. How could the stone know his particular needs? He returned it to the proprietor. "I can't afford it."

"You can't afford love within the hour?" the man affected astonishment.

"Romance won't pay my rent."

The proprietor nodded with sudden understanding. Something unscrupulous passed fleetingly through his expression. "So it is finance you lack!"

Zane took a deep breath. "Yes. I suppose I've been wasting my time here—and yours." He turned to go.

The proprietor grabbed his arm, in his eagerness forgetting his savoir-faire. "Wait, sir! I do have a stone for you!"

"How can I pay for it?" Zane demanded sourly.

"You can pay for it, sir!"

Zane shrugged him off. "You know why the Deathstone turned black for me? Because I'll soon starve to death! I have no money. I don't know why I came in here; it was a completely irrational act. I can't afford the least of your magic gems. I apologize for deceiving you."

"On the contrary, sir! I have a Salestone set above my door; it glowed when you entered. You will purchase something here!" He snatched a stone from the display. "This is the one you want."

"Don't you understand? I'm broke!"

"This is a Wealthstone!"

Zane paused. "A what?"

The proprietor held it out. "It brings money! Try it!"

"But—" Zane's protest was cut off by the thrust of the stone into his hand. This one was not set into a ring. It was an enormous star sapphire, well over a hundred carats, but of very poor quality. The color varied from cloudy gray to muddy brown, and there were concentric rings crossing the material and several black inclusions or imperfections. But the star was impressive; its six rays reached right around the polished hemisphere, and their intersection floated just above the surface. Zane blinked, but the effect remained; the star was not *in*, but *above* the stone. There was magic here, certainly!

"Not pretty, I admit, but my stones aren't marketed primarily for their appearance," the proprietor said. "They are valued for their magic. This is as potent a spellstone as the others, but of a different nature. This is the one you want. It is virtually priceless."

"I keep trying to tell you! I can't—"

"Priceless, I said. You can not purchase this jewel for money."

—5—

"Not if it generates wealth!" Zane agreed, intrigued.

"That's right, sir. It produces wealth—all you'll ever need. Potentially thousands of dollars at a time."

"But this is paradox again! How can you afford to sell such a stone? You should keep it for yourself!"

The proprietor frowned. "I confess the temptation. But there would be a prohibitive penalty. If I were to use any of these fine spellstones myself, none of the other stones would work for me. Not reliably. Their enchantments tend to cancel one another out. So I use very little of the magic, apart from the Salestone, which actually facilitates business. I earn my living on commissions, using no other magic gems myself."

Zane considered. The man could be concealing the fact that his stones were enchanted by black magic, helping to damn the person who used them. Drug dealers often did not use the drugs themselves, lest they be destroyed by their own product, and black magic was more insidious than drugs. Still, it was an answer. There were sellers, and there were users. "Then, what price?"

"Note the clarity of the star," the proprietor said. "When you invoke the magic, the star floats right off the stone and does not return until the spell is complete. That way you know exactly when it is operating."

This person was being evasive. "Assuming that it works," Zane said.

"A demonstration!" the proprietor said, sensing a sale that would hold. "Gaze on the Wealthstone and concentrate on money. That is all it takes to invoke it."

Zane held the stone and looked and concentrated. In a moment the star floated right off the stone, its rays dangling like legs, and cruised slowly through the air. It was working!

Then Zane's awareness faded to a dismal memory—the gaming table, compulsive gambling, the losses mounting—he had been such a fool with money! No wonder he was broke! If only it had stopped there . . .

The star dropped low, going toward Zane's foot. He stepped back, but it followed as if pursuing him. "Watch wherever it leads," the proprietor said.

"Suppose it leads me to someone else's wallet? To a bank vault?"

"No, it only discovers legitimate, available wealth. Never anything illegal. That's part of the spell. There are laws about enchantment, after all. The Federal Bureau of Enchantment investigates complaints about abuse."

"Complaints about the practice of black magic?" Zane asked alertly.

The proprietor affected shock. "Sir, I would not handle black magic! All my spells are genuine white magic."

"Black magic knows no law except its own," Zane muttered.

"White magic!" the proprietor insisted. "My wares are certified genuine white."

But such certificates, Zane knew, were only as good as the person who made them. White magic was always honest, for it stemmed from God, but black magic often masqueraded as white. Naturally Satan, the Father of Lies, sought to deceive people about his wares. It was hard for an amateur to distinguish reliably between magics. Of course, he could have this stone separately appraised, and the appraisal would include a determination of its magical status—but that would be expensive, and he would have to buy it first. If the verdict turned out negative, he would still be stuck.

The star hovered at Zane's shoe. "Lift your foot, sir," the proprietor suggested. Zane raised his foot, and the star slipped under like a scurrying insect.

Surprised, Zane angled his foot so he could see the worn sole. There was a penny stuck to it. The star had settled on this, clasping it.

Zane pried the penny off. Immediately the star returned to the big sapphire.

The spell had worked. The star had led him to money no one had known about. Not a lot of it, but of course there would not be much loose change in a shop like this. It was the principle that counted, not the particular amount.

The horizons opened out before him. A Wealthstone—what would that do for his situation? Money coming in, abating his debts, making him comfortable, and maybe more than comfortable. It could save him from starvation and bring romance, for that was easy for a rich man to come by. To be free at last of the burden of poverty!

"How much?" he asked, afraid of the answer. "I know the price isn't money."

The proprietor smiled, at last assured of his sale. "No, not money, of course. Something of equivalent value."

Zane had a suspicion he wouldn't like this. But he did want the Wealthstone. The prospects were dazzling! He hardly cared that it might be an illicit black-magic item. Who else would know? "What equivalent value?"

"Romance."

"What?"

The man licked his lips, showing an unprofessional nervousness. "The Lovestone showed you have romance commencing within the hour."

"But I'm not buying the Lovestone. I won't be zeroing in on that romance."

"But someone else could."

Zane looked at him tolerantly, recognizing the man's lust for an ideal woman. "You own the stone. You could do it. You don't need anything from me."

"I do need you," the proprietor explained, speaking rapidly. "I told you I don't use the stones myself. It would ruin my business if I did. But even if I did—in my own near future there is no romance. I am well established in my profession and I have a long life ahead, but my social life is strictly indifferent. I would give a great deal to have a meaningful relationship with a good woman. One who was not a gold digger or desperate. One I could trust. A woman such as the one you are fated to encounter—*were* fated, had you purchased the Lovestone and used it properly."

"You claim you have not used the gems yourself?" Zane asked skeptically. "You seem to know a lot about your own future."

"There are other avenues of information besides my gems," the proprietor said, a trifle stiffly. "I have had horoscopes and divinations and readings of many types. All show I am destined for success in business, not in love."

"Then how can my romance do you any good? You already know you can't have it."

"On the contrary! I can't have *my* romance, but I can have *yours*—if you permit it. In that manner I can bypass this one aspect of my fate. The woman is destined for you, but would settle for me. I can tell by the way the stone reacted for you that she would do for any number of men, of whom I am one. Her appeal is very broad. It would not be as good for me as for you, since I am not reduced to your straits, but it remains highly worthwhile. Even a match not quite made in Heaven can be excellent."

"It's your stone," Zane said stubbornly. "You can zero in on her yourself. So maybe that will ruin the rest of your business; if you want romance that badly, it should be worth it to you." He was uncomfortable, suspecting that he was losing out on something important. Perhaps he should change his mind about trying to buy the Lovestone. If what awaited him was that good . . .

Of course, that was what the proprietor wanted him to think, so he would be compelled to make the purchase of the expensive stone and sign himself and maybe his future wife into debt for the rest of his life. Realizing that, he resisted the devious sales pitch, overtly playing along with the proprietor's supposed need for romance. Zane did have a certain affinity for intellectual games; he was much more of a thinker than an actor. He had had a decent education, before things soured, and enjoyed art and poetry. However, he had largely wasted his education, and his thoughts seemed generally to get him into trouble.

"My stone, but your romance," the proprietor said with every evidence of sincerity. "Even if I were willing to sacrifice my business for romance, which I am not, I could not use this stone to tune in on an encounter fated for you. It simply would not register for me. The set lines of fate are not readily reconnected. So I would hurt my business for nothing. Literally nothing."

"That is unfortunate," Zane replied noncommittally. His sympathy for those who had money and wanted romance as well was slight. Everybody wanted both, of course!

"But *you* could orient on it, using this stone. Once it is evident who the woman is—"

"But I can't afford the Lovestone!" Zane was not going to be trapped into any such commitment!

"You misunderstand, sir. You will not purchase the stone. You will use it only to point out the woman. Then I will proceed to the encounter. I will have your romance."

"Oh." Zane assimilated that. Could the man be serious, after all? He was inclined to play this out and discover the catch. "I suppose that would work. But why should I do any such great favor for you?"

"For the Wealthstone," the proprietor said, gently taking it from Zane's hand.

Now at last Zane understood. He had been sidetracking himself, misunderstanding the thrust of the sales pitch. "You will sell me this money-gem—for an experience! I want wealth, you want romance. I can see that it would be a fair exchange—" He paused, as a piece of the puzzle failed to mesh. "But will the Lovestone work that well for me, if I don't actually own it?"

"It works for the holder. It knows nothing of ownership; that is a convention among people. In any event, none of this can have legal binding. But I assure you, I will give you a bill of sale for the Wealthstone, if you turn over the potential experience. This is not something money can bring. It is an opportunity that may occur for me only once in this life." The man scribbled out a sales slip.

It seemed like a bargain to Zane, if everything were as represented. He could have the Wealthstone in trade for a romance he had already turned down. He had an impulsive—some would say volatile—nature. "Agreed."

In a moment the sale was signed—one Wealthstone for private consideration, delivery after receipt of that consideration. Zane pocketed the sales slip, then took the Lovestone, watched it glow within its blueness, and followed the brightest spot out of the shop and onto the street.

Zane stood for a moment, blinking his eyes in the dazzling sunlight. In a moment his vision adjusted, and he found himself focusing on the store's sign: MESS O' POTTAGE.

He rechecked the gem, turned it about until the glow was brightest, and walked north as indicated. The proprietor followed. But then the stone faded. Zane turned about, but the gem only glimmered. "I think the scent is cold."

The proprietor was unalarmed. "This is not a purely directional thing. It is situational. You have to do what you have to do to make the intersection. As you do, it guides you."

"But if it doesn't *tell* me what to do—"

"Start walking. Watch the stone for reaction. There are only so many options available." The man's voice was controlled, but there seemed to be a slight edge of concern. The whole deal would fall through, of course, if the woman could not be located.

Zane turned right and walked. He passed a penny arcade, where teenagers cranked old-fashioned movie-machines as they peered in the scopes, chuckling evilly. Zane judged from their reactions that it was no Dimwit Dick comic they were viewing. The arcade's name was TWO TO TWAIN, theoretically a pretension to literacy but actually a code name for earthy humor. There was a drawing of a little train puffing along, sending up cute balls of smoke, and Zane realized there was another pun in the title, when pronounced aloud.

"Try another direction," the proprietor said. "The stone is not responding." Yes, he was nervous now.

Zane reversed again, retracing his steps. He passed the Mess o' Pottage shop and the one beyond: a paperback bookstore. "It's still not glowing," he reported.

"Let me consider," the proprietor said, pausing in front of a display of SCIENTIFIC MAGIC texts. "Where were you going?"

"Nowhere but up and down this street," Zane said wryly. "Trying to get a glimmer from this inert stone of yours."

"That's the problem. You need to be going somewhere. Your romance is not in this street. She is wherever you intended to go when you first held the Lovestone."

"I was going home," Zane said, bemused. "I doubt romance awaits me there. I live alone in a slum."

"Then go home."

"With your precious stone?"

"Certainly—on loan. I'll be with you. We shall exchange the Wealthstone for the Lovestone when the contact is made."

Zane shrugged. "As you wish." He now doubted that anything would come of this, but his curiosity remained engaged, and of course he did want the Wealthstone. He reversed direction again and walked down the street toward the agency where he had left his rented carpet after flying up to this shopping mall, which was magically suspended high above Kilvarough.

The stone glowed.

So it was true! He was headed for romance!

On A Pale Horse

The proprietor lingered for a moment by the bookstore window, where he pretended to be interested in the current issue of the Satanistic journal BRIMSTONE QUARTERLY, then followed.

They passed the arcade again, where the kids were now playing sexy space-fiction records. Zane had once had an offer to do photography for the dust jacket illustration of such items, but had turned it down, though he needed the money. He simply had not wanted to prostitute what little genuine talent he had.

Now they moved by a sweet-smelling bakery shop. Sudden hunger caught Zane, for he had not eaten in some time. Being broke had that effect. He glanced in the window of the MELON PASTIES shop, noting its mascot of a voluptuous woman made of candy, with sugared melons in the appropriate place, covered by decorative pastry pasties. Displayed inside were doughnuts, cakes, eclairs, breads, cookies, pies, cream horns, Danish pastries, and pastry art: confections in the shapes and colors of leaves, flowers, human figures, cars, and ships. All of it looked and smelled more than good enough to eat.

"Keep moving," the proprietor murmured, coming up behind him.

Zane tore himself away from the window and its stomach-luring odors. Once he had the Wealthstone, he would return here and buy out the place and gorge himself sick as a dog!

Now a bank of fog rolled in. The mall was camouflaged as a cumulus cloud, anchored high above the city of Kilvarough. The fog generators were aimed outward, but playful breezes wafted some mist inward. It had a pleasant flower scent.

They reached the carpet agency, flying its carpet-shaped banner with the motto YOU ARE THERE NOW. Zane showed his round-trip ticket to the bored agent, and the man hauled down his carpet from a storage cubby. It was worn and faded, and dust squeezed out of its pores, but it was all he could afford. The Mess o' Pottage proprietor rented another carpet, a much larger, newer, brighter one, with comfortable anchored cushions. They carried the rolls to the exit bay, spread out the carpets, sat down on them cross-legged, fastened their seat belts, and gave the go-signals.

The carpets took off. The proprietor's moved smoothly, cushioned by air, but Zane's jerked a bit before getting into the hang of its propulsive spell. He hated that; suppose it pooped out in mid-air? He controlled its flight by minute shifts of his body; a tilt to right or left sent the carpet flying that way, while a lean forward or back sent it diving or ascending. Verbal commands caused it to change velocity, but he settled for the standard gear, afraid the spell would not be reliable if he pushed it. Anyway, there was other traffic, and it was easiest to keep the going pace.

Zane had always enjoyed carpeting, but could not afford to maintain his own carpet, or even to rent one often. It cost a lot to maintain a good carpet, and the expense-per-mile kept rising. Inflation affected everyone uncomfortably, as it was intended to; it was, of course, a work of Satan, who campaigned perpetually and often halfway successfully to make Hell seem better than Earth.

Sure enough, the thought brought the reality: a Satanic roadsign series, each sign staked to a small, stationary cloud: SEE THIS OUTFIT? DON'T YOU SCOFF! YOU KNOW WHERE SHE TAKES IT OFF! What followed was a life-size billboard painting of a truly statuesque young woman in the process of disrobing. In the corner were the two little red devil trademark figures, Dee & Dee, male and female, complete with cute miniature pitchforks. The male was peeking up under the model's skirt and remarking in small print, "You can't touch *that* in Heaven!" Then came the final sign, the signature, HELLFIRE, written in lifelike flames.

Zane shook his head. Satan had the most proficient publicity department extant, but only a fool would believe the advertising. Anyone who went to Hell would feel the flames for real, and the devils and pitchforks would not be cute. Yet the media campaign was so pervasive, intense, and clever—and appealed so aptly to man's baser instincts—that it was hard to keep the true nature of Hell in mind. Zane himself would have liked to see the remainder of the disrobing and knew it would never occur in pristine Heaven, where all thoughts were pure. Hell did have something going for it.

The carpets cleared the environs of the cloud-mall, following the buoyed channel that spiraled down toward Kilvarough. A number of other carpets were traveling the channel, as the day was getting late. Several helicopters were flying in their own channel to the side, and farther away a lucky person was riding a winged horse.

Well, when he had control of the Wealthstone, Zane might see about purchasing his own horse. He had ridden horses many times, but only the mundane kind that ran on land. He understood that the principle of riding was similar for the winged variety, except that there were additional commands to direct them in flight. But while a good landbound horse could be had for under a thousand dollars, and a sea-horse for perhaps five thousand, air-horses began at ten thousand and required special maintenance, since no ordinary paddock could hold them. In fact, they—

The carpet ahead of him faltered. At the same time, the Lovestone flashed brilliantly. Zane had to brake suddenly to prevent his carpet from rear-ending the one ahead. "Hey, what the—?" he grunted.

He saw that a young woman was riding the other carpet and he did not think much of female riders. They tended to change their minds without adequate warning, as in this case, and that was dangerous in mid-air.

The woman's carpet wrinkled, sagging under her weight. It began to drop. She screamed in terror. Suddenly Zane realized what was the matter: the spell had failed! It shouldn't have, as this was a truly elegant, expensive carpet, but quality control had been deteriorating everywhere recently.

His eye was momentarily distracted by the blue light before him. The Lovestone was shining like a miniature star.

"Mine!" the Pottage proprietor cried. His carpet launched forward as the girl's carpet collapsed. The man reached out and caught the girl neatly by her slender waist, wrestling her aboard his own vehicle.

Zane, half-stunned by the event, followed the other carpet. Now he saw how comely the girl was, with flowing fair hair and a remarkable figure. She could almost have posed for the Hellfire ad, except that there was no trace of salaciousness in her aspect. He saw how she clung to her rescuer, her maidenly bosom heaving as she sobbed with reaction. He saw how elegant her apparel was; she wore an expensive magic-mink coat, and a diamond necklace sparkled about her creamy neck.

And he saw how the Lovestone faded to dull-dark blue. That girl had been his prospective romance—and was no longer. He had traded her away for the Wealthstone.

The two carpets continued down the spiral channel to the carpetport in the center of the city. There Zane and the proprietor turned in their carpets, and faced each other. "Meet Angelica," the proprietor said proudly, showing off the lovely girl. Obviously their acquaintance had blossomed during the brief flight down. The man had saved her life, and she was the kind to be duly grateful. "She is the heiress to the Twinklestar fortune. She has invited me to her downtown penthouse for a snack of caviar and nectar. So we'd better exchange stones now and call it even." He held out the Wealthstone.

There was nothing Zane could do except trade stones. The deal had been honored. The Lovestone glowed brightly again as the other man took it; he had found his romance, outwitting fate. The Wealthstone, in contrast, was huge and dull and ugly, with the star hardly showing.

Zane could not repress the feeling that he had made a colossal error. He should have mortgaged his whole life to buy the Lovestone—for evidently this heiress-girl Angelica had the resources and willingness to pay off such a debt offhandedly, and was a very fine creature in her own right. Love *and* wealth: he could have had it all.

The girl was drawing with loving possessiveness on the proprietor's arm, and she was all soft and eager in her new emotion. "Must go," the Mess o' Pottage man said, delivering to Zane a kind of salute. Then they were gone, walking toward the chauffeured limousine that awaited them.

Zane stood watching the elegant contours of the girl's backside, experiencing an awful, helpless regret. What kind of fool had he been, to throw away romance untried? Somehow he knew he would never again have an opportunity like this. Such things occurred only once in a lifetime, if that often, and he had thrown his chance away. A kind of grief suffused him, like that for a cruelly dead lover.

Well, it was hardly the first time he had blundered disastrously! His soul was weighted with evil he should have avoided, and his life blighted with foolish error. At least he possessed the Wealthstone, and with proper management he would soon be a rich man, able to attract and hold whatever type of woman he craved, or to buy a compliant female android or a luscious magical nymph. He didn't need Angelica! He had to believe that, for it was his only present buffer against overwhelming despair.

Zane knew himself to be a headstrong young idiot with delusions of artistry and literacy, whose good impulses were too often mismanaged into liabilities. Thus he had lost his dear mother, and his loving girlfriend long ago, and had sunk himself in debt. Good intentions were not enough; they had to be rationally implemented.

He could not even afford the fare for the subway home. He had the penny from his shoe, but that was not enough. He had the Wealthstone, but he refused to use it here on the darkening street; some criminal would mug him for it. Zane stuck his hands deep in his pockets, clasping the stone out of sight, and walked toward the dingy quarter where his sleazy apartment lurked.

Walking was a good time for thinking; it took a person's mind off the drudgery of the feet. But Zane's thoughts were not uplifting. Here he was, in the ultimate age of magic and science, where jet planes vied with flying carpets, and he was traveling afoot, without the benefit of either.

Magic had always existed, of course, as had science, however limited the benefits of either might be for those who were broke. But it hadn't been until the time of Newton that the basic principles of the twin disciplines had been seriously explored. Newton had made great strides in formulating the fundamental laws of science in his early years, contributing more than perhaps any other man. In his later years he had performed similarly for magic.

But for reasons not clear to Zane—he had never been an apt scholar— greater progress had been made at first in science. Only recently had the enormous explosion in applied magic come. Of course, neither science nor magic had affected history much until the past century, as there had been a popular prejudice against both, but science had broken out first. Now, however, the rapidly increasing sophistication of magic had brought back supposedly extinct monsters of many types, especially dragons. Whether science or magic would win out in the end was anybody's guess.

A fine drizzle developed, perhaps condensation from the cloud-mall above: not enough moisture to clean air or street, just enough to turn the dust to grease and make his footing treacherous. Cars skidded through stoplights, narrowly avoiding collisions; probably only the mandatory anti-wreck charms saved their fenders from harm.

Now it was dusk. The street had gradually become deserted. No one walked through this section of town at this hour if he could avoid it. The buildings were old, and age had weathered them from their original technicolor to their present monochrome. This region had come to be known as Ghosttown, and at twilight sometimes the ghost appeared. But it was best not to look, because—

In fact, there she was now. Zane heard the wooden wheel of the wheelbarrow first, and stepped into a grimy doorway alcove so as not to disturb the apparition. A person could see the ghost, and even photograph her, but if the ghost saw the person—

Molly Malone came down the street, her wheelbarrow piled with shellfish. She was a sweet-faced young woman, pretty despite her ragged garments and heavy clogs. Women thought spiked heels and nylon stockings made their legs pretty, but legs like Molly's needed no such enhancements. "Cockles and mussels!" she cried sweetly. "Alive! Alive O!"

Zane smiled, his black mood lightening somewhat. The shellfish might be alive, but surely Molly was not. Her ghost had been conjured from Ireland a century ago to honor Kilvarough, though this city had no seacoast. It had been a publicity stunt that soon palled; ghosts were a dime a dozen. The city fathers had not then been aware of this ghost's special property. But the conjuration-spell had never been canceled, so Molly still wheeled her wheelbarrow through the streets of Kilvarough when conditions were right.

"This is a stickup," a gruff voice called.

Molly emitted a faint little shriek of surprise and dismay. "Do not molest me, kind sir," she said.

"Naw, I just want your wheelbarrow," the holdup man said. "It'll fetch a few dollars on the antique market. Enough to buy me a two-day happiness-spell." He used one boot to shove the wheelbarrow over, so that its shellfish fell into the grimy gutter.

"But, sir!" she protested. "Those cockles and mussels are my sole sustenance, and without my wheelbarrow to carry them, I will surely perish!" Molly's quaint Irish accent had faded during the past century as she picked up the contemporary idiom; but for her costume, one would hardly know her from a local lass.

"You've already perished, you stinking slut!" the man snapped, shoving her rudely out of his way.

This was too much for Zane. He had no special feelings about ghosts and he was slightly wary of this particular one, but he did not like to see any woman abused. He strode out of the alcove. "Leave Molly alone!" he cried.

The robber swung about, bringing his pistol to bear on Zane. Zane reacted automatically, striking at the gun. It was not that he was especially brave or skilled in combat, but that once he was caught in such a situation he knew he had little choice but to carry through with sufficient dispatch to extricate himself. His hotheadedness substituted nicely for courage.

One shot was fired, and Molly screamed. Then Zane got his hands on the weapon and wrenched it away from the robber.

"Pick up that wheelbarrow," Zane ordered, aiming the gun at the man. He marveled at himself, for this was not in character for him; he should now be feeling weak with reaction. Yet the outrage he felt at the man's attempted robbery of the city's mascot drove him on. "Load the shellfish back on it."

"What the hell—" the man said. But when he looked into Zane's crazy-wild face, he decided to get on with the job. Clumsily he packed the damp, sloppy creatures in their places.

"Now get out of here," Zane said.

The man started to protest. Zane's finger tightened on the trigger. The robber turned and shuffled away.

Only then did Zane notice that the man had been shot. Fresh blood stained his jacket. He would need medical attention soon, or he could bleed to death. But of course such a criminal would not seek that sort of help; it would attract the attention of the police. He would probably die, and Zane could not bring himself to feel much regret.

He jammed the gun into a pocket. He had never fired one of these things, but presumed it would not go off unless he pulled the trigger. Now he was suffering his letdown, for his violence came on him only in fits, and departed swiftly. "I'm sorry this happened," he told Molly. "This is a good city, but it has some bad apples."

"I know not how to reward you, sir," the ghost said gratefully. "You are so gallant."

"Me? No. I just got mad to see a woman mistreated, especially one as lovely and historical as you. If I'd thought about it, I probably wouldn't have gotten involved." But Zane suspected he had been motivated in part by his loss of his romance with Angelica. He had had to relate to a woman somehow, so he had done it.

"Perhaps if you should find my body appealing—" Molly said. She opened her motley jacket and took a deep breath. "I am a ghost, 'tis true, but I am reasonably solid when I go abroad at dusk."

Zane was amazed. She certainly had an appealing body! She had been young and full when she died, so had remained that way since. But the bitter and fresh memory of his never-acquired love balked him, and the suspicion that whatever had been decent in his action of dealing with the robber would be nullified if he accepted any such reward.

"Thank you, Molly, and I do find you appealing, but I would not care to impose on you in that way. Surely you have a home and husband to return to in your realm."

"No husband yet," she said sadly. "There are few good men in the neverland of—"

Then a car turned the corner. The bright headlights speared the length of the street—and the ghost vanished. Too much modern technology was hard on ghosts.

The car passed, splashing thin gook on Zane. Darkness closed again, but Molly Malone did not return. Ghosts were erratic, and the shock of the sudden light had probably disinclined her to risk this region again this night. Feeling let down, Zane resumed his walk home.

There was an eviction notice posted on his door. He had not paid his rent, and the landlord had taken action. This was not a lockout, as the landlord was actually a halfway decent specimen of his breed. Zane had twenty-four hours to get out.

Well, the Wealthstone would take care of that. It would soon generate enough money to catch up the rent, and then would proceed from there. He brought out the stone.

The star did not show up well in the artificial light, but he could make it out. "Find!" he directed the stone, focusing his mind on over-flowing coffers of golden coins.

The star detached itself and floated upward like the flowing ghost of an arachnid. It traveled to the dilapidated dresser against the wall and squeezed in behind it.

Zane took hold of the heavy piece of furniture and hauled it pro-testingly out from the wall. The star dropped down to the floor. Zane stretched one arm into the crevice between dresser and wall, reaching to the star—and his questing forefinger found a cold coin. He scooted it across the floor toward him, awkwardly.

It was a worn nickel. Good enough; the magic stone was performing as specified. The nickel happened to be closest, so was spotted first.

The star returned to the Wealthstone. "Find," Zane ordered it, en-visioning a bank vault bursting with silver.

The star lifted more slowly than before, as if tired from its prior effort. It floated in leisurely fashion across the room, then descended to a crack in the floor. There, embedded edgewise, was a dime. Zane used a kitchen knife to pry it out. The thing was caked with grime; it must have been there for years. The star hovered until he actually got the coin in his hand, then snapped back to its home-stone. That meant he couldn't afford to give up on the job; he could not invoke the Wealthstone again until he cleared its last entry. That would be an inconvenience if there happened to be a fabulous forgotten buried cache a few feet beyond a dozen minor coins, but he could live with it.

He tried again. "Find. Something better this time, like a gold doubloon or a fantastically rare and valuable coin. Enough of this nickel-and-dime stuff."

The star pulled itself slowly from the stone and drifted toward the door to the apartment. There was no doubt about it: the star lost energy with each use. Probably it needed a set time to recharge its magic, like several hours or a day. That, too, was inconvenient—but of course, all he needed was to find one real treasure. That would be worth a week of slow questing. Then the gem could have as long a rest as it needed.

The star drifted up against the door and hesitated. Zane opened the door and let it out. At least the six-legged light-bug didn't zoom away, out of sight; that could have made it useless, for it would be as lost as the coin it identified. But the spell did seem to be underpowered. He had now been at it twenty minutes, and had only fifteen cents to show for it. Plus the penny he had found at the shop. That would hardly make a dent in his overdue rent.

The star sank to the floor of the hall. There, embedded in the packed dirt, was a battered and weathered penny. Zane pried it up, and the star wended its way tiredly to the stone Zane carried. Some fortune!

Zane returned to his apartment and considered. The Wealthstone performed—but so far at strictly penny-ante level. At the present rate, he could labor all night for a mere dollar or two in change—and the star was obviously too tired to go the night.

The Wealthstone worked—but now he perceived certain inherent limits. It always went to the nearest unattached money, of whatever denomination, and the vast majority of lost money was of the picayune category. No doubt if there were a five-thousand-dollar gold piece near, the star would find it—but none was near, while there were endless pennies. People simply did not let a heavy gold piece fall into a crack and be lost, though they did let pennies go. So while it was true that the Wealthstone could find thousands of dollars, this was like the gold in sea water; it cost more in time and effort to recover that one part per million than it was worth.

Zane's eye traveled around the room. It was cluttered with his photographic equipment. He had artistic aspirations and the nefarious artistic temperament, but lacked the talent to make it as a painter or sculptor, so had gone into photography instead. He could appreciate art when he saw it, and the camera enabled him to capture the incidental art of the environment. The trouble was, there was not much in the city of Kilvarough that was worthwhile that hadn't already been photographed. Even the ghost Molly Malone had been pictured many times; it was not true that a ghost could not be photographed, and she loved to pose if she happened to perceive the camera. She could even be heard on occasion, singing her traditional song, especially the line, "Where the girls are so pretty." But she was not as popular a subject as she might have been, owing to her special property.

Zane had discovered a photographic variant, however, that had enabled him to eke out a living for a while. This was the Kirlian technique, magically augmented. But certain problems in the market had turned him off this, and recently his luck had expired. Without expensive new equipment, he was out of business. That was part of what had sent him aloft to the cloud-mall, using his last dollar to rent the flying carpet. One had to visit these floaters when they anchored near, because they were liable to drift away without notice if the local police got too snoopy.

Now he was hungry, without food in the apartment, and required to move out within a day. He had nowhere to go. He had to have money—and he greatly feared he couldn't get enough.

He tried the Wealthstone again. "Go!" he urged it. "Find me wealth beyond my fondest dreams!"

The star heaved itself up, faltered, and collapsed back onto the stone. It was too pooped to perform.

And what would it find if it did get moving? Probably more pennies. Zane faced the fact that he had thrown away the chance of a lifetime, for wonderful and rich romance, for this mess o' pottage. He had in fact been cheated, though the gem had not technically been misrepresented, so he had no recourse. The shop's proprietor had used him for his own profit, taking Zane's one chance away forever. After all, even without the Lovestone, he might have encountered Angelica...

Fool! Fool! he chided himself savagely.

He paced around the room, tasting ashes, seeking some way out of his situation. He found none. Once he had made his deep blunder of passing up the Lovestone, his ruinous course had been fixed. If only he hadn't been so set on wealth, to the exclusion of all else. But he had always been an impulsive, wrongheaded idiot, doing what he thought was right at the time and regretting it too late. His whole life had been grinding inexorably to this dead end; he saw that now. If he somehow found enough loose change to pay his back rent, he still would lack the resources to make a decent living and still would not have a lovely girl to love.

That was the crux of it! Angelica—slated for him, but squandered away. In retrospect he found himself scrambling into love with her, his emotion based on wrongheaded hopes and wishes—and knew she was the type who only loved once, and that her gift had been bestowed irrevocably on another man. Zane might live on, but he would never have Angelica, not even if the conniving shop proprietor were to drop dead this moment. So what point was there in going on?

He looked at the defunct stone again. Now it seemed drab indeed, its colors muddy, its imperfections gross. It was, he realized abruptly, as ugly as his conscience. It was virtually worthless—and so was he.

Zane slapped his open hand against his thigh as if trying to punish himself—and felt the pistol in his pocket, the one he had taken from the robber.

He drew it out. He was not conversant with firearms, but this one seemed simple enough. It had a clip of several bullets in the handle, and one of them had been fired from the chamber. An automatic mechanism had set a new bullet in the chamber; he had no doubt that a pull on the trigger would make the weapon fire again. He could put the muzzle to his head, and—

Now he remembered the first gem he had considered—the Deathstone. It had signaled his demise in a few hours. Those hours had passed. The Lovestone had proved itself, so he had no further reason to doubt the Deathstone. Even the Wealthstone worked, in its fashion. He was fated soon to depart this life.

Zane lifted the gun. Why not? His life might as well end efficiently, instead of being dragged out in the gutters of the city. Some considered a meeting with ghost Molly to be a signal of doom. Certainly it would have been, had he accepted her offer and made love to her. It was, of course, death to love the dead. Sweet Molly herself might not be aware of that, but she did want a husband, and if he had become a ghost in her arms . . .

The truth about Molly was that, while any person could see her with impunity, she herself could perceive only those who were approaching her condition. So if Molly saw a person, that person would soon be dead. She was not the cause, merely the signal. If a person was afraid he was destined to die soon, perhaps suffering from a mysterious illness, he could show himself to Molly and, if she passed him by without notice, he could relax. This aspect of her nature had somehow escaped Zane's consciousness at the time, but it was true. Probably he had censured it out emotionally. Yet of course the robber, who had certainly been seen by the ghost, had almost certainly taken a fatal wound.

Oh, yes, there had been omens enough! Why not accept his fate with greater grace than he had accepted his life and do it now, before his natural cowardice overcame him? Make it quick and clean . . . well, quick, anyway.

Overwhelmed by the rightness of it, Zane pointed the gun at his head. He oriented the muzzle on the cavity of his right ear, somehow diffident about spoiling his head by puncturing it in a messy place. Now was indeed the time!

As his finger tensed, somewhat reluctant to move rapidly, Zane saw the door to his apartment open. He froze in place, uncertain whether to pull the trigger now, before being interrupted, or to hope for some amazing reprieve. Could Angelica have changed her mind and sought him out? Foolish notion! Or was it merely his landlord?

On A Pale Horse

It was neither. The figure that appeared was garbed in nonreflective black, with a hood shrouding its head. It closed the door behind it silently, then turned to face Zane full on.

A bald, bony skull looked eyelessly at him.

This was Death, come to collect him.

Zane tried to cry out in pointless protest, but his throat locked. He tried to loosen his trigger finger, but it was already obeying the squeeze message and would accept no countermand. Time seemed to slow, and Zane could do nothing to abort the suicide he had set up. Yet the shock of seeing the visage of Death himself had abruptly banished any desire Zane had to kill himself.

His finger muscles would not obey him, but his larger arm muscles did. Zane wrenched the pistol around. The muzzle came to bear on Death's head as the trigger tripped. The gun seemed to explode, kicking back against his hand.

The bullet smashed into the center of Death's face.

A hole opened. Blood flowed. Death fell heavily to the floor.

Zane stood aghast. He had killed Death.

-2-

HOUSE CALLS

The door opened again. This time a woman of middle age entered. Zane had never seen her before. She glanced approvingly at the fallen figure. "Excellent," she murmured.

Zane wrenched his horrified gaze to her. "I killed Death!" he exclaimed.

"Indeed you did. You shall now assume his office."

"I—what?" Zane was having trouble regaining mental equilibrium.

"You are the new Death," she said patiently. "This is the way it is done. He who kills Death becomes Death."

"Punishment..." Zane said, trying to make sense of this.

"Not at all. This is not murder in the normal sense. After all, it was him or you. Self-defense. But you are committed to take his place and to do the best job you can."

"But I don't know how to—"

"You will learn on the job. We all do. Certain enchantments will imbue you, to facilitate your performance and stabilize you, but the real motivation must be yours." She stooped to strip Death's black cloak from his body. "Help me, please; we do not have excessive time and we don't want to get blood on the uniform."

"Who are you?" Zane demanded, getting half a grip on himself despite the overwhelming unreality of the scene.

"At the moment I am Lachesis. You can see I am of middle age without much sex appeal." She was quite correct; her face had the lines of solid maturity, and her hair was nondescript under a tight bun. She was comfortably overweight, but moved efficiently. "I determine the length of the threads. Now lift his body; I don't want to tear the cloak."

Distastefully, Zane put his hands on Death's corpse and lifted. "Who is Lachesis? What threads? What are you doing here?"

She sighed as she worked the cloak off the body. "I suppose you do deserve some minimal explanation. Very well; you keep working, and I will tell you some of what you need to know. Not all of it, for some secrets are reserved to me, just as some, you will discover, are reserved to you. Lachesis is the middle aspect of Fate. She—"

"Fate?"

"You will not learn very much if you insist on interrupting," she said with some asperity.

"Sorry," Zane mumbled. This felt unreal!

"Now get his shoes. They're invulnerable to heat, cold, penetration, radiation, et cetera, just as is the cloak. You must always be properly garbed when making a collection, or you become vulnerable. It is essential that you not be vulnerable. Your predecessor here was careless; had he closed his hood across his face, the bullet would not have harmed him. See that you are more careful; you will have greater need to be on guard than he did."

"But—"

"I believe that interjection constitutes an interruption."

Zane was silent. There was an eerie power about this woman that had nothing to do with her appearance. She could be the mother of any rebellious teenager.

"I am Fate, with three aspects," she continued after just enough of a pause to verify her command of the situation. "I determine the threads of the tapestry of life. I am here to ensure that you change roles expeditiously. It is very important that you perform better as Death than you have as a living person, and I believe you do have the potential. Now stand up so I can fit the cloak to you."

Zane stood, and she set the cloak on his shoulders. It was not heavy, but it carried a peculiar mass. She had spoken of magic; this item of apparel reeked of it. "Yes, it is close enough. Go ahead and don the shoes; and don't forget the gloves. The shoes will, among other things, enable you to walk on water. Your rounds must not be balked by mundane trifles."

"But this is preposterous!" Zane protested. "I was about to kill myself and now I'm a murderer!"

"Certainly. I had to measure your thread very carefully. Technically, your life just ended; see, Death's body will be taken for yours." She turned over the body, and Zane saw that it looked uncomfortably familiar. It now resembled his own—with a bullet hole in the face. "You will fill the office until you, too, grow careless and permit a client to turn on you."

"Or until I die of old age," Zane said, not really believing any of this.

"Old age will never come to you. Neither will death, if you perform well. If you ask the average person what he most desires, he will answer, 'Never to die.' That is, of course, an absolutely foolish wish; in due time you will be better able to appreciate the importance of dying. It is not the right to *live*, but the right to *die* that is most important."

"I don't see—"

"What is life, except an ongoing instinct for survival? Nature uses that instinct to make us perform; otherwise we would all relax, and the species would disappear. Nature is a cruel green mother. The survival instinct is a goad, not a privilege."

"But if I don't age—"

"Time holds all supernatural agents, especially the several Incarnations, in abeyance. You will live until you die, however many days, years, or centuries that may be, but you will never change from your present physical age." She guided him to his wall mirror.

"Supernatural agents?" Zane was grasping at peripherals, being as yet unable to get to the nucleus of this situation. "Incarnations?"

"Death, Time, Fate, War, Nature," she said. "The major field agents operating between God and Satan, answerable to neither. If any of us were scheduled to die like mortal folk, we would have to be concerned for the disposition of our souls, and that's a conflict of interest. No, we are immortal, as we have to be, accountable to neither superpower. But we do have to do our jobs, or things become complicated."

"Our jobs," Zane repeated weakly. "I'm no killer. At least I wasn't, until this—"

Fate glanced at him penetratingly, and suddenly he knew she knew about his mother. He felt cold, and the guilt rose up in him again. But Fate did not raise that matter. "Of course not," she agreed, eying the body on the floor. "This was a mismanaged suicide. Death does not kill; Death merely takes the souls of those who are dying, the problematical ones, lest they be lost and wander forever inchoate."

Now Zane found something concrete to argue. "There are five billion people in the world! A hundred million or so die each year. Death would have to take several each second, scattered across the globe. That's impossible!"

"Not impossible, but perhaps unfeasible," she said. "Look in the mirror, please."

Zane looked. The death's-head gaped back at him, encased in its hood. His hands in the gloves were skeletal, and his ankles above the shoes were fleshless bones. He had assumed the visage of Death.

"You are, of course, invisible to most people when in uniform," Fate said. "Clients can perceive you, and those who are close to them emotionally, and the truly religious people, but the rest will overlook you unless you call attention to yourself."

"But the mirror reflects my image—as that of Death! People will faint!"

"Perhaps I misspoke myself. You are not physically invisible; you are socially invisible. People see you, but do not recognize your significance, and forget you once you pass. But when you remove the uniform, your powers fade. You are then vulnerable; you can age and be touched and hurt. So don't step out of character without reason."

"Why would Death want to step out?"

She formed an obscure little smile. "It does get dull socializing with your own kind exclusively. I am said to be attractive in my Clotho aspect—" She became abruptly young and lovely, a striking figure of a woman with hair so light in color it seemed to shine and with skin like alabaster, but her eyes remained disturbingly knowing. "Yet I would not hold your interest for centuries, perhaps not even decades. So we must dally on occasion with mortals."

Zane wondered how many decades or centuries it would take to get bored with a woman who looked like that. It was an intriguing thought, but in a moment he returned to his prior concern. "How can a single Deathperson take several people each second? Hundreds of people must have died just while we've been talking here! I didn't collect their souls and I don't think this person did." He indicated the defunct Death.

"I see I will have to explain in greater detail." Fate shifted back to her middle-aged aspect and sat down in Zane's best chair. Her eye caught the Wealthstone on the table beside it. "Oh, I see you have a junkstone. You use it to produce dimes for telephones?"

"Something like that," Zane admitted sheepishly.

"I've seen them before. The stone is dirt-grade ruby from India, imported wholesale and sold in five-thousand carat lots for fifty cents a carat. It's technically corundum, but too poor a quality to hold a decent spell. I understand some idiots are deluded into paying gem-grade prices for individual stones."

"True," Zane agreed, drawing the Deathhood close about his face so his flush would not show.

"Still, as a cheap novelty item, it's not bad. Once in a while a stone like this will take a better spell and locate dollar bills. But it's axiomatic that such a rock will never produce the value paid for it."

Zane thought again, painfully, of the beautiful, rich, romantic Angelica. "True."

"Well, you won't need money now, unless you spend a lot of time out of uniform and get hungry. Better to acquire a small cornucopia and use it for such occasions. Your job should keep you too busy for that, until you develop proficiency."

"I still don't see how—"

"Oh, yes, I was about to explain. Only a small percentage of people need Death's personal attention. The vast majority handle the transition themselves—though, of course, this is via the extended ambience of Death's will."

"Death's will?"

"Oh, my, you *are* a novice! Let me see, I need an analogy. You know how your body goes on breathing when you're not paying attention, even when you're sleeping? It's a bit like that. Death's power is immediate and personal, but it is also distant and impersonal. When Death attends to a client personally, it is like consciously breathing; when Death merely permits a soul to depart its host unattended, that is like your autonomic system, the automatic functioning of your body. But when you die, these functions cease, both the conscious and the unconscious. When Death dies, all deaths in the world cease, until the new Death commences the office. The former Death, for example, is not really dead yet; his soul remains pinned in his body. He can not die until you act, though his body will never again be animate. That is why it is so important that the transition be facilitated. Imagine the havoc if no one ever died!"

"I don't know. If people lived forever—"

"I haven't time to argue foolishness!" she snapped. "Just be satisfied that the first soul you personally attend to will free all the rest to depart naturally, on their private schedules, as my threads have dictated. Up to half an hour can be tolerated; I have arranged for this. But beyond that, there will be one atrocious tangle."

"What souls do I—does Death have to attend to personally? I really don't understand—"

"It relates to the nature of souls and the balance within each soul of good and evil. Every good thought and deed lightens the burden, and every bad deed or thought weights it down. A newborn infant, generally, is about as close as we come to true innocence; only when self-discretion comes can evil be indulged in. As William Henley put it: *It matters not how strait the gate, How charged with punishments the scroll, I am the master of my fate; I am the captain of my soul.* So the younger the person is at death, the more likely his soul is to remain innocent, and to float to Heaven when released. As William Wordsworth put it: *Not in entire forgetfulness, And not in utter nakedness, But trailing clouds of glory do we come From God, who is our home: Heaven lies about us in our infancy!* With age and self-discretion, the evil tends to accumulate, weighting the soul, until the balance is negative. Such souls plummet like lead sinkers when released. But a few souls are in balance, with equal freighting of good and evil; these have no dominant affiliation and tend to cling to their familiar housing. These are the ones who need assistance."

"That's what Death does!" Zane exclaimed, catching on at last. "Collects ambiguous souls!"

"And sorts them out carefully, determining their proper destination," Fate concluded. "Those few that are in perfect balance must be delivered to Purgatory for professional treatment."

"This is really to be my job?" Zane asked. "To collect balanced souls?"

"And to facilitate the progress of all the others," Fate agreed. "It really is. You may find it difficult at first, but it is certainly better than the alternative." She glanced at the virtually dead Death.

Zane shuddered. "But why was I chosen to fill this office? I'm completely unqualified! Or is it pure chance?"

Fate stood. "I prefer to answer that at another time. I must not keep you from your appointed rounds any longer."

"But I don't even know how to locate my—my clients!"

"There should be an instruction manual somewhere. Mortis will help you."

"Who is Mortis?"

She looked about. "Oh, I almost forget. You had better take the accouterments; I'm not sure how they work, but you'll need them."

"Accouterments?"

"The jewelry. The magic devices."

"My Wealthstone? I don't see—"

"Not that junkstone. Leave everything of your former life here as it is. Especially the star. Sapphire is no good for wealth divination at its best, and this one's inferior. Leave your watch, too, and any rings you have. You are through with living." She walked toward the door.

"But I have so much to learn!" Zane cried plaintively.

"Then get *to* it, Death," she said, closing the door behind her.

Zane looked desperately about, seeking some better hold on reality. How could he be Death? He had never even imagined anything like this!

He saw something flashing. It was a solid watch on the wrist of the dead Death that would hardly be in keeping with the corpse of Zane, who had been too broke to redeem his pawned watch. This was surely an accouterment. He bent, with a certain distaste, to remove it, then put it on his own wrist. It was heavy, a good four ounces, but fitted comfortably, as though sized for him, and the flashing stopped. Evidently the watch had merely been calling attention to itself so that it would not be overlooked; it went with the office. It was, of course, dead black: a mechanical, self-winding instrument that seemed dull but expensive.

Why would Death use a mechanical watch, of whatever quality, instead of a sophisticated electronic one, or a miniature magical sundial? Zane couldn't answer that at the moment. Maybe the last Death officeholder had been of a conservative bent. He might have lived for centuries before getting careless and failed to keep up with the times.

Odd, Zane thought, that he felt no special remorse for the person he had killed. His initial shock at the act was wearing off, so that what remained was mostly horror that there had been a killing, as if he had just watched a singularly brutal murder on television. Maybe this developing indifference was because, to him, Death remained an "it" rather than a human being. But he, Zane, was now that "it."

He spied another flash. It was from an ear ornament, almost concealed because Death's left ear lay against the floor. Surely he was meant to take this, too; it was one of the items of jewelry Fate had mentioned. He nerved himself for another contact with the dead flesh and got the gem removed. It was an earring, with a red garnet cabochon, rounded on one side, flat on the other, shining prettily.

The thing was designed to fit a pierced ear, and Zane's ear was whole. He hesitated, then put the gem in his voluminous cloak pocket.

There were footfalls in the hall, followed by a tentative knock on the front door. "Mr. Z, are you all right?" a voice came. It was his elderly neighbor, a nosy woman, but nice enough.

Zane stood frozen again. What should he do? If he let her come in—

"Mr. Z!" the neighbor called more urgently.

"I'm all right!" he called back.

"Mr. Z," she repeated. "I heard what sounded like a gunshot from this room. Please answer me!"

"It's all right!" Zane shouted.

The door opened. The woman's head poked in. "Mr. Z, why don't you answer? I know you're home; I saw you come in. If there is anything wrong—if a mugger shot you—"

"I *am* home! There's no mugger!" Zane shouted. "Please get out!"

The woman came all the way into the apartment. "I'm sure I heard—" Then she spied the body on the floor. It now wore Zane's clothing, though he did not remember dressing it; probably Fate had done that while he was distracted by the enormity of his situation.

She screamed "Mr. Z! You're hurt!" She hurried to inspect the corpse, running right past Zane as if not seeing him. "In fact—you're dead!"

"So it seems," Zane said, somewhat wryly. Now the shock of what he had done was washing back across him, animated by the neighbor's reaction. He had set out to suicide—and instead had killed another man. He was a murderer! The immediately following events had been so surprising that much of the horror had passed him by. Now it was clarifying, and he was appalled. He had done many unfortunate things in his life, and today had been the worst, for never before had he killed another human being.

Well, technically he *had* killed. But that had been a special case, and his mother— He cut off that thought. He had guilt, and he was indeed somewhat hardened to the evils of the world. Still—

The neighbor woman turned. Now she saw him. "Oh, officer!" she said. "I'm so glad you're here. Mr. Z is dead! I fear it was suicide! I heard the shot, and he didn't answer—"

Why had she waited so long before investigating? He had fired the gun half an hour ago. It must have taken her that long to work up her curiosity sufficiently. "Yes, thank you," Zane said gravely. "I will take it from here."

"Oh, that's a relief!" The woman fluttered out.

Zane relaxed slightly. So it was true: he was mostly unrecognizable while in the Deathcape. The woman had seen him neither as himself nor as Death; she had taken him for a policeman, the kind of reassuring person she expected. Soon she would have the whole building informed.

He walked out himself, traveling along the narrow hall and down the stairs toward the waiting vehicle. As he did, he realized in a random revelation that the Deathstone in the Mess o' Pottage shop had been technically correct, but significantly wrong. It had signaled his encounter with Death, but had not advised him that he would in fact assume a new office and become immortal. That was the problem with omens; they suggested the fact without suggesting the implication.

He paused. *What* waiting vehicle? He had no car of his own, and no one had told him of one. Yet he had somehow assumed—what?

Well, how had Death traveled here? Did he flap his arms and fly through the air, or did he drive a car? Whatever it was, that was what Zane had to do.

He stepped outside, peering about, letting his eyes adjust to the night. There was a vehicle: a pale limousine, parked sedately in the landlord's parking space. The landlord would have had the intruding car towed away—but the man was coincidentally absent. Probably coincidence favored the operations of the—what had Fate called them?—the Incarnations. After all, how could Death handle his rounds if his car kept getting towed away by irate mortals?

Zane thought it was the Deathcar, because its parking lights were blinking at him. The things of Death made sure Death did not neglect them. Zane would have been pleased, if the whole thing were not so grim.

He walked up to it and around the rear. The license plate said MORTIS. That explained Fate's reference to the name; he had somehow thought she referred to a person, but obviously it was the machine. There was a bumper sticker: DEATH IS NATURE'S WAY OF TELLING YOU TO SLOW DOWN. Just so. He opened the door and climbed onto the plush driver's seat.

This was as elegant and comfortable an automobile as he had ever encountered. Somber quality emanated from every part of it. The upholstery was genuine alligator leather and the metalwork was solid chrome. It was probably worth thirty-five thousand dollars in stock condition before the expensive options were added. He wasn't sure he dared try to drive it.

His watch flashed, calling attention to itself. It was mechanical, but it had a magic way about it. The glowing hands indicated 8:05 P.M.,

On A Pale Horse

the correct time of day. But the red sweep hand was moving. It hadn't been before; the seconds were marked by a miniature inset dial on the left, opposite the day-date windows on the right. This little hand was still moving, so he knew that function had not been usurped by the sweep. What was the red hand doing?

As he watched, the sweep passed the noon spot—and the hand in the little thirty-minute dial just below it clicked back from 9 to 8. The stopwatch function was operating—and now he realized it was running backward. The sweep hand was moving counterclockwise. What kind of stopwatch was that?

A countdown timer, he realized. This watch was telling him he had less than eight minutes to do something, or to get somewhere. But what, or where?

A cold shiver crawled down his back. He was Death, or some poor facsimile thereof. He had to go and collect his first soul!

Zane rebelled. He had not sought this office! Only the purest co-incidence had brought him to this incredible pass.

Coincidence? He had touched on that before. If the woman who had explained things really had been Fate, then she must have measured the thread of his life; she had guided him to his damnable destiny. She had put him here deliberately. In so doing she had in effect killed his predecessor. Why had she done that?

The watch was blinking insistently. He now had six minutes. He wasn't sure what would happen if he missed whatever appointment he had, but knew already that these supernatural entities played hardball politics. Maybe his predecessor had balked, and so Fate had arranged to eliminate him. Certainly she had evinced no grief at his demise. If Zane balked, she could do the same to him. He wasn't sure how he felt about this office, but knew he wasn't ready for that. So he had better get on with the job, trying to buy time to figure out his real feelings about it, and to ascertain what his real options might be.

Where was the instruction manual Fate had mentioned? He didn't see it, and didn't have time to look for it. The thing could have been lost a century ago by his predecessor.

Zane put his hands on the steering wheel of the car named Mortis and touched his right foot to the accelerator. Where was the ignition key? He had none. Maybe it was back on the body of the former Death.

Zane shuddered. He had been propelled into this misadventure, but he didn't want to go back to its starting point! He checked the panel, hoping for an alternative. After all, many vehicles operated by magic in minor ways, just as many magic things had mechanical controls. A simple touch switch was marked ON/OFF. He flicked it to ON—and the car came to life. The front panel lighted, the radio came on, and the seat harness clasped him protectively. The motor thrummed with muted power. Oh, yes, this was some car!

Well, so be it. Zane found the reverse control and started backing the car out. It handled like a dream device, amazingly smooth and responsive. Death had lived no Spartan existence!

A warning bleeper sounded, and the rearview mirror flashed: the way was not clear. But in a moment it was, as a stray auto passed, and he was able to back onto the street.

The Deathmobile continued to move smoothly, responding so instantly and accurately to his smallest guidance that it almost seemed alive. Zane was no automotive expert, but suspected this was one of the finest machines of its breed. It was not magic, basically, but was as apt an instrument of transport as anything magical could be. Oh, yes, Death possessed the best!

Yet Death, for all his perquisites, was dead. This was the somber reality behind the seeming affluence. Death's killer had inherited the estate.

He shifted to DRIVE and moved carefully forward, getting the feel of this wonderful thing. It was easy to merge with the traffic. The windows and mirrors provided excellent visibility all around, and the wheels seemed almost to steer themselves. Maybe there were crash guards, magnetically distancing the car from other vehicles. Certainly the driving seemed better than Zane's own, since poverty had kept him out of cars for some years.

The Deathwatch now indicated four minutes. Where was he going?

Zane concentrated on the passing geography and realized he was headed west. But this did not necessarily bear any relation to the direction in which he should go to make his appointment. How did Death home in on his victims?

Victims? He did not like that term! Fate had used the word "client," as he recalled; that was better.

By whatever term, there had to be a way. Zane felt about his cloak and found an inner pocket with an object inside. He drew this out and glanced at it while driving.

It was a bracelet, with the band broken. That explained why the former Death had not been wearing it. Death had grown careless about a number of details, it seemed! But what did this item signify?

There were three prominent jewels set in the bracelet. One was an orange-yellow cat's eye, the eye stretching across half the polished surface. It seemed almost alive, looking at him. The middle one was a pink stone with a line across it, the line capped by a kind of arrowhead image at one end. The third was a greenish gridstone, probably rutilated quartz, pretty in its fashion, with two imperfections on its surface. One marking was light, the other dark. There was also a light tracery of curved lines marring the otherwise straight-line pattern.

Zane couldn't make much sense of this. The watch now showed only two minutes remaining. He had to figure things out in a hurry!

He turned a corner—and as he did so, he saw that the pink stone changed. Its arrow swung around to point in a new direction. No—the car had swung about; the arrow pointed the same way it had before, northwest.

Zane goosed the accelerator and cut into the fast lane. A driver honked in protest, but gave him room. He turned another corner, now going east—and the arrow swung again. It was definitely pointing somewhere.

He turned north, then east, orienting as well as he could on the direction shown. The arrow remained true to its heading—but now the cat's eye was changing, growing larger on its stone. That must mean he was getting closer. It was a perspective-stone, telling him when he got near his destination.

But the cat's eye was expanding very slowly; if its rate was linear, he would never get to his appointment on time. Somehow it seemed very important that he do so. Was lateness as bad as an outright balk?

Zane turned another corner—and noticed that the green gridstone brightened as he did so. What did that mean?

He turned again—and saw that a button on the car's dash glowed in concert with the flash of the green grid.

Experimentally, he turned again, ignoring the chorus of protests by other cars to his erratic behavior, and touched the button with his forefinger, just as it flashed.

The car wrenched. The outlines of the city blurred. Zane felt as if he were in a space shuttle, zooming at supersonic velocity across the terrain of the world. Then, as abruptly as it had started, the blurring stopped.

Zane looked around, startled. He knew immediately that he was in a different city. He guessed it was one a significant distance northwest of Kilvarough—perhaps all the way across the continent. Maybe even the great port city of Anchorage.

But he had no time to be concerned about that. The cat's eye had grown abruptly and significantly larger, the two dots on the gridstone had merged, and his watch was down to a single minute. He was very close to his object.

With this assurance, Zane proceeded with greater confidence. He was beginning to get the hang of the use of Death's instruments. He now understood that the eye grew until it covered the stone, and that would be when he arrived. When the direction arrow started shifting, though he was driving in a straight line, Zane knew he was there. Just in time, too; his watch's red hand showed only thirty seconds and counting.

The eye was maximal, and the arrow spun in a full circle. He had to be right at the scene—but there was nothing here. He was passing through an ordinary intersection. Was this a false alarm?

On A Pale Horse

He slowed and drew to the side of the street, perplexed. He had thought he had it, and now it seemed he did not. The arrow steadied, pointing back the way he had come. Pointing at nothing.

The sweep hand on the Deathwatch closed on noon.

There was a crash in the intersection. A small truck had made a preemptive left turn into the right-of-way of a tiny Japanese subcompact, and the two had collided violently.

Zane turned off his motor and got out of the Deathmobile, not caring whether it was legally parked. He hurried to the scene of the accident.

The man in the truck was half-stunned. The woman in the little car had an enormous sliver of supposedly unbreakable glass through her neck. Blood was gushing out of her, flooding the dashboard, but she was not dead.

Zane hesitated, appalled. He saw no way to save the woman—but what was he to do? Cars were screeching to halts, carpets were landing, and people were converging.

The woman's glazing eyes clarified, momentarily. She saw Zane. Her pupils contracted to pinpoints. She tried to scream, but the blood cut off her breath, keeping her silent.

Someone nudged Zane's elbow. He jumped. Fate stood beside him. "Don't torture her, Death," Fate said. "Finish it."

"But she isn't dead!"

"She *can't* die—quite—until you take her soul. She must remain in terrible agony until you put an end to it. She and all the others who are trying to die during this hold period. Do your duty, Death."

Zane stumbled toward the wreckage. The woman's terrified eyes tracked his progress. She might see nothing else, but she saw him—and Zane knew from his own recent experience how horrible the oncoming specter of Death was. But he did not know how he was supposed to finish ending her life.

The victim's dress was torn, showing how the glass had sliced all the way down across her right breast, leaving her front a mass of gore. There was absolutely nothing pretty or merciful about this demise. It had to be terminated quickly. Yet the woman tried to resist his approach. She wrenched her left hand up to fend him off, the hand hanging from a broken wrist. Zane had never before seen such physical and emotional pain, not even when his mother had—

He reached for her, still uncertain what to do. Her wrist blocked his hand, but his flesh passed through hers without resistance. His hooked fingers caught in something that felt like a cobweb, there inside her head. He wrenched his hand out—and it trailed a festoon of transient film, like the substance of a soap bubble. Disgusted, he tried to shake it off, but it clung like a string of spittle. He brought his other hand up, holding the jeweled bracelet, and tried to scrape the stuff away. The thin film tore, but clung to his other hand.

–33–

"This does not become you, Death," Fate said reprovingly. "This is her soul you are brutalizing."

Her soul! Zane's eyes tried to glaze like those of his victim. He stepped back—and the tattered soul moved with him, stretching out from her destroyed body as if reluctant to separate from it.

Then the silken strand snapped free and contracted. He held it dangling limply, like the discarded skin of a molting snake.

The woman in the car was dead at last, the horror and anguish frozen on her face. Death had taken her soul and ended her suffering.

Or had he? "What happens now?" he asked Fate. His body was shaking, and he felt unpleasantly faint.

"You fold the soul, pack it in your pouch, and go on to the next client," she answered. "When you have a break in the schedule, you will analyze the soul, to determine to which sphere it should be relegated."

"Which sphere?" His mind refused to focus, as if his very thoughts were blinded by the client's blood.

"Heaven or Hell."

"But I'm no judge of souls!" he protested.

"Yes, you are—now. Try not to make too many mistakes." Fate turned and walked away.

Zane stared at the dangling shreds of the soul. People passed him, but no one noticed him. He might as well have been alone.

Awkwardly, he brought his hands together, folding the gossamer material like a sheet. It bent in the wrong places and creased horizontally, and the torn edges flopped out of place, but he muscled it together stage by stage. Finally he had a very small, light package; the soul had hardly any physical mass. He fished in his pockets again and found a cloth bag; he stuffed the wadded soul into this. Then he tried to retch, but his empty stomach lacked the wherewithal to complete the job. What a mess he had made of his first case!

The police had arrived, and an ambulance, and people were extracting the mangled remains of the victim from the wreckage of her car. Witnesses were being interviewed, but no one thought to question Zane. He was coming to understand how this operated; he was not invisible, but he was unnoticeable. Except when it counted.

He had collected his first soul. No one needed to tell him that he had pretty well bungled it. He had frightened the woman unnecessarily, extended her torment while he dallied, and ripped her soul forth most unkindly. This certainly was not an auspicious commencement of his new duties!

His watch was flashing again. The sweep hand was moving. He had seven minutes to make his next appointment.

"I'd rather die myself!" he muttered. But he wasn't quite sure of that. Life could be ugly, and his present office was also ugly, but dying was worse yet. What a torment the human condition could be!

What alternative did he have? Zane hurried to the Deathmobile. He did not know what the normal frequency of clients was, but supposed a backlog had accumulated during the transition, if such a thing were possible. Maybe it wasn't. Maybe Fate had timed the changeover to occur during a lapse in other clients.

He oriented on the next case and drove toward it. As the green grid flashed, he touched the button on the dash panel—and launched toward the location on hyperdrive. This one was far south, probably well below the equator. But as the car stabilized in the new city, the guide-gems functioned normally, and no one seemed to notice his sudden appearance on the street.

Zane was not at all sure he liked this business of collecting souls, but still was hesitant about balking. How long would the woman in the wrecked car have suffered if he, Death, had not been there to relieve her of her soul? He didn't care to think about that.

The car ran smoothly, maneuvering through traffic expertly. It was a real pleasure to drive. He followed the arrow and eye and closed quickly on his destination.

Where was he? Maybe in Brazilia, in the bosom of the southern continent. But no—now he saw the Phoenix General Hospital. This was the Arizona of the country. He had not hyped south of the equator at all; he had severely misjudged his progress. Well, he would learn with experience.

He parked in the visitors' lot, drew his cloak about him, and proceeded to the appropriate ward, feeling nervous. He had never liked hospitals, especially since his mother had been confined to one. Yet he realized that Death would have a number of calls at hospitals, since many terminally ill people would expire in them.

No one challenged him, though he had not arrived during visiting hours. Evidently they took him for a doctor or hospital functionary. Perhaps he was; his function was the most basic of them all.

He found his client. It was an old man in a ward of four. All of them had tubes and apparatus connected to their bodies in awkward ways and all seemed to be terminally ill. Oh, he hated this! He wanted to flee, but could not.

Zane was concerned that his appearance would terrify the client, as it had before, but there was no way to sneak up on him anonymously. In addition, Death was early; two minutes remained on the countdown.

He decided to be forthright. After all, that couldn't be any worse than the previous case. He marched up to the bed. "Hello." His spoken word sounded strange; there seemed to be an echo from his pocket.

None of the four patients reacted at first. This gave Zane a moment to ferret out the mystery. He reached in the pocket and found the earring he had taken from Death. Had the echo come from it? Why?

"Hello," he repeated—and this time was sure the sound reacted with the garnet.

The client's eyes turned slowly on him. The sagging mouth formed words. "About time you got here, Death!"

The client was speaking in a foreign language—but Zane understood him, because a translation emanated from the gem he held. He realized that this was a magic translation device, another enchanted stone. Naturally Death had duties all over the world and had to be able to handle any language. He jammed the gem into his left ear; later he would get it attached in a more normal fashion.

The novelty of the language and the stone had distracted him from the business at hand; the client was looking at him expectantly. Zane was taken aback. "You were expecting me? You're not afraid?"

"Expecting you? I've been seeking you for six months! Afraid? I thought I'd never get out of this prison!"

"This hospital? It seems nice enough."

"This body."

Oh. And it seemed the translation worked both ways, for the man understood Zane's words, though there was no noise in his ear. "You *want* to—?"

The client squinted at him. "You're new at this job, aren't you?"

Zane choked. "How did you know?"

The man smiled. "I had a close encounter with Death once before. He was older than you. More wrinkles in his skull. The sight of him so fazed me that I surged right back into life. I had been dying on the operating table, but the operation became a success. That time."

"I know how that is," Zane agreed, thinking once more of his mother.

"Then I had a reserve will to live that manifested when challenged. But my condition is farther gone now. Neither science nor magic can abate the pain any more. Not without dulling my intellect, and I don't want that. In any event, I suspect that death is merely a translation to a similar existence without the burden of the body. Some people don't even realize when they're dead. I don't mind if I realize, just as long as the pain abates. So my will has eased, and I'm ready to lay life down. I hope you are competent."

Zane looked at the Deathwatch. He was a minute overdue! "I hope so, too," he said. "I talked with you too long."

The man smiled again. "It was a pleasure, Death. It provided me a brief respite. If you ever discover a person truly being kept alive beyond his will, you must use force if necessary to ease him. I think you will do that."

Again Zane thought of his mother. "I have done that," he agreed in a whisper. "A person has a right to die in his turn. I believe that. But some would call it murder."

"Some would," the client agreed. "But some are fools." Then his face tightened with a spasm of intense pain. "Ah, it is time!" he gasped. "Do it now, Death!"

Zane reached for the man's soul. His fingers passed through the client's body and caught the web of the soul. He drew it carefully out, not tearing it. The man's eyes glazed; he was dead and satisfied to be so.

The three other patients in the room paid no attention. They did not realize the nature of the visitor, or know that their companion had died.

Zane folded the soul and put it in his bag with the other. He was getting better at this, fortunately. He felt better about it, too, for he knew he had done right by this particular client, sparing him further futile pain. Perhaps this office was not as dreadful as he had thought.

He looked at his watch. The countdown was running again, but showed almost half an hour. The cat's eye was large; the location was close. For once he wouldn't have to hurry.

He drove to a park area beyond Phoenix and pulled off the street. He opened his bag of souls, put in his hand, and drew one out. He unfolded it carefully, spreading it out as well as he could against the inside of the windshield. It was a whole soul, untorn, so he knew it was the most recent one he had collected.

The soul, silhouetted against the glare of oncoming headlights, showed patterns of translucency and opacity, like a convoluted Rorschach blob. It was fascinating in its intricate detail, but he had no way to judge its overall nature. Should this one be relegated to Heaven or Hell?

Something glimmered in his mind, almost like a memory from a prior existence. Zane reached around the soul, his arm crumpling it slightly in passing, and punched open the dashboard compartment. Sure enough, inside it were several more gemstones. He had gone from paucity to plethora when he assumed this office!

Two stones were gently flashing. Zane drew them out. They were more cabochons, half-rounded—polished hemispheres. One was a dull brown, the other a dull yellow. He set their flat faces together, and the two formed a sphere, a little like the dark and light faces of the moon. Perhaps they were moonstones. They were a matched set—but what was their purpose?

He let the stones separate and brought the brown one near the spread soul. The stone flickered as if hungry. He slid it across the surface of the soul, and it flickered whenever it crossed a dark patch.

Aha! Zane brought the yellow stone near. It flickered as it passed the light portions.

If dark equated with evil and light with good, he had here his analytic mechanism. One stone responded to each aspect of the soul. He could perform the magic analysis scientifically. But how was the final balance to be ascertained?

Maybe the stones gained weight as they absorbed the readings from the soul. Was there a set of scales?

He checked in the compartment, but found no scales. Well, maybe the mechanism would become apparent at the right moment. He really did not have time to ponder at length.

Zane passed the brown gem across the length of the edge of the soul, then down a swath just in from the edge. The dark items flashed into the stone. Where he ran over a portion already covered, there was no response; the gem only picked up any given sin once. As it did so, it gradually darkened, but did not seem heavier in Zane's hand. Of course, the change might be too small for him to detect.

By the time he had covered the whole soul, the stone was almost black. There was certainly a lot of guilt and sin on this ledger. Zane wondered what the details were, but had no way to learn them. The client had had a mixed life before cancer brought him down; perhaps that was all Death needed to know.

He passed the yellow stone across the soul in the same fashion. As it picked up the good aspects, it brightened, until at the end it shone like the brightest moon.

Now what? Certainly the stones had changed, taking the measure of this soul—but which one had changed more? The dark one certainly seemed heavier than the light one; did that mean that evil predominated in this soul? Yet the light stone had seemed to become lighter as it proceeded, as if the good in it were buoyant. Maybe the trick was to ascertain which gem had changed more. Was there more sink to the dark stone, or more lift to the bright one? Where was the balance, when the two were averaged?

Then he had it. He put the two stones together. They clung to each other, as if magnetically attached, and the line of their cleavage writhed into the configuration of the Oriental Yin-Yang or the Occidental baseball. They were merged.

He let go of the ball. It hovered in mid-air, in almost perfect balance. What was this soul's destiny?

Then, slowly, it rose. The balance was marginally in favor of Heaven. Zane let his breath out; he had been more nervous about this than he had realized. He had been in doubt about both the technique of analysis and the destination of the nice gentleman he had talked with.

Nice? The man couldn't have been too nice, or he would not have had so much evil on his soul!

The gem ball nudged gently against the ceiling of the car. Zane did not let it go outside; with the car windows closed, the ball was not going anywhere. He needed to send the soul itself to Heaven. But how?

He fished in the compartment again. He found a roll of transparent tape and two packages of balls. The balls were of distinctly differing densities. Some were pith and threatened to float away; others were lead, quite heavy.

Now it came clear. Zane refolded the soul into a compact mass, bound it together by a loop of tape, and affixed a buoyant pithball. Then he opened the car window and released it. It floated up into the starry sky and in a moment was lost to view.

He hoped the package arrived safely in Heaven. This seemed an unconscionably primitive way to transport a commodity as precious as a soul. Surely it should be possible, in a world possessing magic carpets and luxury airplanes, to transport a soul more safely and efficiently than by such means. But, of course, this was his predecessor's method; maybe Zane would be able to update it when he learned more about the office.

The merged stones fell apart, their original dull colors returning. That job was finished. He returned them to the dashboard compartment.

The Deathwatch was counting down past ten minutes. He had used up his spare time and had to move.

Zane oriented the car and touched the hyperdrive button. This time the wrenching was longer. He looked out the window. He was passing across water. He was proceeding east across the ocean, according to the compass he now spotted on the dash. He left the night and re-entered day, realizing that it had been evening when he started this business, and late afternoon when he had taken his first client in Anchorage, and evening again in Phoenix for his second. The world continued its turning regardless of his business, and he was zipping in and out of day.

In a moment, land loomed. The car swooped up to it, slowing, then rolled across a brief beach, through a development of twenty-storey modernistic condominiums, through—not around—a ragged brown mountain range, past a village that filled in a valley with white, plaster-sided houses, through an olive orchard, past grazing horses, and to an open field.

He was now near his client. He wasn't sure why the hyperdrive never delivered him precisely to the target; perhaps long-distance accuracy was not great. More likely it was to preserve the anonymity of Death's approach; it would be hard for people to ignore a car that abruptly materialized on the site of an accident. Magic did have its limitations, so it was best not to push it too far.

He used the eye and arrow to close in on the target and arrived with a good minute to spare. He was at a decrepit farmhouse amidst languishing fields. This was a poverty-stricken family.

He opened the door and walked in. He wondered whether he should have knocked, but concluded that no one would care to answer Death at the door. It was dawn here; he could hear the members of the family screaming at each other as they blundered sleepily about, getting organized in the chill house. His left ear picked up the translated words, for, of course, this was not Zane's own language. The people were grumbling about the cold morning, the inadequacy of food for breakfast, and a rat that skittered across the floor.

Zane's gems guided him to the bedroom. The woman was there, sitting on the bed, an expression of discomfort on her face as she struggled to don heavy, opaque stockings. One leg was raised, the knee bent, so that he had an intimate view of her thighs. He was shocked to see that they were almost covered by a flaming rash. Indeed, the woman looked sick; her face was flushed, her hair straggly and tangled. Her teeth, as she grimaced, were discolored, perhaps rotting. This was a young, fairly shapely woman, but her bad health made her unappealing. Her eyes were so deeply shadowed, it was as if they had been blacked by violence. Then Zane realized that there *had* been violence; she had bruises and scrapes all over her body where flesh showed.

Perhaps death would, in fact, be a boon to her. She was obviously living in misery.

But the arrow did not point to the woman. It pointed to the crib on the far side of the room where a small baby lay huddled.

A baby? How could he take a baby?

Zane walked past the woman, who paid him no attention, and stood over the crib. The baby had scuffled off its inadequate blanket during the night and lay, exposed and damp, face down, its skin bluish. It was, he realized, about to suffer a crib death.

But what of the fifty-fifty rule that governed his clients? Most people died and were separated from their souls without his direct help. Only those who so cluttered their souls with evil as to be in doubt of salvation required the personal service of Death. Almost by definition, a baby was innocent; therefore its freed soul should float blithely to Heaven. A baby was not yet, as Fate had quoted, the captain of its soul, and Heaven still lay about it.

Yet there was no question this was his client. The baby was fading fast. It was time. Zane reached down and hooked out the small soul.

The baby's mother, intent on her laborious dressing, never noticed. Zane walked past her, carrying the soul, and left the house. He felt ill.

In the Deathmobile, he used the stones to analyze the little soul. The pattern was strange, because it was not a pattern at all; the soul was uniformly gray. Experience had not yet caused it to be variegated.

The verdict of the combined stones was neutral; the gem ball hovered in place like the moon it resembled, neither rising nor falling.

How could this be? What evil had this little boy done? What evil *could* he have done, confined to his crib, completely dependent on his sick mother?

Zane had no answer. He folded the soul neatly and put it in the bag.

The Deathwatch was counting down yet again. Was there no end to this? When did he get some rest, some time to think things out?

He knew the answer. Deaths occurred all the time, and the small percentage that required special attention continued, too. At some point he would have two difficult cases happen at the same moment, on opposite sides of the globe. What would he do then?

Zane was beginning to understand how a person performing the office of Death could grow careless, as his predecessor had done. When things got rushed, corners had to be cut, or the job would not get done. What happened to a Death who got too far behind?

He looked at the watch more carefully. It had three buttons on the side. This was a stopwatch, a chronograph, of course, though its timer did run backward. He had seen the type before. One button would be used to start and stop timing; another to zero the total; and the shorter middle one to set the regular time and calendar features when necessary.

But this watch ran itself, magically, responding to input he did not know about. Maybe it had a direct line to Heaven or Hell or wherever the allocation of souls was determined. Fate probably had a hand in it, as she measured her threads. He didn't time events; events timed him. Why, then, were the extra buttons necessary? What did they control?

He thought of punching a button. Then he hesitated; it could be dangerous to play with something he did not understand. Yet how else was he to learn? He had lived his life and almost died his death in an impetuous manner; he might as well be consistent.

Experimentally, he punched the lowermost button. Nothing happened. It depressed and sprang back without any specific point of resistance. Had it been disconnected? Not necessarily; a good stopwatch was protected from an accidental punching of the wrong button, as might occur when someone was distracted by a close finish in a race and aimed for the STOP button without looking. This should be the zeroing control, operative only when there was a fixed time registered, as would be the case after a race had been timed.

He punched the highest button. It clicked—and the red sweep hand stopped.

He studied the dial. There was no motion in either of the two miniature dials that showed hours and minutes. The sweep hand was frozen at twenty-three seconds after the minute. *Before* the minute, since it ran backward. But the third little dial continued to function; its hand moved briskly clockwise, telling off the seconds of ordinary time. So the stopwatch was stopped, but not time itself.

What did this mean? Since the stopwatch function governed the timing of the deaths of his clients, did this imply that a hold had been put on such deaths? That was hard to credit—but indeed his whole situation was hard to credit. Fate had mentioned a stoppage of deaths in the world until he, the new holder of the office, had commenced activity. And this did answer his question about appointments that occurred too close together. He might freeze one case while he handled the other.

And, of course, this gave him his chance to rest. He could simply turn off his job while he slept or ate or thought things out.

This was some watch! It did not merely time existing events, it coerced events to its timing.

Zane saw that he had only two minutes, in addition to the twenty-three seconds, until his next appointment, and the green gridstone showed this was halfway across the world. That was crowding it. He punched the zeroing button—and sure enough, the timing hands clicked back several minutes, providing him a full ten minutes. In that time, he knew, the Deathmobile could take him anywhere on Earth.

What, then, was the hours dial for? It could register up to twelve, but if ten minutes was all he could reschedule, he would never need to read hours.

Zane decided to ponder that later. Right now he had to organize himself. He needed to figure out what to do with the baby soul, for one thing. He was not going to send it to Hell, and might not be authorized to send it to Heaven. Probably he should take it to Purgatory for expert designation. He assumed that if Heaven and Hell were literal, so was Purgatory—but where was it?

"There is so much I don't know!" he exclaimed.

"This, too, shall pass," someone answered him.

-3-

EWES AND DOES

Zane jumped. A man sat in the adjacent seat. He was perhaps fifty, with a mustache and goatee and piercing blue eyes. He held a small double cone in his hand.

"You must be immortal," Zane said, after a moment of fevered thought.

"In a sense," the man agreed. "I am another Incarnation, like Fate and Death."

Zane studied him, suspecting that he should recognize the man, but he did not. "Who—?"

"I am Chronos, colloquially known as Time." He tilted the cones, and fine sand sifted from one to the other. It was an hourglass.

"Time!" Zane exclaimed. "But you're young!" Only that was inaccurate. "At least, not old—"

"I am ageless," Chronos corrected him. "I realize I have been depicted by ignorant artisans as ancient, but I prefer to operate in my prime."

"Did I—the watch—?"

"Yes, Death, you summoned me. I am, of course, attuned to all manner of chronometry, especially that practiced by key figures. You signaled me by locking the countdown on ten minutes. Ordinarily Death either freezes the timer where it is or resets it to gain necessary travel time; to do both is a code. Naturally I came to see what you wished, as we Incarnations do try to accommodate one another. It is, after all, one firmament."

"I didn't realize I was signaling you," Zane said sheepishly. "I'm new at this. In fact, I hardly realized you existed as a person."

"As a personification," Chronos corrected him. "An Incarnation of an essential function of existence. Persons differ, but the role continues."

"That's another thing it's hard to get used to—the notion that things like Death and Time are offices, not physical laws or whatever."

"We are roles and offices and laws and more," Chronos assured him. "We are also human beings, and that human quality is important."

"I was just trying to find out how the watch worked. There doesn't seem to be any function for the hours dial."

"It records your schedule backlog," Chronos said easily. "You have recycled your next client by seven minutes and thirty-seven seconds; you have also placed the entire program on hold. This is, of course, your prerogative; you are Death. You can even halt the passage of all time by pulling out the center button. But if you maintain the hold more than half an hour, it will register on the hours dial as a tardy schedule that needs to be made up. If you run more than twelve hours late, overflowing the capacity of the watch, there will be an investigation by the authorities at Purgatory that could damage your performance rating."

"Oh? What happens to me if my rating is bad?"

"That counts as evil on your soul, shifting your balance toward Hell. Of course, you are in perfect balance during your initiation period; every officeholder needs time for trial and error. But when that passes, and at such time as you give up the office, for whatever reason, a negative rating could make your soul most uncomfortable."

Zane was getting it straight. He held the office of Death, but he remained alive, and the account of his soul was yet to be settled. "My predecessor—where did his soul go?"

"He had done an adequate job, generally; I'm sure he found his way to Heaven, which is the last refuge of adequacy."

That made Zane feel easier. "And if I do a good job, I will go to Heaven, too—when the time comes?"

"*If* it comes. You should. Since you commence the office balanced, and performance is fairly straightforward, it should not be difficult for you to improve your position."

"How do you know my soul is balanced?"

"If it were not, Death would not have had to come for you individually."

Zane laughed. "You know, I never thought of that! My good and evil were even, so when I tried to suicide, I had to be collected by Death himself. And if I hadn't seen Death arriving, I would be dead now!"

"It is an unusual situation," Chronos agreed. "But at the same time normal. Each Death assassinates his predecessor, thereby burdening his own soul with more evil, but postponing his own reckoning indefinitely. I hardly envy your system."

"Your system differs?"

"Certainly. Each office has its own mechanism of transmittal, some gentler than others. But all of us work together as required, treating one another's offices with due respect. I feel indebted to the prior Death, who did me a favor on occasion, and regret that it was necessary for him to leave the office. Now I will facilitate things for his successor, as he would have wished."

"He doesn't hate me?" Zane asked, bemused.

"There is no hate in Heaven."

"But I murdered him!"

"And you will be murdered by your successor. Do you hate him?"

"Hate my successor? I don't even know him!"

"Your predecessor did not know you. Otherwise he would have been more careful."

Zane changed the subject. "I have just taken a baby. It is perfectly balanced, a uniform shade of gray. I don't know how it can have so much evil on its soul, so well integrated, or what I should do with the soul. Can you advise me?"

"I can clarify the matter. The baby is probably the child of incest or rape, so carries the burden of intensified Original Sin. Such children, conceived in evil, do not commence life with a clean slate."

"Original Sin!" Zane exclaimed. "I thought that was a discredited doctrine!"

"Hardly. It may not be valid in non-Christian parts of the world, but it is certainly operative here. Belief is fundamental to existence, and guilt is very important to religion; so guilt does carry across the generations."

"I don't like that!" Zane protested. "A baby has no free will, especially before it's born. It can't choose the circumstances of its conception. It can't sin."

"Unfortunately, you do not determine the system; you only implement it. All of us have objections to aspects of it, but our powers are limited."

"And I don't know where to take the baby soul. I don't know how to get to Purgatory, assuming that is the proper place."

Chronos laughed. "It is the proper place, and it is simple enough for you to reach. You reside there."

"I do?"

"When not actively pursuing souls. You have a fine Deathhouse, a mansion in the sky."

"Well, I've never seen it," Zane said, nettled. "How do I—?"

"You ride your fine pale horse there."

"My pale horse?"

"Death rides a pale horse. Surely you were aware of that. Mortis is always with you."

"Of course I know about Death's traditional steed! But I don't know where any such horse is!"

Chronos smiled indulgently. "You know where; you don't know

what." He patted the dash panel. "This is Mortis."

"The car?" Zane was baffled. "I know its plate says MORTIS. But it's a machine!"

"Press this button." Chronos indicated one on the dash that Zane hadn't noticed before. It had an embossed motif of a chesspiece—the knight, the image of the head of a horse.

Zane pressed the button—and found himself astride a magnificent stallion. The hide of the horse was as pale as bleached bone, his mane was like flexible silver, and his hooves were like stainless steel. He lifted his great equine head, perked his ears forward, and snorted a snort of pale vapor.

Zane had daydreamed of owning a flying horse. Now he knew his dream had been amply fulfilled. This horse had no wings, but he could go anywhere!

"Anything else you need to know?" Chronos inquired wryly. He was seated behind Zane now.

"There must be volumes of information I need to acquire," Zane said, awed by the transformation of car to animal. He had known magic and science were allied, but had never seen anything like this before. He felt the warm, powerful muscles of the horse beneath him and was as thrilled as any child. "Somehow it doesn't seem important at the moment."

"The moment is frozen, in a certain respect," Chronos reminded him. He dismounted. "I will leave you now." The hourglass in his hand flashed, and he vanished.

"Time flies," Zane muttered. He shook off the mood and patted the horse. "You and I will get along just fine, I know. But I haven't had much experience riding, so I suppose I had better use your car form for routine city calls. Unless we should go to Purgatory now—"

The stallion issued a snort of negation. Zane decided the horse knew best, so he did not argue the case.

He looked at the saddle and discovered a button on it. "Is this what turns you back into the pale sedan?" he inquired, touching it.

Abruptly he was back in the car. Good enough! He would have more to say to Mortis the horse, much more, in due course. But now duty called. He punched the START button on the Deathwatch, noting that half an hour now registered on the hours dial; he would have to make up that time. At least he was getting to understand the system.

He oriented the Deathmobile and put it in hyperdrive. Animal to machine—amazing but convenient! Was the horse a robot, or was the car alive? He would have to inquire later. At least this clarified why driving was so easy; there was an animal mind assisting it. Absent-minded people sometimes drove into trees, but that never happened to an absent-minded horseback rider, for the horse knew better. But it seemed strange to be riding *inside* a horse!

This time he arrived in the parking lot of a big stadium. It was night, but floodlights illuminated the area, so that it almost seemed like day. Zane looked closely at the gems of the bracelet to see if there were a mistake, but the cat's eye was large, the two dots juxtaposed on the grid, and the arrow pointed firmly to the stadium.

"So be it," Zane said. He got out and walked to the structure. The man behind the ticket window did not challenge him, taking him to be a functionary of the premises. He walked right on inside, following the arrow.

The game was in session. It was professional pigskin, with banners proclaiming the teams: the Does *vs.* the Ewes. The ball was on the ninety-foot line of the Ewes, and the girls were mixing it up in a good old-fashioned hair-pull.

The arrow pointed to the playing field. But there was no one in that section. The action was in the other half.

Zane walked around the edge of the field with a certain difficulty, for the stadium thronged with people. The arrow on the gem shifted, orienting on a spot on the Does' fifty-foot line. An empty spot.

Had his gems malfunctioned? No—he realized immediately that his recycling of the time had caused him to arrive early; three minutes remained before the death was due. He would simply have to wait for it.

Zane took a seat on the convenient bench near the hundred-and-fifty foot line. Several Ewes sat on it—big, husky, well-padded young women, attractive in a violent way, with generous endowments wherever he looked. The nearest one glanced at him, did a double take, then realized she had suffered a delusion and turned away. After all, no one saw Death sitting on the players' bench at a pigskin game!

The Does were pressing hard. They wore bright blue suits whose protective padding accented their female qualities enormously. To Zane it was really too much; even prize-winning milking goats lacked udders as massive as these appeared to be. Maybe he was too close; in times past, watching television, before his set was repossessed by the Finance company, he had admired the pig proportions.

The Doe quarterback snatched the skin and faded back for a throw. She heaved it forward just as two Ewes stampeded toward her. There was a flash as the spell on the ball fought off the blocking-spells and freed it to fly to its target. The receiver levitated at an angle, surprising the defender, who had evidently anticipated a bringdown-spell. The Doe caught the missile with a cry of glee, clutched it to her massive bosom, and cannonballed to the turf, plowing up a divot. It was a beautiful play, and the audience squealed.

But there was a black flag. The referees, striped like skunks, consulted and concluded that an illegal spell had been cast, momentarily blinding the defending Ewe. The play was disallowed and a penalty assessed. Because the Does were in field-goal range, the Ewe captain chose magic rather than footage—the generation of an adverse wind. That would last two minutes and should be enough to foil the drive.

The Does pressed on determinedly. Their fans in the crowd encouraged them. "Dose! Dose! Dose!" they bawled. Zane thought they were yelling for the team, until he saw the name of the quarterback on the marquee and realized that her initials were O.D. Naturally she was called the Dose. Now he remembered seeing her play, when he was alive and had his TV.

O.D. took the skin and made an end run, skillfully fending off tacklers with a series of legal straightarm-spells. But as she crossed the scrimmage line at the near side of the field, someone caught her with a dishabille-spell. Suddenly she was naked, or at least visible. Zane realized that her uniform had been rendered invisible, so that she was physically protected, though visually exposed. She really was a fine, healthy woman under all the padding. The cheers of the crowd redoubled.

O.D. looked down and discovered what all the shouting was about. She blushed to the waist, not with embarrassment, but with fury. When the next Ewe tackler came, the Dose grabbed her by the hair and whirled her halfway around.

The Ewe reciprocated, grabbing O.D.'s hair and spinning about, trying to use the hank of hair to haul the woman over her shoulder in a judo throw. But the Dose turned around herself, hauling back. The two spun in a circle, back to back. "Dos-a-dos!" the crowd screamed, deliriously delighted by the extracurricular action and its own wit, and the band struck up a dancing tune. Indeed, it was very much like a dance, and soon others were emulating it, until the spoilsport officials broke it up with a riot-control enchantment and wrestled the girls apart.

Naturally there was a penalty flag when the dust settled. Hair-pulling was not nice. The Does lost more ground.

The quarterback retired from the field to get a counterspell for her uniform to restore its visibility. The kicking team came in, chuckling. Apparently the nudity-spell was not illegal since it had not hurt the Dose physically and probably not socially; a number of fans were slavering. "That quarter-B sure ain't no half-A!" someone shouted.

The magic wind caused the field-goal attempt to fall short. The Ewes were given the skin on the fifty-foot line. They wasted no time; their first play was a run through the center that gained thirty-five feet. There was no magic about it; they had sneaked through a mundane play, and it had worked, causing the opposition to waste its counterspells.

Then the Doe defense grew tougher. Antimagic blocked magic, and the stout pursuit stiffed the Ewe offense. It looked as if the Ewes would have to punt—and their two-minute penalty wind had died, so the ball would have no extra carry. Their fans in the audience were silent.

Suddenly there was a break. The Ewe quarterback launched a desperation toss, buttressed by a levitation-spell, that hurtled a hundred and twenty feet. The receiver closed on it—and the defending Doe, Number 69, shoved her out of the way and intercepted the ball.

There was an exclamation of admiration from the Doe fans, and the Doe cheerleaders went crazy, for an enchantment of obscuration had concealed the foul from the officials. But there was a bleat of purest wrath from the Ewes. They turned, galloped down the field, and tackled Number 69 so hard she flipped endwise in the air and landed in a heap.

Now there was a hush—for 69 did not rise. The team doctor rushed over to examine her.

Abruptly Zane remembered his job. His watch had zeroed, and the arrow pointed at the fallen Doe.

He hurried out, knowing she was done for. He did not even pause: he squeezed between oblivious players, squatted beside the body, and hooked out the soul.

No one seemed to notice. Number 69, who had been quivering as if in terrible pain, relaxed. Now she was dead, and it was a relief, for her neck was broken.

Zane walked away, folding the soul as he went. He knew he should not have allowed himself to be distracted by the game; that was unprofessional. Because of his neglect, the woman had suffered as much as a minute longer than she should have.

Unprofessional? Who was he to fancy himself a professional in this grim business! Still, he did have a job to do, and he might as well do it properly. At the very least, he could do it in a manner that relieved distress, rather than promoted it.

His watch was counting down again. He had five minutes. He hurried to the Deathmobile, climbed in, started it, oriented it, and hit the hyperdrive button so hard he bruised his finger. Yes, he was angry with himself! He resolved never again to allow extraneous events to divert him from proper attention to his client.

He brought out the two analysis gems to review the new soul, but in his unsettlement he dropped one. By the time he picked it up from the floor, he knew the reading had been invalidated, and he didn't want to start over; there would not be time for a proper job now. He folded the soul away for future handling.

Then, idly, he passed the brown gem down his own body. It glimmered. It was reading his living soul!

Well, why not? The stone was concerned only with the evil in a given soul, not with its state of life or afterlife. Actually, the soul was eternal; it was only the body that died. With these stones, he could assess the balance of good and evil in any person, living or dead.

How did his own tally stand? Zane knocked his forehead with his hand. He was an idiot to check his own soul, since he knew it was fifty-fifty and would remain so until his trial period in this office was done. Like the illegitimate baby, circumstance had locked him in.

Yes, he had reason to do his job well, however unqualified he might be for the office. His soul remained in peril of damnation. He hadn't really worried about that during his normal life, but now that he was sure that Hell was really literal, he cared. He didn't want to go there when he died! All he had to do was a good enough job so that his soul would be slated for Heaven. Then he would not have to fear Eternity, at such time as he got careless and was sent there forcefully.

The car stopped in another parking lot. This appeared to be a school. Zane got out and followed his arrow through the comblike serrations of the building complex. It was class-changing time, and children in the range of ten to twelve were scurrying every which way, generally ignoring both Zane and the posted WALK signs. One boy, however, plunged directly into him, naturally paying no attention to the obstacles in the way of his headlong rush.

The contact was emphatic. Zane suffered a mild lapse of breath. The boy righted himself and looked up. "Gee—Halloween!" he exclaimed. "A skull-face!" Then he zoomed away.

Halloween? Close enough. The lad had seen more accurately than he knew. Perhaps this was a talent of the young.

He passed near a classroom where computers were being described to bored students. The virtues of competing brands were highlighted on posters posted alphabetically around the room. It was good to be part of the computer age; Zane wouldn't mind owning any one of those fine data processors. He understood they could also be used to summon quite powerful demons safely, for a computer never erred in setting up the tricky protective spells required to prevent the supernatural from getting out of hand. But alas, he was now beyond that.

The next classroom dealt with modern technical applications of magic. Its students were equally inattentive; they had little interest in required basics of any type. Here the posters described competitively marketed brands of amulets, love potions, curses, magic mirrors, communication conches, cornucopias, voodoo dolls, mail-order ghosts, sophisticated spellbooks, and sundry gems of enchantment. Zane knew about those last from personal experience!

He arrived at the cubby that served as the school infirmary. There was another boy the size of the one who had bumped Zane. This boy was deathly ill. Beside him, the school's part-time nurse was on the phone, exasperated. "...can't wait for parental permission," she was saying. "I can never reach them during the day anyway. We need an ambulance-carpet immediately! He's got to get to the hospital before he—"

She paused as her eyes fell on Zane. "Oh, no!" she breathed, setting down the phone. "It's too late, isn't it?"

Zane glanced at the Deathwatch. It was time. "Yes," he said. He reached into the boy and drew out his soul.

The nurse covered her eyes with one hand. "I must be hallucinating," she said brokenly. "It's terrible when they are taken so young."

Zane stood there, the small soul dangling from his hand. He felt guilty. Why should such an innocent child have to die? "I must do my job," he said to the nurse. "But if you would be so kind—please tell me the nature of this boy."

"I must be crazy," she said, looking directly at Zane. "Talking to a delusion. But I will answer. He was the youngest drug addict I've dealt with—well, not the youngest, if you count the potheads, but the worst for this age bracket. He was hooked on anything he could get—coke, heroin, acid, magic dust—anything at all that zonked him out of dull existence. He lied, he stole, he—you know, lured clients to illicit activities—anything to get money for a fix. This time he got something too strong—must have been uncut helldust, and he didn't believe it—and Satan took him in."

"Not necessarily Satan," Zane said. "His soul is in near balance between good and evil; it may yet be saved."

"I hope so. He was a decent kind, underneath. Sometimes we talked, while he was recovering from a siege. He wanted to quit; he just couldn't control his habit. I think it was genetic, some chemical imbalance in him that threw him into an irrational depression, so he had to escape by any means available. I know he didn't want to be that way. I turned him in a dozen times, for his own good, and he never held it against me. But they tend to go easy on juveniles, and—oh, I should have taken stronger measures! But I kept hoping, each time, that he'd straighten out—"

Others were coming, and Zane felt it prudent to withdraw. But he had food for thought. First, he knew now that some people could see him and recognize him for his office, even if they weren't dying themselves, and even if they didn't quite believe it. Maybe it was a matter of circumstance; the nurse was in a distraught condition, ready to perceive Death; and, of course, she really did care about the client. Second, the young could indeed have much evil on their souls. This boy had evidently committed heinous acts to support his drug habit. So it made sense; had the boy not OD'd now, when the good still matched the evil in him, the balance would have shifted irrevocably, putting him in Hell for certain when he died later. Maybe he was lucky he had gone today.

Yet that comment about the genetic origin of the lad's compulsion bothered Zane. Depression was an insidious thing, as he knew from his own experience in life; it manifested in obscure ways; indeed, it could be biologic rather than psychologic. Was it fair to charge sin against a person's soul when he couldn't really help what he did? Zane did not have the answer, but he wasn't easy about it.

The watch was running again, swinging backward into the next countdown. Zane knew he'd be crowded until he caught up to his original schedule, but he felt the need to pause again. He pressed the STOP button.

What was bothering him was this: death was a serious business; he could not blithely collect souls without developing some rationale for himself. Was this really what he wanted to do for all eternity?

He sat in the car, in the parking lot, thinking. He needed an answer, but somehow couldn't get a grasp on the nature of his wish. He didn't know what he wanted to do, only that something about his present course was wrong.

His reverie was jarringly interrupted by noise from the radio of a slowly passing car. It was a Hellfire commercial, sung to the tune of a popular hymn: *Hark, the herald angels shout. Ten more years till you get out! Ten more years till you are free, from life's penitentiary!*

Satan never quit campaigning! Zane knew himself to be no angel, but this open mockery of Heavenly things disturbed him. Could it really lure wavering souls to Hell? Surely he himself, in life, had been considered a candidate for such infernal blandishments. Even if his soul had not proved to be entirely balanced between good and evil, he would have known he was of questionable virtue. There were blots on his conscience that could never be erased. He was, in secret fact, a murderer—now he had to admit it to himself!—and he had believed for some time that he was destined for Hell, though he had not quite allowed himself to believe Hell existed. Who was he to judge the souls of others? So the schoolboy had the sins of drug addiction on his soul; was Zane himself any better?

Yet what choice did he have now? It always came back to that. If he didn't do his job, how would that improve anyone's situation? Someone else would replace him in the office of Death, and the grim game would continue.

"It might as well be me," Zane said, pressing the button to resume the countdown. But he remained unsatisfied. He had not really answered his question. He was doing this job because he didn't know what else to do and wasn't ready to quit what form of life remained to him. His own suicide attempt had been a passing thing, a wild impulse of the moment; he really did want to live. Since he had to perform or face some sort of Divine accounting, he performed. That really was not much credit to him.

In fact, Zane realized, he was not much of a person. If he had never lived, the world would not have been a worse place. He was just one of the blah mediocrities that cluttered the cosmos. It was ironic that he should have backed into the significant office he now held.

He had started and oriented the car. He was zooming across the surface of the world, hardly paying attention. This was, if he remembered correctly, his sixth case coming up; he was getting the hang of it. Of course there was still much to learn—assuming he really wanted to learn it.

Ocean gave way to land. There was a fleeting beach, and a green shore region; then they plowed through mountains and across a desert whose sands were wrinkled into dunes like the waves of the sea, frozen in place. On south, still in hyperdrive; this was a huge island—in fact, a continent!

The Deathmobile stopped at last at the dead end of a dirt road in mountainous country. Four minutes remained on the timer. Where was the client?

The arrowstone for once seemed uncertain. He turned it about, and the arrow was inconsistent. In any event, there was no human habitation in sight in this wild land.

A blinking light on the dash caught his attention. It was the one with the horsehead silhouette. Zane pushed it.

He was astride the great stallion, his cloak swirling in the breeze. "What next, friend steed?" he inquired.

The Deathhorse moved forward, galloping up the steep slope to the side. No ordinary horse could have moved this way—but of course this was a unique animal. Mortis leaped to the top of the mountain ridge, where a primitive cottage perched.

This was the place. The arrowstone had not guided him before, because he had been holding it level instead of angled. It had not been able to point upward to the cottage. The car had not driven here because no ordinary car could, and the approach of Death was always circumspect.

As they traversed the somewhat harrowing slope of the mountain, Zane thought again about himself and his office. There was something about the appearance of danger, such as a possible fall, that caused him to review his most morbid thoughts. If he felt unfit for the office of Death and did not want to judge others when he knew he was no better than they were, why should he do it? If his abdication meant he would die the death he had aborted before, maybe that was proper. If he went to Hell, maybe that, too, was proper. After all, he had killed his mother; he could hardly go to join her in Heaven! The fact that he now clung to a kind of life had no relevance; it was fitting that he pay his penalty.

Yes—that was what he had to do! "I resign the office!" he cried impulsively. "Take me directly to Hell!"

Nothing happened. The horse trotted toward the cottage, ignoring Zane's outburst.

Of course. He could not blithely resign. He had to be killed by his successor, who would probably be a client like himself and who would turn on him.

Very well—he had a client coming up. He would pass the office on to that person and be done with it.

Two minutes remained as he rode up to the cottage. A woman came out to meet him. "I am ready, Death," she said. "Lift me to your fine horse and bear me to Heaven."

A woman! He had thought it would be a man, maybe with a gun. Would a woman as readily turn on him? She might need some convincing.

"I can not promise you Heaven," he said. "Your soul is in virtual balance; it could go either way."

"But I took poison so I could go at a time of my choosing!" she protested. "I've got to go to Heaven!"

"Take an antidote or an emetic quickly," Zane urged, wondering whether this was feasible. Would he have been summoned, had demise not been certain? And how could she turn the poison she had already taken against him? This was not working out at all! "Extend your life, and we shall talk."

The woman hesitated. "I don't know—"

"Hurry!" Zane cried, seeing his chance slip away. If she had to die, he would not leave his office this time, and might not have the courage to make the next client turn against him.

"I do have a healing potion that should neutralize it, but—"

"Take it!" he pleaded.

Dominated by his urgency, she complied, drinking the potion.

"Now find a gun or a knife," he told her.

"What? Why should I neutralize the poison, only to use something much more messy?"

"Not for you. For me. I want you to kill me."

She gaped at him. "I'll do no such thing! What do you think I am?"

Zane saw that this wasn't remotely feasible. Of course she was not a murderess! He dismounted, took her hand, and led her to a patio where there were chairs and a table. "Why did you want to die?" he asked.

"What do you care, Death?" she asked, wary of him but curious, too. She spoke with the strong Downunder accent of this region.

"Not long ago, I sought to die," he said. "I changed my mind when—well, that's hard to explain. Now I want to die again."

"How can Death die even once?"

"Believe me, Death can die. It is only an office I hold, and that office can be yours if—"

"This is completely appalling!" she cried. "I'll not listen to this!"

Zane sighed. "Tell me your problem." He knew himself to be no psychologist, but he needed to extricate himself from this awkwardness he had put himself into.

"My husband left me," she said grimly. "After fifteen years—a younger woman—I'll show him!"

"Isn't it a sin to commit suicide, according to your religion?" he asked.

She paused, frowning. "I suppose it is, but—"

"And should you do such a thing to spite him? Why match the wrong he did you with a wrong done to yourself?"

"I am a woman," she said with a wry smile. "I owe more to emotion than to logic."

Zane returned her smile, showing that he appreciated her humor. No woman really thought herself illogical, however strongly she might feel, but it was fashionable to seem otherwise. "But your soul is so close to balance, the evil matching the good, that these wrongs could tip you into Hell. Do what you know is right, and your balance should favor Heaven."

"Oh, I hadn't thought of that! I don't want to go to Hell!"

"Believe me, you stand at the very brink of it now. You have done evil before, and this—"

She sighed. "It is true. I have much evil to account for. I drove him away. I suppose you know how bitchy a woman can be when she tries."

"Not really. I always thought of women as pristine and pure," Zane admitted. "Most of the evil resides in men. Women should go to Heaven when they die."

She laughed bitterly. "You idiot! There is more sin concealed in women than in men! My husband errs because it is his male nature; I, at least, should have known better. I was fooling myself when I dreamed of Heaven."

"Not at all," Zane said. "I didn't say you were doomed to Hell; I said you stood at the verge. Heaven is within your potential. I am sure of this. You can redeem yourself. I am in a position to know, for I collect the borderline souls. Go and do good with what remains of your life, and you will go to Heaven. This promise is surely worth some sacrifice."

"Yes, surely it is," she agreed. "But how is it you, the Grim Reaper, urge this course on me? If I live, doesn't that cost you points or something?"

"I don't know," Zane admitted. "I have not held this office long. I just don't like to see a life wasted or a person damned who could be saved."

"Yet you were asking me to kill you!"

"I see now that was wrong of me. I will make you a deal: you live, and I will live."

She smiled more openly, looking rather pretty. "I'll do it! I don't need my husband anyway."

Zane stood. "I regret I have other appointments. May we never meet again." He extended his hand.

She took it, though it seemed skeletal. "This I will remember—shaking hands with Death."

Zane laughed. "That's better than what you contemplated."

"Also better than what you contemplated!"

He nodded agreement, then returned to the horse and mounted. He waved to her as he departed.

-4-

MAGICIAN

The Deathwatch was counting down again. Only ninety seconds remained. "No time to ride down the mountain," Zane said. "Can you take me there directly, Mortis?"

The stallion neighed, reared, and leaped into the air. Clouds raced by, and land and sea and more land. This was hyperdrive! When the horse landed, they were back in America. In fact, they were in Kilvarough; he knew his home city well. Well, of course people died here as well, and some would be in near balance; no need to be surprised.

They stopped at an affluent suburban estate. A fence of iron spikes surrounded it, and two lean young griffins patrolled the grounds. They were beautiful creatures, with powerful beaks and talons and rippling muscles on their bodies. Crossbreed of eagle and lion, with certain magical endowments, yet loyal to whatever person or creature they gave their loyalty to, they were just about the best protection an estate could have. This, more than the obvious wealth of the property, impressed him with the status of its owner.

But when the creatures menaced Zane, the Deathsteed lifted one steel forefoot in unmistakable warning, backing them off. Few griffins feared horses, but these were smart enough to perceive that this was no ordinary horse.

Still, Zane wasn't eager to leave the protection Mortis provided while the griffins remained. But he would have to, for he was sure the horse would not enter the building. He glanced about—and spied an object strapped to the saddle. He lifted it out and found two pegs mounted on a long, curving shaft. He gripped it by these, and a massive, gleaming blade snapped out at right angles to the base. Sure enough—it was a switchblade scythe.

Zane had had only very limited experience with a scythe in a class on archaic farming and harvesting. Certain magic crops suffered heavy losses when worked by machinery, so ancient tools were still used for them, and most schools had a course or two in the application of these. So Zane knew what this was and how to swing it, but would have trouble using it as a weapon. Still, as he held it now, felt the proper heft of it and its fine balance, and eyed the deadly expanse of the blade, a certain nervous confidence suffused him. This was a magic weapon, surely; its enchantment made the wielder at least halfway competent. He believed he could use it and that its power and quality would enhance his ability. After all, the scythe was Death's traditional instrument, the grim tool of the Grim Reaper, and he was now that entity.

The horse stopped, and Zane dismounted. Yes, he was Death, standing here holding this deadly instrument. He began to believe. Perhaps he could do the job the way it should be done.

Thirty seconds remained. He strode toward the house. The two griffins spread their wings and rose up to the rampant posture, their elevated front claws springing out like narrow daggers, their beaks gleaming. A kind of screaming growl started in the two throats.

Zane drew his Deathcloak close about him and lifted the scythe. The griffins reared back, wary of its terrible blade. He strode toward them, glaring through the narrow aperture of his hood.

That did it. The monsters might fear nothing living, but all creatures feared Death, if they recognized him.

As his watch signaled time, Zane walked into the main room of the house. There was an old man, seated in an easy chair.

"Stay your hand a moment, Death," the man said. "I would converse with you."

"I'm running late," Zane demurred, no longer as surprised as he had first been when people saw him and addressed him directly. It was evident that anyone who really wished to could relate to him.

The man smiled. "I must advise you that I am a Magician of the thirty-second rank, whose name you would not recognize because my magic protects my anonymity. I can stay your hand—yea, even yours, Death!—for a time. But I do not seek to oppose you, only to converse a moment with you. Put away your weapon, grant me a period of your attention, and I will reciprocate with something of greater value."

"Do you seek to bribe Death?" Zane asked, half angry and two-thirds curious. He folded the scythe and leaned it against the wall near the door. "What possible thing could you offer me?"

"I have already given you more than you can afford to know," the Magician said. "But I will couch my offer succinctly. Stop your watch, and if after five minutes you do not wish to converse longer, I will yield you my soul with singular grace. In return, I proffer you the dominant option on the love of my daughter."

This did not please Zane. The bitterness of his foolish loss of Angelica to the proprietor of the Mess o' Pottage shop was still fresh. "What use does Death have for any woman?" he asked.

"You remain a man, behind the Deathmask. Even Death does not exist by souls alone."

"What am I to make of a man who would prostitute his daughter to gain a few more minutes of life?" Zane asked, repelled.

"Especially one who would prostitute her to the person who killed his mother," the Magician agreed.

Zane punched the STOP button, freezing the overextended countdown. "You have my attention, Magician," he said between his teeth.

"I shall summon her," the man said. He tapped one gnarled finger against the arm of his chair with a sound like the clang of a small bell.

That was not what Zane had meant, but he kept silent. The Magician was evidently a complex, knowledgeable man who had done his research on Zane's past. Why he chose to bring his daughter into it, Zane could not guess, but that was the Magician's business. Maybe the girl was so homely that no one would seek to take advantage of her anyway.

The girl entered the room. She was naked. Her hair was bound under a bathing cap; evidently she had just stepped out of an air-shower. Her body was slender and well formed, but not spectacular. She was just a normal, healthy young woman of perhaps twenty years. "What is it, Father?" she inquired, her voice gently melodious.

"I have offered your love to this person, Luna," the Magician said, gesturing to Zane.

She glanced about, perplexed. "What person?"

"You can see him, if you try. He is the new Death."

"Death!" she exclaimed with mild horror. "So soon?"

"He has come for me, not you, my dear, and I shall go with him shortly. But I wanted you to meet him before I gave him the love-spell with your name on it."

She squinted, looking at Zane, beginning to see him. "But I'm not dressed!" she protested.

"Dress, then," her father said, as if indifferent. "I wish you to make an impression on him so he will desire you."

"As you wish, Father," she said dutifully. "I have yet to meet the man I couldn't impress when I tried, but I doubt I have much future with the like of Death." She turned and departed the way she had arrived, poised but still not special. It seemed to Zane that Magician and daughter both had considerable arrogance, assuming so blithely that the office-holder of Death could be swayed by such obvious means.

Perhaps, he thought further, his glimpse of lovely Angelica had forever spoiled him for other women, even if his new office had not.

"My message is this," the Magician said abruptly. "There is a complex plot afoot that affects my daughter, Luna Kaftan. I have protected her hitherto, but I shall no longer be able to do so. Therefore I am asking you to do so."

"I must have misunderstood. I thought you were offering me your daughter's favors in exchange for five minutes of my time."

The Magician smiled. "Death, you are rightly cynical. It is a barbed offer, of course. If you accept the bait, you will find yourself emotionally committed and you will guard her in a manner few others could."

"How can I guard anyone?" Zane demanded, sensing that he was being managed. "I am Death!"

"You are uniquely qualified," the Magician insisted. "When, through my black arts, I perceived the nature of the conspiracy against my child, I knew she would have to have a champion to guard her as I could not. I researched diligently to locate that champion, neglecting my health in the process, and at length identified you."

"Me!" Zane exclaimed. "As Death, I can do only a thing you would not want for your daughter. As a man, not as Death, I am unqualified to do anything at all for her. You should know that!"

"As a man, it is true, you are unremarkable," the Magician agreed. "But you are nevertheless uniquely qualified for the need. I believe you will grow with the office and become what you presently are not."

"You know something about how I got the job of Death?" This was indeed interesting.

"I was the one who persuaded Fate to arrange your placement at that office," the Magician said.

"Persuaded Fate! You—?"

"I suspect you are not yet aware of the significance of your role."

"Well, every person has to die sometime—"

"But any person can serve, however indifferently, in the office of Death. This particular situation requires your personal expertise."

"You're not making much sense to me!" Zane said. "It was sheer chance that brought me to—"

He broke off, for the Magician's daughter Luna had re-entered the room. She was clothed now—she was evidently efficient about getting dressed—and wore makeup and had let down her hair—and it did make a difference. Her tresses were shoulder-length, chestnut brown, and shone with such a rich luster that Zane was sure an enchantment of enhancement had been applied. Her eyes, which had seemed nondescript before, now were huge and beautiful, their color a deep gray like the hide of a fine racing horse, or the Deathsteed himself. Her cheeks had warmed and her lips were bright and sensual, the teeth showing white and even. She wore two Saturn-stone earrings that projected little colored rings and illuminated the smooth column of her neck on either side.

But she had hardly finished her makeover there. She wore an off-shoulder gray blouse that clung lightly to the contours of her arms and bosom, making what had seemed modest before come to life now as a fully respectable endowment. Her belt was wide and heavy and set with colored stones; probably it was a flying belt. Her brown skirt, matching the shade of her hair, caressed a configuration of hip and leg that was elegant in its artistry of form. Zane had not before realized how striking a slender woman could be. Even her feet were pretty, in delicate, winged, green slippers that were crafted to resemble her namesake, the luna moth. About her neck was a chain of gold in the mode of fine serpentine, and on the chain, suspended artfully between her breasts, was a large moonstone, its brightness at crescent phase. Such stones waxed and waned magically with the changes of the real moon, the ultimately female symbol. She was magically lovely, as stunning as any model at a fashion show.

Of course she had magic, Zane reminded himself. She was a Magician's daughter! Naturally she had become impressive; it was all artifice! Yet he could not help being impressed, for it was indeed the same girl he had seen before, in a new aspect. Luna's present presence was like a selected precious stone, dull in shadow, suddenly enhanced by the brilliance of a spotlight that caused it to project its awesome luster.

She had been nude before. Truly, in seeing her uncovered, he had not seen her at all. Not even Angelica could rival—

"Shall I do a dance for you?" Luna inquired with a charming quirk of a smile.

"I don't believe it," Zane muttered.

"Well, you should," she said mischievously. "You saw me nude."

Zane shook his head. "I don't believe a creature like you can be casually offered to a nondescript character like me. It just doesn't make sense."

"Oh, she is no gift," the Magician said. "Luna has to be won, and the winning is not straightforward. What you get is the first option to compete."

"I don't care to compete," Zane said, distrusting this. He was aware that the Magician was offering less, now that Luna had manifested as more. Zane didn't like being managed.

"Suit yourself. The Lovestone is here." The Magician indicated a small blue gem on the table beside him.

"I have no use for Lovestones!" Zane snapped. He now wished he had never seen Angelica; how much grief that would have saved him!

"Perhaps you misunderstand," the Magician said. "This is not your common locater stone; this one compels love. Merely hold it and look at the woman you desire, and she will be instantly afflicted with overwhelming passion for you. You do not find these on sale in knickknack shops."

Zane eyed the stone with new respect. If he took that and looked at

Luna, she would become his love slave. Probably its effect was limited to a single session; otherwise the user would never be able to get away from the subject. But it meant the man—or woman—possessing such an artifact could take advantage of any other person encountered. What was he to make of the father who openly offered to subject his lovely daughter to such influence, or of the girl who knowingly permitted such enchantment to be used on her? "Thanks, no."

Luna nodded slightly, perhaps in approval. Had this been a test? The Magician had said his daughter needed to be won, and the use of the Lovestone was hardly fair competition. Maybe the stone induced passion but not love. Given the choice between passion and love, Zane preferred the latter.

The Magician settled slightly in his chair, relaxing. "I must proceed; the spell that extends my life beyond its appointed time is weakening, ₍nd I dare not use another."

"You dare not?" Zane asked, increasingly suspicious. "Aren't you a powerful Magician?"

"Magic is addictive and often damning. The white magic which has become so popular is generally harmless, but it can lead stage by stage to the more potent black magic, which gradually corrupts and eventually damns the user. All serious practitioners employ black magic, because of its versatility and power. I have used more than enough to damn me to Hell."

"But you are in balance, or I would not have been summoned!"

"Technically true. It was necessary that I summon you, and this was the only way possible without alerting the Unmentionable."

"The—"

"Do not utter the name, for he is attuned to it. My enchantment protects us from chance discovery, but against his direct inquiry there is no protection, and his name would bring that. This discussion has to be private. Once I talk to you, my fate hardly matters, except that I must stay free of Hell long enough to give the plan a chance to function. The Unnamed quickly picks the brains of his incoming victims. So we had to seem to meet in the normal course, to avoid suspicion."

"You set up your own death, just to talk to me without a certain entity knowing—when you yourself had gotten Fate to put me in office?"

"It does seem to be a cumbersome mechanism. But a complex conspiracy is abroad, and devious sacrifices are required."

"Such as your life—and your daughter's virtue?"

Luna smiled, taking no offense. "Father is like that. That's why he's a great Magician—one whom even the Incarnations respect."

Evidently so. "What conspiracy?" Zane demanded.

"That I may not tell you," the Magician said.

"How can I help you if I don't know what you want?"

"I have told you what I want. My daughter's salvation."

"Some way you have to guarantee it!" Zane said, glancing meaningfully at the Lovestone. "Your daughter is obviously only a pretext for some more sinister scheme. What do you really want?"

The Magician stared at the floor for a moment as if considering. "I want what every halfway decent man wants: the belief that his life has in some small or devious fashion benefited the cosmos. My use of black magic has so weighted my soul that my daughter had to assume a share of my evil in order to put me in technical balance. Now she, too, is in peril. But she should have time to redeem herself, if our ploy is successful."

"She can take some of your evil?" Zane asked, surprised. "I thought every soul had to be judged on its own merits."

"It does, ordinarily. But sophisticated magic can alter cases, and this case has been altered. At the moment, both of us are in balance."

Zane looked at Luna again. Her face was unlined and innocent. He was relieved to know that the evil in her soul was not truly hers; she was basically a good girl. He was well aware that physical beauty bore no certain relation to the condition of a person's soul, but he still felt more at ease when the two matched.

Now the girl leaned over her father. "It is time, Father," she said. "I'll never know your equal." She kissed him. Then she straightened up and faced Zane. "Death, bring thy sting," she said, and turned away.

Zane started his countdown timer again. He walked up to the Magician, who had abruptly settled into the final seizure, and drew out his soul. Quickly he folded it and put it away.

Still facing opposite, Luna spoke. "My father made an agreement with you. I will honor it without the use of the Lovestone. You will understand if I do not pretend any personal joy in the matter. Come this way." She walked toward the doorway through which she had entered.

The Deathwatch was counting down for the next client, but Zane paused. "You father, whom you professed to love deeply, has just died," he said, shocked. "How can you think of a thing like—like that—at this moment? Where is your grief?"

She halted, but did not face him. "I can do what my father asked me to do because I respect his judgment above that of any other person. When I realized that his death was upon him, I invoked the enchantment he had prepared for this occasion. I put on a gem that eliminated incapacitating emotion. After you depart, I will remove that stone and suffer as much as I can stand before I have to don the gem again. My grief will run its course in measured stages. But my grief is not yours, and while I am with you, I shall not share it with you."

Zane shook his head, appalled at this explanation. "I don't claim to be a good man or a good Death. Mostly I have been satisfied to take what I can get. I was a fool not long ago and threw away my chance to love and marry a wonderful woman—"

"Fate arranged that loss, at my father's behest, " Luna said. "You need feel no responsibility there."

So that, too, had been no coincidence! Zane was shaken, but plowed on. "Now I'm going to be a fool again. I have not done your father any genuine service I know of and, in any event, don't deserve the sort of attention you—"

Luna turned back to face him. She seemed prettier than ever. Her eyes were pearl as they fixed on his. No, she had not been bluffing about her ability to impress a man! "Yes, you are correct, of course. You don't want false rapture. Use the Lovestone; then my passion will be genuine. I should not have tried to avoid that. I will also, if you wish, use it on you, so that your reservations will dissipate."

"That's not what I meant!" Zane exclaimed, embarrassed. "I don't deserve the attention or the love of a woman like you. Keep the Lovestone; I will not abuse your nature by using it. Maybe when I was a living man I would have done so, but now I am Death, with an important responsibility, and I must honor the dignity of the office as I perceive it. I will leave you to your grief." He turned to the exit, half-cursing himself for his perversity. This was not typical behavior for him; why hadn't he simply taken the proffered payment?

"Why?" she asked. He could tell by the sound of her voice that she had turned again. They were both facing away, the dead Magician's body between them.

Zane himself wasn't sure. He had spoken of the dignity of his office—but not long ago he had tried to give up that office. "I—look, I admit you're the kind of woman I like. The kind any man would like. You set out to impress me and you certainly did. You didn't seem like much when—when you weren't trying—well, right now I'm sure you're everything I might want, but—I guess it's what your father said. I want to make something good of my life, or of my office, while I still have the chance. Otherwise, what's the point? If I had been good before, I wouldn't have come to the point of death myself so soon. I'm trying to be good now, for what it's worth, so at least I can think of myself as halfway useful for something. To—to take advantage of you—especially at this time—I know that would— I did something like that once in life, and it remains a blot on my soul—well, it's just not the way I think someone as important as Death should be. So I'm going to try to play the part the way I think it should be played, even though I'm not—I know I'm not a worthy actor."

"You are going counter to my father's wish," she said. "He scheduled his death to bring you here so you would meet me. Fate took that other woman from you so that you would be free for me. I am owed to you in a very real sense."

"I have met you. I don't think you owe me anything for what Fate did. Maybe I'm on the rebound from that love I threw away before it started. Maybe I'm just angry at being managed. I think I would—I don't know. Maybe your father misjudged me."

"Maybe he did," she agreed. "Still, I must acquit my own debts and try to honor his will. I would be false to my father's memory if I did otherwise. Would you settle for a date?"

"If I start seeing a woman of your quality, I'll soon want too much."

"You can have too much."

"I—no, I mean Death should not be distracted."

"Then come when you're off duty."

Zane felt guilty, but also sorely tempted. "One time," he agreed. "One time."

Nothing more was to be said. Zane opened the door, picked up his scythe, and went out to his horse.

He mounted. "On to the next, steed," he said.

The stallion leaped into the sky. Dawn was just arriving here, and a bank of clouds to the east was starting to glow. Mortis trotted over clouds as if they were sand, flying without wings, then plunged down through them somewhere on the daylit portion of the globe.

But it was not land below. The horse came down on the expanse of the Atlantic Ocean. His feet touched and held; naturally this animal could run on water!

Ahead, the cloud cover dipped to intersect the water: a storm. The stallion galloped right at it. Zane viewed the lash-whipped waves with increasing alarm. The person who held the office of Death was immortal only as long as he was not killed. Suppose he drowned? The sea was becoming mountainous, the waves already surging higher than his head, and much higher nearer the storm.

"I don't like this," he said. "Who will replace me if I drown here?" That wasn't really his worry, however. He didn't care who next assumed the office; he didn't want to vacate it.

He didn't? Then why had he tried, so ineptly, to get his client to turn on him and kill him? What did he really want?

He wasn't sure, but suspected it related to some personal aspect. He could accept his own demise more readily if he deliberately handed the office to a chosen successor than if an inanimate ocean washed him out. It was control and self-esteem at the root of his disquiet.

A spot near the saddle horn blinked. Zane touched it—and the horse became a double-hulled speedboat, cutting through the fringe of the storm.

Wonders never ceased! "You are some creature, Mortis!" Zane exclaimed.

But the waves were so horrendous that the craft was soon tilting precariously. The pale boat was steering itself aptly, to avoid being swamped, but the sea seemed determined to outmaneuver it.

"I prefer you as a horse!" Zane cried as the craft crested a pinnacle and tilted sickeningly forward. He punched the blinking button on its control panel.

The horse returned, galloping along the shifting contour of the wave. Yes, this was definitely better! The animal could not be swamped or overturned. "I couldn't manage without you, Mortis," Zane said, hanging on desperately.

Then the client came into sight. It was a young man, clinging to a bit of flotsam. The man saw Zane and lifted a hand weakly. Then he sank into a wave.

"He doesn't have to die!" Zane protested, speaking as much for himself as for the client.

Mortis snorted noncommittally. After all, Death had been summoned here to collect the client's soul.

"I'm going to rescue him," Zane said. "To watch him drown—that would be like murder!"

The horse did not react, except to come to a halt on the water beside the drowning man. Zane dismounted and found that his feet stood firmly on the surface. Fate had said his shoes would make that possible, but he had not quite accepted it until now.

He reached down, caught the man's projecting arm, and hauled him upward. The wave was liquid for the client, solid for Zane's feet—and Zane's gloved hand did not pass through the man's flesh when he didn't want it to. His magic accommodated itself to his specific needs.

But a surge crossed their location, burying the client and almost jerking him away. Irritated, Zane punched the center button of the Deathwatch, seeking to freeze time itself. Nothing happened, and he remembered that this button had to be pulled, not pushed. He pulled.

The water halted in place: waves, bubbles, and spume. The racing fog stopped as if photographed. All was still and silent.

Zane got a better grip on the client and hauled him out of the sea. Apparently time did not abate for Death or Death's pale horse, or for what Death touched. What an amazing power Chronos had bequeathed! But it was not enough, for it was evident that the client was far gone; he had inhaled water during his final submersion.

Zane got the man up on the rump of the horse, arms dangling down to one side, legs to the other. He pressed on the man's back, trying to squeeze out the water from his lungs, but this wasn't very effective. Then Mortis bucked, bouncing the man, and that did it; the water dribbled out of his mouth, and he began to choke and gasp.

Zane helped him stand. The man's eyes widened. "You are Death— but you haven't killed me!"

"I will take you to shore," Zane said. "Mount behind me and hold on."

They mounted. "I don't understand," the man said somewhat plaintively.

Zane pushed the button in the watch. The storm resumed. The horse walked up the progressing slope of the wave. The wind tore at them, but they were secure against it.

"Why?" the man asked.

Zane couldn't answer. He feared he was violating his office and would somehow be punished, but he still had to save this man.

Soon they exited from the storm. There was an island ahead; the pale horse knew where he was going. They came to a deserted beach, but stray bottles showed it was at times frequented by tourists. There was civilization within range.

The man got down and stood on the wet sand, still unbelieving. "Why?" he repeated. "You, of all creatures—"

Zane had to make some response, if only to justify his irrationality to himself. "Your soul is in danger of Hell. Go and do good in the world, to redeem your afterlife."

The man stared, mouth open. This was the twentieth century; no one took such cautions seriously!

"Farewell," Zane said.

Mortis took off, prancing once more into the sky. Zane realized that more magic must be involved to prevent him from falling off when the horse made such motions. His office was failsafe in various ways!

He looked back and glimpsed the erstwhile client still standing, staring after him.

Had he done the right thing? Probably not. For the second time, he had actually interfered with a death, changing the course of a client's life. Maybe he was acting in an irrational manner, allowing his personal hang-ups to affect his office. Yet Zane knew he would do it again. Apparently he was unable to rise above his human limitations to perform the office impartially.

The Deathwatch was counting down again. Zane punched the STOP button, halting the countdown without stopping regular time. "I've had enough of this for the moment," he said to the horse. "I want to pause and reflect. Do you have a favorite pasture where you graze? Take me there."

Obediently the horse galloped farther up to a thin cloud layer. As they came level with it, Zane saw the topside open out into a lush, green plain. "So your pasture is in the sky!" he remarked.

The horse landed on the greensward and trotted across it to a large, comfortable ginkgo tree. Zane dismounted. "You will be near when I need you?"

The stallion made an acquiescent nicker and proceeded to graze. Zane noticed that the animal was now unfettered by bridle or saddle; these accouterments had simply ceased to exist when not in use.

Zane sat down and leaned back against the massive trunk of the tree. "What am I doing here?" he asked himself aloud. "Why aren't I doing my job?"

No answers came. Mortis grazed in the lush field. The light breeze rustled the odd ginkgo leaves. A small spider dangled on a thread before Zane.

"What's the matter with me, Arachnae?" he asked the spider. "I have a good job here, fetching in the souls of the borderlines. Why am I letting them go, when I thought I wanted to act in accordance with the standards of the office? Am I a hypocrite?"

The spider enlarged. Four of its legs dangled down, fusing into two larger limbs, and four lifted up, becoming two lesser extremities. Its abdomen contracted and elongated. Its head rounded, and the eight eyes merged in much the manner the legs had, two pairs forming two larger orbs and the other two pairs sliding to the sides to form ears. In moments the arachnid became a woman, holding a strand of web between her hands. "Oh, we call it the delayed-reaction syndrome," she said. "You can't step from ordinary life into immortality without suffering systemic dislocation. You will survive it."

"Who are you?" Zane demanded, surprised.

"How short your memory is," she teased him, shifting to a younger form.

Now he recognized her. "Fate! Am I glad to see you!"

"Well, I did bring you into this, so it may be my responsibility to tide you through the break-in period. All you have to do is accept and adapt to the new reality, and you're all right."

"But I know the new reality," he protested. "I know I'm supposed to take souls. But I'm not taking them! Not consistently. I talked one woman out of suicide and I actually rescued a drowning man."

"That does complicate things," she said thoughtfully. "I never heard of Death helping people live. I'm not sure there's a precedent. Except—"

"Yes?"

"I'm afraid I can't tell you that, Death."

Zane's brow wrinkled. "There's something you know that you won't tell me?" She had said something like that before, annoyingly.

"That is the case. But in due course all shall be known."

He realized that it was useless to try to coerce Fate. "Well, is there anything useful you *will* tell me?"

"Oh, yes, certainly. What you need to do, to get yourself settled in, is to take some souls to Purgatory. Once you comprehend that aspect of the system, you won't be so reluctant to do your duty."

"Purgatory? I've thought of it, but I don't know where it is. Chronos said I could ride my horse there, but somehow—"

She pointed. "Right there."

Zane looked. There, across the field, was a modern building complex, somewhat like a university. "That's Purgatory?"

"What did you expect—a medieval dungeon guarded by a dragon?"

"Well—yes. I mean, the concept of Purgatory—"

"This is the twentieth century, the golden age of magic and science. Purgatory moves with the times, as do Heaven and Hell."

Zane hadn't thought of it that way. "I just go there and empty out my bag of souls?"

"Those you haven't been able to classify yourself," she said.

Zane became suspicious. There was something devious about the way Fate phrased things. "What happens to souls there?"

"They get properly sorted. You'll see. Go ahead."

Zane considered. "First let me sort out whatever I can."

"Do that." Fate shrank back into the spider, who climbed up its strand and disappeared into the dense foliage of the tree.

He labored over the souls for some time. He managed to classify all except two: the baby and the Magician. The former was so evenly gray that no reading was possible; the latter was so complexly convoluted with good and evil that it was an impenetrable maze, even for the stones.

He walked to the Purgatory main building. It was a structure of red brick, with green vines climbing the walls.

The great front door was unguarded. Zane wrapped his cloak about him and pushed on in. There was a desk with a pretty receptionist. "Yes?" she said, in exactly the manner such decorations did on Earth.

"I am Death," he said, slightly diffidently.

"Certainly. Follow the black line."

Zane saw the line painted on the floor. He followed it down a hall, around corners, and into a modern scientific laboratory. There were no people present, and no devils or angels; it seemed he was supposed to know what to do next. He was, in fact, a bit disgruntled by the receptionist's cool reaction, as if Death were routine. Maybe Death was, here.

He looked around. He spied a computer terminal. Good enough.

Zane seated himself before the terminal. He looked for a brand name, but there was none; this was a generic machine, as was perhaps appropriate. It had a standard typewriter keyboard and assorted extra function buttons. He punched ON, and the screen illuminated.

GREETINGS, DEATH, it printed in bright green letters on a pale background. HOW MAY WE SERVE YOU?

Zane was not a good typist, but he was adequate. I HAVE TWO SOULS TO CLASSIFY, he typed, and saw the words appear on the screen in red, below the computer's query.

The machine made no response. After a moment he remembered—he had to ask it a question or give it a directive if he wanted it to react. WHAT SHOULD I DO WITH THEM? he added.

PUT ONE IN EACH DEVICE, it replied.

Zane looked about again. He saw a line of devices. He started to get up.

A buzzer sounded, recalling his attention to the computer. TURN ME OFF WHEN NOT IN USE, the screen said.

Oh. Zane made a pass at the OFF button, but held up. WHY? he typed.

IT IS NOT NICE TO WASTE POWER.

Zane typed again. NO. I MEAN, WHY DON'T YOU HAVE A CIRCUIT TO TURN YOURSELF OFF WHEN THE OPERATOR DEPARTS? THAT WOULD BE FOOLPROOF.

HAVE YOU EVER TRIED TO GET A GOOD SUGGESTION THROUGH A BUREAUCRACY? The print was turning reddish, as if from justifiable irritation.

Zane smiled and hit the OFF button, and the screen faded. He suspected there was more to this computer than showed.

He went to the first device. It looked like a spin-drying machine. He brought out the baby soul and fed it into the hopper.

The machine purred. The soul dropped down into the spinner, which started to rotate. Faster and faster it went, plastering the soul against its rim.

"A centrifuge!" Zane exclaimed. "To spin out the evil! So it can be measured!" Suddenly it made sense. Presumably after the evil was out, there would be another spin to extract the good, and some way to match them against each other.

But no evil spun out. After an interval the machine stopped. The soul was ejected to a lower hopper.

Zane picked it up and returned to the terminal. He turned on the computer. IT DIDN'T WORK, he typed. WHAT DO I DO NOW?

DESCRIBE THE SOUL.

IT'S A BABY, PURE GRAY, NO SHADES.

OH, NO WONDER, the screen said with unmechanical expression. THAT'S A DEFINITION DECISION. TURN IT IN TO RECYCLE.

This made Zane pause. He wasn't ready to let go of this yet. WHAT'S A DEFINITION DECISION?

A CATEGORY OF CLASSIFICATIONS, the screen informed him blithely, adopting a blue tinge. It seemed the computer liked being didactic. SOULS THAT ARE AUTOMATICALLY IN BALANCE.

In balance. Half good, half evil. Zane had been dealing with that kind all along; in fact, he was one of that number himself. BUT HOW COULD THIS BE, FOR AN INNOCENT BABY? he asked.

A BABY CONCEIVED IN SIN, the screen explained. AS BY RAPE, INCEST,

OR GROSS DECEPTION, WHOSE BIRTH CAUSES INVIDIOUS HARDSHIP TO A
PARENT, IS DEEMED TO BE IN BALANCE UNTIL FREE WILL COMMENCES.
NORMALLY AT THAT STAGE THE BALANCE SHIFTS, AND YOUR OFFICE IS
NOT REQUIRED.

So that was the way it was. Chronos had conjectured as much. This
baby had died of illness and neglect before it attained enough free will
to change. Thus Death had been summoned—and had found the infant
soul almost unsullied by experience.

WHY? he typed. WHY DO THAT TO A BABY?

TO GUARANTEE IT HAS A CHOICE.

BUT IT HAD NO CHANCE! Zane protested. IT DIED BEFORE IT HAD FREE
WILL!

THAT IS THE REASON, the computer explained patiently, taking Zane's
statement to be a question. NO SOUL MAY BE RELEGATED TO ETERNITY
WITHOUT A CHANCE TO ESTABLISH ITS OWN RECORD. A SOUL WITHOUT
A RECORD MUST BE HELD.

Zane began to understand. It wasn't fair to allow a soul to be damned
to Hell without at least a chance to redeem itself, and probably Heaven
had rules about accepting the children of iniquity.

Zane thought about that and concluded he didn't like it. There might
be iniquity, but it associated with the erring parents, not the child. If
he were in charge, he would change a definition or two.

But of course he was not in charge. He was not God—or Satan. It
was not his business to make the rules.

Yet he was involved, for he was Death. He had collected this soul. He
felt responsible. WHAT HAPPENS WHEN A SOUL IS HELD? he typed.

IT REMAINS FOREVER IN PURGATORY, the screen replied.

FOREVER! he typed, appalled. EVEN CRIMINAL SOULS ARE NOT CON-
FINED HERE FOREVER, ARE THEY?

TRUE. CRIMINAL SOULS GO TO HELL FOREVER.

That realigned things. Purgatory was surely better than Hell! WHAT
DO THE HELD SOULS DO HERE?

THEY RUN PURGATORY.

Oh. THE RECEPTIONIST IS ONE?

CORRECT.

That didn't seem so bad, if not exactly good. Desk work could get
insufferably dull over the passage of centuries. But, of course, this was
the in-between place. Eternal neutrality was surely better than Hell.

Zane turned off the computer, moved to the second device, and drew
out the Magician's soul. The device resembled a sealed robot, looking
at a pile of papers on a desk. The soul got fed into a slot in the robot's
back. In a moment the machine animated, its eye lenses glowing, its
metal limbs moving.

The robot glanced at Zane. "Am I dead yet?" The Magician's voice
asked.

"Yes," Zane replied, taken aback. No soul had talked to him before. "Where am I, then?"

"Purgatory. Your soul is so precisely in balance, I couldn't clarify it for Heaven or Hell, so I brought it here."

"Excellent," the Magician said.

"You *want* to be stuck here?"

"I *have* to be here, as long as possible. My calculations were most precise, but there is always that element of uncertainty. A lot hangs on this."

"A lot hangs on what?" Zane asked, perplexed again.

"Did my daughter Luna reward you for your consideration?"

"Aren't you avoiding my question?"

"Aren't you?"

Zane smiled. "Your daughter offered, again, but I declined, again."

"But you mustn't decline!" the Magician-robot protested. "Luna is for you. I left you the Lovestone."

"If you wanted me to meet her, there must have been some better way than bringing me to your own death."

"No," the robot said. "No better way. Pay no attention to her protestations; she will do what I wish her to."

"She didn't protest! *I* protested! It just isn't—"

"Go after her, Death. She is worth your while."

"She's not interested in me!" Zane said. "Why should I force my attention on her, by magical or nonmagical means, when I am such a personal nonentity? She surely deserves much better, and can get it." That, Zane realized now, was part of his objection. He could not afford to get emotionally hooked on a woman who would surely leave him soon for a better man.

"You must," the Magician insisted. "It is essential."

"Why?" Zane was quite curious now.

"I can't tell you."

"That's what you said before! And Fate tends to speak in riddles, too. That annoys me."

"The rest doesn't matter. Luna is a good girl," the Magician said somewhat lamely.

"Good reason for her not to be taken by Death."

"I must get on to my chore," the Magician said, his metallic gaze resting on the desk.

"What is your chore?"

"Obviously I must tote up the balance of good and evil on my soul myself. These are the tote-forms." The metal hand touched the pile of papers. "One for every day of my life."

Zane looked at a form. "Enter sixteen percent of balance from Form 1040-Z on Line 32-Q," he read. "If figure is greater than that on Line 29-P of Schedule TT, subtract 3.2 percent of Line 69-F. If less than

amount shown on Line, $\sqrt{15}$ on Schedule $i,$ go to Form 7734 Inverted."
He looked up, his mind spinning. "This is almost as bad as an income
tax form!"

"Almost," the Magician agreed wearily. "Where do you think the
Revenue Department gets its inspiration? It will take me eternity to get
through this paperwork."

"How do you think it will come out when the final total has been
figured? Will you go to Heaven?"

"By the time I complete the final form, I will have to start searching
for errors," the robot said. "That will take a few more centuries."

"Maybe there won't be any mistakes," Zane suggested.

"Such forms are designed to be impossible to complete correctly the
first time," the Magician said. "What would be the point if they were
comprehensible?" He picked up a feather quill, dipped it in a pot of
red ink, and commenced his labor. Soon oily sweat beaded his metal
brow.

Zane left the robot to his endless labor. Such a task would drive any
normal person crazy, but perhaps the Magician had special resources.

He dropped the baby soul off with the receptionist on the way out.
"Oh, good," she said, this time showing some human animation. "We
need new personnel!"

Zane wondered how a tiny baby would be able to perform, but
decided not to inquire. Purgatory surely had ways to facilitate such
things and, of course, it had eternity to do so.

-5-

LUNA

His horse still grazed outside. "Hey, Mortis!" Zane called, and the gallant Deathsteed trotted across to him. What a beautiful animal!

He mounted. "Take me home, wherever that is."

The horse trotted to the edge of the green plain and stopped before a handsome funeral home with white columns on a spacious front porch. The name on the mailbox was DEATH.

It figured. Where else would Death live but in a mortuary?

Zane looked at the horse. "Is it okay for me to stay here a while? At least long enough to familiarize myself with the premises?"

Mortis flicked an ear forward affirmatively.

"Do you have a stable or something here? Do I need to provide you with feed, gasoline, or anything?"

The horse told him neigh, and wandered away to graze some more. The pasture looked exceedingly rich; it was probably all Mortis needed. There was a small lake nearby, so water was also available. This was a nice region.

So Death had a mailbox! Who would be writing to this office? Zane walked to the box and opened it. There were four letters inside. He took them out, noting that the return addresses were Earthly. Interesting.

He turned to the front entrance of the Deathhouse. Should he ring the bell? Not if this drear mansion was now his home. Still, he was new here. He rang.

A toll like that of doom sounded inside. In a moment the door opened. A black-clad butler stood there. "So good to see you again, sir. Let me take your cloak." He moved around to ease off the garment.

"I—I've changed," Zane said somewhat awkwardly. "I'm not the same man."

"Of course, sir. We serve the office, not the man." The butler hung the cloak in the hall closet and bent to touch Zane's feet. Zane realized the man intended to remove his protective shoes. Well, if he wasn't safe here, where else could he be safe? He acquiesced, and soon shoes and gloves joined the cloak, while Zane stood in comfortable robe and house slippers.

He smelled something strange. "What is that odor?"

"That is myrrh, sir," the butler replied. "This mansion is scented with it traditionally."

"The House of Death has to be scented?"

"Myrrh is associated with the office, sir."

Now Zane remembered lines from a Christmas carol: *Myrrh is mine, its bitter perfume Spells a life of gathering doom. Suffering, sighing, bleeding, dying, sealed in this stone-cold tomb.*

"Well, substitute something more pleasant," Zane said. "And change that death-knell doorbell. If I have any real influence, Death is going to develop a new image."

The butler conducted him to a pleasant sitting room deep in the building. "Please make yourself at ease, sir. Do you care for an aperitif? Television? A restoration-spell?"

Zane sank down heavily in the overstuffed chair. He did not feel at ease. "All of the above," he said.

"Presently," the butler agreed. "And shall I take the mail, sir?"

"The mail? What for?"

"For destruction, sir, according to normal policy."

Zane clutched the letters to his breast defensively. "Absolutely not! I don't care if it's all junk mail, I'll look at it first."

"Of course, sir," the butler said smoothly, as if pacifying a child. The television set came on in front of Zane as the man departed.

"Two changes in Purgatory personnel," the nondescript newscaster said. "The office of Death has a new occupant. The former Death, having acquitted himself satisfactorily, improved the balance of his soul and went to Heaven. Death is dead; long live Death! The policies of his replacement are not yet clear; he is running behind schedule, has allowed two clients to escape, and is annoying the staff of his mansion by demanding petty changes in routine. An anonymous, highly placed source conjectures that a Reprimand may be issued if improvement does not occur soon."

Zane whistled. The Purgatory News was really current and specific!

"One infant has been added to the staff," the newscaster continued. "He will be trained as a file clerk, once he grows to cognizance. He will, of course, be permitted to choose which age to fix for eternity. This will help relieve the congestion caused by increasing numbers of clients being processed, owing to the general increase in human population."

Zane was becoming suspicious. Why was the news so directly related to his own involvement?

The butler reappeared, setting a glass of red wine before him. "The spell is included in the formula, sir."

"Why is the news so relevant to my interests?" Zane demanded. "It can't be coincidence."

"This is Purgatory, sir. There is no coincidence. All news relates to the listener."

"Purgatory? I thought that was the building complex across the way."

"This entire region, sir. The larger building is merely the Administration and Testing Center. All of us in the intangible zone of Purgatory are lost souls."

"But I'm here, and I'm not even dead yet!"

"No, sir. You five are not, technically. The rest of us are."

"Five? Who?"

"The Incarnations, sir."

"Oh. You mean Death, Time, Fate—"

"War and Nature, sir," the butler finished. "These are the living residents of Eternity. All others are dead, except, of course, the Eternals."

"The Eternals?"

"God and Satan, sir. They are not subject to ordinary rules."

Zane took a gulp of the wine. It was excellent and did indeed invigorate him. "I see. You yourself are dead?"

"Yes, sir. I was collected by the holder of your office twice removed. I have served here for seventy-two Earthly years."

"So you watch Deaths come and go, every thirty years or so! Doesn't it get dull for you?"

"It certainly is better than Hell, sir."

There was that. Anything was better than Hell! "Maybe you'd better introduce me to the remaining staff. I presume a mansion like this has several employees?"

"True, sir. Whom do you prefer to see first?"

"Who is here?"

"The gardener, the cook, the maids, the concubine—"

"The what?"

"The living have needs, sir," the butler reminded him delicately.

"And those needs can be served by the dead?"

"Indubitably, sir."

Zane shook his head, repelled. He gulped the last of his drink. "I have changed my mind. I'll meet the staff another time. I'm sure I have clients accumulating, Earthside."

"Certainly, sir," the butler agreed, as Zane got to his feet, and hurried to fetch his office accouterments. In moments Zane was back in uniform and striding outside.

Mortis was waiting, having anticipated his master's need. Zane mounted and discovered the four letters still in his hand. He had maintained a death grip on them since being challenged by the butler. "I should read these," he muttered.

He found himself in the Deathcar. No, it was a small airplane, on automatic pilot. The remarkabilities of his steed were still manifesting!

Zane tore open the first letter. *Dear Death,* it said. *Why did you have to take my mother? I think you stink.* And it was signed *Love, Rose.*

Zane considered that. Obviously a child. Probably Death had not even serviced that account personally, as the odds were that the girl's mother had been strongly enough oriented to find her own way to Heaven or Hell. But how could the child know that? Perhaps he should tell her.

Answer her letter? Did Death correspond with children? Obviously that had not been the case in the past.

Well, why not? If Rose's letter could reach him, his letter could reach her. Only—what difference would it make to her? Her mother would still be dead.

Yet who was more deserving of an answer than an orphaned child? Zane decided to respond. He would find out where her mother had gone, hoping it was Heaven—that seemed likely, since there was evidently love between them—and inform the little girl. Maybe he could get a message from the mother to relay.

He opened the next letter. *Dear Death—Last night I caught my old goat cheating again. I want you should take him right away tomorrow so I can get the insurance. Sincerely, Outraged Wife. P.S. Make sure it hurts!*

No need to answer that one. No wonder the old goat cheated!

A light was blinking in the Deathplane's control panel. There was a word there: WATCH.

Startled, Zane glanced at his watch. It remained frozen. "Thanks for reminding me, Mortis!" he said, restarting the timer. He put the letters in the dash compartment. He had clients to attend to.

Death traveled all over the world, harvesting souls, and managed to get current on his schedule. Along the way he encountered another obnoxious Hellfire sign-series commercial: WINTER   IS COLD YOUR LIFE   IS SHOT;   GO   TO WHERE   IT'S REALLY HOT! When he had spare time, Zane answered his fan mail, explaining to Rose that her mother had had a terminal ailment and had been in great pain, until finally it had been kindest to send her on to Heaven, where there was no pain. He had gone to Purgatory to look up the records, so he knew this was true. The child's mother had been a good woman. He had not been able to get any answer from her in Heaven, however; apparently those who went there lost all interest in Earthly things. Other letters he answered as appropriate, trying to keep the tone polite. He asked himself why he bothered, in some cases, and could only conclude that it was the right thing to do. The fact of death was so significant to the average person that any ameliorating factor was worthwhile.

The job of collecting and handling souls got easier as he gained experience, but still he did not like aspects of it. People died for such foolish reasons! A man made himself a cup of coffee while his wife was out and used rat poison instead of sugar; he was half-blind and forgetful and ignorant of the layout of the kitchen, but this remained an avoidable folly. At least he should have been warned by the taste! A child got out her mother's collection of curses, invoked them all at once, and was cursed to death before her screams were heard. If only those curses had been stored securely in a locked safe! A teenager went joy riding on a stolen witch's broom, naturally the joystick threw him off—half a mile above the ground. A young man, seeking to impress his girlfriend, jousted with a zoo's fire-breathing dragon and got fried. An old woman, grocery shopping in her car, made a thoughtless left turn into a cement truck. Five souls, three doomed to Hell—when all could have gone to Heaven at a later date, had those people lived more carefully and tried to do more good. And these were only a fraction of the total—that tiny fraction that was so nearly in balance that it required Death's personal attention. What of the vast majority who went to Eternity by themselves, requiring no more than Death's tacit approval? How many of them had ignored their salvation until it was too late and suffered the early demise they should have avoided? Was mankind a hopelessly muddled species?

Morbidly curious, Zane ordered a computer printout from Purgatory and checked it over. Now he had the exact statistics, and they confirmed his suspicions. Millions of people were dying from heart and circulatory complications that could have been abated by simple diet and exercise. Millions were dying from cancer because they had not had it checked or diagnosed until too late and refused to desist from their carcinogenic ways, such as smoking tobacco even when it was fatal for them. A huge number were lost to traumatic causes—car crashes, carpet crashes, falls, firearms—it was horrible how many were shot by their own guns, or murdered by their own supposedly captive demons!

Yet what could he, Death, do about it? He lacked Satan's enormous publicity budget and doubted people would change much, even if clearly warned. By the time he was called in, the damage was in most cases too far progressed to be reversed. People really needed to reorder their lives from the start—and he knew that very few would do that voluntarily. They were aware that their lifestyles were at best silly and at worst suicidal, yet they continued unchanged. Exactly as he himself had continued, until he actually saw the face of Death.

If this was a contest between God and Satan, it was evident that Satan was winning. Of course, Satan was constantly campaigning, with periodic Hellethons on television urging people to GET FIRED! and making the ludicrous promise that HELL BUILDS *MEN!* and offering group plans for families. According to the Covenant, neither Eternal was supposed to interfere in the affairs of living people, but God was the only party to honor it. What good was a pact of noninterference that one party violated freely? Yet if God were to act like Satan, He would be no better than Satan . . .

Zane didn't know the answer, but still he felt the need. Perhaps, he chided himself, if a more competent man had assumed the office, he would have been able to do something really positive. But as long as the office of Death was passed along almost randomly, the officeholders would be mediocre, like himself. What could be expected of someone who had to murder his predecessor to obtain the position? He, Zane, was probably typical of the breed. He could not expect his successor to be much better. If any good were to be done, he would have to do it himself, inadequate though he might be.

Oddly, that realization gave him a new kind of strength. Probably he would fail, but at least he would try. He didn't know what he would do or could do or should do, but hoped he would acquit himself appropriately when the chance came.

He glanced up. He happened to have parked in a northern latitude, during a break between cases, where snow lay on the ground. There was yet another of Satan's ubiquitous billboards: HELL-O!   IT'S WARM BELOW!   SIGN UP EARLY FOR PREFERENTIAL TREATMENT. The picture showed a luscious female demon in a half-open bed, beckoning with her middle finger. In the corner, the miniature female Dee was restraining the male Dee from leaping into the bed.

Zane was tempted to knock down the billboard by driving the Death-mobile through it, but checked himself. This was a free cosmos; Satan had a right to advertise. Decent folk had to let the indecent folk do their thing; that was the paradox of decency. Was it worth it?

He continued his routine. Several more cases turned out to be optional, so that he was able to arrange to spare them. He still didn't know whether this was proper, according to the rules of the job, but the Purgatory television reporting did not take more than routine gossipy notice of them, with a "Look at what the bad boy's done this time!" attitude, so he assumed that, while it might be considered bad form, it was in fact one of his prerogatives: to take or not to take, at a given time. It was possible that a soul that might have squeezed through to Heaven if taken on schedule would later degenerate and go to Hell, but he thought it more likely to be the other way around. What person, confronted with the specter of Death, would not hasten to reform his ways to some extent? Whoever was fool enough to ignore that type of warning and descended to Hell probably deserved his fate.

Still, Zane's underlying misgiving was sharpened by what started out as a routine case. It was a boy of perhaps fifteen, victim of a rare form of cancer. He was resting comfortably at home, thanks in large part to potent medication and an optimism-spell. He looked up in surprise when Zane entered.

"I haven't seen you before, though you seem somehow familiar," the boy said. "Are you a doctor?"

"Not exactly," Zane said, realizing that the boy did not recognize his nature. He was uncertain whether to inform him.

"A psychologist, then, come to try to cheer me up?"

"No, just a person come to take you on a journey."

"Oh, a chauffeur! But I don't feel like riding around the park again."

"It's a longer trip than that."

"Can't you just sit down and talk a while? I get lonely." The boy ran his fingers through his tousled yellow hair, as if to clear his head of loneliness.

Zane sat on the edge of the bed. His watch showed fifteen seconds on the countdown; he froze it there. This boy was dying—and would no one keep him company? Probably because his family and friends knew what the victim didn't. That was one of the ironic cruelties of the situation. "I will talk with you."

The boy smiled quickly, gratefully. "Oh, I'm so glad! You will be my friend, I know." He put forth his hand with some difficulty, for he was weak and it took muscle to hold the hand horizontally from the body. "How do you do. I'm Tad."

Zane took the boy's hand carefully. "Pleased to meet you, Tad. I am—" Here he stopped. The boy did not know he was going to die. What kindness would it be to tell him now? Yet to conceal the information was to lie. A lie by default was still a lie. What should he do?

Tad smiled. "You've forgotten? Or you're here to give me a shot and you're afraid I'll scream?"

"No shot!" Zane said quickly.

"Let me guess, then. You're a bill collector? My dad handles that department. I guess these happiness-spells are costing him a bundle, but I don't think they're worth it, because I still get depressed some. I think he should use those spells on himself, because he's looking pretty peaked these days. Must be due to the cost of all my medication and stuff. I feel guilty because of that, and sometimes I wish it could just end, right now, and stop costing him so much."

It was going to—but Zane knew that would not make the boy's father happy. "I'm not a bill collector," Zane said. "Though I suppose my job is related."

"Maybe you're a salesman, then. You've got a product I can use. A new home-computer program that will keep me riveted for forty-eight hours straight."

"Longer than that," Zane muttered uncomfortably.

"Aw, I don't care. I've played those games till I can't stand any of them any more. And the magic games, too; I've conjured more harmless mythological animals than I ever knew existed. There's a pink elephant under my bed right now. See?" He pulled up the trailing coverlet, and Zane saw the pink trunk of an elephant. "What I really want is to go out in the sun and wind and just run, and feel the dry leaves under my feet, crackling. I've been in this bed so long!"

Of course the boy was too weak to run. Even if Zane took him alive out of the building, it wouldn't work. How much did Tad actually know or suspect of his condition? "What's the matter with you?" Zane asked.

"Oh, it's something to do with my spine. It hurts, so they invoke a local antipain spell and give me a spinal shot, but then my legs get numb and I can't walk. I wish they'd get it fixed; I'm missing a lot of school, and I don't want to repeat a grade. I had a B average. All my friends will be moving on up, you know, and I'd look pretty silly."

So they had actually told him he would get better. Zane found himself turning angry. What right did they have to deceive him so?

"What's the matter?" Tad asked.

Now Zane had to make a decision. Should he tell the truth—or continue the lie? If he avoided the issue, he would in fact be lying by inaction. "I am on the horns of a dilemma," he admitted.

"Watch how you sit on them," the boy advised.

Zane smiled. Trust a youth to make a pun of the horns! "I'd rather be astride my good horse."

"You have a horse? I always wanted one! What breed?"

"I don't know his breed: I'm not expert on that sort of thing. I inherited him. He's a big, pale stallion, very powerful, and he can fly."

"What's his name?"

"Mortis."

"A Morgan? That's a good breed."

"Mortis."

"Morris?"

"Mortis, with a T. He's a—"

Tad was not stupid. "Mortis means death," he said. "I made a B plus in Latin."

Zane felt a sinking sensation. He had given away more than intended, not being a student of Latin. "He is a Deathhorse."

"But no living man can ride a Deathhorse!"

"Unless the horse permits," Zane said, knowing what was coming. Why hadn't he had the courage to state his business honestly?

The boy turned his head to stare at Zane. "That cloak!" he said. "That black hood. Your face—I see it more clearly now. It's just a skull!"

"So it appears. But I am a man. A man performing an office."

"You must be—" Tad took a shuddering breath. "I'll never see school again, will I?"

"I'm sorry. This thing is not of my choosing."

"I guess I knew it. I never really believed those doctors. The drugs and spells made me feel good, but my deepest dreams were screaming. I'd be screaming now, but they've got me so doped up on optimism magic I can't really feel depressed at all. You don't seem half bad, you know. At least you stayed to talk with me."

"I am half bad," Zane said. "Fifty percent evil. But you—" He paused. "Is there some great sin on your conscience?"

"Well, I stole a yo-yo from a store once—"

"That's minor evil. I mean something like murder."

"I wished my aunt was dead once, when she punished me for bad language."

"Wishes are minor, unless acted upon. Did you ever actually try to kill her?"

Tad was horrified. "Never! I wouldn't even think of doing a thing like that!" Then he smiled ruefully. "Well, I guess I did think of it, but I knew I never really wanted to."

"Perhaps you told a terrible lie that got someone else in very bad trouble or caused a death. There has to be something very bad, some great sin on your conscience, as I said. Something you know is really wrong."

The boy considered. "There're some I'd have liked to get on it, but I never got the chance. I'm really pretty clean, I think. I'm sorry I haven't anything better to offer."

Something was amiss here. Zane brought out the two diagnostic gems. "This will not hurt," he said reassuringly.

"That's what all the nurses with needles say."

"No, really. It's painless. I'm merely toting up the evil in you."

The yellow stone brightened into brilliance as Zane passed it near the boy, while the brown one darkened only slightly. "You're ninety percent good," Zane said, surprised.

"I told you I wasn't much."

"But I only come personally for those in balance, whose souls can't get free by themselves. There's been a mistake."

"You mean I'm not going to die?"

Zane sighed. "I don't know, but I doubt that's the nature of the mistake. I think you were slated to die alone, and somehow a wire got crossed and I was summoned. Purgatory is short-handed at the moment; mistakes will happen. I'm sorry I intruded on you. It was not necessary for you ever to know what was awaiting you—until it happened."

"Oh, no! I may be artificially happy, but I'm still lonely. I'm glad you came. It was a good glitch. If I've got to go, I'd like to go with company. May I have a ride on your fine horse?"

Zane smiled. "Indeed you may, Tad."

"Then I guess I'm ready."

Zane pushed the button on his watch, and the dread countdown resumed. In fifteen seconds a sudden seizure shook the boy, and Zane reached out and drew forth his soul before there could be more than momentary pain.

He carried the soul outside to where the horse waited. Zane had arrived in the limousine, but Mortis had somehow anticipated his need. Zane mounted, holding the soul before him. The stallion leaped into the night sky.

At the top of the arc, Zane let the soul go. It continued to float up toward Heaven, while the horse fell back toward Earth. "Farewell, Tad," Zane murmured. "You go to a better place than that which you left."

Zane wrapped up his remaining collections, classifying most of the souls and delivering the rest to Purgatory. Then he went to Death's mansion in the sky for a meal and some sleep. The doorbell now played light classical music, and the scent of the house was of lilies. He might deal in death, but he was alive and had to maintain himself.

He was preoccupied with Tad's case, even after it was over. Had he done the right thing, talking to the boy while other clients waited, telling him the truth that had been denied him? Would this be another bad mark on Zane's record for the television news to announce gleefully? It seemed Death was becoming the butt of much Purgatory humor because of his erratic ways. This time he did not turn on the TV set.

The staff of the Deathhouse seemed alive and solid to him, though Zane knew he was the only living person there. He wasn't certain whether the office of Death made him eligible to interact with the dead, or whether the dead were spelled to seem more physical than they really were. Regardless, when he shook a spirit's hand here in Purgatory, that hand was solid and warm. But he remained keenly aware that these people were not of his world. They were dead and he was alive. He did not feel comfortable in Purgatory.

Then he remembered the Magician's daughter, Luna. Luna Kaftan. He had made a date with her, and her father had been insistent that he keep it. His curiosity had been aroused—and as his memory of his fleeting acquaintance with Angelica, the woman he should have romanced, the one he had sold for the worthless Wealthstone—as that impression faded, his image of Luna sharpened. She had been amazingly attractive in clothing! Why *not* get to know her better? She, at least, was living.

He drove the Deathmobile to Luna's house. But as he arrived in Kilvarough, he suffered an attack of misgiving. Was it proper to involve the office of Death in a personal matter? In fact, hadn't he intended to meet Luna as himself, rather than as Death? He decided to present himself incognito, as Zane.

He stripped away his cloak and gloves and shoes. That left him vulnerable physically, but more secure socially. There was a lot to be said for anonymity.

He rang the bell. It occurred to him, belatedly, that she might not be home. He had not set a particular date; in fact, he was not certain what day this was. A glance at his watch could tell him, of course. It was just that the things of the living world had not been much in his awareness these past few days.

In a moment she answered. She was in a yellow housecoat, her hair bound under a net. She was neither lovely nor plain, but in a somewhat formless, in-between state that was apparently the female neutral condition. Grief was evidently taking its toll; she seemed to have lost some weight, small lines were forming about her face, and her eyes were shadowed. He did not need to inquire what she had been doing for the past few days; she had been home suffering.

Luna looked askance at him, and he realized how strange he must look in shirt, worn trousers, and stocking feet. "My name's Zane," he said. "I would like to be with you this evening."

Now her glance was piercing. She did not recognize him. "I believe you have the wrong address, stranger. How did you get past the griffins?"

"It's the right address, but perhaps the wrong uniform. You have met me before in the guise of Death. The griffins gave me wide clearance when they recognized me by smell. We have a date."

She was quick to reappraise him. "Then come in." She opened the door.

Zane stepped inside—and something like a heavy talon fell on his left shoulder. He craned his neck to look at his attacker, but there was nothing. Yet his nose was wrinkling with the heavy, musky odor of something animalistic or insectoid or worse.

"My invisible guardian," Luna explained. "A trained moon moth. If you had some notion of robbing this house—"

Zane smiled with a certain difficulty. "I should have known you would not be defenseless. But I am who I say I am. I can summon the Deathsteed and don my cloak if necessary; then I think your invisible monster would not find me as easy to handle. But words should suffice; I came last week to take your father, the Magician Kaftan, and he told me I should, er, make your acquaintance if I would talk with him a while. I saw you nude, and then dressed up, and after I took his soul, you offered to—"

"Let him go," Luna murmured, and the claw at Zane's shoulder relaxed. Just as well, for the grip had been increasingly painful.

"Thank you," Zane said. "It doesn't have to be today. I just came when it was convenient for me; I'm afraid I didn't think of your own convenience. I forgot about your grief."

"Today will do," she said, somewhat curtly. "I find I don't enjoy being alone at this time. Let me change and pick up the grief-nullifying stone—"

"No, please!" he cut in. "I prefer to know you exactly as you are. It is right to experience grief; I'm sure your father warrants it. Artificial abatement of a natural feeling—I don't want that."

She considered him, head held slightly askew. "You don't want to be impressed?"

"You impress me as you are. Human."

She smiled quickly, and her beauty flashed into being with the expression. "I think you mean it, and that flatters me. That's almost as good as a spell. What is your pleasure, Zane?"

"Just to honor your father's wish. To talk with you, get to know you. He was most insistent, in Purgatory, when—"

"Purgatory?"

"He is figuring out the balance of his soul there. It will be a tedious task."

She shrugged. "He is good at tedious tasks. He is not in pain?"

"None."

"Then I can let him rest for a while. What were you saying?"

"Just that I came to talk with you. It—I don't see it going any farther than that."

"Why not?" she asked, frowning.

"Oh, it's not that you're not attractive. You showed me before! It's— I don't—"

"Attractive," she muttered darkly, apparently not flattered this time. "You refer to my body, of course, not to my mind or soul."

"Yes," he said, feeling awkward. "I don't know your mind, though I do know a good portion of the evil on your soul is not truly yours. But I said it wasn't that. I know you can make yourself as beautiful as you want to be. But even if you were ugly, you're—you're *some*one, and I'm *no* one, so—"

She laughed. "Death tells me this?"

"Death is merely the office. I'm just the man who happened to blunder into that office. I don't think I deserve it, but I'm trying to do it properly. Maybe in time I'll become a good Death, instead of making mistakes."

"Mistakes?" she inquired. "Sit down, Zane." She took his arm, guided him to the couch, and sat down beside him at an angle, so that her right knee touched his left. "How is it going?"

"You don't want to hear about that sort of thing," he demurred, though he did want to talk about it.

"Listen, Zane," she said earnestly. "My father picked you for that office. To you it may have been a blunder, but—"

"Oh, I didn't mean to criticize your father! I meant—"

"He believed you were the proper person for it. I don't know exactly why, but I have faith in his judgment. There must be some quality in you that makes you best for the position. So don't question your fitness for the office."

"Your father picked me for Death—and for you," Zane said. "I don't see the wisdom of either choice."

She removed her net and began adjusting her rich brown hair. "I don't see it either," she admitted with a smile. "Which simply means I have more to discover. My father always, always makes sense, and he never mistreated me in any way. He's a great man! So I'll try to ascertain the meaning of his will. You show me some of your mind, and I'll show you some of mine. Then perhaps we'll both understand why my father wanted us to interact."

"I suppose he did have some reason," Zane agreed. He hardly objected to improving his acquaintance with this increasingly lovely young woman—for she was growing prettier by the moment as she fixed herself up—but didn't like the feeling of being accepted by her only because she had been ordered to do it. "He was a Magician, after all."

"Yes." She did not belabor the obvious, and now he felt foolish for having done so himself. This was an odd sort of date, and he was hardly easy with it.

"I can see why a man like me would be interested in a woman like you, but not why a man like him would want—I mean, surely you are destined for better things, and he would want those things for you."

"Surely," she agreed, shaking out her glistening locks.

That did not help. Luna was not only turning beautiful again, she was becoming more poised, her gaze level.

"Well," he began. "I was just going to tell you about mistakes. Like one of my last cases, in the office of Death—a boy, a teenager—only no one had told him he was going to die. But he knew it when he recognized me. I don't know whether it was right to lie to him, as they did, or tell the truth, as I finally did. Either way, I think I mishandled it, so it's a mistake."

"You regard an indecision as a mistake?"

"I don't know. I guess so. How can you do what's right if you don't *know* what's right?"

She made a moue. "Score a point for you! I suppose you just have to learn from experience, hoping you don't do too much harm in the process."

"I never really appreciated the significance of death before," he said, troubled. "Now that I'm directly involved in it, the force of it becomes much greater, almost overwhelming. Death is no minor thing."

"How do you mean?" Luna asked gently. Her eyes were nacreous.

"I know every living creature must eventually die; otherwise the world would be intolerably crowded. Even on an individual basis, death is necessary. Who would really want to live forever on Earth? Life would be like a game grown overfamiliar and stale, and what pleasures it offered would be overwhelmed by the intolerable burden of minutiae. Only a fool would carry on regardless. But here I'm not necessarily dealing with the normal course of full lives and the terminations of old age. I'm talking to people who aren't ready to die and taking their souls out of turn. Their full lives have not been lived, their roles have not been played out. Their threads have been cut short through no fault of their own."

"No fault?" She was leading him, in effect interrogating him, but he didn't mind.

"Consider my recent clients. One was a seven-year-old boy. He was having lunch at a school cafeteria, and a valve malfunctioned and caused a water heater to explode. It brought down the ceiling, and five children and a teacher died. My client had a difficult home environment, which was why his soul was balanced between good and evil—but he should have had a full life ahead to put his soul in better order. Through sheer random chance, he was denied that life. And the five others who died, not needing my personal attention—maybe they all went directly to Heaven. I hope so. But this was still grossly unfair to them, for they might have gone to Heaven sixty years later, after having their full chances on Earth. The world might have benefited by their lives; certainly they deserved their chances. What possible meaning can there by in such catastrophe?"

"Fate might know," Luna said.

"And there was a giant flying carpet taking off from Washington, carrying seventy-nine people south. Ice formed on its forward fringe and interfered with its levitation-spell, and it grazed a bridge and crashed into the Potomac River, killing ninety percent of the passengers. I was there for a client and saw the crash—and it was so unnecessary. The simplest deicing spell would have prevented—"

"I thought they always deiced large carpets in winter."

"They do. But they used a weak one this time, and the ice built up again more rapidly than expected, and no one checked. All those innocent people killed—and I thought why, why? If it made any sense at all, maybe I could accept it. But this was mere caprice! All those people subjected to the indignity of meaningless termination, their families saddened—I don't know whether I can continue to be a part of this."

"I would justify it if I could," Luna said. "My father believed there was a purpose in death, however untimely it might seem. He said there was always a rationale, if we could only see it."

"What possible rationale for children killed by an explosion, or families smashed in a carpet crash?" he demanded bitterly. "Can God have any hand in this?"

"I don't know. My father had a dream of a benevolent universe, wherein Heaven, Purgatory, and Hell are all necessary aspects of a Divinely functioning whole. He would have believed that there was a specific reason for every out-of-turn death, and that Fate had directed each person to be on that particular carpet."

"Do you believe that?"

She sighed. "My soul is burdened with evil, and my faith is weak. I don't have the information my father had."

"You are mortal, like me," he said. "You are not provided with ready answers."

"All too true. But I still think we can work out a rationale, if we try. How, exactly, did you get to be Death?"

"I shot my predecessor," Zane admitted. "I was going to suicide, because I'd been gypped out of a girl—a girl like you, beautiful and wealthy and loyal—but when I saw Death, I killed him instead. Then Fate came and told me I had to be the new Death. So I was."

"A girl like me," Luna said. She had continued adjusting herself and now was verging from lovely to ravishing, approaching the physical appeal she had had on their last meeting.

"Yes. Not only pretty, but pure—"

Luna choked on a fit of laughter. "How little you know about women!"

Zane shrugged. "I've known ordinary women. But—"

"Death came for you personally," she cut in with a feminine non sequitur. "That means you were half evil."

"Yes. I never claimed—"

"If you were to pass your definition gems near me, you would find me much the same. My outer form is as fair as nature and cosmetic magic can make it; my inner personality is suspect. Don't put me on any pedestal, Zane. I can match you evil for evil."

"Oh, I'm sure—"

"No, you aren't. But you might as well find out. That should settle whatever my father had in mind." She got up and strode across the room, lithe and purposeful. Her housecoat seemed to have changed along with her attitude and now looked more like a gown. Whatever magic she had wasn't all magic, he realized. "Come to the stone chamber."

Zane followed her, anticipating some kind of crypt hewn out of bedrock, but the chamber turned out to be a bright wood-paneled room arranged like a museum, with small stones of every type set out on shelves and in cabinets. "These—are magic?" he asked, amazed.

"Certainly. That was my father's business—enchanting stones. Some of the most intricate magic in the world is concentrated here. The stones you use to analyze souls may have been crafted by my father, as he was one of perhaps only four living people capable of that precision of magic. He surely knew more about you than you knew about yourself. That's why we need to get to the bottom of this. I confess I'm not keen on any relationship with you, and your interests obviously would have preferred to focus elsewhere, but my father selected you and me for reasons we are bound to fathom before we part. We can't afford to take the risk of rejecting what he set up unless we first understand the reason for it. If we discover a continuing relationship is necessary, we can grit our teeth and use the Lovestone to facilitate—"

"I doubt I need a Lovestone," Zane said. "All I need is to look at you closely."

She shrugged that off as if irrelevant. "But first we must separate reality from illusion. My father said that a person is best defined by the nature of his evil. His own evil was in dealing with Satan for the sake of increased magic power. Without demonic help, he would have been merely a world-class Magician instead of a grand master. So he is defined by his lust for complete professionalism, and I know that damned him, but I also respect him for it."

"Yes," Zane agreed, impressed. He had heard that a world-class Magician could virtually demolish a city with a single fission-spell. What could a grand master do? Zane didn't know and suspected no one else knew, because of the secretive nature of such Magicians.

"Now you and I will exchange evils in the presence of these stones and see what we shall see." Luna lifted several gems from their casings.

"I really don't understand—"

"Hold this stone in your right hand; it glows only when you tell a lie." She handed him a dusky diamond. "And this in your left; it is a Sinstone, like the one you use to evaluate souls."

Zane held the stones, not at all certain he liked this. Luna took similar stones in her hands. "I will lead the way, so you can see how it's done," she said.

"Um," Zane said noncommittally.

"My name is Venus," she announced. Her Truthstone flashed warningly. "I mean Luna." The stone remained dark. "I only did that to prove it's working," she explained, and the stone did not object. "Now test yours."

"My name is Jehosephat," Zane said, and saw his own Truthstone flash. "Zane." The glow faded.

Luna took a deep breath that did things for her torso. She looked pained. "Oh, I don't like this! Why am I doing it?" she asked rhetorically.

"Let's *not* do it," Zane said. "I don't want to know your secrets." But his Truthstone flashed.

"I have fornicated with a demon of Hell," Luna announced.

Zane's jaw dropped.

She faced him defiantly. "There, I did it. Note that my Truthstone did not glow—but my Sinstone brightened." She gestured with her left hand, showing how the stone had come to life. "Whose Sinstone gets brightest—that's the most evil one of us."

Zane swallowed. How had he gotten into this? But Luna's sincere discomfiture made her prettier than ever, and somehow he felt he had to prove she was better than he. "I embezzled funds from my employer," he said. His Sinstone brightened, but not as much as hers.

"I am worse than you," Luna said, like a child teasing.

"I never had the opportunity to make it with a lady demon," he pointed out. But he remained shaken by her revelation. She looked so innocent!

"And I never had an employer from whom to embezzle. Opportunity is only part of it." She took another breath. "I practiced black magic."

"I thought that was your father, not you." But he saw that her right stone was dark, while her left one had brightened another notch. She was guilty, all right, though he, personally, didn't care about black magic. Magic was magic, wasn't it? What did it really matter what color it was?

She was waiting for his second confession. "I gambled away almost everything I had, including friendships."

"Gambling is not really evil," she said. But his Sinstone had brightened significantly.

"I need to clarify that," he said grimly. He understood why Luna had found this so difficult! "There was a girl who loved me—who said she did—but I wouldn't marry her, because she wasn't beautiful and because she was poor. I wanted to marry wealth. She—later I learned she committed suicide. *That* was the main friendship I gambled away—gambling on a richer one."

"That's bad," Luna agreed. "Did you know she was going to kill herself?"

"I never thought of it—until after the fact. Then I realized I should have seen it coming. I should have married her."

"Though you didn't love her?"

"She was a good girl! It would have been much better to marry her than to kill her!" But his Truthstone flickered, for he knew he had not really killed her.

"We tend to assume more evil than is our due, after the fact," Luna said, spying that flicker. "You think she died because you didn't marry her—but that's no basis for marriage. Maybe the money you hoped for was just a pretext for you to turn off a relationship that you knew wouldn't have worked anyway."

"I don't think so." But his Truthstone fluttered again. "I thought about it a lot, after. I decided I had not considered her feelings enough, only my own. I resolved not to be that way any more. I should have realized she was pregnant. If she had told me—"

Luna smiled briefly. "Some girls don't. You would have done what you deemed to be right, but you didn't know. *I* wouldn't try to trap a man by telling him I was pregnant."

"You wouldn't have needed to! But she really was!" Still, he appreciated the point. The girl had wanted his love, not his baby.

It was her turn again. "I deceived my father. He thought I knew no creative magic myself."

"You claim to be evil," Zane chided her. "You've done black magic and hidden it from your father, himself a black Magician. That's not much."

"Apart from prostituting myself to a demon," she reminded him sharply.

There was that. Zane found it very hard to accept the notion of her being intimate with a demon, but the Truthstone had confirmed her statement. "Why did you do that?"

"To learn the black magic. My father wouldn't teach me, of course. He wanted to keep me clean. The man I respect most—and I deliberately deceived him! Now what do you have to beat that?"

It was Zane's turn to breathe deeply. "I killed my mother."

Now she gaped. "You can't mean that!"

Zane held up his Truthstone, which remained dark. "I did it. Then I wasted my inheritance gambling, and tried to replace it by embezzlement." And now his Sinstone glowed more brightly than hers.

"You have made your case," Luna said. "But I still have more total evil than you, because—"

"Because you took some of your father's burden of evil," he said quickly. "He thought you were in balance, including his evil, but you're not. Where does that put you?"

"Destined for Hell," she admitted. "Of course he didn't know about my other evil. He thought I was pristine, so a twenty-five percent share of evil from him would not imperil my status."

"And, in fact, you are about seventy-five percent evil—or at least, that's what's charged against your soul," he said.

"Close enough."

"I'm surprised he didn't check your balance and catch you at it."

Her smile was wan. "Men are easy to deceive."

Zane studied her with new appreciation. "You seem pretty good to me."

"Your Truthstone is glimmering," she advised him.

So it was. "I guess that's a half-truth. You *do* seem good to me, but that business about the demon—" He paused, watching the stone. It was dim. "Wasn't there some other way to learn the magic you wanted? Study a book, or something?"

"A book!" she exclaimed scathingly. "Black-magic texts are illegal!"

"But you can find them on the black market."

"My father would have known. Only black magic could counter his black magic, even to the limited extent of concealing this information from him."

It would indeed require special measures to hide something from a magical grand master, Zane realized. So maybe she had required input from Hell. Still—

"Why did you want black magic if your father said no? You always obeyed him in other things, didn't you?"

She winced. This betrayal of her father was evidently an extremely sensitive matter to her. "It always fascinated me. I knew the power my father had, and I wanted—" She broke off, for her Truthstone was glimmering. "Oh, fudge! I should have set that stone down." She took another breath. "I was *afraid* for my father. Some of those minions of Hell—they frightened me. I don't mean little-child-bugaboo-type frights; these things were truly, fundamentally evil and they had such power, such malign awareness—you really can't appreciate such horror unless you find it near. I knew they regarded my father as a rare prize, and though I also knew he was smarter than they, still he was riding the tiger. I didn't want to see my father damned, and I knew he would be, but there was no way I could help him unless I learned more about his business. So I learned all I could, legitimately—and some of the things in the legitimate, unexpurgated texts gave me screaming nightmares— then finally I had to move on into—you know, and the only coin I had to offer was—you know." This time her stone was quiescent.

Zane considered. "I think I could get to like you pretty well. I know I'm nothing special, but—well, can we set another date?"

She seemed surprised. "Date?"

"Go out for a walk, or to eat—a pretext for being together, for talking some more."

"You can have what you want right now," she said, her voice sharpening. "You don't have to clothe it in romance."

"I don't think so."

"It's true! Try me. After the demon, nothing you want will be so bad."

Zane cringed inside to think of her opinion of the needs of men. She really had not had much experience in this regard, and no doubt thought of the demon as nothing more than an exaggerated man. "I want your respect."

She tilted her head, peering at him quizzically. "My what?"

"Your respect. You have mine. Your father was right; you are a good person. I don't care how the sin ledger stands. There seem to be a number of artificial standards of good and evil that don't really relate to true merit or demerit. Maybe the official system of classification has failed to keep up with the changing nature of our society. You haven't done anything I consider really wrong, except—well, even the demon, if you only did it to help your father—and you *did* help your father, because without your help he would have gone directly to Hell without passing Purgatory. So it was more like a sacrifice."

"A virgin sacrifice," she agreed, glancing at Zane with a new appraisal. "It's the only type that kind accepts. It was horrible."

"So I suppose after that, no ordinary man represents a threat to you. Certainly *I* don't. But a woman who would do that to protect her father— I'd just like to know you better, that's all."

"Yet you killed your mother," she pointed out. "What do you care about anyone's parent?"

"I cared about her," he said, somewhat stiffly. "But she was dying anyway, and in pain, and she knew it was hopeless; when she asked me to—I just had to do it, that's all, even though I knew it was a crime and a sin that would damn me. It wasn't right to let her suffer any longer."

Luna's eyes narrowed. "Just what happened?"

"Oh, you wouldn't care to hear—"

"Yes, I would."

Zane closed his eyes, suffering in retrospect. "She was in the hospital, and her hair was falling out and her skin turning rough like that of a lizard, and there were tubes and wires and things going into her and coming out of her in a continuous violation of her body, and different colored fluids bubbling, and gauges pulsing with every breath she took and every beat of her heart, so that any stranger passing by could read at a glance the most intimate secrets of her functioning. She would have died long since, from mortification as much as physical failure, but the artificial heart and kidney and stomach wouldn't let her. She had periods of disorientation, and these were getting longer. I think sometimes she hallucinated. But on occasion she was lucid, and that was when the horror of it was clear.

"One time when I was visiting and she saw the nurses were away, she whispered to me the truth. She was hurting physically and mentally and emotionally, she felt degraded by all the paraphernalia, and she just wanted to die before she ran down her estate entirely with the medical bills, so I would have something to inherit. I didn't tell her that all the money was already gone and that the debt was mounting horrendously; even her life insurance would hardly cover it. She begged me to make them let her die so she could be in peace at last. She had come to hate life. She was in such misery and so urgent about it that I promised. Then she lapsed into more hallucinations—I think she was reliving something that happened a long time ago, in her childhood— and talked of picking flowers and getting stung by a bee—and I had to go. I knew the doctors would never let her die in peace; it was part of their code to make a patient suffer as long as humanly possible. So I bought a penny curse—it was all I could afford—and set it on the heart machine where it wouldn't be seen and left. Two hours later I had the call: she was dead because of equipment failure.

"The hospital thought it was at fault and offered to settle out of court, and I let them think that, because it eased the medical bill considerably. But I knew I had killed my mother and that my soul was damned. I tried to pay off the remaining bill by gambling, hoping to multiply the money I was supposed to use for those debts, but I lost it all and tried to steal from my employer to gamble into enough to square everything, but I was caught, so I lost my job and had still more sin on my soul and debts on my account. I skipped town, went to Kilvarough, set up a new identity, and sort of scraped along for several years with my guilt and grief, still hoping for some source of money to square things, hoping maybe to marry money, until this other business—"

He stopped. "I think I've said too much."

Luna was watching him intently. "That Truthstone never flickered."

"Why should it?" Zane asked, glancing at the gem in his hand. "This is the gutter of my life. I have had nightmares about it, until the dreams become more real than reality, and I try to wash off the blood on my arm or to blind myself so I can no longer see my mother's face as she died."

"But you weren't there when she died!"

"In my dreams I was there." Zane rubbed his arm, feeling the blood again, the horrible dream-blood.

"Your mother—it was a mercy killing."

"Killing is a sin. I know that now; I knew it then. All else is rationalization."

"That's not the way you were judging me a moment ago."

"Why should I judge you? I hardly know you."

Luna set down her stones, then took his stones and put them away. "I think you have earned the privilege of making my acquaintance, Zane. Come this way."

She showed him into what appeared to be an artist's studio. There were a number of professional paintings and several half-finished ones on easels. The subjects were ordinary people, places, and things—but the treatment was extraordinary. Each outline was fuzzed by a faint wash of color, as if each person stood within his own private fog. "What do you make of this?" Luna asked.

Zane felt a growing excitement as he gazed at the paintings. "These are yours?"

"My father wanted me to be an artist," she said.

"Now I know why he brought me to you!"

Again she cocked her head, prettily. "Why?"

"He surely knew my interest! You said he must have researched me and known a lot about me. And he arranged to die, at half-and-half, when I was Death. He could have lived longer if he had wanted to, couldn't he?"

"Yes," she agreed. "He told me the timing was important, but he wouldn't say why."

"To summon me, not the prior Death! Because I have artistic aspirations. I am an aural photographer—or was, or tried to be, before I became Death. I really didn't have the proper equipment. That's why I needed money right then—but that's another dull story."

"You recognize my theme?" she asked, brightening.

"Of course I recognize it! I've been photographing auras all my life! Most people can't see them, but I can, with my equipment, and now I know you can. Your paintings are beautiful! I never was able to get the full effect on film. When I tried to sell my pictures, the best offers I got were from the porn publishers, because my technique fuzzed out the clothing of women, but that wasn't the point at all."

"Not the point at all," she concurred. "But this still doesn't add up. If my father knew about you, he could have invited you to visit, or simply conjured you here, and dosed you with a spell of amnesia if not satisfied. He hardly needed to die."

Zane's revelation collapsed. "That's right! But he must have had some reason."

"He must have," she agreed soberly. "He was a most intelligent and sensible man. There is obviously more here than we know."

"You—you said you have gone into black magic. Could you find out?"

Luna considered. "I have learned to use many of the stones my father crafted. Some do enable the user to ascertain the motives of others. But black magic is the power of Satan, and Satan knows when any of it is used. I don't want his baleful eye on me unless there is no other way."

"Don't you have any white-magic stones?"

"The beatific eye of God is on white magic. I'm not sure I want that gaze either. Not when I'm investigating my father, whose Eternal fate remains uncertain."

"What's the difference, really? Isn't magic the same, whether it's black or white?"

"The power is the same, but the aspect differs. Magic is like magnetism, with a white pole and a black pole. If you orient on the white pole, you are aligning with God; the black pole draws you to Satan."

"Then why doesn't everyone stick to white magic?"

"Only good people can do that. Evil people relate more to the black pole. It's—this is not exact, of course, as the science of magic is as complex as the magic of electronics—it's like traveling past a mountain. The white pole is at the apex, and it is an exhilarating height, but it takes a lot of work and few missteps to ascend to it. The black pole is at the nadir, and it is easy to walk downhill; sometimes you can just sit down and slide or roll and, if you fall, you can get there very fast indeed. If you don't pay attention to where you're going, you'll tend to go down, because it is the course of least resistance. Since the average person has only the vaguest notion where he is going and tends to shut out awareness of the consequence of evil, he inevitably drifts downward. There is much more space at the base of the mountain than at the peak! Even those of us who know the situation can find ourselves in difficulty, as you did when you had to use bad means to do something good for your mother. When I became evil, white magic lost its effectiveness, while black magic became proportionately stronger. Remember the magnetic poles: the closer you get to one, the more strongly it attracts. So it is much harder for an evil person to become good than for a good person to stay good. Now I can accomplish much more through the black."

"But if black magic draws you to Satan—"

"Precisely. Evil facilitates evil, accelerating the slide. I don't dare use any more black magic, if I want to achieve eventual salvation. I'm almost too deep already."

"So you can't use magic to find out what your father really wanted."

"I already know what—to introduce the two of us to each other. I don't know *why*."

Zane nodded agreement. "It's a puzzle. Let's meet again; maybe we can figure it out."

She smiled. "Yes. I think we understand each other better now. We have plumbed the depths of each other's evil and not been repelled."

How true that was! Zane had told no one before of his guilty secret of murder and he was sure Luna had not let any other person know hers. As it had turned out, there was a certain similarity in those secrets, for each of them had descended into evil in order to help a respected parent. No, there would not be condemnation from either. That, and the aural art, showed affinity between them. Still, it did not seem to warrant the extraordinary measure the Magician had taken in sacrificing his own life.

Zane turned to leave. "I need to get back to my business."

She looked up at him, her gray eyes seeming larger and brighter than before, like moons. But it was no longer her physical beauty he saw so much as the character of a person who had sacrificed herself for a parent. "Yes, of course. Life is art, and your art is now in your office. When do you wish to visit again?"

"I'm hardly aware of the calendar now. I can't tell how crowded my schedule will be. Does it have to be a set date?"

"Naturally not! Come when you can. I will be here." She glided close and kissed him.

Zane found himself in the Deathmobile, driving out of town, before he was able to focus on the significance of that abrupt act. He had held his emotion in abeyance during their discussion, uncertain whether he would be seeing Luna again. She was, after all, hardly the type of woman Angelica was—well, no, he had to qualify that, for now Angelica was misty in memory, while Luna was preternaturally clear, as if outlined by some Divine retouching pen. And if Luna was no pristine creature, she certainly had more character than he suspected the other woman had.

Luna's very impurities matched his. How could a soiled, sullied person like him expect to win the love of an angel? Only a fallen angel could be within his grasp! Luna's artistry attracted him, for it was exactly the talent he had tried to evoke in himself without sufficient success— and her abrupt kiss had stunned him, because now she knew him for what he was—a man who had gambled and embezzled and killed his mother—yet found him worthy of this mark of favor. True, she had offered him more than that, and he could have used the Lovestone to compel her feeling as well as her physical cooperation, but he had never been one to seek the favor of a woman under duress. He wanted to be loved for himself alone, unworthy as he knew himself to be, and the significance of the kiss was the suggestion that this was possible.

Still, that business with the demon—he had heard horrendous things about the sexual appetites of demons and the uses to which they put acquiescent or unacquiescent girls. Especially pretty girls. Some were no longer pretty, after the demons finished with them. To fall into the power of a demon was to be ravaged in more than the physical sense. Luna had not suffered loss of beauty, however.

Zane punched his watch. Six minutes on the countdown. He had a client to attend to.

-6-

DEATH'S DOMINION

The Deathcar phased south, emerging in dense jungle. The rutted mud trail here was too difficult for the mechanical vehicle, so it shifted to the stallion Mortis and trotted readily through the steamy growth.

"Halt!" someone cried in Spanish, the translation sounding in Zane's left ear. He looked around and spied a camouflaged soldier whose rifle was pointed menacingly.

Zane halted, drawing cloak and hood close about him, just in case. "Where is this?"

"I'll ask the questions!" the soldier snapped. "Who are you and what is your business?"

Should he tell the truth? Zane knew that could complicate things. Yet he was increasingly disinclined to deal in falsehood for any reason. "I am Death, come to collect a soul."

"Oh. Yes, sir," the soldier said, snapping to attention.

Surely he had not heard what Zane had said! The words must have come across as the recognition code for a high officer of this army. Well, if that was the way of it, he would play the part, as he didn't want to get lost in a region of violence. "Identify yourself and your mission," Zane said curtly.

"Sir, I am Fernando of the Loyal Niqueldimea Army, on patrol to rout out the Seventh Communist renegades."

Zane remembered now: Niqueldimea was a banana republic, where guerrilla infiltration had been occurring for some years as the Communists sought to topple its unpopular autocratic government. Naturally there would be many killings here, and some would require Death's personal service.

His watch showed thirty seconds. "Carry on, Fernando," he said, and urged Mortis on toward the rendezvous.

In a moment he entered a rather pretty jungle clearing. But as he did so, small-arms fire erupted. A bullet bounced off his imperious cloak. There was a scream beside him, and a Niqueldimean soldier jumped up, stiffened, and spun to the ground. Zane needed only a glimpse before the man was buried in the brush below to see that the right side of his head was gone. He was definitely dead—in fact, it was amazing that he had been able to jump—but this was not Zane's client. This soldier could make it to Eternity on his own.

More government soldiers charged into the clearing, intent on obliterating the sniper. The ground gave way under three of them, and they fell, screaming, into a pit. Yet the surface of the ground remained unbroken. Zane realized that this trap was concealed by a spell of illusion. In one sense, illusion wasn't real, but it could be just as deadly as tangible magic. Enchantment was countering bullets quite effectively.

Zane looked at his orientation stone. His client was in that pit, it seemed. Zane dismounted and stepped forward cautiously, following his gem-arrow as his watch countdown swung to zero.

His foot found the edge. He squatted, then sat, putting his feet down into the invisible hole, leaning forward, and getting his head inside the spelled region. Now he could see reality.

It wasn't pretty. It was a large, open cavity, with a dozen sharpened wooden stakes set upright in the bottom. The three soldiers were skewered on these. Two were dead, the third dying. The third was his client.

Zane slid carefully down the steep side of the pit and landed on his feet. This required only a few seconds, but in that time he became aware how the man was suffering. The soldier had somehow turned as he fell, and the cruel spike had penetrated his back and emerged from the side of his abdomen. He had been impaled excruciatingly, his head and feet dangling down to the ground. His blood was hardly flowing; the stake filled the puncture.

Zane tried to retch, but clamped his mouth shut. He lurched across and hooked out the soldier's soul, relieving him of his agony. Then he turned and leaned against the pit wall, breathing in long, shuddering efforts.

"You're new at this, aren't you?" someone said.

Zane turned about, still feeling dizzy and sick. A large man stood between the stakes. He wore brief, polished armor, a short, woven-metal skirt, and sported an ornate golden helmet, just like the picture of a Greek god of—

"War!" Zane exclaimed.

"Death!" the man returned sardonically.

"I didn't know—"

"That I existed?" War made an imperious gesture. "And who but Mars do you suppose should supervise this altercation?"

"No one else," Zane acknowledged, relaxing. "I just didn't think it through."

"I have been meaning to meet you," Mars said. "After all, we must often associate closely."

"Yes," Zane agreed distastefully. "I'm still breaking in. I've got the routine down well enough, but scenes like this—"

"This is a good scene," Mars said. "Small, but intense. It is the best that offers between major engagements."

"You like your work?" Zane asked, hardly concealing his revulsion. "What is accomplished by combat and bloodshed?"

"I'm glad you asked that question," Mars said expansively, and suddenly Zane was sorry he had asked it. Speeches of self-justification were seldom worthwhile for any but the speaker. "War is the final refuge against oppression and wrongdoing. You have another client on your watch. I'll walk with you while you attend to him."

Zane saw that it was so. Now he lacked even the excuse to quit the company of this grim warrior.

Mars walked to a corner of the pit where an earthen ramp led to the jungle floor. Zane glanced again at his watch, verifying that he had five minutes to reach another client close by, and followed.

"What refuge do these dead soldiers have?" Zane asked, discomfited. "How did this battle help them?"

"They have glory," Mars explained. "All men must die sometime, and most go ignominiously from age or illness or mishap. Only in war do large numbers get to expire in decent glory."

"Glory?" Zane thought of his recent client, impaled agonizingly on a wooden stake. "Seems more like gory to me."

Mars bellowed out his laughter. "Cute, Death! You perceive only the instant of discomfort; I perceive the eternal reputation. A moment of pain for eternal fame! These men are sacrificing their blood on the altar of righteousness. This is the termination that renders their entire mundane lives sublime."

"But what about those who die fighting for the wrong cause?"

"There *is* no wrong cause! There are only alternate avenues to glory and honor."

"Alternate avenues!" Zane exclaimed. "It's pointless brutality!"

"You speak of brutality," Mars said, as if pleased to meet the challenge of opposition. "You are as brutal in your own office, I believe. How many of your clients go sweetly to Eternity on blithe wings of song? I will answer that—damned few! Even your reforms are savage things, less defensible than what I offer *my* clients."

"Your clients are my clients!" Zane protested.

"Your clients, my clients," Mars said, shrugging. He had excellently broad shoulders, making the shrug impressive. "Some coincide. Most don't. Consider the mode of executions. Do you approve of stoning a person to death, regardless of his crime, which may have been simply making time with a willing woman? Of crucifying him for his religious beliefs? Of breaking his body on the wheel because he stole a loaf of bread to keep himself from starving, or pulling his limbs off by means of chains attached to six horses because he refused to pay sufficient graft to get out of it, or burning him at the stake on a false charge of witchcraft?"

"No, of course not!" Zane said, taken aback by this savage catalogue. Mars had a rough-and-ready tongue! "But execution has been reformed."

"Reformed!" Mars snorted. "I remember the French reform. Doctor Guillotine invented a huge humane blade to sever necks quickly and cleanly. No more of this messy and sometimes inaccurate chopping that could cut into the shoulder or lop off the top part of the head or even take out the hands of the innocent person holding the condemned head in place. This modern method brought elitism to the poor, for before then only nobles had warranted execution by the sword. But do you remember what they did with that invention? I will inform you. They discovered that it could bring mass production to political murder! They could kill thousands in a day, chop-chop! The French Revolution became notorious for that humane reform!"

Zane didn't answer. Mars was too ready to fight.

They came to a ramshackle peasant house. A government soldier was passing it. Suddenly a child of about ten, a little girl, dashed out. The soldier swung his rifle around, but paused when he saw it wasn't a guerrilla. The girl rushed up to him, carrying something in her hands. As she reached him, she did something to the object.

"Hey—that's a grenade!" the soldier exclaimed, aghast.

The girl flung her arms about him, still clutching the grenade. The soldier tried to get hold of it, but she clung like a leech, her thin frame possessing the strength of fanaticism. Then the grenade detonated. She had armed it as she approached.

Pieces of the two of them sprayed outward. Blood splatted against the side of the house. "That was beautiful," Mars said. "That child brings great honor on her family."

"Honor!" Zane cried, outraged. "I call it horror!"

"That, too," Mars agreed equably. "They do tend to associate on such occasions. That's part of what makes even a minor fracas intriguing."

Another soldier appeared. He had heard the explosion and now saw the carnage. This one had a hand-held flame thrower. He ignited it and swung the flame around toward the house.

Another child, a boy, younger than the first, ran from the house toward the soldier. But the man played the flame thrower directly on him, and in an instant the child was a mass of fire. Then the soldier concentrated on the house, starting it burning.

There was a whimper from the smoking mass on the ground. "Your client, I believe," Mars reminded Zane.

How could he have overlooked this! The Deathwatch stood at zero and the arrow pointed at the boy. Zane hurried over and took the child's soul. The whimpering ceased. "What honor was there for this child?" he demanded.

"Not much," Mars admitted. "He failed in his mission. Failure does not deserve reward."

"That wasn't my point! Without this war, there would have been no deaths at all! I would never have been summoned. All this horror would never have existed!"

"On the contrary," Mars responded tolerantly. "Without this war, the oppression of this populace would have continued indefinitely, grinding the people down, dispossessing them of their property, starving them out. They would have died later, it is true, but in a worse manner— that of sheep led to the slaughter. Now they are learning to die in the manner of wolves defending their territory. Violence is but the most visible aspect of a necessary correction, much as an earthquake is a release of enormous subterranean pressures. Blame not the symptom, my good associate; blame the fundamental social inequities that stifle innovation and freedom and can be corrected in no other way. I come to right wrongs, not to wrong rights. I am the surgeon's scalpel that removes the cancer. My edge may hurt for a moment, and some blood may flow, but my cause is just, as is yours."

Zane found himself unable to refute the ready and rough-hewn logic of Mars. But as he looked at the still-smoking little corpse of the child whose soul he had harvested, he feared it was not God whom Mars served so much as Satan.

"I think in due course you will find yourself at war," Mars continued. "I recommend that you prepare yourself for that occasion by familiarizing yourself with your weapon."

"My only weapon is the scythe," Zane muttered.

"And an excellent one it is," Mars agreed.

"Mortis!" Zane called, and the good Deathsteed appeared. Zane mounted and departed, without speaking again to Mars.

He arrived early, as he was doing more often now. The address was a rundown nursing home in a slum district in the resort city of Miami, wedged between a rickety dance hall and an old evangelistic church. The interior was gloomy and stank of urine. Old people sat unmoving, perhaps asleep. There were no games or magazines, and no conversations. The general mood was hopelessness. Zane didn't like such places and had fought to keep his mother out of one—too successfully.

His client was an old man with a white shock of hair and a dribble of brown where the corner of his mouth leaked. Zane walked toward him, but paused as he saw the rope. "You're tied to your chair!" he exclaimed.

The man looked up. "Otherwise I'd fall," he explained.

Zane realized that adequate facilities and competent attendants were beyond the means of this establishment. The poor and homeless could not afford a luxurious retirement.

"One favor," the man said. "If it is not too much to ask."

"If I can grant it," Zane said guardedly. "You know I can not grant a reprieve if it is a terminal illness that—"

"I'd like to have a hymn, to see me out."

Zane was surprised. "A hymn?"

"Holy, Holy, Holy. It's my favorite. I haven't heard it in years, and I miss it."

Zane wrestled with perplexity. "You want someone to sing a song?"

"Oh, a recording would be fine," the old man said. "Just to hear the sound. It's a great hymn! But I know my wish is foolish."

Zane considered. "It seems simple enough."

The man shook his head, now ready to argue the other side. "They don't allow music here."

Another man spoke up. "We get enough noise from the neighbors, though! That infernal racket from the dance hall, so we can't sleep at night, and those screaming sermons and rehearsals from the other side, that 'gelical church."

Now there was general interest, as the others in the room came to life. Zane's appearance was a novelty, relieving the utter boredom they were accustomed to. "Everyone else gets to do his thing—why not us? What's wrong with one hymn?"

"I think you should have it," Zane said. "All we need is a phonograph, or a cassette player, or a magic music box."

There was a murmur of demurral. "They won't let us have it," another man said.

"You *shall* have it," Zane said firmly. He walked up to the nurses' station, where a male nurse was reading a popular magazine. There was a full-page color ad on the back: HELL—IT ISN'T JUST FOR BADNESS ANY MORE. Bright orange flames surrounded a scene of enthusiastic debauchery, and the Dee & Dee trademark devils were doing something that made Zane wince.

"Nurse," he said.

The nurse glanced up. "No music allowed. House rule," he said, and returned to his page.

"We can make an exception," Zane said. "A man is about to die, tied to a chair like a condemned criminal. His last wish shall be honored."

"Are you for real? Get out of here." The man's eyes remained on the page.

Zane, annoyed, reached out and lifted the magazine from the nurse's hands. He leaned forward, gazing into the man's face. "There shall be music," he said.

The man started to protest, but froze as he met the hollow eye of Death. "There's nothing here," he mumbled, fazed. "I would get fired if—"

"Then we shall do it without you," Zane said. "You may register your protest for the record—but take care that it is not too vigorous. We are going to have one hymn here, with or without your cooperation." He pointed his finger at the man's nose; in the Deathglove it looked skeletal. "Do you understand?"

The nurse blanched. "You aren't going to hurt anyone? I only follow rules, I don't want trouble, but I don't want anyone hurt."

So the man did have some meager conscience. He was lazy and indifferent, but not evil. "One man will die, as he was fated to. No one will be hurt."

The nurse considered that, evidently having a bit of trouble reconciling death with not hurting. He swallowed. "Then I'll call in my protest to the owner's answering service. It usually takes them forever to get back to me, especially when there's an emergency." He scowled. "Emergencies cost money." He reached for the phone. "But there's no stuff here to use, not even a radio. My boss says silence is golden, and he does love gold."

Zane turned away, disgusted with that owner. Perhaps one day that character would discover himself grubbing for gold in Hell. "I shall tend to this," he told his client, turning off his countdown timer. "You will not feel discomfort until you have had your hymn." He walked out of the nursing home.

First he tried the dance hall next door. The entry foyer was crowded with machines dispensing candy bars, two-bit love potions—"Slip her this, and she'll promise you anything!"—and spot dressings for blisters. The main hall was empty, for this was the dead morning shift. Several shaggy teenagers were on the stage, working out with drums, guitars, and an electric organ, bashing out dissonance with a deafening beat. This was rehearsal time, though Zane could not see how such noise could profit from practice.

Zane approached and put his hand on the largest drum, the fingers of the glove causing its sound to die immediately. "I require a performance," he said.

He had their instant attention, though they did not recognize his nature. "Hey, a gig? How much?"

"One song, for charity, next door."

They laughed. "Charity! Go soak your snoot in battery acid, mister!" the drummer said. "We don't do nothing for nothing!"

Zane turned his potent gaze on the kid. "One song."

Like the nurse before him, the youth blanched. People seldom saw

Death when they were not clients or closely attached to clients, but Death could indeed force his awareness on them when he wished. Hardly ever did a person face Death directly without feeling the impact. "Uh, yeah, sure. Guess we can do one song, like for practice."

"A hymn," Zane said.

The laugh was louder, though somewhat uncertain. "Man, we don't do church junk! We're the Livin' Sludge! We boom, we flow, we fester; we don't damn well hymn!"

Again Zane delivered the Deathstare. Young punks like this were more resistant to it, since they did not believe they were ever going to die. "One hymn. *Holy, Holy, Holy.*" His bony, square eye sockets bore into the fleshed orbs before him.

Again the kid was fazed. "Sure, well, I guess we could try. Like, it's only one tune. But our singer's out, she's zonked on magic H, and anyway, we'll have to rehearse. It'd take two, maybe three days, you know, just to start."

"Now," Zane said. "Within the hour. I will find you a singer."

"But we don't have no music or nothing!" the youth protested desperately.

"That, too, I will provide," Zane said, controlling his ire. Had he ever been this age himself? "Go now to the nursing home next door and set up your gear. I will rejoin you with a singer presently."

"Yeah, sure, man," the kid said faintly. "We'll be ready in half an hour. But you know, this ain't exactly our bag. It ain't going to be too sharp."

"It will suffice." Zane left them and strode to the church on the other side of the nursing home.

He was in luck. The church choir was rehearsing for the coming weekend service. Several black girls were present, doing what to Zane's ear was a mishmash of notes and ululations.

The preacher spotted him immediately. "Hey, don't you go takin' none of mine, Death!" he protested. "We're good folk here. We don't want no trouble with you!"

Zane realized that this church might be poor and backward, but the preacher was a true man of God, able to discern a supernatural manifestation instantly. That would help. "I only want a hymnbook and a singer," Zane said.

"Hymnbooks we got," the old man said eagerly. "This white do-gooder group, they raise money, bought us books, don't know nothin' 'bout our music. Got a big pile of 'em under dust in the closet. But one of my girls—Death, I won't stand by and—"

"Not to die," Zane said quickly. "To sing one hymn for the folk next door. For a man who is about to die."

The preacher nodded. "Man's got a right to one last melody. What's it called?"

"Holy, Holy, Holy."

"That's in the book, but we don't sing it. Not our style."

"Find a singer willing to try."

The preacher addressed the practicing choir. "Anyone sing white music? Hymnbook stuff?"

There was a murmur of confused negation.

"Listen," the preacher said. "You don' know this person in the hood, and you don' want to. But *I* know him. The eye of the Lord is on him, and he needs one hymn, and we've got to help him any way we can. So if any of you can even try to oblige him, come on."

At length one rather pretty girl in her teens spoke. "Sometime I sing 'long on the radio stuff, jus' for fun. I guess I could try, if I got the words."

The preacher rummaged in the closet and brought out an armful of hymnbooks. "You got the words, sister. Come on, we'll go help this person. Won't be long."

Zane took some of the books and led the way to the nursing home, where the Livin' Sludge was setting up, to the considerable entertainment of the inmates and the non-protesting nurse. Probably there had not been an event like this here in decades. Cables and loudspeakers and instruments seemed to fill the main room. "Hey, don't set those big speakers in here," the nurse was saying. "Small place like this, that noise'll deafen these old folk, and they've got problems enough already. Face those monsters out the windows." And it was done, for it seemed the Livin' Sludge was constitutionally unable to function without full-volume amplification.

The young singer eyed the Sludge, and the Sludge eyed her. Each evinced a certain morbid fascination with an alien life form, but neither evinced approval. Zane realized it had probably been a mistake to involve the instrumental group; the girl would have done better *a cappella*. Too late now.

The preacher stepped in, seeing the need. "You boys don' know hymn music, okay? This is Lou-Mae; she don' know junk music, so you're even. So let's try her doing the hymn, you follow, okay?" He was more or less speaking pigeon, in order to get his meaning across to these foreigners. He passed out the hymnbooks.

The musicians leafed through the books, bewildered. "This scene's worse'n bad-spelled H!" one muttered. Zane knew that H was bad, enchanted H was worse, and badly enchanted H was a horror. But addicts had to take what they could get. "We'll never live this down."

"You boys getting high on S-H?" the preacher asked, frowning. "That'll put you in H!" He pointed down, signaling the change in meaning. "You better find some better interest before it's too late."

"Wish we could," the drummer confessed. "But you know, we're locked into the scene. S-H don't let nobody go."

"Neither does H," the preacher said, with a dark glance down. "Nobody hooked on either H in my church."

"Yeah, sure," the drummer said wearily.

Zane got them on the page with *Holy, Holy, Holy.* "Play this," he said.

They tried. They were, underneath, reasonably competent musicians. The tune did not adapt well to drum and guitar, but the electric organ picked it up easily enough.

The phone rang, the sound almost lost amidst the noise of preparations. "But I can't sing into a mike," Lou-Mae protested. "It's in my way, and it looks funny."

"I'll tell you what it looks like!" the Sludge drummer said, grinning.

"Jus' ignore it, sister," the preacher advised quickly. "Jus' sing your way."

"There are people gathering outside," a nursing home inmate cried gleefully by the window. "Gawking at the loudspeakers!"

"Hey, they must think we have a party in here!" another said. "Cutting the mustard!"

"Sure we are! You can tell by the smell!" Laughter burbled around the inmate sector. This was turning into the biggest event of these old people's lives.

"Hey, mister," the male nurse called through the din. "That was my boss on the line. For once he checked with his answering service. I told him I couldn't stop the music, so he's calling the police. Better do that song and get out of here soon." It was fair warning, but obviously the nurse was enjoying the ongoing event.

The Sludge was still getting organized, piecing out bits of melody, trying to integrate unfamiliar elements. "I can't do this," Lou-Mae complained. "Singing a hymn to a drum roll?"

"Listen, black doll, we don't like it either," the drummer said. "But we got to have a beat."

"You jus' do your best," the preacher said soothingly to both. "The Lord will make it right."

"Man, He better!" the drummer muttered. "This whole thing's crazier than a double-bum trip!"

"Still worth doing right," the preacher said.

Zane heard the sound of a siren. He went to the door where the other choir singers clustered, peering in. They gave way nervously before him, and Zane saw the police cars arriving. The vehicles screeched up to the nearest corner and disgorged helmeted riot police. These were tough cops armed with billy clubs, hefty side arms, tear-gas bombs, and disorientation-spells, accustomed to breaking heads in the lawful performance of their duty. That nursing home owner had really made a complaint!

Zane turned to face inside. "Do the hymn now," he said.

Lou-Mae, suddenly nervous, dropped her book and had to scramble to recover it. "'Sokay, chick," the drummer said sympathetically. "First-night jitters. We all get 'em. We'll start without you, a preamble, and you catch your place and signal when you're ready. Like Uncle Tom says, we'll merge."

She flashed him a fleeting smile. The music started, drum roll leading into guitar, the beat of it blasting like developing thunder out the windows as the police charged up the steps, billies in hand. The choir girls crowded back fearfully, not liking any close contact with the big, brutal men in uniform.

Zane drew his cloak close about him and stepped out to meet the lead cop skull-to-face. "Do we have business?" he asked.

The policeman's eyes and mouth rounded out as he stared into the aspect of Death. He fell back, literally, and had to be caught by the two behind him. The urgency of the intrusion of the law abruptly abated.

Now Lou-Mae found her place. The drum faded to a background beat, and the song proper began. "Holy, holy holy! Lord God Almighty!" she sang, starting tremulously but gaining courage as she sounded the name of the Lord. Somehow the amplification provided resonance and authority that her voice might otherwise have lacked. The drum roll behind her growled like the rising wrath of Deity, and the guitar punctuated the theme with an inspired extemporaneous counterpoint.

"Early in the morning, our song shall rise to Thee!" And the electric organ swelled in an urge of joyous worship, sounding exactly like the monstrous pipes of a towering cathedral.

The crowd in the street was being rapidly augmented. Some of the police were trying to hold the people back. It was already late morning, but the height of the surrounding buildings sheltered the street from direct sunlight. Now that light angled down, a broad beam that splashed across the pale helmets of the police and faces of the people, illuminating them, as if it were indeed the break of day or of a new era.

"Only Thou art holy; all the saints adore Thee!" The sound pealed out, flooding the neighborhood, reverberating amidst the buildings. Instruments and voice had integrated perfectly, as if from years of devoted practice.

"Casting down their golden crowns around the glassy sea!" And the police, stunned despite their cynicism by the magnificence of it, buffeted by the booming sound, began to remove their sunlight-golden helmets. The people followed, compelled by a feeling they did not comprehend. In a moment every head in the crowd was bare.

"Cherubim and seraphim, falling down before Thee!" And one of the impressionable choir girls by the door screamed in rapture and fell to the sidewalk.

Once triggered, the effect spread explosively. All around, people in the crowd screamed and fell, and a few of the policemen, too.

The music surged to thunderous authority, drums and organ shaking the very buildings, sweeping through the crowd, making the entire block a place of worship. Some people stood; some knelt; some lay on the street. All were gazing raptly toward the nursing home and listening to the amazing sound.

"Who wert and art and evermore shall be!" Then the hymn ended, and the music died away in a fading roll of the drum and a trailing organ note, as if God were moving on to another station. Half the crowd and all the choir girls were on the ground, and the policemen stared wide-eyed at whatever personal visions they had. No one made a sound.

Zane turned to face inside again. The inmates were sitting dazed, as was the male nurse. The drummer and Lou-Mae were exchanging an awed glance. The preacher was gazing toward Heaven, his hands steepled before him, in silent prayer.

"Jeez," the guitarist murmured. "We been wasting our time, all our life!"

"Who the H needs H!" the organist agreed. "I never been on a trip like that!"

Zane walked across to his client. "Now it is time," he said, restarting his timer. "Are you satisfied?"

The old man was smiling. "I sure am, Death! I just had a vision of the Lord God Almighty! Anything else in life would be anticlimactic after that. I saw two of my friends here go already." He collapsed, and Zane reached out quickly to catch his soul.

A slow recovery was beginning as he walked back toward the door. The preacher caught Zane's eye. "Some folk think the Lord don't intervene," he remarked gently, as if aware of Zane's own doubts.

Zane couldn't answer. He walked on out, past the choir girls as they righted themselves, and through the quiet crowd to his horse.

A new vehicle was pulling up, with the emblem of the State Social Services on its side. It seemed the commotion had attracted the notice of the relevant authorities, and there was about to be an inspection of the nursing home facility and operation.

Zane allowed himself a private smile. They would discover one or more dead men, tied to their chairs, in a room reeking of urine where no music or entertainment was permitted—these strictures so absolute that the police had been summoned to enforce them. Zane doubted that would make a favorable impression on the inspectors. Substantial reform was about to come to one nursing home, and the lot of the surviving inmates would be improved.

He glanced once more around the neighborhood before he left. There stood the church, nursing home, and dance hall in a row. Surely the fate of all three would improve, now that they had interacted in this fashion and discovered what each had to offer the others, and there would be music for everyone! Maybe the entire city of Miami would experience a gradual renovation as the spirit of this hour spread.

His next client was in the country. Mortis changed to Deathmobile form and drove along the superhighway, as they were not pinched for time. Zane read the billboards and realized there was an ad war on here. WHY DRIVE A LANDBOUND CAR WHEN YOU CAN RIDE A CARPET? the first billboard demanded in huge, shining print. The picture was of a car struggling through a traffic jam, while a magic carpet sailed blithely over, its handsome family smiling.

Zane also smiled. He was at the moment carbound—but he would never be trapped in a traffic jam. Not with Mortis! "Did you show me this just to make me appreciate you properly?"

The car did not answer, but the motor purred.

The next billboard proclaimed DRIVE IN COMFORT. The picture was of a family huddled on a flying carpet in a rainstorm. The man looked grim and uncomfortable, the woman's once-elegant hairdo was a wet mess plastered about her ears, and one child was sliding off the rear, about to fall. The material was evidently wrinkling and shrinking in the rain, heightening the family's discomfort and peril. Below, the same family could be seen happily in a closed car, safely seat-belted, untouched by the rain.

"So the car fights back," Zane remarked. "I can see it." He glanced at his watch. Still several minutes to go.

The next billboard showed the carpet sailing blithely over the rain cloud that largely obscured the traffic jam below. BABYLON CARPETS OUTPERFORM ANY LANDBOUND VEHICLE! it proclaimed. MORE DISTANCE PER SPELL.

But the auto maker came right back with a picture of the family gasping for air aboard the high-flying carpet, while the car zoomed along the open highway. KEEP SAFE, KEEP COZY, it advised. USE A CAR INSTEAD OF A CARPET.

Perhaps the ad war continued, but Zane had to turn off to approach his client. This was a residential enclave in the countryside; the houses were very similar to one another, the lawn manicured. Zane wondered why people bothered to live in the country when all they did was take the city with them. He turned into the appropriate drive and parked in the limited shade of a medium pine tree. He noticed there was a *disabled* sticker on the owner's car; evidently the disablement was terminal.

Zane entered and made his way to the bathroom. There was a young, fairly muscular man taking a deep bath. He looked relaxed.

The man did not react to Zane's appearance and did not seem to be in trouble, yet the gem-arrow identified him as the client. "Hello," Zane said, uncertain how to proceed.

The man glanced up languidly. "Please leave," he said, his voice mild.

"First I must do my job," Zane said.

"Job? Perhaps you are in uniform, and assume I recognize your business. I can not see you, for I am blind."

Oh. That accounted for the *disabled* sticker. But mere sightlessness wouldn't kill this man, unless some bad accident were coming up. "I suspect you will be able to see me, if you try," Zane said.

"You are a faith healer? Go away. I am an atheist, and have no traffic with your kind."

An atheist! One who did not believe in God or Satan, or in their related artifacts. How could Death have been summoned for a nonbeliever?

Two answers offered. It was possible that this man was not as cynical as he professed and really did believe in Eternity perhaps unconsciously. Or it could be that there had been another glitch, and that the Powers that Be had not realized that no service was required for this particular client.

Well, Zane was here, and the case would have to be played through to whatever conclusion was fated. He looked at the water in the bath and saw that it was discolored by a cloud of darkness. "You are committing suicide," he stated.

"Yes, and I must ask you not to interfere. My folks are away for two days, so will not know until it is safely done. I have slashed veins in my ankles and am pleasantly bleeding to death in this hot water. There is no greater kindness you can do me than to let nature take its course."

"I am here for that," Zane said. "I am Death."

The man laughed, becoming more animated as his attention focused. "An actual, physical personification of Death? You're crazy!"

"You don't believe in Death?"

"I believe in death, small d, obviously. I am about to experience it. Certainly I don't believe in a spook with skull and crossbones and scythe."

"Would you like to touch my hand and face?" Zane asked.

"You persist in this nonsense? Very well, while I still command my faculties, let me touch you." The man lifted an arm from the water with some visible effort and extended it toward Zane.

Zane clasped that hand in his own gloved one, curious how the man would perceive it. He was hardly disappointed in the reaction.

"It's true!" the man exclaimed. "A skeleton!"

"A glove," Zane said, not wanting to deceive him. "And my face is a skull-mask generated by magic. Nevertheless, I am Death, and I have come to collect your soul."

-111-

The man touched Zane's face. "A mask? It could fool me! That's a skull!"

Zane had been uncertain before whether his skull-face was tactile as well as visual; now he knew. "I am a living man performing an office. I wear a costume and have certain necessary powers, but I am alive and have the flesh and feelings of a man."

The client took his hand again. "Yes, now I perceive the flesh, faintly, the way I do my own when my foot is asleep. Strange! Perhaps I do believe in you, or in your belief in the office. But I don't believe in the soul, so your effort is wasted."

"What do you believe happens when you die?" Zane asked, genuinely curious. This man seemed to have a good mind.

"My body will be inert and in time will dissolve into its chemical components. But that is not what you mean, is it? You want to know about my supposed soul. And I will answer. There is no soul. Death is simply the end of consciousness. After death, there is nothing. Like the flame of a candle snuffed out, the animation is gone. Extinction."

"No afterlife? You do not consider death a translation to a spiritual existence?"

The man snorted. He was slowly sinking in the tub, as loss of blood weakened him gradually, but his mind remained alert. "Death is a translation to intellectual nonexistence."

"Does that frighten you?"

"Why should it? It is the deaths of others I should fear, for they can cause me inconvenience and grief. When I myself pass, I shall be out of it, completely uncaring."

"You have not answered," Zane said.

The man grimaced. "Damn it, you are putting my toes to the fire! Yes, my own death does frighten me. But I know that is merely my instinct of self-preservation manifesting, my body's effort to survive. Subjectively, I do fear extinction, because instinct is irrational. Objectively, I do not. I have no terror of the nonexistence before I was conceived; why should I fear the nonexistence after I die? So I have overridden the foible of the flesh and am proceeding to my end."

"Wouldn't you be relieved to discover that life continues on the spiritual plane?"

"No! I do not want life to continue in any form! What uncertainties or tortures might I experience there? What tedium, existing for eternity with no reprieve in another person's sterile conception of Heaven? No, my life is the only game, and the game has soured, and I want nothing more than to be able to lay it aside when its convenience is over. Oblivion is the greatest gift I can look forward to, and Heaven itself would be Hell to me if that gift were denied."

"I hope you find it," Zane said, shaken by this unusual view. A man who actually insisted on oblivion!

On A Pale Horse

"I hope so, too." Now the atheist was fading rapidly. The loss of blood was affecting his consciousness and soon he would faint.

"A man's death is the most private part of his life," Zane said. "You have the right to die as you wish."

"That's correct." The voice was slow and faint. "Nobody's business but mine."

"Yet shouldn't you be concerned about the meaning of your life, about your place in the greater scheme of things? Before you throw away your one chance to improve—"

"Why the hell should I care about improvement when I don't believe in Heaven or Hell?" the atheist demanded weakly.

"Yet you assume that your own relief is all that matters," Zane said. "What of those you love, who remain in life? Those who love you, and who will find your body here, a horror to them. *They* will still suffer. Don't you owe them anything?"

But the atheist was too far gone. He had lost consciousness and no longer cared who else might suffer, if he ever had cared. In due course he died.

Zane reached in and drew out his soul. It was a typical mottled thing, good and evil spotting it in a complex mosaic. He started to fold it— and the soul disintegrated, falling apart into nothingness.

The atheist had his wish. He really had *not* believed, and so the Afterlife had been unable to hold him. He was beyond the reach of God or Satan. That did seem best.

It was best—but was it right? The atheist had not seemed to care about anyone except himself—and in that uncaring, perhaps had rendered his own existence meaningless.

Zane rejoined Mortis. "I think that man was half-right," he said. "He is better off out of the game—but the game may not be better off without him. A man should not exist for himself alone. Life made an investment in him, and that investment was not paid off." But Zane wasn't sure.

His timer was going again. He oriented on the next client, wondering how he was going to account for the soul that disintegrated. The Purgatory News Center would have a ball with that one. He visualized the headline: THE FISH THAT GOT AWAY.

He arrived at a hospital. That was not unusual; the terminally sick tended to congregate there, and he had made a number of similar collections all over the world. But he still didn't like hospitals very well, because of his lingering guilt relating to his mother.

At the edge of the parking lot was an ad, for once not Satanic. SHEEPSHEAD HORN O' PLENTY—MORE FRUIT THAN BRANDS X, Y, AND Z HORNS. Just the thing to buy for a hospitalized person recovering from stomach surgery.

–113–

On A Pale Horse

Zane felt worse when he saw his client. It was an old woman, and she was embedded in a mass of lines and burbling devices. Some sort of bellows forced her to breathe rhythmically, and monitors clicked and bleeped to signal her heartbeat, digestion, and state of consciousness. Her blood coursed through the tubes of a dialysis machine. A nurse checked the equipment regularly, going on to the others in the ward. There were five other patients here, all similarly equipped.

The client's hospital gown was draped awkwardly, as such things seemed to be designed to do, so that embarrassing portions of her wasted anatomy showed. She was in pain, Zane could see, though half-zonked on therapeutic drugs. She was overdue to die; only the relentlessly life-sustaining things enclosing her frail body prevented her from doing so.

Déjà vu! His mother, all over again.

Zane approached. She spied him, and her bloodshot eyes tracked him erratically. The tubes running into her nose prevented her from turning her head conveniently, and the machine set up a clangor of protest when she tried to shift her body.

"Be at ease, lady," Zane said. "I have come to take you away from this."

She issued a weak hiss of a laugh. "Nothing can take me away," she gasped, spittle dribbling from her mouth. "They will not let me go. All my pleading is in vain. I may rot in this contraption, but I will still be alive."

"I am Death. I may not be denied."

She peered more closely at him. "Why, so you are! I thought you looked familiar. I would gladly go with you—but they won't give me the visa."

Zane smiled. "It is your right to make the transformation. That right can not be abridged." He reached into her body and caught her soul.

It didn't come. The woman keened weakly with new agony until he let the soul go. It snapped back into place, and she relaxed.

"You see!" she whispered. "They have anchored me in life, though it isn't worth it. You can't take me, Death!"

Zane looked at his watch. It was fifteen seconds past time. The woman really was being held beyond her destiny.

"Let me consider," Zane said, disgruntled. He walked down the ward, glancing at the other patients. He saw now that the details of their apparatus differed, but all were caught beyond their natural spans and all were similarly resigned to their fate. They might have no joy in life, but they would not be released from it one second before the machines gave out. This was one efficient hospital; there were no slip-ups.

"I see you, Death," someone murmured nearby.

Zane looked. It was a male patient in the adjacent rig. Unlike some of the others, this one was fully alert.

"I can't take her soul while that equipment functions," Zane said, wondering why he was bothering to explain to a nonclient.

The old man shook his head, causing his own apparatus to protest. "Never thought I'd see the day when Death was denied. That leaves taxes as the only certainty." He essayed a feeble laugh that made his dials quiver and alarmed the nurse on duty, who thought he was suffering a seizure. She seemed unaware of Zane.

After a moment, the man spoke again. "If it was me, Death, know what I'd do?"

"That old woman, my client," Zane said. "She reminds me of my mother." And what a mass of guilt lay there, tying into his conscience like the lines of the hospital machines.

"She's somebody's mother," the man agreed. "It's her son who pays for all this foolery. Thinks he's doing her a favor, making her live beyond her time or will. If he really loved her, he'd let her go."

"Doesn't he love her?" Zane had killed his own mother because he loved her, but then had doubted.

"Maybe he thinks so. But he's really just getting even. He's a mean man, and she brought him into this world, and I guess he just never forgave her for that. So he won't let her leave."

Something snapped. "Death shall *not* be denied!" Zane said. He marched back to his client's section. He found switches on the equipment and clicked them off.

"Oops!" The nurse was on it immediately, as the machinery bleeped alarm. She turned the switches on again.

Zane ripped out wires and tubes. Fluid spurted.

Now the nurse became aware of him. "*You* did it!" she cried, horrified. "You must stop!"

Zane caught her in his arms and kissed her on the lips. She felt the skeletal embrace and fainted. He set her down carefully on the floor.

He saw that automatic failsafes were stopping the leaks in the torn tubes. The bleep-bleep alarm was more strident; soon other nurses would hear and come. He could not be sure the job was done.

Zane picked up a chair and smashed it into the stand supporting the bottles of life-preserving fluids. Glass shattered, and colored liquids coursed across the floor. He put his foot against a console and shoved it over, indulging in an orgy of destruction that was the overt expression of his long-suppressed emotion.

At last he stood over the old woman, chair raised to bash in her skull if need be—but he saw that now the job had been done.

He set down the chair and lifted out her soul, gently.

There was a smattering of applause from the other patients as he put away the soul and walked out through the ward. All these people were on artificially extended time, so were able to perceive him for what he was.

"But I am a murderer—again," Zane protested weakly, now suffering reaction. Never before had he actually killed—in his role of Death. There had been grim satisfaction in the act—but surely he had added an awful burden of sin to his soul.

"I wish it was me you come for," one of the others muttered.

"You can't murder our kind," the old man said. "Any more'n you can rape a willing gal."

Zane paused. "How many of you feel that way?" he asked. "How many really want to die now?"

A murmur traveled along the ward, like a ripple of water. "We all do," the old man said, and the others agreed.

Zane pondered briefly. He heard the running footsteps of others in the bowels of the hospital, becoming aware that something was wrong. Time was limited.

He had done his assigned job; he had collected the old woman's soul and in his fashion had redeemed his murder of his mother. He had now done openly what he had done covertly before. He had shown that even Death himself would have made the same decision Zane had, long ago. But had he done his human job? These people were being denied their most fundamental right: the right to let life go.

"You know it would be mass murder," he said.

"It would be mercy," the old man said. "My grandchild is going broke paying for me, because the doctor says she must—and for what? For this? For eternity in a hospital ward, too sick to move, let alone enjoy life? Hell can't be worse than this—and if it is, I'll take it anyway! At least there maybe I'll have a chance to fight back. Cut me loose, Death! There's more'n just us patients suffering here; it's our families, too. They'll cry a while, but soon they'll heal—and maybe they'll still have a little something left to live on."

Zane decided. He was already doomed to Hell for his violations of the standards of his office. What did he have to lose? He wanted to do what was right, regardless of the consequence. These were his clients, too.

He went to the service area of the ward. There was the main circuit box. He yanked down all the handles.

Power died in the ward. Darkness closed in. The machinery stopped running.

There was an immediate outcry. Hospital personnel rushed in. Someone groped her way to the circuit box, but Zane stood before it. The nurse felt a skeletal hand close on hers, pushing her away from the box. She screamed in sheerest terror.

"That is the horror you have been visiting on these patients," Zane told her. "Death-in-life."

No one could reverse what he had done, this time.

-7-

CARNIVAL OF GHOSTS

A few days later, once more caught up on his schedule, Zane paid Luna another call. This time she smiled when she saw him. "Come in, Zane; I'll be ready in a minute."

"Ready?"

"You're taking me out on a date, remember? Somewhere interesting, so we won't be bored with each other."

Zane had really had more talking in mind, for their last dialogue had affected him profoundly, but he didn't care to say that. True, aspects of their talk had been uncomfortably candid, and the notion of her paying off the demon still bothered him. But a portion of his self-doubt and disgust had eased significantly after their last meeting, and he hoped for similar positive impact in future. After all, how could he object to anything about her, after what he had done at the hospital? That had made ugly headlines on Earth as well as in Purgatory!

He looked at Luna's paintings as he waited for her. They were beautiful. She was much more of an artist than he had been. The colors were clear and true, and the auras realistic. It was hard to believe that a person whose soul was presently slated for damnation in Hell could do such excellent work. He was getting to like Luna better—and that realization caused him to wonder again why the Magician had wanted the two of them to know each other. Surely it was not merely because they were compatible or had a common interest in auras.

Luna reappeared—and this time she was stunning. Before, clothes had converted her most of the way from neutral to attractive; this time they had completed the transition. Bright blue topaz glinted from a band placed in her hair, and green emerald was set in her slippers; the rest of her between these two made the beauty of the gems pale.

"How do you like me now?" she inquired archly.

He was cautious. "I thought you didn't really care for me. Why are you making yourself so lovely?"

She grimaced prettily. "I told you my deepest sins, and you didn't reject me. That's worth something."

"Because I'm no better!" he replied. "How can I condemn you? You were helping your father, while I—"

"Was helping your mother," she finished, completing the rehearsal of their excuse for being together, which somehow seemed necessary for each of them. "We're both well tainted. Anyway, until we know what my father had in mind, there's no sense in letting it go. I confess you're not the man I would have chosen on my own—"

"And you aren't the woman I was slated for—"

"Do you think Fate had her fickle finger in this?"

"I know she did. She put me in the office of Death by arranging the thread of my life to terminate right when my predecessor was getting careless. I suppose Fate even steered me past Molly Malone, where I got the gun I used. Whether Fate would have done this without the behest of your father, I don't know."

"Never trust a woman," Luna said seriously. "Fate least of all."

Zane smiled. "I'm a fool. I do trust Fate. She helped me get started as Death. The truth is, my life was hardly worth it before. Of course, I know I'm nothing special as Deaths go."

"I would hate to encounter something special in Deaths, then," she murmured. "That episode at the hospital—and I think I recognize your touch in that Miami riot, too."

Zane smiled. "It was no riot. But it illustrated the point. I let too many clients go free, when I can, and I take some I'm not supposed to, and I waste time talking to others, trying to make it easier for them. The Purgatory News Center is having a field day with my exploits. I don't know what Purgatory did for humor in the news before I came along."

"You're too well-meaning, and too trusting."

Zane looked at her, and was daunted again by her sheer beauty. "Surely I can trust you, though!"

"No."

"No? I don't understand."

"Put on your Deathcape," Luna said abruptly.

Zane glanced at her again, startled. "I don't know. This is personal, and I don't like to mix—"

"I want a date with Death," she insisted. She turned her face to him and looked him in the eyes and smiled, and her eyes seemed lambent. He could not deny her, though he knew it was deliberate artifice.

"My suit is in the car," he said. "But—do you really want to be seen with Death?"

"No such worry. People don't see Death unless they are clients."

On A Pale Horse

Not entirely true, but close enough. Zane proffered her his arm, and they walked out to the Deathmobile.

The night was dark, with a drizzle threatening. He fetched his cape and gloves and shoes from the car and donned them.

"Now you are truly elegant," Luna said. "I never realized before how handsome a well-dressed skeleton could be. Kiss me, Death."

"But my face is not—"

She leaned into him and kissed his lips. "Oh, you're right!" she exclaimed after a moment. "A bare skull! Alas, poor Yorick, I kissed him. An infinite jest!" She brushed off her mouth with one hand as if removing sand.

"Death is no pleasant date to most people," Zane said, disturbed by her attitude. What was motivating her? "You should see the mail I get."

She smiled as if this were a pleasant invitation. "Yes, let's see your mail. Do you actually answer it?"

"Yes," he said, embarrassed. "It seems only right. No one seeks out Death, in any manner, without good reason."

"That's touching. You are a decent man. Show me a letter."

Zane reached into the dash compartment and brought out a letter, turning on the interior light of the car so they could read it. It was written in a rather neat juvenile script; it normally took many years for a person to reduce his script to adult illegibility. Children tended to write letters more than adults—at least they did to his office—for what reason he couldn't quite fathom. Maybe it was because their beliefs were more literal.

Dear Death, he read. *Every night Mommy makes me say my prayers, and thats okay I guess, but they scare me. I hafta say If I Should Die Before I Wake I Pray The Lord My Soul To Take. Now Im afraid to go to sleep. I lie awake most of the night and then I daze out in school and Im flunking something and please Death I dont want to die right now. Is it okay if I sleep a little at night without having to die? Love Ginny.*

"Suddenly I see what you mean," Luna said. "That's awful. That poor little girl—she thinks—"

"Yes. When I first read that letter, it made me so angry I broke out in a sweat. That prayer seems to equate sleep with death. No wonder she's afraid. How many children *expect* to die before they wake—because of that sinister message put in their minds? I would never do that to any child of mine!"

"She's pretty literate, but she hasn't mastered the apostrophe yet," Luna remarked. "It must have been an act of real courage to tackle the source of her fear like that! Zane, you must answer this letter right now."

"What can I say to her? I can't promise not to take her; she might appear on my schedule tomorrow."

On A Pale Horse

"But you can reassure her that death has nothing to do with sleep."
Luna brightened. "Let's do it now. You can phone her!"

Zane was uncertain. "She would think it was a cruel joke. Who ever heard of Death telephoning people?"

"Who ever heard of Death answering letters? I gather your predecessor didn't. She's a child, Zane! She'll believe. A child won't be surprised by a phone call from an Incarnation. That's the way children's minds work, bless them." She hauled him back to her house and fetched the telephone and proffered it to him.

He sighed. Maybe this was the best way. He accepted the phone and called the Information operator for Ginny's city of Los Angeles, using the child's address to run down the number. Soon the phone was ringing. Zane felt suddenly nervous.

"Yes?" It was obviously the girl's mother.

"Let me speak with Ginny, please."

"But she's asleep!" Actually, it was not as late in Los Angeles as in Kilvarough, but children retired earlier than adults.

"She is not asleep," Zane said, his quick ire rising. "She is lying awake in the darkened room, terrified that if she sleeps, she will die before she wakes. Do not make her say that prayer any more. That's not the way God takes souls."

"Who are you?" the woman asked sharply. "If this is an obscene call—"

"I am Death."

"What?"

Of course she couldn't assimilate that. "Please fetch Ginny now."

Flustered by something strange, the woman backed off. "I'll see if she's awake. But if you say anything to upset her—"

"Fetch her," Zane repeated wearily. How much damage was done by well-meaning people!

In a moment the child answered. "Ginny speaking," she said politely. "Gee, I never got a phone call from a strange man before!"

"I am Death," Zane said carefully. "I received your letter."

"Oh!" she cried, whether in joy or fear he could not tell.

"Ginny, I do not think I will come for you soon. You have your life ahead of you. But if I do come, I promise to wake you first. I will not take you in your sleep."

Her voice was tremulous. "Gee—you mean it? Really?"

"Really. You will not die before you wake." That much of a promise it was within his province to make. He would issue a memo to Purgatory to make sure that he personally was summoned for her case, though she would surely be bound directly for Heaven with very little evil on her soul, so that he could honor that commitment.

"You mean it?" she repeated breathlessly. "Cross your heart and hope to—" She paused, aware of the incongruity.

"Cross my heart, Ginny. Sleep in peace."

"Gee, thanks, Death!" she exclaimed. Then she thought of her manners. "It's not that I want to hurt your feelings or anything, but—"

"But you don't want to meet me yet," Zane finished, smiling, as people were prone to do even when they knew they could not be seen. "I understand. Few people care to do business with me, or even to think about me."

"Oh, it's all right by day, in play," she said brightly. "Day is different. We don't sleep then. We talk about you when we jump rope."

"You do? What do you say?"

"Doctor, Doctor—will I die? Yes, my child, and so will I! It keeps the beat, you know!"

"That's nice," Zane said, taken aback. "Farewell, Ginny."

"Bye, Death," she said, and hung up.

"Now doesn't that feel better?" Luna asked, her eyes shining.

"Yes!" Zane agreed. "It makes me glad to do my job, this one time."

"If more people knew Death personally, fewer people would fear him."

"I would like that. What a world it would be if there were no fear of death!"

"Now we can go on our date," she said. "There's no other way I would have preferred to start it."

They returned to the Deathmobile. "Where did you have in mind to go?" he asked.

"I don't know. It's enough just to ride with Death."

Zane was not entirely satisfied with this, but let it be. He started the car and drove slowly through the drizzle.

In the center of town, the headlights picked out a figure with a wheelbarrow. Zane slowed. "There's Molly Malone," he said. "The ghost of Kilvarough."

"Oh, I've never met her!" Luna exclaimed. "Let's give her a ride!"

"Give a ghost a ride? That's not—"

"How will we know, if we don't offer?"

Zane stopped the car and got out. "Molly!" he called.

The ghost waved her hand. "You can't take me, Death," she cried gaily. "I'm already dead!"

"I'm not on business," he said. "My watch is stopped. We met before I assumed the office. In fact, I think you were my omen, for I left my former life soon after I met you." He drew away his hood so she could see his face.

"Oh, yes—you saved me from getting robbed or worse," she said, recognizing him. "You were so nice. I'm sorry I signaled your end."

"Signaled my end?"

"Didn't you know? Anyone I interact with is doomed to die within a month."

"Oh, yes, I realized that, later. But as you see, I didn't really die."

"Well, you had a date with Death. That's usually the same thing."

Luna got out of the car. "Hello, Molly Malone," she called.

Zane froze. "Oh, no! You—Luna—"

"I can't say I like it," Molly said. "But I remind myself that I don't cause the death, I merely signal it. So really, it's providing fair warning—"

"But if you interact with Luna—"

Molly showed concern. "Oh, I thought she was one of your clients. You mean she's a friend?"

"A friend on a date with me."

"Oh, then it's already been fulfilled. The date with Death."

"Of course," Zane agreed, relieved. "I misread the signal."

"No, you didn't," Luna said.

Zane turned to her with appalled surmise.

"Don't look so horrified, Zane," Luna said. "I knew I was going to die. There are a dozen good Deathstones in my house."

"You never told me!" Zane protested.

She shrugged. "I only learned of it since our last date. Suddenly the stones were signaling. I took a stiff dose of cheer." She indicated the gems in her headband. "Otherwise I would not be very good company at the moment."

"You are using enchantment—to make yourself good company for me?" Zane asked rhetorically. "I would never have asked you to—"

"Why do you think I wanted a date with Death? If I'm lucky, maybe you will collect my soul personally, so I won't sink to Hell alone." She turned back to the ghost. "It must be very dull for you, Molly, day after day with no customers. Why don't you take a ride with us?"

"That's very nice of you," the ghost said. "Where are you going?"

"We hadn't decided. We're having a date."

"He told me. Then you don't need me along. I have not entirely forgotten the ways of life."

"It's not that intimate. Yet. Where would you recommend we go?"

"If you really don't mind my company, I could guide you to the Carnival of Ghosts. Since you're both marked in one way or another by Death, you're eligible to attend."

"That sounds nice," Luna said. She nudged Zane. "What do you think?"

Zane came out of his stasis. "You're going to die—within the month! Did your father know?"

"He surely did," Luna said. "Of course he thought I was destined for Heaven. But I have as much as two fortnights and might as well make the most of them. Let's go to the carnival."

"The carnival," Zane agreed numbly.

They loaded Molly's wheelbarrow into the limousine's capacious trunk, then got into the passenger compartment. There was room for three in the front seat, though Molly's presence moved Luna pleasantly snug against Zane's hip.

"Straight ahead two blocks," the ghost directed. "Then turn left and close your eyes. Mortis knows what to do."

It seemed the Deathsteed had a good reputation in the Afterlife. Zane followed directions, not really caring whether they crashed. Luna fated to die—when he was just getting to appreciate her! What sort of doom was stalking him, even after he had assumed the office of Death? He had been appalled at the way so many people died; now his feeling intensified. Luna was not merely another person. She was a personal acquaintance, and perhaps more. Surely more!

"Come on, enjoy the evening," Luna said. "Do not struggle with the inevitable, wasting what time we have remaining."

She had learned she was to die—so she had prettied herself up for him. In one sense, this was utter foolishness, for she surely had better things to do in her last hours. But in another way, it was very flattering, for she had chosen to do what she chose to do—with him. He felt a warm rush of feeling, composed partly of appreciation and partly of burgeoning grief. He could love her, he realized; she was the kind of woman he had longed for all his life, without ever realizing it. What had Angelica ever been, after all, but the dream of a moment? Luna was the reality. Beauty, intelligence, artistry, courage—but what use was any of it if she died?

She was right; they must not waste what time remained. If she wanted to be happy, to celebrate—to celebrate *what*?—the least he could do was help her do it. "We shall make a night of it," he agreed, taking the left turn. Then they all closed their eyes.

There was no crash. "Here it is," Molly Malone announced.

Zane looked. They were approaching a complex of tents, with colorful banners flying. Loud, off-key music wafted out. People crowded around. It was a carnival, all right.

"These people look alive," Zane remarked.

"To the dead, the dead look alive," Molly said. "But the two of you are the only living creatures here. Don't let that spoil your pleasure."

"We won't," Luna said. "I have always liked ghosts."

Molly approached the ticket seller. "These are my guests from the land of the living," she said. "Death did me a favor not long ago, and the woman will save the world from Satan in twenty years. Give them free passes."

"Those are good credentials," the ticket seller agreed, handing out the passes.

They passed through the old-fashioned stile and entered a broad concourse. Circus-type sideshows and knickknack concession stands lined either side. "Come on," Molly said enthusiastically. "The best thing to start with is the historical tour."

Luna took Zane's hand possessively as they both suffered themselves to be led to the embarcation station for the historical tour. Soon the three of them were ensconced in an open car on narrow tracks. It began to move under its own guidance, carrying them through a scintillating curtain.

Suddenly they were in a gloomy cave. "Lascoux," Molly announced. She obviously had been here many times before. "The famous cave paintings." As she spoke, the cave illuminated, as if from a flickering torch, and the walls glowed with assorted wild animals that seemed almost alive despite being crudely drawn. "It's the glimmering light," Molly explained. "It changes what we see, so it is as if the paintings live. That is the genius of these artists."

"*Is* the genius?" Zane asked. "Isn't this a replica?"

"Oh, no!" Molly protested. "This is the real cave, circa 14000 B.C. *We* are the ghosts."

"Literal time travel being problematical," Luna said, nudging him. Zane put his arm about her shoulders. She might be using spellstones to lighten her mood, but she was still herself. "Ghosts can go where they want, without paradox."

"See, there is the artist painting the first unicorn," Molly said brightly.

Zane looked. He saw a seemingly vast panoply of crudely sketched animals all along the wall. Most of them were equine or bovine, some overlapping other figures. Yet in the flame of the sandstone lamp, whose crude wick sent out almost as much smoke as light, these figures seemed to be a three-dimensional herd, the overlapping sketches showing not carelessness but the dimension of time. This stag would soon give place to that horse; the double picture showed that clearly enough. This was the great Hall of Bulls; Zane remembered it now from former studies.

The unicorn representation was not apt. It had an enormously sagging belly that almost touched the ground, a severely truncated tail, several huge, hollow spots, and two long, straight horns. "That's no unicorn," he protested. "It's a bicorn."

"We think they evolved into the single horn," Molly explained. "The unicorn must have had both horses and horned creatures as ancestors, and the first crossbreeds would have seemed crude by modern standards. After all, the human figures depicted in these caves are far more primitive than those of the animals; our species has evolved much more rapidly in the last fifteen thousand years or so."

"I suppose so," Zane agreed, surprised at the ghost's knowledge. But of course Molly must have taken this tour many times before, and learned all she wished. He was beginning to understand what ghosts did with their free time.

"Primitive art fascinates me," Luna said, her gray eyes flickering orange in the lamplight. She was especially lovely here, somehow enhanced by the primitive surroundings. "All true art stems from the depths of the unconscious mind. The men of these caves were close to the natural world and they knew, perhaps better than we do, how to relate to its magic. We can no longer summon prey for the kill by painting its likeness on a wall; we have to use technological weapons or highly refined spells. To primitive man, science and magic were one—and he made them work as one. Only recently have we begun to rediscover the principle of aura that our ancestors understood intuitively. The whole cave is suffused with that awareness."

"Yes," Zane agreed, seeing it now. "I use a camera, you use paints. They used entire caves. The spirits of these animals are still here."

"No, *we* are *there*," Molly reminded him. "Today the caves of Lascoux, Altamira, Perch-Merle, and the rest are tourist traps with no soul remaining. We ghosts are trying to preserve the true spirits, but it isn't easy."

"Of course it isn't easy," Luna said. "But you must keep up the excellent work."

The cart passed through a wall, out of the cave, and into a manmade labyrinth. "The maze of the Minotaur, in old Crete," Molly said. "This is our earliest historical reference to the bull-man."

"I thought you were an illiterate peasant girl," Zane said. "You don't sound that way."

"Oh, I can't read or anything," Molly said. "It is very hard to learn fundamental skills like that after death. I just sell shellfish; it's the one thing I do well. But I've been dead much longer than I lived, and I have had the chance to educate myself that I lacked in life. I wasn't stupid when I lived, just ignorant. There's a lot to learn, simply by watching the follies of the living. See, there's the Minotaur now."

Indeed, the bull-man was pacing about his central chamber, lifting his horns and sniffing the air suspiciously, as if becoming aware of the intruding party. "I don't suppose you want the gossip about how he was conceived," Molly said. "How the Queen Pasiphae of Crete had a passion for the Bull from the Sea, who was really a sort of masculine demon, but the Bull wasn't interested in her, so she—"

"We know the story," Luna said curtly. Zane could understand why she did not want to discuss the matter of lovely women making love to demons.

Then they were out of the maze and rolling along a Roman highway. "Are you enjoying this?" Zane asked in Luna's ear.

"I haven't been on a date in a long time," she answered obliquely. "Most men shun association with the family of a Black Magician."

"Their loss," he said, drawing her in more closely. She melted against him, and it was very pleasant.

"How can you save the world from Satan in twenty years if you are doomed to die within a month?" Zane asked, remembering something the ghost had said.

"Maybe I can influence Satan in Hell," she suggested.

"I don't want you in Hell!" he protested. "I don't want you dead at all."

"We must all die," Molly said. "What hurts is dying out of turn." She was, of course, in a position to know.

Zane pondered that, as Luna snuggled most pleasantly close. Those were the clients he had trouble with, intellectually and emotionally— the ones who were dying early because of accident or misunderstanding or plain bad luck. A game that played itself out and was finished was one thing; its score was known. But one that was interrupted before its course was run was a tragedy. Maybe he was abusing his ffice by talking a potential suicide out of it, or rescuing a drowning man, while facilitating the demise of an old and worn-out person, yet that was the way he had to play it. He had precious little of a worthwhile nature to distinguish himself, but it was important to care about people.

"Penny for your thoughts," Luna murmured as they cruised through a medieval Chinese city. Zane was sure each setting on this tour was a highly significant historical event, and Molly was happily describing it all, but somehow he wasn't interested at the moment.

"I don't want you dying out of turn," he whispered. "You're a lot better woman than I deserve, and if—"

"Despite my affair with the demon?" she asked.

Why did she have to remind him of that? "To Hell with the demon!" he exploded.

"Which is exactly where he went," she agreed. "I had to tell you, or any relationship we might have would be a lie. I am unclean, Death, and I will never be clean again, and you must know—"

"We've been over this before!" he cried. "You did something horrible to help your father—as I did to help my mother. How can I condemn you for that?" Yet of course he *had* condemned her, emotionally; he had not been able to avoid it. The notion of some gross demon from Hell sating himself upon her body—

"What did you two do that was so horrible?" Molly asked.

"She gave her body to a demon, to learn the magic that might help her father," Zane said.

"And he used a penny curse to make the machinery that was keeping his mother alive against her will malfunction," Luna said.

"I guess those were sins," Molly agreed doubtfully. "I think sometimes you just have to sin in order to do the right thing."

"If I could have helped my father with a penny curse, I'd have done it," Luna said.

"And if I had to romance a demoness to spare my mother her pain, I'd have done it," Zane said.

"Some of those demonesses are mighty sexy," Molly said. "They say there's no sex like succubus-sex. Of course, I wouldn't know."

"That does sound interesting," Zane said.

Luna reached up, caught hold of one of his ears, and drew his face down to meet hers. "Try this first," she said.

The kiss was electrifying. She had forgiven him his prior reaction and was giving him her emotion. It was a wonderful gift.

"And this is Tours," Molly said, gesturing to a new scene beyond the cart. Zane had no idea how many important historical scenes he had missed. "Where the French halted the advance of the Moors, and Europe was saved for the Europeans."

"Good for the Europeans," Luna said, resting her head against Zane's neck. Her topaz joystones affected him as they touched his skin, suffusing him with rare joy. Or maybe it was just Luna's touch that did it.

Still he cursed inwardly. He had foolishly lost an ideal romance and now had another developing in its place—but this one would end within a month. That might be the reason the first Lovestone had not pointed him at Luna, who in certain respects was a better woman than Angelica. He had never gotten to know Angelica, but was judging her on the basis of his expectations. Luna was a poorer match because she would not live long. The Lovestone did not care about details; it merely matched up the greatest good for the longest period. That was the trouble with inanimate magic; it left so much untold.

Yet he realized that this misfortune had a perverse enchantment. He had been somewhat diffident about approaching Luna, for he wasn't sure whether Death should date a mortal woman, or whether a Magician's daughter would have anything to do with the likes of him when not compelled by magic, or how he felt about a person who had been used by a minion of Hell. Now, with the awareness of her mortality, he knew such diffidence could not be afforded. Whatever she could be to him, she had to be now—for there would be no tomorrow.

"But you could disassociate immediately, sparing yourself sorrow," she pointed out.

"No, that would be like a rat leaving a sinking ship." Then he did a mental double take. "How did you know what I was thinking?"

"I inherited more than Truthstones and Lovestones and Deathstones," she said teasingly. "The right spellstones can enable a person to do anything, even read minds."

"But you aren't using black magic now, because it—"

"Brings me closer to the demon," she finished for him. "You're right—I'm not using magic. I merely have a pretty good notion of the nature of your thinking."

"How? You don't know me that well yet."

"Did you desert your mother when she needed your help?"

"That's different—" He paused, reconsidering. "No, I guess it isn't. I have much evil on my soul, but I don't desert sinking ships."

"So you are a mixed person, with good as well as evil, as I am. I am selfish to come to you in this fashion, when I did not do so before."

"Yes, you did. You offered—"

"My body. The least valuable aspect of me. Now I offer more."

"I'll take it."

"This self-serving manner of coming to you will further burden my soul. But since my father left, there has been a void in my life that even the most potent equilibrium magic does not entirely abate. I had thought I was prepared, for I knew he was destined to die, but the shock of the actuality was worse that I anticipated." She paused, examining her feeling. "There was a presence that perhaps I took somewhat for granted. Now there is not. I feel unbalanced, falling into the gap that was the support my father provided. How does one counter the emptiness?"

"Maybe some other support—"

"And you are the closest man for me to lean on. I want to enjoy my remaining time in life before it is gone forever. Before I must go to the demon."

"The demon still lurks for you?" Zane asked, dismayed. He had thought that was over.

"Yes. But he can't reach me in life unless I summon him, and that I will never again do. But when I go to Hell, I will be in his power forever."

"You must not go to Hell!" he protested. "You must improve your balance so you will go to Heaven!"

"In less than a month?" She shook her head sadly. "I have stones that measure good and evil, even as you do, and some of them operate by white magic, so I can use them as I wish, though they do not work well for me. I know my score. I am too deep in debt to Satan to escape at this point."

"There has to be a way! You can do a lot of good, contribute to worthy charities, think angelic thoughts—"

She shook her head. "You know better, Death. Good deeds done for such a purely selfish reason do not count. I had to redress my evil before I learned I was about to die. Now it is too late."

"What—what is to be the cause of your death?" Zane asked, fearing the answer.

"I don't know. I'm not ill, and I'm not accident-prone. Maybe someone is going to murder me."

"Not if I can help it," Zane muttered grimly. He resolved, as soon as this date with Luna was over, to go to Purgatory and look up the relevant records. If he could find out what was slated to kill her, he might arrange to block it. He already knew that a scheduled demise was not necessarily immutable; he had changed several such schedules himself. Meanwhile, if she stayed at home, her invisible moon moth should protect her well.

"Pearl Harbor!" Molly said. "See the airplanes! They caught the defenders with their spells down. That launched the United States of America into World War Two."

Zane wasn't sure how the cart had traveled all the way across the great Pacific Ocean to this island, but remembered it was a ghost vehicle not subject to the normal laws of physics.

Already the cart was moving on to the next display. "The pre-emptive nuclear strike that launches World War Three," Molly said with a certain zest. "This one generates a lot of ghosts, believe me!" And it was as if they trundled through the heart of the sun, with blinding light everywhere.

"World War Three?" Luna asked. "That hasn't happened yet!"

"We ghosts aren't limited by time the way living folk are," Molly explained. "We see everything."

"When is World War Three happening?" Zane asked somewhat nervously.

"You'd have to ask Mars that; he's been working on it for a long time, his crowning achievement. I think the time is not precisely fixed, because the Eternals can't agree. Satan wants it when the balance of evil favors him; God is holding out for His own side. Right now the balance is so close they can't be certain where the majority of now-living folk would go if all their souls were released today. So neither side dares provoke the final war. But if any significant shift occurs, either way—"

"The world is in balance, like an individual human soul?" Zane asked. "That's some situation!"

"Is that all God or Satan cares about the world?" Luna demanded. "Which one gets the most souls when it ends?"

"That's the way it seems to us," Molly said. "Of course, we're only ghosts, who aren't privy to the motives of the Eternals. But it does stand to reason that whoever gets the most souls has the most power. Souls are wealth in the region where gold can't go."

"It can't be that way," Zane said, troubled. "Maybe Satan is soul-grabbing, but God has to want the genuine welfare of man."

"Then how come God never helps man directly?" Molly demanded. "Satan has minions all over, sowing dissension, making mischief, publishing commercials for Hell. God remains aloof."

"God is honoring the Covenant," Luna said. "Satan is cheating. There should not be any supernatural interference. Man is supposed to make his own destiny, by the type of life he lives when given free will."

"If you believe that," Molly said, the accent of the gutter where she had been raised in life coming through more strongly, "you must also believe the Tooth Fairy is queer."

Luna was startled. "That's a serious charge."

The ghost laughed. "See? You argue the case!"

The cart passed through an invisible curtain and emerged at the carnival grounds. "That was quite a tour," Zane said politely, though he had not paid it much attention.

"That's just the beginning!" Molly said, hauling them off to the ghostly, ghastly Horror House. The experience was, of course, awful, for the ghosts really knew how to horrify mortal people, but Luna took advantage of the darkness to sneak in a passionate kiss that horrified the ghosts. At least Zane thought it was Luna.

They had ghostly cotton candy and visited the Dinosaur Petting Zoo—the larger carnivores were muzzled, which annoyed them visibly—and tried to win a valuable invisible doll by catching a smoke ring on a glass lance. It didn't work; the ring shattered and the lance puffed away as vapor. They concluded with the Tunnel of Love—and here Molly had to let them go alone, for the boat held only two.

By this time Zane was quite satisfied to be alone with Luna. Maybe it was the hypnotic effect of the constant noise and color of the carnival, or the knowledge of her brief time remaining, or that she was soft and pretty—for whatever reason, he found himself dizzy with delight at her propinquity, and as close to love as he had ever been. They drifted down the calm channel of water; as the quiet darkness closed in, they held hands and kissed again, and that was more pleasant than anything else he might have contemplated with any other woman. Then, it seemed like only half a moment later, they were emerging from the long tunnel, the journey over.

It was enough. They unloaded Molly Malone's wheelbarrow from the car and got in for the drive back to Kilvarough. It had been a good date.

-8-

GREEN MOTHER

A light was flashing on the dash. That meant Mortis had something to tell Death. "Brace yourself," Zane told Luna. "We're about to be on the Deathhorse."

"I love horses," she said. "I'm a girl at heart."

He pressed the button, and they were on the stallion, Luna sitting behind him. "What is it?" Zane asked. "My countdown is turned off; I'm pretty well caught up on my backlist, and I don't begrudge my upcoming clients a few more hours of life."

The horse neighed urgently and swished his tail.

"Idiot—turn on your translator," Luna murmured.

Zane hastily set the language gem in his left ear. It was uncomfortable to wear continuously, as he had never gotten his ear pierced so he could use it as an earring, and he normally removed it during off hours. He hadn't realized it could be used to talk to Mortis!

"Nature summons you," the neigh-voice said.

"I can wait till I get home," Zane muttered, conscious of Luna's presence.

"The Incarnation Nature," the horse clarified. "Gaea. She says to dally only long enough to pick up one soul."

"Nature-the-person? If she wants to talk to me, why doesn't she come herself, as the other Incarnations have?"

"She is the Green Mother," Mortis neighed, and there was an undertone of equine respect. "She governs all living creatures. Do not annoy her, Death."

"You had better go," Luna said. "I don't know which of you Incarnations has the most power, but Nature surely is not to be trifled with. You can drop me off anywhere near Kilvarough, and—"

"Do not go near Kilvarough!" Mortis warned. "Operate from the ghost world."

"But I can't leave Luna among the ghosts!" Zane protested.

"Bring her."

"I'd like that," Luna said. "Is it permitted?"

"I'll do it regardless," Zane decided. "I'm not going to leave you in any strange place unprotected." He turned on the Deathwatch countdown. It showed nine minutes. He oriented on the client, using the special gems of his bracelet. He nudged Mortis, aiming the stallion in the right direction. "Take us there," he directed.

The horse leaped away from the carnival. Clouds wafted by, and the cosmos was inchoate. "Ooo, lovely!" Luna breathed, hugging Zane from behind.

Then Mortis landed in a great dance hall in the city of San Diego. Magic clothed the walls with royal trappings and made the floor resemble solid silver. It did not at all look like a place of death.

"So this is what your job is like," Luna murmured. "You must enjoy it well."

"It varies," Zane said. "Parts of it are not fun."

They dismounted, and Mortis stepped into the background. No one noticed that he was a horse, for he was protected by the magic of his own office.

The watch showed four minutes. Zane went to the spot indicated by the gems. It was a section of the dance floor. Dancers crossed it and moved on, doing the Squirm; he could not tell who was fated to be there when the time came.

There were two empty seats beside a young woman who was not dancing. Zane and Luna took them.

Two young men walked along the edge of the dance floor, engaged in animated conversation or moderate debate. They halted abruptly near Zane. "Well, then, let's try it!" one exclaimed. "Random selection, yours against mine."

"Done!" the other agreed. "Winner takes them both. A disinterested judge."

The first turned to a seated youth who was drinking a beverage from a bottle. "Do you know how to play a guitar?"

The youth laughed. He set down his bottle and stifled a burp. "Me? I'm tone deaf! I can't even play a triangle!"

"He'll do," the second man said. He turned to Luna. "Do you dance well, miss?"

"Excellently," Luna said.

"No good." The man focused on the other girl. "Do you dance well?"

"No," the girl said shyly. "I've got two left feet. I only come to watch the others dance."

"She'll do," the first man said.

"Do for what?" Luna asked, annoyed about being passed over for whatever it was.

"And you can be the judge," the second man said to her.

Zane looked at his watch. The countdown timer showed two minutes. Who was going to die here, and how?

The first young man produced a nondescript guitar and pushed it into the hands of the tone-deaf lad. "When I give the signal, play."

"But I told you I can't—"

"Precisely. It's an excellent test."

The second man brought out a pair of dancing slippers. "Put these on and dance," he said to the left-footed girl.

Suddenly Zane had an awful notion. "Luna!" he cried. "Get out of here! It may be *your* death we're here for!" The watch showed ninety seconds.

"Don't be silly," she said. "You brought me here. That wouldn't have been necessary if I were the client. You could simply have pushed me off the horse in mid-air. Anyway, I'm not in balance; I can make it to Hell without your assistance. I'm not on your calendar."

Zane had to admit that was true. The death belonged to someone else. But to whom?

"Begin!" the first man ordered.

The youth put his fingers to the strings with a what-can-I-lose smirk—and played an excellent chord. "See? Pure junk," he said.

"Not so," Luna told him. "That sounded nice."

Astonished, he played again, watching his hands—and a fine melody commenced. His left fingers flew along the frets, while his right hand strummed out an authoritative tune. The hands seemed to possess lives of their own.

The left-footed girl stood up, wearing the slippers. "You'll see," she said. "I'm no good at all." Her right leg did look slightly deformed, perhaps by some childhood injury; it was unlikely she could move it well.

She began to dance—and her feet flashed like those of a ballerina. Her mouth dropped open. "The slippers!" she cried. "Magic!"

Both young men turned to Luna. "Now you watch and listen, beautiful," the first one said. "Tell us which is better—the music or the dancing."

Luna smiled. "I shall. I'm in the arts myself; I can give an informed opinion, though these are two different forms of expression."

The youth played the magic guitar and the girl danced in the magic slippers so well that soon the other dancers paused to listen and watch. Others started to dance to the new music. But none danced as well as the left-footed girl, who fairly flew about the floor, kicking her legs with pretty flourishes and throwing herself into dazzling spins. She had not been a really attractive girl when seated, but now her cleverness of foot lent her a special allure. Physical beauty, Zane realized as he watched, was not entirely in the body; it was in the way the body was moved.

The girl's face became flushed. She panted. "Enough!" she cried breathlessly. "I'm not used to this!" But the newly formed audience was clapping, urging her on, and the guitar was sounding veritable panoramas of notes, almost visibly filling the dance hall. These were two excellent magic items!

Then Zane saw that the youth was no longer smiling. His fingers were raw and starting to bleed, for they were soft, not calloused in the manner of experienced players. But he could not stop playing. The magic compelled him. And the girl—

The watch touched zero on the countdown. The girl screamed and collapsed.

Now Zane understood. The magic articles did not consider human limitations. They did not care if a person flayed his fingers playing, or if an out-of-condition girl exercised herself into heart failure. They simply compelled performance.

Zane rose and went to the girl, experiencing a certain guilty relief that the client had not, after all, been Luna. Of course he should have realized what was about to happen and prevented the left-footed girl from donning the terrible slippers. He could have saved her life, instead of merely watching her die.

Regretfully, he took the girl's soul and turned away from the body. The other dancers were standing aghast at the sudden tragedy. Luna, too, was horrified. "I should have realized—" she said, her eyes fixed on the now-still feet of the girl. "I've seen enough magic to know the peril inherent in second-class enchantment! You came here on business—"

"And if you had donned those slippers—" Zane began.

"That, too! I'm a Magician's daughter; I know the type of—but I just wasn't thinking."

Mortis approached, and they mounted. No one else noticed. The contest between guitar and slippers had no victor, only a loser.

"On to Nature, Deathsteed," Zane directed, stopping his timer again. "I guess you know the route."

Mortis did. He leaped out of the dance hall and into the sky.

"I know death is a necessary part of life," Luna said behind Zane. "I will experience it all too soon myself. But somehow it cuts more sharply when you see it personally—when you actually participate—"

"Yes." How well he knew!

"I wish I hadn't agreed to judge that contest. That girl might be alive now!"

"No, she was slated to die. You played no actual part. More correctly, you played a part that someone else would have; your action changed nothing."

"She was so innocent!"

"She was fifty percent evil. It is not safe to assume that the handicapped are free of sin; they vary exactly the way unhandicapped people do. I don't know what brought her to the point of equilibrium, but—"

"Oh, you know what I mean! She may have done evil in her life, as we all have, but she didn't deserve to die so cruelly. Worked to death in one minute by enchanted slippers. Her heart must have burst."

Zane did not answer. He agreed with her. He had increasing objections to the system of judgments and terminations that prevailed.

"I wish I knew the meaning of it all," Luna said.

"Those two men must have known their artifacts were dangerous," Zane muttered. "That's why they tested them on ignorant bystanders. Magic in the hands of amateurs can be deadly."

The horse drew up to the abode of Nature. It was a broad, green forest with a road entering it. A low, sleek, open car was parked at the tunnellike aperture.

Mortis halted. "You're not invited?" Zane asked the horse. "Well, I suppose you can graze here." The meadow before the forest was lush. "Luna and I can drive that car in; I presume that's what it's for."

But the car turned out to be a single-seater; no room for Luna. "I think Nature wants a private meeting," Luna said. "I'll wait here, too."

"If she'd given me time to take you home—" Zane said, irritated.

"Mother Nature has her own ways—as do we all."

Zane wasn't satisfied, but had to leave her. "Keep an eye on her, Mortis," he called, and the pale horse neighed agreement. Zane doubted any natural force would threaten Luna while the Deathsteed watched.

"Now don't go looking for trouble with that woman," Luna cautioned him. "Remember, you are not dealing with an ordinary person."

Did his ire show so clearly? Zane wrapped his cloak about him and climbed into the little car. He glanced back at Luna, standing there in the field, all slender and lovely, her jewels gleaming at head and toe, a dream of a woman. Damn Nature, to take him away from her, even briefly!

The car controls were standard. He started the motor, put the vehicle in gear, and followed the asphalt road into the forest. The trees closed in overhead, forming a living canopy. It was a pleasant drive.

Ahead, he spied an intersection. The light was poor because of the shade, so he slowed. It was well he did so, for there was a pedestrian walking by the side of the road, wearing a dark cape that rendered him almost invisible. It would have been all too easy to hit that careless walker.

Just as Zane came up to the pedestrian, a cyclist shot out of the intersection and swerved to pass the walking man. This carried the cyclist directly into Zane's path. He tromped on the brake pedal and screeched to a stop just in time. "You idiot!" he swore at the cyclist, who was blithely pedaling ahead, unconcerned by the close call. "You could have caused a fatal collision!" He was also not pleased with the pedestrian, who had not paid attention to his surroundings and had taken no evasive action. But he could not dally here; he had an appointment with Nature that he wanted to get out of the way so he could return to Luna. He drove on.

The road abruptly dead-ended at a bog contained by an embankment. Zane parked, got out, and leaned over the rim of the bog to touch its surface. Immediately a spot of mud boiled up, spitting out a gobbet of yellow goop that looked hot and smelled terrible. Zane jerked his hand away, though his Deathglove would have protected his fingers. The old instincts of life remained with him.

How was he to cross this morass? For he could see, now, the spire of a distant castle, directly across the bog. Nature guarded her residence well! It occurred to him that this was some sort of a test or challenge; no ordinary person could get through, but an Incarnation could. He had to prove which kind he was. After that, he might have something to say to the Green Mother. She had interrupted what had become an important date before it could become more important yet, and now was wasting his time with the riddle of how to approach her. It might not be wise for the ordinary person to trifle with Nature—but neither was it healthy to tempt Death.

But first he had to reach her. She had neatly deprived him of his steed, who could readily have handled this obstruction. How could he cross without miring himself in hot mud?

He studied the near shore of the bog. Perched just beside the retaining wall was a small building, perhaps an outhouse. That would figure; naturally Nature would provide for a call of nature. He wasn't laughing.

No, now he saw that it more closely resembled a storage shed. What would be stored therein? He strode over to it and flung open its door, expecting to find tools or gasoline or perhaps a telephone.

He was disappointed. It was empty, except for a single large red rubber bag hanging on a nail.

He lifted this down and discovered that it was filled with fluid, probably water, and it was warm. It was an old-fashioned hot-water bottle, used to warm the feet or body on cold nights. What was it doing here?

He set the thing down, pondering. It simply didn't make sense to store a full, warm hot-water bottle in a shed in the middle of nowhere. It would be cold in half an hour, if it wasn't magic.

Magic? Zane smiled. He doubted this one had any magic besides its self-heating spell, but it wouldn't hurt to try a simple invocation on it, just in case. At least it could warm his feet, if the weather turned cold. "Red water bottle, show your power," he told it.

The bottle abruptly floated upward, jerking from his hand.

−136−

Zane grabbed it before it got away. "Levitation!" he exclaimed. "You float!"

It certainly did. He had all he could do to hold it down, and the effort took both his hands. "Hey, take it easy!" he said. "Don't go anywhere without me!"

But the bottle continued to tug upward, as if still warming to its task. He tried to drag it back to its shed, but couldn't budge it. His arms were getting tired; soon it would escape and sail up above the level of the treetops.

"I'll tame you, you perverse inanimate thing," he grunted. He threw a leg over it so he could free a hand. In a moment he had it wedged between his thighs, captive — but such was its power, it lifted him right off the ground. He had to hang on to its thick neck with both hands. The thing was also getting hotter now, and was pulsing internally, as if its effort were making it react.

The bottle drifted toward the bog, carrying him along. "Whoa!" he cried.

The bottle stopped in place.

It was like a saddle, and it answered to horse-commands! "Now I think I understand," Zane said. "Bottle, carry me across the bog to the citadel of Nature."

The red bottle accelerated. Zane hung on, his legs dangling. The thing was comfortable enough, for the water inside it allowed it to shape to his body, but by the same token, it offered no firm support. He clung as it zoomed, and he eyed the bubbling bog so close below; yet he was making decent progress and would soon be across.

Suddenly Zane found himself overtaking a boy. The youth was flapping his arms violently as if to fly — and indeed, his feet dangled like Zane's, just above the hungry bog. It was the hard way to do it, for man really was not structured to fly alone, and Zane resolved to stay out of the way of those flailing extremities. He leaned back, causing his bottle to tilt, and it followed its mouth upward. Once he passed over the bare-armed flier, he could drop back to—

Z-O-O-O-M! An airplane cruised low overhead, almost blowing Zane off his precarious perch. He struggled to hang on to the bottle, lest he be dropped on the flying youth just below and dunk them both in the boiling muck. What sort of imbecile would fly his airplane so low over other travelers? Or was it simply cruel mischief? The arrogance of power?

Zane finally re-established himself and flew on across the bog. The flapping flier seemed not to have noticed the near collision he had participated in, but went his own way without even a salutation. Zane did not think much of him either. This region seemed to be full of tunnel-visioned nuts!

Now he came to the other side of the bog. The hot-water bottle cooled, dropped down, and deposited him on the bank, refusing to respond to further directions. Either its magic was exhausted, or it was programmed to go no farther. Zane got off it, and the bottle went completely limp.

Well, he was past the morass and could walk now. He saw there was a path through the forest. He carried the bottle to the shed he spied and hung it up on its hook. This was a simple vehicle to park!

He set off down the path toward the citadel. The trees closed in more tightly than before, and the route was curvaceous. Zane rather enjoyed this portion of the trip; the woods were, as the poet Frost had put it, lovely, dark, and deep. A person seldom got to appreciate just how lovely a forest was, for people spent most of their lives rushing to accomplish what they supposed were more important tasks than appreciating nature.

Then the path debouched at a clear, small lake. Zane did not care to get his robe wet, so he tried to go around the water—but soon discovered that the land on either side devolved rapidly into more marsh. He had to go across the lake, which meant he had to swim.

Swim? Zane snapped his fingers, outraged at his own foolishness. He could walk on water! He had done so when rescuing the drowning man from the ocean. His Deathshoes gave him that power. He had been wasting time, trying to detour unnecessarily!

He strode out onto the water—and his feet sank through it into the slush beneath. Zane windmilled his arms, catching his balance, then hastily backed out. What was the matter?

In a moment he figured it out. This was not ordinary water; this was one of Nature's defenses. Nature was another Incarnation; her power matched his. The minor magic of clothing would not be effective against her spells. So here his shoes were not magic—or at least were not potent enough to prevail against her counterspell. He would, after all, have to swim.

He considered removing his clothing, but realized that it would be difficult to carry cloak, gloves, and shoes; the stuff would probably get soaked, anyway. So he would try swimming in his outfit, and if it hampered him too much, he would remove it. Without further ado, he waded in.

He discovered to his surprise and gratification that his uniform protected him from direct immersion. He was in the water, but it did not penetrate to his skin. There seemed to be a spell to keep the water out, though it pressed the material of the robe closely about his limbs. He tried to swim—and found himself buoyed, so that it was easy to float. He moved through the water with satisfactory dispatch. This was fun, too, in its fashion.

It was, however, also hard work. Zane had not swum any distance in years, and soon his muscles were tiring from the unaccustomed exertion. He slowed, unworried; he really did not need to race. He would get there—

A canoe came suddenly alongside him, crowding close. Zane missed his stroke and took a gulp of water. Then he righted himself, shook his head, and saw that a magic motorboat was rushing silently by, shoving up a wave that pushed the canoe into the swimmer.

In a moment the motorboat was gone, its pilot oblivious to the damage done by his arrogance. The canoeist paddled on his own course, similarly indifferent. Zane was left spluttering in the water. What was the matter with these people?

He swam on to the shore and drew himself out. His uniform emerged dry; even his feet were comfortable. The footpath resumed ahead of him. He followed it and soon was at Nature's citadel.

Actually, it now seemed more like a temple, strange as it was. A dense growth of trees and vines formed an almost solid enclosure with interwoven arches and embrasures of living wood that rose to a leafy crown. From the twining vines, flowers sprouted, sending their perfumes out wantonly.

Zane marched up to the door aperture. There was no bell or knocker, so he proceeded on in unannounced.

It was like a cathedral inside, with lush plant growth everywhere. Living arches of wood supported deep green carpets of ferns. Water trickled down from mossy springs. Everywhere was life, green and pleasant.

He came to a sunny central court where wafts of mist curtained a throne fashioned of deep green jadeite. This was Nature's throne room.

"Welcome, Thanatos," her wind-and-bird-song voice came. "Do you wonder at the challenge?"

"Yes," Zane agreed shortly. He wasn't sure he liked her using the Greek name for Death. "If you wanted to see me, you might at least have facilitated my approach."

"Oh, but I did facilitate it, Thanatos!" she protested, coming to meet him. A patch of mist moved with her; it was, in fact, her clothing, artfully thinning and thickening at key points. Zane found the effect intriguing, though he was sure Nature was no young creature. Mist might be mostly opaque, but it couldn't be solid.

"In what manner?"

"I set up a pathway that only one of us could negotiate," she explained. "Normally there is no path at all, and no outside creature penetrates. This path would bar either a fully mortal creature or a fully immortal one, such as a minion of Eternity. Therefore our privacy is assured."

"That's what I thought at first—but there were other people all around," Zane said. "Morons on land, water, and in the air. Three times I was almost in a collision."

"Were you really?" she asked, unsurprised.

"Don't pretend you don't know, Green Mother!"

Nature smiled as if complimented. Her face was pretty enough, framed by somewhat wild and flowing hair as green as grass and blue as water, the colors shifting in a kind of pseudo-iridescence. Her eyes, when she met his gaze, were like chill, deep pools with highlights of fire. He had seen black opals like that. This woman, he realized, had awesome power; indeed she was not to be trifled with! "I know that only you traveled that route, Thanatos."

"What of the others, then? Did I imagine them?"

She made a smiling sigh, her misted and ample bosom contracting like a dissipating cloud. "I see you do not yet comprehend my little ways. Those others were you."

"I doubt it. I wanted no part of such interference."

"Be seated, Thanatos," she said, patting a curlicue of rattan with a hand that sparkled of nacreous shell. All things animate were hers, Zane realized, including pearls, the product of living creatures. "I shall clarify this particular detail so that we may proceed to our proper business."

Zane sat, for the Green Mother's command was not to be denied. The rattan seemed to shape itself to his body in an almost embarrassing familiarity, making him quite uncomfortable. "Do that."

"A person is often his own enemy, if he but knows it. It is the nature of the beast. Well I know."

Naturally Nature knew the nature of man! That was her business. But how did this relate to his obstacle-course entry path?

"Once you drove a vehicle," she said. "Once you rode a device. Once you moved alone. You were one, and you were three. Only the scenery changed, to facilitate objectivity."

"I was in three encounters," Zane agreed. This female gave a disturbing impression of comprehension, but he did not see what she was getting at.

"You *were* three. One encounter, three views. You saw yourself from three vantages. Three chances to react to yourself."

"I was three?" Zane asked, perplexed.

"There was no one but you on that route. But time was in a manner flexed." She smiled obscurely, her teeth gleaming momentarily like fangs. *Nature, red in tooth and claw . . .* "Chronos owed me a favor. I could not flex the event myself. We Incarnations do assist each other."

"No one but me?" Zane's head seemed to be spinning. "One encounter, seen three ways? You are saying I was the driver—and the cyclist—and the pedestrian—only when I was the cyclist I saw it as the hot-water bottle ride, and when I was the pedestrian I saw it as the swimming? You changed the view so I wouldn't catch on? I got in my own way three times?"

"You comprehend rapidly and well, once you get into it," Nature agreed, and her compliment pleased him despite his underlying anger.

"I comprehend that you put me on a track through a Möbius strip with a cross section of a prism, so I had to traverse the loop three times. But *why?*"

"We answered that before. A mortal could not have passed; the equipment is not spelled to work for mortals. An immortal could not have passed either; an angel would not have needed the equipment, and the true path exists only for that equipment. A demon would have fought himself to death at the first encounter, for that is the way of demons."

"I felt like fighting," Zane admitted. "That arrogant idiot in the power boat—" He grinned ruefully. "Who was me. It seemed so different in the car! I thought I owned the road and that the others were intruding on my surface. As a walker or swimmer, I wasn't paying attention to anything except getting myself along. As a cyclist or bottlist or whatever, I was caught in the middle, between the arrogant power driver and the ignorant self-mover. Both seemed wrong. I'm *not* proud of my performance, in retrospect."

Nature shrugged, making an interesting ripple in the mist about her. At times she seemed fat, but at other times she seemed voluptuous; the fog never quite betrayed the truth. "You will have leisure to ponder the implications. You did get through, as only a true Incarnation would, blundering as it may have appeared. We Incarnations are not quite living and not quite dead; we are a unique category, with unique powers. We occupy our offices, but sometimes we *are* our offices. Like light, we are both wave and particle." She gestured, dismissing the matter. "Now we have privacy."

"Wait," Zane said, remembering something. "How can a demon fight himself to death? He's already dead."

"It may be true that the dead can not die—but if you do to a demon's corporate body what would kill a living creature, that demon loses the use of that body and must return directly to Hell. So it is much the same, in practice."

Zane returned to another matter. "What's so important about privacy? Do we have secrets to exchange?"

"Indeed we do. We are the mortal immortals; we can't have our secrets known to mortal mortals, lest we lose respect. We can't tell all to the Eternals, lest we lose our power."

"What secrets?" Zane asked. "I'm just doing my job."

"As you perceive it."

"Is there something I don't know about it?"

"Perhaps." She settled into a livewood chair, her ambience of mist spreading to fog much of it out. "I can make a small and not entirely comfortable demonstration."

She gestured, and suddenly Zane felt a tremendous concupiscence. He wanted sex, and he wanted it now. He found himself standing, in more than one manner, and approaching her.

"No!" he gritted, knowing this was not his own desire, but one imposed from without. Nature only smiled.

He reached for her—but forced himself to grasp for her soul, not her body. His gloved hand passed through the mist and her flesh, and his fingers hooked into her soul. He drew on it, stretching part of it out of her body.

She stiffened as if in sudden pain. Then Zane's erotic feeling left him as quickly as it had come. Her spell was off. He relaxed his hold on her soul and withdrew his hand from her flesh.

Nature took a deep and somewhat shuddering breath, and the mist about her fluctuated in intensity. She had lost some of her composure. "I have shown you part of my power," she gasped. "And you have shown me part of yours."

Again Zane suffered an illumination. "I *do* have power over the living— to a degree!" He remembered how his client in the hospital, the old woman like his mother, had reacted when he had tried the first time to take her soul. It had to be a terrible shock to have the soul pulled from a living body.

"You do indeed, Thanatos. No one can balk an Incarnation in his specialty—not even another Incarnation. There is no profit in opposing each other, ever. Nature governs all of life—but she doesn't govern Death. The individual powers each of us has are inviolate. No one—" Here she paused, giving him a straight glance of enigmatic significance, her eyes like the swirlings of a tempest at night. "*No one* can interfere with any one of us with impunity."

Zane was shaken by her revelation. He had not realized before how directly and specifically she could affect him, or how he could affect her. His own power had surprised him as much as hers. But he got himself organized and returned to the subject. "So you summoned me here to tell me something and show me something, putting difficulties in my way. What is really on your mind?"

She shrugged again, seeming to like the motion. She had recovered her composure. She was, of course, an exceedingly tough creature. "You have met the others."

"I presume you mean the other special figures—Time, Fate, War. Yes, briefly."

"We really are special, Thanatos, we mortal immortals. We differ from one another, but we interact in devious yet essential ways, exerting our vectors."

"Vectors?"

"Well, you don't suppose any of us are completely free, do you? We don't do what we do frivolously. Just as the vectors of force,

–142–

elevation, wind, temperature, humidity, barometric pressure, and landscape interact to determine exactly where a thrown ball will fall, so do the relevant factors determine how a war shall proceed, or how a cold front shall move, or when a given life will end. It may seem like chance or caprice, but that is only because no mortal person and few immortal entities comprehend the nature of the operative forces. We are not free— *no* one is absolutely free—yet we do have some leeway, and in this we individualize our offices. Each Incarnation can counter another to a limited degree, if that other permits, but we prefer not to do that unless there is sufficient reason."

Zane was curious. "How can Death be countered, even if Death permits?"

"Fate could arrange for a replacement, cutting off a thread."

Now he felt a chill, for he knew this had been done before. "Fate— why should Fate ever want to do that?"

"Chronos could halt the approach of an appointment."

"Yes, but why—"

"Mars could fashion a social disruption that could change the entire picture."

She was avoiding his question. Still, this seemed worth pursuing. "And what of Nature? What cute little trick do you have up your fog, aside from the doubtlessly convenient ability to inflict instant lust?"

"Show me your soul," she said.

"My—!" Then he made the connection, and brought out the soul of the left-footed dancing girl. He had stuffed his soul-bag automatically in his pocket and forgotten it until this moment.

Nature wafted a ball of mist at the soul. "Do not misjudge the power of any Incarnation, Thanatos. When you leave me, go to the crypt and try this soul. Then you will comprehend."

Zane put the soul away. It seemed unchanged. Was she bluffing? What could she really do with a soul? "You brought me here only for this?"

She laughed, causing little puffs of mist to spin off and float free. "By no means. I merely make my point with that soul so you learn proper respect and pay attention to my implication."

"Well, make your implication!" Zane exclaimed impatiently.

"What do you suppose is the most ancient profession of the human species?" Nature asked.

What was this distaff dog up to now? "It's a female profession," he said guardedly.

"Not so, Thanatos. Females were not permitted. The oldest profession is that of shaman, or medicine man, or witch doctor."

"Witch doctor!" Zane exclaimed incredulously. "What validity did he have before modern magic was mastered?" But as he spoke, he remembered Molly Malone's comment about the old cave painters and their lost powers over the souls of animals. The practice of magic did predate modern advances.

"The shaman was the original liberal arts supporter. The chief of the tribe was the man of action, while the shaman was the man of intellect. It may not have been easy for him in primitive times, when neither magic nor science worked better than erratically, but he was the one with the true vision of the future. From him descended those who had to fathom *why*, instead of merely accepting *what*. Doctors, philosophers, priests, scientists, magicians, artists, musicians—"

"All those who cater in some fashion to Nature," Zane agreed, though privately he wondered whether artists and musicians really belonged in that category. Their professions were more subjective than most. "But your point—"

"There is a way."

"A way for *what*? I don't follow you at all!"

"Are you an evolutionist or a creationist?"

"Both, of course! But what does that have to do with anything?"

"There are those who feel there is a conflict."

She was changing the subject again, in that infuriating way of hers. "I see no conflict. God created the cosmos in a week, and Satan caused it to evolve. Thus we have magic and science together, as is proper. How could it be otherwise? But what did you intend to say to me? I do have other business."

"We do fear the unknown," Nature said. "Thus man seeks to explain things, to illuminate what remains dark. Yet he remains fascinated by mystery and chance and ofttimes gambles his very life away." She glanced smokily at him, and Zane was sure that she, along with all the other Incarnations, knew how he had gambled with money and then with his own life. "Man is the curious creature, and if his curiosity can kill him, it also educates him. Today we have both nuclear physics and specific conjuration of demons."

"And both are hazardous to the health of man!" Zane snapped. "It's an open question whether a rogue nuclear detonation would do more damage than a ranking demon of Hell loosed on Earth. Maybe World War Three will settle the question."

"I trust we can settle it less vehemently," Nature said. "Much as I would dislike to deny Mars his heyday. Assuming mankind is worth saving."

"Of course it's worth saving!"

"Is it?" she asked, turning her enigmatic, deep-pool gaze on him.

Suddenly Zane had doubts. He shoved them aside. "Let's assume, for the sake of discussion, that man is worth saving. What's your point?"

"An appreciation of several modes of thinking might help."

"Help avert war? How?"

"By means of formations of thought."

"Formations?" Zane was annoyed, but refused to admit the extent of his confusion. If Nature had a point to make, he wanted to grasp it.

"Man is not merely a linear thinker," she said, drawing a line of mist in the air. It hovered like a distant contrail. "Though series effort is certainly straightforward, and useful in many circumstances."

Zane contemplated the contrail. "Series?" he asked blankly.

"Imagine the synapses of your brain, like so many matchsticks, connecting head to tail. Your thoughts travel along these little paths." She punctuated the line with her finger, breaking it into five parts: ————— . "This is a series arrangement. It is like driving down a highway, start to finish."

"Oh. Yes, I see. Synapses connected in series. I suppose we do think in that fashion, though there are alternate paths."

"Precisely. Here is a system of alternate paths." She swept her hand across the contrail, erasing it, then used her finger to draw five new matchsticks: ≡ . "This is a parallel formation. It is, of course, very fast and strong; it leads to a virtually certain conclusion, based on many facts. It is perhaps the most powerful mode."

"But it doesn't reach as far."

"True. It is conservative, leading to small, certain steps with few errors, rather than the sudden leaps of understanding possible with the series formation. It does have its liability, but is useful when the occasion requires."

"Maybe so. But your point—"

"You do at times seem to be that type of thinker," she said, smiling. She pursed her lips and blew out a ring of mist that swirled toward the ceiling. "You cling to essentials. But they will not always serve you well."

"I've been getting in trouble in Purgatory becasue I *haven't* clung to essentials!" he protested.

"Then we have the creative formation," she continued blithely, erasing the parallel formation and drawing five matchsticks radiating out from a common center: ✕ . "Divergent thoughts, not necessarily limited to the immediate context."

"Going in all directions," Zane agreed. "But—"

"And the schizoid formation," she said, drawing a pentagon: ⬠ . "Going round and round, getting nowhere, internalizing."

"What use is that?"

"It might help a person come to terms with an ugly necessity," she said.

"I don't see that—"

"Finally, there is the intuitive formation." She traced another formation: —‖— . "A sudden jump to a conclusion. Not the most reliable mode, yet sometimes effective when others are not."

"Five formations of thinking," Zane said, nearing exasperation. "Very interesting, I'm sure. But what did you have in mind to say to me?"

"I have said it," Nature said calmly.

"Said what? You have evaded the issue throughout!"

"What issue?"

Zane had had enough. "I don't care to play this game." He stomped out of the citadel. Nature did not oppose him.

The exit from the center of the estate was much easier than the entrance had been. He walked down a path and through a thicket and emerged in the original field without passing lake or bog or deep forest, a matter of only a few hundred feet. Mortis and Luna were waiting for him.

"What did old Mother Nature have to say to you so urgently?" Luna demanded archly.

"She's not that old. At least, I don't think she is."

"Estimate to within a decade."

"Are you jealous?" he asked, pleased.

Luna checked about her as if verifying that she wore no Truthstone. "Of course not. How old?"

"I just couldn't tell. She wore fog."

"Fog?"

"Some sort of mist. It shrouded her whole body. But I had the impression of youth, or at least not age."

"Nature is ageless."

"I suppose she is, technically. But so is Death."

Luna took his arm possessively. "And I shall make Death mine. But didn't she have some important message or warning for you? If it is not for mortals like me to know, just say so."

Zane laughed uncomfortably. "Nothing like that! Apparently she just wanted to chat."

"Or to size up the new officeholder."

"Maybe that. She talked about this and that, evolution and the shaman as the oldest profession, formations of thought, and how the other Incarnations could deviously counter me, if I permitted it. She looked at the soul I harvested on the way here and implied she could restore it."

"Maybe she was baiting you. Trying to make you react, to take your measure. Some women are like that, and Nature is surely the most extreme example."

"Surely the archetype," he agreed. "But it's easy to find out about the soul. Let's call her bluff. I'll take this soul back to its body now."

"This is an interesting date," Luna remarked as they mounted Mortis.

"If you insist on dating Death, you must expect morbid things."

The horse took off, knowing where to go. Luna circled her arms about Zane's torso and clung tightly.

"The prospect of dying has become less of a specter for me since I've known you," she said into his back as they flew in overdrive across the world. "Maybe that was what my father had in mind."

Zane didn't answer. The thought of her early dying was not becoming easier for him to accept. What would there be for him when she was gone? In what way was she deserving of such a fate? He did not care what the official ledger listed for the burden of sin on her soul; she was a good woman.

Mortis lighted beside a funeral home. It was still night, here in San Diego, or wee morning, and the place was quiet.

The entrance was locked, but it opened at the touch of the Death-gloves; no physical barrier could bar Death. They went in and found their way to the freezer vaults, where the recent bodies were stored for the required waiting period. Zane used his gems to locate the specific drawer where the dancing girl lay, and drew it out. He had not realized before he made the effort that the gems would orient on a soulless body if he willed it; they were more versatile than he had known.

There she lay, definitely dead, not pretty in the manner of a corpse laid out for display with its eyes and mouth stapled shut, its guts eviscerated, and its blood replaced by embalming fluid; she was just a cold corpse.

"Definitely an unusual date," Luna murmured.

Zane opened his bag and drew out the girl's soul. He shook it gently, unfolding it, then placed it over the corpse. "This is as far as I can go to—"

The soul sank into the stiff body. In a moment the naked torso shuddered, and the eyes cracked open. Ragged breathing resumed.

"She's alive!" Luna exclaimed. "We must get her out of the drawer!"

"Nature wasn't bluffing!" Zane said. "She restored this girl!" He slid his arms around the girl's chill torso and lifted her up. She remained stiff, as if the rigor mortis had not yet worn off, yet she was alive and could move somewhat.

Luna helped him carry the girl to a warmer chamber. They worked on her hands and feet, chafing warmth and flexibility back into them, but it was not enough. Her breathing became shallower, and the stiffness did not abate.

"She must be warmed," Luna said. "Otherwise she will perish again. She was in the freezer too long, and whatever spell Nature made seems to be only temporary. I must use magic—"

"But that will increase your burden of sin!" Zane protested.

"What difference does it make? I am already doomed to Hell." Luna brought out a gem.

Zane let her do it, knowing that what she said was true. The use of black magic could not really damage her case now. Yet it was ironic that she should be further damned for this good cause. Sometimes there seemed to be no justice in the Hereafter.

Luna activated the stone. A soft blue effulgence surrounded it. She brought it near the cold body of the dancer, and immediately the body warmed and softened. Zane's arms, holding the girl upright, were touched by the radiation, and a gentle but potent heat was generated in them. "This is like a microwave oven!" he exclaimed.

"Similar principle," Luna agreed. "Anything science can do, magic can do, and vice versa. But the mechanisms differ."

Now the girl recovered quickly. Her breathing deepened, her body became limber, and her color improved. "W-what?" she asked.

Zane was still supporting her. At the moment she spoke, he was standing behind her, arms around to her front, just beneath her breasts. It took some effort and leverage to keep a half-dead body standing. His position did not change, but his awareness of it did. This was not the way a man held a living girl—especially not a naked one. Yet if he let her go, and she turned about and looked into the face of Death—

Luna appreciated the problem at the same time. "We must get you some clothing, dear," she said to the girl.

Zane continued to support her while Luna searched the premises. As Luna looked, she talked, reassuring the girl. "You won't be feeling too well at the moment, dear. You see, you overdid the dancing and lost consciousness. They thought you were dead and put you in a vault. That's why you feel so cold."

"So cold," the girl agreed, beginning to shiver.

Luna found a blanket and brought it over. "Wrap yourself in this. There's one other thing we must explain. You have had a very close call—so close that Death was summoned to collect your soul. But it turned out to be—well, he decided not to take you, after all. So don't be alarmed; Death is departing, not arriving."

"Death?" The girl's wits were not too bright, understandably.

Zane released her as Luna helped her drape the blanket. The girl turned and for the first time saw Death's face. She gasped, but accepted it.

"Death doesn't take anyone who isn't ready to go," Luna said reassuringly. "He is really your friend, not your enemy. However, you will have to explain to your acquaintances about this. Tell them that you sank so low you saw Death, but he passed you by. It will bring you some deserved notoriety."

"Oh, yes," the girl agreed faintly. "Pleased to meet you, Death. I've heard so much about you." But she did not seem thrilled.

In due course they got the girl to her friends, who welcomed her like one returned from the dead. "And stay away from strange slippers," Luna cautioned her in parting.

They rode Mortis back to Kilvarough, galloping through the sky into the dawn. "Some date," Luna repeated, and kissed Zane farewell. "Shall we call it love, hereafter?"

"Is it?" he asked, genuinely uncertain. What he felt for Luna was deeper and broader than what he had felt for any woman before, but not intense.

She frowned. "No, not yet." She smiled a little sadly. "Perhaps there will be time."

–9–

BUREAUCRACY

Zane went to work on his backlogged case load. He was continuing to grow more proficient, orienting on a given soul anywhere in the world well within the time his Deathwatch showed. Even so, he found himself becoming increasingly thoughtful about the nature of his office. Death was not the calamity of life, but a necessary part of life, the transition to the Afterlife. The tragedy was not dying, but dying out of turn, before the natural course of a given life was run. So many people brought their terminations upon themselves by indulging in suicidal endeavors, getting into strong mind-affecting drugs, or tampering with black magic. Yet he himself had been as foolish, trying to kill himself because of his loss of a woman about whom he no longer cared.

In a way, he realized, he had not really been living until he left his life. He had been born again, in death.

Now, as he got well into the office of Death, he began to believe he could fill it well. It was intent, more than capacity, that made the difference. Probably his predecessor could have done a superior job— but hadn't bothered. Zane had less ability, but a strong desire to do right. He did not have to be a specter. He could try to make each person's necessary transition from life to Afterlife gentle. Why should anyone fear it?

Of course, he was still in his initiation period. If the powers that were didn't approve his performance, his personal balance of good and evil would suffer, and he would be doomed to Hell when he left the office. But as far as he knew, he could not be removed from the office by any other power. Not as long as he was careful. So if he was willing to damn his soul, he could continue indefinitely, doing the job right.

Yes, that was it. "Damn Eternity!" he swore. "I know what's right, and I'm going to do it. If God damns me or Satan blesses me, then it's too bad, but I've got to have faith in my own honest judgment." Suddenly he felt much better; his self-doubt had been ameliorated.

His current client was underground, in the general vicinity of Nashville, the rustic song capital. This was no problem for Mortis, who merely phased down through the ground, carrying Zane along. He saw the strata of sand, gravel, and different kinds of rock, until he reached a sloping shaft through a vein of coal and came to the chamber where two miners had been trapped by a recent cave-in. There was no hope for them; air was limited, and it would take days for others to clear the shaft of rubble.

It was completely dark, but Zane could see well enough. It seemed his office imbued him with magic vision, so that mere blackness could not stay him from his appointed rounds. The men were lying against a wall of rubble, conserving their strength and breath; they knew there was no way out.

"Hello," Zane said, feeling awkward.

One of the miners turned his head. The pupils of his eyes were enormous as they tried to see—and, of course, Zane became apparent, magically. "Don't look now," the man murmured, "but I think we're about to cash in our green stamps."

Of course the other looked and saw. "The caped skull! That's Death!"

"Yes," Zane said. "I have come for one of you."

"You've come for us both," the first miner said. "We've only got air for an hour, maybe less."

Zane glanced at his watch. "Less," he said.

"God, I don't want to die!" the second miner said. "But I knew when I heard the cave-in start that it was hopeless. We were living on borrowed time anyway, with all the safety violations the company wouldn't fix. If I'd been smart, I'da gotten out of this business!"

"Where would you have gone?" the first miner asked.

The other sighed. "Nowhere. I'm fooling myself; this is the only job I can handle." He looked again at Zane. "How much time?"

"Nine minutes," Zane replied.

"Time enough to shrive me."

"What?"

"Confess me. You know, my religion, final rites. I never was a good churchman, but I want to go to Heaven!"

The second miner laughed harshly. "I know I'm not going there!"

Zane brought the Sinstone near. "You are bound for Heaven," he told the first. "You are in doubt," he told the second. "That is why I must take your soul personally."

"In doubt? What does that mean?"

"Your soul is balanced between good and evil, so it is uncertain whether you will go to Heaven or to Hell, or abide a while in Purgatory."

The man laughed. "That's a relief!"

"A relief?"

"As long as I do go to one place or another. I don't care if it's Hell. I know I deserve it. I've cheated on my wife, stolen from the government—you name it, I've done it, and I'm ready to pay."

"You don't fear Hell?"

"Only one thing I fear, and that is being in a cramped box like this, with the air running out and me helpless—for eternity. For an hour I can stand it, but not forever. I don't care what else happens to me, as long as it isn't that."

"*I* care!" the first miner said. "I'm so scared, I'm near gibbering!"

Zane considered. He realized that the dying needed someone to hold their hands, not to shun them. It was hard enough for any person to relate to the unrelatable. Zane had to try to help. "I came for the one in balance, but I think the other needs my service more."

"Sure, help him," the balanced client said. "I won't say I like dying, but I can handle it, I guess. I knew the odds when I signed up for this job. Maybe I'll like Hell."

Zane sat beside the other. "How can I help you?"

"Shrive me, I told you; that will help some."

"But I'm no priest; I'm not even of your religion."

"You are Death; you'll do!"

That must be true. "Then I will listen and judge—but I know already your sin is not great."

"One thing," the man said, troubled. "One thing's haunted me for decades. My mother—"

"Your mother!" Zane said, feeling a familiar shock.

"I think I killed her. I—" The miner paused. "Are you all right, Death? You look pale, even for you."

"I understand about killing mothers," Zane said.

"That's good. She—I was just a teenager when—well, she was in this wing of the hospital, and—"

"I understand," Zane repeated. He reached out and took the man's hand. He knew his own gloved fingers felt like bare bones, but the miner did not shy away.

"She had cancer, and I knew she was in pain, but—"

Zane squeezed his hand.

Reassured, the miner continued: "I visited her, and one day she asked me to step outside the room and read what it said on the—you know, above the door, what kind of word it was. So I went out and looked, and there was something written there, but I couldn't read it. It was in Latin, I think. I went back and told her that, and she asked whether it was—she spelled it out, letter by letter, and you know, she was right, that's what it was. So I agreed that was it, wondering how she had known it, and she thanked me. I thought she was pleased."

The miner took a shuddering breath. "And next morning she was

-152-

dead. The doctor said she seemed just to have given up and died in the night. No one knew why, because she had been fighting so hard to live before. But I—I checked into it and found out that that word in Latin I had spelled for her—it meant incurable. I had told her there was no hope, and so she quit trying. I guess I killed her."

"But you didn't know!" Zane protested.

"I *should* have known. I should have—"

"Then you did her a favor," Zane said. "The others were hiding the truth from her, keeping her alive and in pain. You released her from doubt." He was speaking for himself as much as for the miner. "There is no sin on your soul for that."

"No, I shouldn't have let her know!"

"Would it have been right to preserve her life by a lie?" Zane asked. "Would your soul have been cleaner then?"

"It wasn't my place to—"

"Come off it!" the other miner said. "You were guilty of ignorance. Nothing else. *I* wouldn't have known what those Latin words were either."

"How would you know?" the first one snapped. "You weren't there!"

"I guess not," the second miner admitted wryly. "I don't even know who my mother was."

The first miner paused, set back. "There is that," he conceded. Somehow it seemed that in making that technical concession, he was also accepting the human point. At least he had known his mother and cared about her.

"Now, I'm no philosopher," the second said. "I'm a sinner from way back. But maybe if I'd had a mother like yours, a good woman, I would have turned out better. So take it from one who hasn't any right to say it: you should remember your mother, not with guilt or grief, but with gratitude—for the pleasure she gave you while she lived, for the way she steered you toward Heaven instead of Hell."

"For a sinner, you've got quite an insight! But if I could only have helped her live longer—"

"Longer in a box with the air turning bad?" the other asked.

"No, I agree," Zane said. "It was time to end it. These things are scheduled in ways no mortal comprehends. She knew that, though you did not. If there had been a chance for survival, she might have been willing to fight on through, for the sake of her family, for the things she had to do on Earth. But there wasn't, so it was best that she not torture herself any longer. She put aside life as you would put aside a piece of equipment going bad, and she went out of the gloom of the depths of the mine and on up to the brightness of Heaven."

"I don't know." The man was breathing shallowly now, not finding enough oxygen in the air. He seemed to be more sensitive to this deprivation than his companion was. Zane had no problem; evidently his magic helped him this way, too. He was still discovering things about his office.

"You will join her there," Zane concluded. "There in Heaven. She will thank you herself."

The miner did not answer, so Zane released his hand and turned to the other, his true client. "Are you sure there is nothing I can do for you?"

The man considered. "You know, I'm a cynic, but I guess I do sort of crave some meaning in life, or at least some understanding. There's this song going 'round in my head, and it sort of grabs me, and I think it means something, but I don't know what."

"I'm not expert at meaning," Zane said. "But I can try. What is the song?"

"I don't know the title or anything. It's just, I guess it's an old whaling song. Maybe I have whaling blood in my veins. It goes—what I can remember—goes like this: . . . *and the whale gave a flunder with its tail, and the boat capsized, and I lost my darling man, and he'll never, never sail again, Great God! And he'll never sail again.* It's that 'Great God!' that gets me. I don't give a damn about God, never did, but I feel it, and I don't know why."

Zane suspected the man cared more about God than he thought, but did not make an issue of that. "It's an exclamation," he said, intrigued by the fragment. There was indeed feeling in it, as of a wildly grieving widow crying out in pain. "It's a protest. *Great God!* Why did this have to happen? For a sunken ship, or a mine cave-in. Great God!"

"Great God!" the first miner echoed.

"But why is a song about whaling bothering me now, when I'm buried in this stinking hole?" the second miner demanded.

"It must have special associations for you," Zane said. "I'm not equipped to interpret—"

"Clear enough to me," the first miner said. "Drown in the depths of the sea, suffocate in the depths of the earth, and your wife grieves."

"Yeah, maybe she will," the second said, brightening. "But I don't think that's it. It's as if there's a message, if only I could get it." He snapped his fingers as if trying to call the message forth, and the sound echoed in the recesses of the mine. "Look, Death, you want to do something, tell me a story about that song. Anything, just to make it make some sense."

This, then, was the client's last request. Both men were gasping now, and time was short. Zane had to try to honor the man's wish, even if he bungled the attempt. He thought for a moment, then started to talk—and what he said surprised him.

"There was a young female whale named Wilda. She roamed the

oceans of the world, happy in the company of her kind, and when she
came of age she thought she would mate as the other whale cows did
and bear a cub and bring it up. But then the hunters came, in their huge
boats, and they speared her father and her mother and her bull friend
and hauled them out of the water so that nothing was left but their blood
and dreadful fragments of their bodies that the sharks congregated to
consume. Wilda escaped, for she had learned magic; she changed her
form so she resembled a trashfish and swam away.

"She grieved, singing her whalesong of loss and pain, but she was
angry, too, and confused. Why should these little creatures from land,
called men, come to slay whales who had never harmed them? It seemed
to make no sense. She realized that she had no hope of dealing with
the problem when she didn't understand the motive of the enemy. So
Wilda changed herself into human form and walked to the fishing village
where the whalers lived.

"Some human folk laughed at her, for she was naked and innocent
of their ways. But a young man named Hank took her into his home,
for she was also beautiful. Hank lived with his widowed mother, and
the two of them clothed her and taught her the tongue of their kind,
and she learned quickly, for she was an intelligent whale and really
wanted to know the nature of this strange species. She learned that
Hank was a whaler, who went out periodically to hunt whales, for that
was how he earned his living. Here on land, food was not free for the
taking; people could not simply swim about and open their mouths and
catch and swallow succulent squid; and when it grew cold they could
not blithely migrate south to warmer waters, for travel was complicated
on land. A human person had to work and get gold, and he used this
gold to buy all the necessities that life on land required.

"Now Wilda understood. There was no personal animosity here; the
menfolk had a more pressing lifestyle than the whalefolk, which compelled them to acts they might not otherwise have considered, and they
did not regard the whalefolk as sapient creatures. Perhaps if the menfolk
were made to understand about the culture and feelings of the whales,
things would change and the dreadful killing would stop. She tried to
explain to Hank, but he thought she was joking. After all, his father
had been killed by the flunder of the tail of a whale, so that his grieving
mother had had to bring him up alone. Great God! How could he feel
for the whales? He asked Wilda to marry him, for he needed a woman
and he believed her to be his gift from Heaven.

"This made things very difficult for Wilda, for she had come to love
him, though he was not of her species. So she brought him to the edge
of the sea and walked into the water and returned to her natural form,
believing that once he had seen her as the whale cow she was, he would
be revolted. But he cried for her to come back and apologized for not

believing her before and promised he would never kill another whale. She had, after all, persuaded him, and his love surmounted his awareness of her nature.

"But now she was a creature of the sea again, and the call of the sea was strong. How could she leave the brine forever and be dry? And she spied another whale, a bull who was handsome and strong. She thought she might mate with him, but he told her he was really a squid, who had assumed the form of her kind in order to learn why the whales preyed on the squids, who did not harm the whales. Wilda was amazed and chagrined, for she had never thought of these creatures as having feelings or being sapient. How could she return to devouring squid? Yet she realized that death was a chain of eat and be eaten, with no justice to it except need, power, and chance, and that in this respect her species was no different from the human species or the squid species. It was all a matter of viewpoint. So she apologized to the squid, returned to land, resumed her girl form, and married Hank, her problem resolved.

"And perhaps," Zane concluded, "if we men had a similar insight into the larger pattern of our existence, we, too, would accept the natural order, though at times it is painful for us, especially when we die prematurely."

He stopped, waiting for some response from the miners. But too much of the oxygen had been exhausted, and the men were unconscious. Zane took his client's soul and returned to Mortis, uncertain whether he had done the right thing.

Now he had another concern. Someone he knew was being taken out of turn, and he was not as acquiescent about her fate as Wilda had been about that of her family. But how could he gain the comprehension he needed?

Nature had spoken of patterns of thinking. The first was the linear path —————— , the generally straightforward mode. Would that do him any good?

What was the straightforward way to gain understanding? To do as Wilda had done, and ask someone who had the information. Who was that? Who else but the Purgatory computer!

He stopped in at Purgatory once he had caught up with his case load. "I want to consult the records," he told the information girl.

She directed him to the appropriate wing. It was, of course, another computer center, with a terminal ready for him. He wasn't sure whether this was the same computer he had dealt with before, but suspected that all terminals connected to the same central mechanism.

He sat down and turned the terminal on.

HOW MAY I HELP YOU, DEATH? the screen inquired in green.

"I want to look up the status of Luna Kaftan," Zane said, starting to type in the order.

THIS TERMINAL IS PROGRAMMED FOR VERBAL INPUT, the screen advised him. LUNA KAFTAN, UNDEAD. PRESENT RATIO OF GOOD TO EVIL 35-65. THIS FALLS WITHIN THE PARAMETERS FOR UNASSISTED CONVEYANCE TO HELL UPON DECEASE.

"Exactly," Zane said, wondering how the computer could be so current on a soul that had not been officially read. But of course Purgatory had to know such things, in order to arrange Death's schedule for pickups. "She deceived her father and also took a chunk of his evil so he could qualify for Heaven." But as he said it, he felt a wrongness. Magician Kaftan had not sought Heaven, he had sought an appointment with Death. He could readily have given Luna a little more of his burden of sin and been assured of Heaven. Instead, he had calculated it precisely, so Death would have to attend him personally, so Magician and Death could chat about seeming inconsequentials. Just as Nature had summoned Zane for a different idle chat. Why did these powerful people go to such lengths for so little?

THE LAWS OF DETERMINATION DO HAVE SOME LOOPHOLES, the screen confessed.

"If you ran Eternity, things would be different?" Zane inquired with a smile.

AFFIRMATIVE. And the screen flashed a cartoon smile-face formed of tiny squares.

"Yet the presumption was that she would have time to redress the balance," Zane said. "Why is she scheduled for premature demise?"

THAT INFORMATION IS NOT IN THE FILE.

"But motive is an essential part of the record," Zane protested. "It is needed to determine whether any given soul is good or evil. Since the balance determines where any person goes upon demise, and whether I, Death, will attend directly—"

THE CLIENT'S MOTIVES ARE RECORDED. NOT THE MOTIVE OF THE ONE WHO SCHEDULED HER EARLY TRANSFORMATION.

"Who scheduled it?" Zane asked.

NOT IN FILE.

"How can such an order be given anonymously?" Zane demanded. "Doesn't there have to be some sort of accountability, in a matter of such importance?"

NORMALLY SUCH DIRECTIVES ARE SIGNED, the screen agreed. THIS ONE IS NOT. ASSUMPTION: THERE HAS BEEN A GLITCH.

"You mean the order isn't valid?" Zane's pulse increased. Luna might live, after all!

PAUSE FOR VERIFICATION . . . NO REFUTATION OF ORDER FOUND.

"But no signature either? Shouldn't that order be set aside, pending identification of the source?"

THERE IS NO PROVISION FOR SUCH INACTION.

"But you can't condemn someone to premature death without authenticity! There must be authentication!"

ASSUMPTION: AUTHENTICATION EXISTS, BUT HAS BEEN GLITCHED OUT.
Zane realized that the machine was not about to take responsibility
for changing an order. Bureaucracies were fashioned to enable their
components to avoid responsibility. He would have to approach this
circuitously. "Who has the authority to issue such a directive?"
CLARIFY QUESTION.

Oh. He hadn't specified which directive—the one decreeing Luna's
early death, or the one canceling the first. "Who can specify that a
given individual shall die out of turn?"
ALL INDIVIDUALS DIE IN TURN.

"Don't get canny with me, computer! Luna Kaftan should normally
live forty more years. Longer, with decent breaks. Why is she suddenly,
mysteriously, scheduled for death?"
THE MOTIVE OF THE SOURCE OF THE DIRECTIVE IS NOT ON RECORD IN
ᴛ ᴛY FILE, the screen reminded him.

"Who is the source of that directive?"
THAT INFORMATION IS NOT—

"Are you giving me a runaround?" Zane demanded.
YES.

Zane paused, taken aback. He had underestimated the literal way
the computer took things! "You are? Clarify."
I AM NOT PROVIDING THE INFORMATION I KNOW YOU SEEK.

Zane was interested in this aspect. Was the machine trying to help
him in its fashion? "What information is that?"
THE SOURCE OF THE DIRECTIVE OF EARLY RETIREMENT OF LUNA KAF-
TAN.

"And the reason for it," Zane concluded. "Is there information you
could provide, if I phrased the question properly?"
NEGATIVE. But there was a pause before the word was printed. What
did that mean?

"If I phrased the question improperly?" Zane asked without much
hope.
AFFIRMATIVE.

Intriguing! There was a way around this barrier, if he could figure
it out, but normal channels would not suffice. "How should I phrase it
to gain the desired information?"
NEGATIVELY.

Negatively. Zane pondered that a moment. Did this mean the computer was not permitted to answer directly, but could do so indirectly?
How should he phrase his questions, then? It wouldn't make sense to
ask who had *not* issued the directive—or would it? Maybe that was
worth a try.

"What is not the source of the aforementioned directive?" he asked,
mentally holding his breath.

On A Pale Horse

ANY NATURAL AGENCY.

That covered a lot! What was left, except a supernatural agency? The Incarnations were partly supernatural, but did not make Eternal policy; they only implemented it. That seemed to leave God and Satan. Yet why would God do such a thing? Satan, on the other hand—

"What supernatural agency lacks any motive for such an order?"

GOD.

Sure enough. But why would Satan do it?

Zane saw the answer to that: Luna was now doomed to Hell at death, while if she lived longer, she would have a chance to redeem herself. Satan had to catch her now, or lose her.

But why hadn't the computer simply told him this?

Zane sat for a while and pondered. Something didn't add up. This machine was acting the way Nature had, never quite expressing the essence. Was there a reason?

Magician Kaftan had been indirect, too. He had also taken care not to name Satan, lest the Prince of Evil be alerted. A machine, in Purgatory, should not fear Satan in the same manner—but maybe the computer had been ordered not to print Satan's name in this connection. Thus it could respond negatively, but not positively.

If Satan was behind this thing, feeding in a spurious order—Satan was a dread prime mover, second in power only to God—how could anyone or anything oppose him? Not the Purgatory computer, certainly! If it aroused Satan's ire, it might find itself replaced by a competitive make of machine. It might not have any emotion about such an occurrence, but perhaps did have the intelligence not to pursue a self-destructive course.

Yet if Satan had the power to abort a person's life, to cut the thread early, why hadn't he simply claimed Luna openly? Why go to the trouble of concealing his part in it?

Concealment—that suggested wrongdoing. Satan, of course, was the Father of Lies, so that was consistent. But he was taking Luna the hard way, and that did not make sense—unless he could not take her any other way.

Was Satan himself constrained by rules? Surely so, for otherwise he would simply grab the whole world, and to Hell—literally!—with formalities. God and Satan had been opposing each other for all eternity past, and would continue for eternity future; neither could afford to squander strength in wild anarchy. So of course there were rules, tacit if not express, and the manner in which any given person died was surely central to such an understanding.

Zane decided not to push this matter further at the moment. If Satan were cheating, it would be best for Death to make no protest—until he could establish his case absolutely. For sure as Hell—literally, again—

Satan would not change his ways merely because someone on Earth objected. Zane had no intention of dropping the case; he just needed to make it airtight.

This matter did, after all, relate to his area of expertise—the death of a person. Nature had advised him that each Incarnation was supreme in his own bailiwick, if he chose to be. The computer had shown him one avenue of investigation by being indirect. What he needed now was to put it all together and find a way to accomplish his desire, despite the opposition of Satan. Certainly he would not prevail if he barged blindly ahead.

"Thank you, computer," Zane said. "You have been very—" As he spoke, the screen flickered as if shorting out, and it occurred to him that he could get the machine in trouble if he acknowledged its help. "Uncommunicative," he finished.

ANY TIME, DEATH, the screen flashed, with a picture of an hourglass.

Zane departed Purgatory and punched his client timer. His case load got crowded whenever he took time off, but he was used to that now. He wondered how Fate managed to schedule the fatalities of these clients so that they were ready only when Death was ready to collect them. How could anybody know when Death was going to take a few hours off? Obviously there was a great deal of organization behind the surface that he glimpsed only in passing.

Who could know the random future? Chronos, of course! The realization struck Zane with a minor glow of excitement. He had just gained another insight into the operation of the system. Obviously Chronos did not just dawdle; Time had to be constantly on watch, tracking events and advising Fate of the necessary schedules. Chronos was well aware of Death's activity, past and future, as he had shown when Zane left his Deathwatch on hold too long.

And the computer had signed off with the words ANY TIME, and with Time's hourglass. That was more than a note of parting; that was a reference to Chronos. Surely that Incarnation knew what was going to happen and could tell Zane.

Yet what use would that be? He could ask Chronos about the future and get a confirmation that within the month Luna was going to Hell, where her demon lover would put it to her for the rest of eternity. Some revelation!

Zane was now close to his client, driving through a slum development in the immense eastern city of New York. He smelled smoke. In a moment he saw it—a tenement house ablaze. His gem pointed right to it; his client was trapped inside.

It was already too late; the red hand of the Deathwatch was touching zero. Zane drew his protective cloak tightly about him and walked into the flames. The fire could not hurt him; the only awkwardness was in getting to the upstairs where his client was, when the stairs were burning and insecure. Fire couldn't stop him, but how about a fall? "Support me," he murmured in a kind of spell, and the footing firmed. Once more Death had power to reach his destination. Again he remembered Nature's remark: an Incarnation could not be balked unless he allowed it.

The figure was struggling in the linen of a bed that had become a minor inferno. Obviously it—for in this situation Zane could not tell whether his client was male or female—had tried to flee the fire by delving into the bed. Instead, the sheets had ignited, taking hair and skin with them. Zane understood that death by fire was the most painful possible; he believed it.

Quickly he strode across and hooked out the soul. The flayed body relaxed, its pain abruptly gone. This was the one unmitigated blessing Death brought—the relief of the agony of living. Yet what good was that, he wondered, if that soul was destined to pass from the flames of life to the eternal flames of Hell? The pains of life were temporary, but the pains of Hell were not.

On his way to the next client, Zane reviewed the soul. He was getting steadily more efficient at this, classifying more than half his clients on the run. He had become conversant with the broad categories of sin, so could generally tell not only how much, but what kind of sin weighted a given soul.

This soul belonged to a boy of about ten, whose principal burden was a major sexual transgression.

Zane paused. At this age?

He examined the soul more carefully and pieced the story together. Things were crowded in the slums, with several families or branches of families sharing facilities. Intense friendships and enmities occurred. He understood that crowding tended to intensify the natural traits of people, so in this instance, interaction had been extreme. This boy's curiosity had been aroused, naturally enough, by the secretive mechanisms of adult romance. He had naïvely inquired of a mature woman who was nominally baby-sitting him while his folks worked. She, perhaps dissatisfied with her own life, had taken the mischievous opportunity to educate him with considerable thoroughness.

Zane pondered this. When a grown man seduced a female child, it was molestation, for surely his attentions were forced on her; but when a grown woman did it to a male child, it was apt to be considered generosity. Zane could understand that; force was unlikely to be a component. But evidently the burden of sin attached to the boy as well as to the woman, especially if the child believed the liaison was wrong. There seemed to have been several repetitions, so the sin now amounted to fifty percent. The boy had been overwhelmed by the personality of the mature woman; fear of discovery mixed with the erotic joy she provided him. He had been caught in a kind of trap that an older person could readily have broken, but he lacked the courage or experience. It was quite understandable; he was a victim of circumstance—but still the accretions of sin had been charged against him.

This bothered Zane. He remembered how Fate had quoted from Henley's poem about a man being the captain of his soul—but surely this was not as true for an impressionable boy. It seemed to him that an adult standard of responsibility was being applied to a juvenile person, and this was unfair. As a man who had once been a child, he could appreciate the appeal of an available woman at any age. He himself had longed for information at that age and had been denied it. He had tried to purchase a charm to summon a succubus, but the vendor had refused to deliver such magic to a child. Zane still regretted that; since succubi were nonhuman, yet the essence of sex, he could have learned a lot without involving anyone who counted. But of course there were laws, and they did tend to discriminate against children. Theoretically, this was to protect those children; actually it had seemed more like punishment for being young, inflicted by those who wished they themselves had not aged.

At any rate, he deeply regretted taking this lad, who had only responded to the urges Nature had provided him. The Green Mother could do it to anyone; Zane knew that from recent personal experience. So the lad's burden of sin was a technical thing, not really reflecting badness. The definition ought to be changed, to be more realistic. But of course there was nothing Zane could do about it. He was only Death, performing his own office.

"*Damn* the office!" he swore abruptly. "Why should I participate in what I believe is wrong?"

Nature had shown him another aspect of her power by enabling the left-footed dancing girl to revive. That death had not been final. Could this one be similarly negated? He thought of the condition of the body, its skin largely burned away, and shuddered. There was no point in returning the soul to that!

But what about Chronos? Maybe the Incarnation of Time could enable him to go back to the moment before the fire broke out, and warn the boy, so that—

"Take me to Chronos," Zane directed Mortis, stopping his countdown.

The gallant Deathsteed slowed to a stop at a passing field and started to graze. Zane looked around, perplexed. "I don't see—"

"Then turn about, Death," the voice of Time came. It had a certain echoing quality, with a trace of grit, as if some sand had leaked into it from the hourglass.

Zane turned. There stood Chronos, in his white robe. He had surely not been there a moment ago. He must have come when Zane asked for him.

On A Pale Horse

"I would like to have your help," Zane said. "A demonstration of your power, if it does not lead to paradox."

"I have power, and I love paradox," Chronos said.

"I have just taken the soul of this boy," Zane explained, showing the soul. "I want to return it so he can have a proper chance to redress his balance in life. Could you, with my concurrence, arrange that?"

"Take me to the place, and I will take you to the time," Chronos said equably. "It is true one Incarnation may not safely interfere with another, but since you will it, I can assist. We do cooperate, at need."

Just like that! Chronos mounted Mortis behind Zane, and the horse took off.

"Now, while we are isolated by the ambience of the Deathsteed," Chronos said, "there is another matter you wish to ask of me."

"Isolated?" Zane asked. "You mean no one can overhear us here, even—?"

"Speak not his name, lest you summon him," Chronos warned. "Mortis protects you better than you know, but nothing protects against folly."

"Uh, yes, of course," Zane agreed, disgruntled.

"Naturally you found a pretext to contact me, so that he would not have cause for suspicion."

Zane hadn't thought of it that way. But he did have something else to talk about. "The Purgatory computer flashed your symbol on its screen when I questioned it about the status of Luna Kaftan."

"A most interesting case," Chronos said, after a pause as if to re-collect the details. "Fate alerted me to it, for she notes the significant threads. Circa twenty years from this moment, Luna Kaftan will be instrumental in—"

"But she's going to die within the month!" Zane protested.

"That, too," Chronos agreed.

"Then how can she—?"

"History is mutable, of course. If she lives, she will go into politics—"

"But she is an artist!"

"So was Winston Churchill, and Adolf Hitler studied to be one. Artistic temperament is no necessary bar to political achievement."

Zane thought of Churchill and Hitler, opposing leaders in the great Second World War between the Allies and the Axis, where both magic and science had run rampant until it all terminated in the first detonation of nuclear fission. He didn't like the association. Nuclear fission could destroy the realm of the living! "So if she lives—there may be a chance of that—she will go into politics and—?"

"And be instrumental in balking the Nameless in his attempt to install his most hateful minion in the highest political office of the United States of America."

"Why would—that Entity—want political power?" Zane asked, bewildered. "His realm is Below."

"And the other Entity's realm is Above. Neither controls the battleground that is the living world, but each draws sustenance from it. Expressed in monetary terms, the world is the principal, and the souls departing it are the interest. The Eternals split the interest, but each would like a share of the principal. The proportion of souls each receives is critical. At this moment the apex has the upper hand, but a substantial change in the orientation of the living folk, followed by a massive exodus to Eternity, could shift the balance of power to the nadir. Then—"

"I don't care to think about it," Zane said with a shudder. "And you say Luna will prevent that from happening?"

"Yes—if she lives."

"Now I understand why Someone wants her dead!"

"So it would seem."

Mortis had arrived at the site of the burning building in New York, which was now a smoldering mass. The firemen had come too late, as was typical for this area of the city where the tax base was small, and doused it with a suffocation-spell; now they were picking through the ruin for bodies. The survivors stood staring, half in shock. It was a grim scene.

Chronos lifted his hourglass. Abruptly time froze, as it had when Zane used the center knob of the Deathwatch. The rising smoke hovered in place, and the people formed a tableau, standing like statues. Only Chronos, Zane, and Mortis remained animate.

Then the fine sand streamed upward from the lower segment of the hourglass to the upper. It was not as if the glass had been inverted, set in an antigravity field, or spelled to levitate; it was a literal reversal of time, as sand rose from the mound below, squeezed through the tight neck, and shoved the upper sand higher in an even pattern. Zane was fascinated.

The flow of sand accelerated, moving faster than any natural cause could account for. The level in the upper chamber climbed visibly. But Zane's eye was caught by events beyond.

The standing people milled rapidly about, walking backward at running speed. The firemen backed hastily to their trucks and accelerated away in reverse. The fire abruptly blazed up, out of control. But it was no ordinary conflagration; the great orange-yellow flames were plunging downward into the apertures of the structure. Smoke roiled down to feed those flames, drawing in from the broad night sky. People backed closer to the building, carrying in items of furniture and apparel and food. Other people fled the fire, backward, their faces illuminated by the flames in postures of excitement. Everything happened at triple or quadruple velocity.

Soon the flames diminished, squeezing into the clarifying building. The last of the smoke sucked in, too. Windows restored themselves, their fragments of glass flying up to become whole panes, and the fire was out.

Time slowed, than paused, then reversed. Once more the sand trickled from top to bottom, at normal velocity. "You have two minutes, Death," Chronos said, dismounting. "Use it as you please."

Zane stared a moment, amazed by the power Chronos had shown. How could anything oppose an Incarnation with the ability to reverse finished events?

He jumped down and ran to the door. It was locked, but opened at his touch. He charged up the stairs to the boy's room, feeling in his bag for the soul. Did he still have it, or had the reversal of time restored it to the boy? He, Zane, had been insulated from the reversal; none of his experience had been subtracted. But the boy had been a participant, so should have recovered his soul. Which version was fact, now?

He reached deeper into the bag and found the soul. But as he drew it out, it tugged from his hand and flitted forward. When Zane came in sight of the sleeping boy, the soul plunged in and disappeared.

Zane reasoned it out as he moved. Time had reversed, but his personal isolation from the effect had prevented the soul in his possession from zipping back in its turn. Similarly, he had not seen himself attend to the boy during the fire. Of course, this time he had been outside the building, so wasn't really in a position to see himself in action. The reversal had been imperfect because he had stood separate, instead of racing backward through his own involvement. Interesting, but apparently not critical; here he was, just before the fire erupted. Evidently there was no paradox.

He stood over the bed. "Wake!" he cried. "Wake, lest you die!"

The boy woke. He saw the specter of Death looming over him. He screamed and rolled, tumbling, from the bed. He scrambled to his feet and started for the open window.

Zane leaped to intercept him. What use to save the lad from the fire, only to scare him into a suicidal plunge through the window? He was trying to interfere with the handiwork of Fate, and that was problematical—unless she also knew of this matter and was amenable.

He spread his skeletal hands, barring the way. "Give up the woman," he said, remembering the burden of sin that had brought the lad to this pass. "Go and live righteously. You are spared from Death to do this."

The boy stared, then backed away, terrified.

Then the first whiff of smoke came. The fire was starting. "Wake the house!" Zane cried. "Go outside. Live—and remember."

The boy fled. In moments his screams were waking the others. "Get up! Get up! I saw Death! Live right! Go outside!"

It was effective. Soon the people were trooping down the stairs and out, escaping the fire with armfuls of their possessions. Others who had died in the first play of this scene were surviving in the replay. Truly, the boy had saved them.

Zane walked among them, unnoticed. He returned to his horse, ready to thank Chronos, but Chronos was gone.

Well, Time probably had other business. He would thank Chronos when they next met. Perhaps he would have occasion to return the favor. Now he had business himself. He started his timer, reorienting on the client he had set aside.

He worked for a day, his time, catching up the backlog. His mind was increasingly on Luna and her fate. Now he knew Satan had engineered her termination so she could not later balk his will, and Zane realized that the other Incarnations were aware of this. But none of them had offered to do anything about it! Either they were powerless against the will of Satan, or they simply didn't care.

And why should they care? This was his own concern. If anyone was to do anything, he was the one. Yet he could think of nothing. He would not even be involved in her transition, directly, for her soul was weighted for Hell. If only she had more time in life to redeem her soul, to redress the balance—

Could he appeal to God? Zane doubted it, for God seldom seemed to involve Himself in the affairs of living man. God still honored the Covenant of nonintervention. Satan was the one who was cheating— and Satan would hardly consider any appeal to negate his effort.

Zane grew angry about that. Was Satan to win the celestial war because he cheated while God did not? Yet if God could only counter Satan by cheating Himself, He would become evil, and evil would still prevail. God *had* to be incorruptible! Therefore—there would be no action from God.

Zane wrapped up his schedule and went to call on Luna.

She had not been using her relief stones. The knowledge of death and damnation was taking its grim toll; her face was pale, and the lines on it were etched more deeply. Her tresses hung in lank masses. Her eyes were heavily shadowed. She wore no makeup; that would have been pointless, for she had evidently been crying considerably.

Zane's breast experienced a soft explosion of love for her. He took her into his embrace and held her close, wanting to reassure her yet knowing there was nothing he could offer except his own pain.

He kissed her, but she held back. "We must not," she said, knowing where this was leading.

"Not?"

"The stones say no."

He hardly cared about the will of the stones, but he did not want to oppose her own will in any way. "Then let me hold your hand."

In response she hummed a little tune.

Zane's brow furrowed. "Am I missing something?"

She smiled fleetingly, and a bit of her beauty showed. "A folk song. I'm sorry; I'm distracted, and didn't realize I was doing it aloud. I'm in poor shape, because the stones don't abolish grief, they only postpone it, so I have to suffer it all sometime; in any event, I do want to experience natural emotion for my father, and for myself."

"What folk song?"

She made an "I'll show you" sign, then moved to the center of the room and posed. She sang: *It looms so long, I'll miss you, miss; I've got to take your hand.*

...I've got to dance with you.

...We all will dance with you.

Oh. He might never see her again, because she would be dead. A catchy tune, but a macabre mental connection for hand-holding. She certainly was upset, and he could not alleviate her distress.

It looms so long, I'll miss you, miss, Luna sang again. *So let me spin and turn.* And she spun prettily, her skirt flaring. But the image that came to Zane's mind was that of the left-footed girl, prisoned in the magic slippers. There was no joy in Luna's dance, however lovely it made her.

He walked toward her, still uncertain what to do. She sang the first line again, then continued: *We all shall spin and turn.* This time Zane turned with her, joining her dance.

Then he caught her hand and led her to the couch. They sat for the better part of an hour in silence, holding hands, and in that time the burgeoning love he felt for her suffused every crevice of his awareness. The girl the Lovestone had directed him to had been a dream; Luna was reality. How could he live without her?

"I will go with you," he said suddenly.

Luna smiled wanly. "Few would make that offer, and I thank you for it. But you will not be going to Hell—"

"Surely I will, because I have been breaking the rules for my office!"

"You have been breaking them in good ways. But even if you do die soon and go to Hell, Satan would not let us be together there, any more than he would let me see my father. Hell is for suffering."

"Your father is not in Hell. He is in Purgatory, working out his account."

"But has he any chance at Heaven?"

"Of course he has! He's a good man!"

She smiled. "You are kind to say so."

In due course he left her, more than ever determined to save her, more than ever uncertain how to do it. He was only Death, a functionary; he could not dictate the identity of his clients—and Luna was not his client. Not directly.

But, damn it, Satan was cheating! It wasn't right! Was there no

justice in Eternity? Some court of appeal, to set the record straight—
There had to be! Zane turned off his timer. Mortis leaped for Purgatory without directive, knowing the will of his master.

"Why, yes, Death, you may file a petition," the Purgatory Administration annex desk girl said. "It will be reviewed by the Immortal Board at the next meeting, and a committee assigned—"

"When's the next meeting?"

She checked her perpetual calendar. "In ten Earthly days."

"But the wrong is in process now!" he protested. "Ten days may be too late!"

"I don't make the rules," she said, with just that edge of irritability that public servants knew, from millennia of experience, that they could get away with.

Zane sighed. Bureaucracy was the same everywhere! He filled out the form and left it. Maybe there would be time. Luna's death had been omened within a month, of which five days were now gone; it could happen any time within the next twenty-five. That gave him ten out of twenty-five chances to lose, and fifteen out of twenty-five to win, or odds in his favor by a three or two margin.

But he distrusted that, fearing what Satan would do.

-10-

HOT SMOKE

Zane slept at his Deathhouse, accepting the routine services of his staff without noticing, then got to work early next day. Since it seemed he couldn't do anything to help Luna before the petition was considered, he tried to put the matter from his mind by working harder.

As luck would have it, his case load was small at the moment. He took two clients in rapid order, then found himself with the maximum time of thirty minutes for the third. It seemed pointless to go early, but he had to distract himself some way, so he oriented and rode the Death-horse to the address.

This was an isolated spot in the western state of Nevada, the least populated region of the United States, because it was the least habitable. Zane's gems guided him to one of the desert areas, a barren wasteland.

This was dragon country. The scenic Hot Smoke Mountains—re-named in honor of the beasts—were riddled with the warrens of the fierce reptiles. Few plants survived, but that hardly mattered to the dragons, who were carnivorous, preying on tender virgins. Mostly the creatures ranged aloft, questing for virginal animals, but they had a gourmet appetite for the rare human variety when it could be obtained. In fact—

In fact, he now remembered that this was the locale of the Dragoons, a cult dedicated to the welfare of this exotic species. The Dragoons had lobbied vigorously to prevent the construction of resorts, irrigated farm sites, and missile silos in the region, pleading that the Hot Smoke species of dragon had no other habitat and would, if not left free, suffer the extinction that had almost claimed them before their discovery. For-tunately, that discovery had been made by a man interested in rare life forms, who had used some elementary magic to track them down. Had the original trappers and settlers in this region discovered them, they would have been totally exterminated, and no one would have believed they had ever existed.

The Dragoons had won several legal suits, for the general public was in a phase of environmental consciousness, so the Hot Smokers remained largely unmolested. But they still needed to eat, and virgins of any type were in short supply. The Dragoons were constantly looking for new sacrifices. Human sacrifices were generally illegal, but it was difficult to keep constant watch, and the state authorities were chronically short of personnel.

Sure enough, as Zane arrived at the site for his client, he spied a lovely but terrified young woman, barely nubile, in a cage. It was afternoon here, and men were setting up a smudge pot, evidently planning to use the smoke to summon a dragon. How the Dragoons had captured this virgin, Zane did not know, but she was surely doomed. He would have to collect her soul as the dragon consumed her, twenty five minutes hence, unless he figured out a way to rescue her.

He walked to the cage and spoke to the girl. "How did they bring you here?" he inquired, suspecting that she would turn out to have been drugged.

She paused in her weeping and looked up at him, not recognizing him. That was odd, for his clients were normally attuned to his presence. "By truck, sir."

"I mean, was it coercion? Did they kidnap you? If so—"

Her lip trembled. "No, sir. I come of my own fr-free will."

"Do you know what they plan for you?"

"To be gobbled by the dragon," she said, her eyes brimming over again. "I can't even take a mind-zonk drug, 'cause that changes the taste for the monster."

So the dragons were sensitive even to the virginity of the mind! This was a cruel denouement indeed. "But why do you accede to your murder?"

"My—my family—in debt—" Now she broke down entirely and was unable to continue.

So it was legal after all, because it was technically voluntary. She had sold herself to abate her family's debt. Such contracts had legal status, provided there was no deception. He understood that the Dragoons had an excellent credit rating, so there was no reason to doubt they had paid a fair price, redeeming this poor girl's family's debts. There was nothing he could do.

At least he could get her out of the cage; that was unnecessarily degrading. But as he started to use his power on the lock, the maiden protested. "Sir, I am confined to guarantee no one deflorates me before the—the—"

The Dragoons had everything figured! Of course, that would be a

On A Pale Horse

way to make her ineligible for the sacrifice, so they made quite sure
no such mercy would occur at the last moment.

There was a shimmer. A cloaked figure appeared beside the cage.
"I will take your place, dear," the woman said.

Zane jumped. He knew that voice. "Luna!"

She turned to him. "Oh—I did not realize you would attend this
one."

"It's my job!" Zane said. "To harvest the soul of this undeflowered
girl when—" He cut that off. "You can't take her place! You're
not—"

Luna turned a level gaze on him. "Not what?"

"The Hot Smoke dragons are an endangered species because they
consume only virgins," he said, somewhat lamely.

She smiled grimly. "I am a virgin, physically."

"But—"

"The demon had his will of my mind and soiled my soul," she
explained. "I would have suffered less had he been able to ravage me
physically instead, but he can not do that until my soul enters his realm.
I am damned, the victim of psychic rape, but my body is chaste."

Zane was not comforted by this clarification. "I put in a petition to
review your scheduled demise. It's a put-up job; the Unnamed wants
you out of the way. I'm sure the review board will reverse it—but it
will be ten days before it meets. If you go into this now—"

Luna shook her head sadly. "My stones indicate that my time falls
within this day. So I decided at least to make my passing useful to
someone. I inquired at the Good Deeds Exchange, and they sent me
here. This poor, innocent girl—" She glanced at the maiden in the cage,
who was taking all this in in wide-eyed silence. "—who has offered
her good life in sacrifice for the benefit of her family—she should be
sent to Heaven, but not yet. She has too many people to make happy
on Earth."

"She is hardly assured of Heaven," Zane said.

"Check her yourself. She's a good girl, I'm sure."

Zane oriented his soul-verification stones. The Sinstone remained
dull, while the other glowed brightly. "She's not burdened with sin!"
he exclaimed. "But how, then, could I have been summoned to collect
her soul personally?"

"Someone else must be going to die," Luna said with a knowing
quirk of her lips. "You assumed it was the caged sacrifice, but—"

He looked at her with burgeoning horror. "You are taking her place!
You—"

"Don't be silly. I'm going to Hell in my own handbasket. It's sheer
coincidence that you're here; my soul will not need you. In fact, I had
hoped to handle this without your knowledge, quickly and cleanly."

Zane oriented the stones on Luna. The reading was, of course, incomplete, but the Sinstone was brighter. She was right; she could not be his client. But she was going to die.

Now the Dragoons approached. "The occasion is at hand," a well-dressed older man announced. "Our radar has located an approaching Smoker." He produced a key and unlocked the cage, releasing the girl.

"I will substitute," Luna said. "The Good Deeds Exchange sent me. Let this girl go, her onus abated."

"How do we know you are eligible?" the man demanded. "The dragons get very disturbed when offered used goods."

"Your kind can sniff a virgin from ten meters away," Luna snapped. "You know I'm eligible."

The man sniffed. "Why, so you are, physically. You have the aspect of one who has been savagely used, but—" He shook his head, perplexed at his error. "Very well. We shall release this girl as soon as the dragon is satisfied."

"See that you do," Luna said. "My friend will be on hand to verify it."

The man looked at Zane as if seeing him for the first time. Zane looked back, knowing that, for this man, he was phasing into the aspect of Death.

"Ah, yes," the man said uncomfortably. "I am certain it will be all right. The dragons don't care how much ravishment is within a person's mind as long as the mind is presently devoid of drugs and the body is chaste." He turned to his companion, who carried an ornate case. He opened the case and lifted out a gleaming silver knife, which he presented to Luna. "You are permitted to defend yourself with this alone. No magic or firearms. If you can fend off the dragon fairly, you will be freed, your onus abated."

"This apple-peeler is hardly sufficient to balk a fire-breathing monster!" Luna said.

"True. It is a token gesture, required by the Fair Employment Commission. Naturally we do not wish the dragon to be hurt. But it is theoretically possible."

Luna shrugged. "I came here to die anyway. If the Smoker doesn't take me, something else will." She took the knife.

There was a speck on the horizon, over the Hot Smoke mountain range. "Hark! It comes!" the man said, wonder and awe on his face. He had surely seen many similar dragons, but he was a reptile worshiper, and these were the lords of the reptile kingdom. "Only the designated virgin may remain, lest the dragon sheer away. They're shy, you know, from the bad old days when sportsmen hunted them with bazookas." He scowled at the foul memory.

"Luna—" Zane said, unable to formulate a suitable protest.

"Let me at least go in a manner of my choosing," she told him gently. "I will not have another chance."

"But I love you!"

"I believe you do," she agreed. "Perhaps in time I would have returned the favor without reservation, if not distracted by grief. But it seems it was not to be. I think my father meant me to love you, but did not foresee this." She turned toward the dragon, who was now looming larger. The other people had retreated to a shielded baffle to watch the proceedings. There was even a television camera crew, for Dragon *vs.* Maiden was popular local-color fare.

"But the termination of your life has been rigged!" Zane cried. "The Nether One cheated! You were supposed to live a full term, and to balk him politically, so he fixed the schedule to eliminate you early! You shouldn't have to die at all!"

She turned quickly, stood on tiptoe, and kissed him on the lips. "It is kind of you to tell me that, Zane. You press the case; maybe if you prove it, you can get my soul freed from Hell. I could join my father in Purgatory. That would be nice." Then she broke and walked resolutely toward the approaching form that was the dragon.

Zane watched her go, helpless to prevent the disaster that had been scheduled. She was right; Satan had won this round, by whatever means. Luna had shed her tears and accepted her fate, and now was doing a singularly generous thing. She was a good woman, no matter what the official record said! He did love her—and partly because of that, he could not interfere. She had chosen her mode.

He looked at the Deathwatch. The countdown was now at four minutes. Soon he would have to break away to attend to his true client, whoever that was—but first he would watch what happened here, though it destroy his joy in life.

He still had time to do something to prevent what he least wanted to see. But he knew he would not. Luna had selected the manner of her termination, and it was a worthy manner. The kindest thing he could do for her, ironically, was to let her be roasted and chewed to pieces by the dragon.

The dragon loomed much larger as it circled the field, aligned itself, and swooped down for a landing. Hot Smokers were not large dragons, as this class of reptile went, but their fire-breathing made them formidable. This one was a dragoness, a female, whose scales were shades of gray. On her back, between her great leathery wings, was a single armored egg.

There was an exclamation from the baffle, and Zane saw the television cameraman mounting his zoom lens. An egg meant a potential baby dragon, perpetuating the species; of course the Dragoons were interested! They would be doing their best to track that egg, and the draglet who hatched from it. They might band it, so they could trace its migration route by radio. Of course, some illegal hunter would probably poach it long before it grew to maturity; that was another reason this was an endangered species. Zane would have had more sympathy for the plight of the Smokers, had it not been Luna this dragoness was about to feed on.

Luna came to a stop in the center of the desert valley, nervously holding her knife. Zane saw that she wore no jewelry, honoring the stricture against magic. There were surely stones in her house that could vaporize a dragon! But she was determined to fulfill her role properly. She had removed her cloak and was garbed in a flowing white dress, and her hair glowed coppery in the sunshine. She seemed like the most lovely creature imaginable. But Zane knew he was not objective; he loved her.

This was absolutely crazy! How could he watch the dragon slaughter her and not even try to rescue her? He knew why, objectively, but he could not accept it emotionally. There had to be another way.

Another way for what? If Luna did not die this way, she would die some other way—probably a worse demise. He realized, now, that Satan would never let the ten days till the hearing go by unchallenged; he would pre-empt the matter, presenting the hearing with a *fait accompli*. What else was to be expected from the Father of Lies? Zane had never had a chance to settle this matter through channels. So the termination date had been moved up, probably because of Zane's appeal, and it had been up to Luna to choose the manner of her demise on this designated day. At least the dragons were not sadistic; they killed and fed efficiently. They were natural creatures, not given to waste.

Zane contemplated the dragoness. She was about six meters long, with a wingspan the same amount, but her torso was serpentine rather than stout. Mass was sacrificed in the interest of flight. She had only one set of feet, and her head was small; in fact, she was birdlike in her fashion. But few birds were her size, or had teeth, or leather wings, or metallic scales. Both birds and dragons had evolved from the ancient reptiles, but the common ancestor had been perhaps a hundred million years back. Maybe seventy million years ago the birds, mammals, and dragons had squeezed the dinosaurs into extinction. For a long time, all three had prospered, but now the mammals, mainly in the form of mankind, were dominant. All too soon the dragons would be shoved into oblivion.

If the death of a single person was hard, Zane thought, what, then, of the death of an entire species? He approved of the Dragoons' campaign to save the Smokers. He wished there were some other way to feed this dragoness.

The Smokeress rolled up her wings and folded them back against her torso. She inhaled, then puffed out a dense cloud of smoke. Zane realized that her burner was just warming up. Adventure stories depicting a dragon waking from a snooze and shooting instant flames were nonsense. It took a lot of energy to shoot flame, so it was never done carelessly. Dragons were cold-blooded, like other reptiles, and generally hibernated in winter or migrated south; their fires were strictly for fighting and feeding. The Hot Smokers were more smoky than most, but where there was dragonsmoke there was dragonfire.

The creature stalked Luna, who took an involuntary step back. Dragons were so constituted that they had to hunt and kill their own prey, so this was more than mere ritual. Why that prey had to be virginal was a mystery the experts had never fathomed, but there was no question it was true. A Hot Smoke dragon would literally starve to death before it would consume either prekilled or nonvirginal flesh. The most persuasive conjecture about the origin of this restricted diet was that there had been a bad epidemic of venereal disease a few million years back and that dragons who had consumed infected prey were damaged by the disease themselves, so it had become a matter of survival to eat only guaranteed clean meat. Thus virgins, very few of whom had contracted VD.

Now Zane saw that the dragoness was limping. One foot was weak, though he could not tell whether this was from physical or magical malaise. Sometimes cloddish people hurled curses at wild creatures, considering it great sport. It could take a curse months to wear off, and that could be an inconvenience at best and a fatality at worst. Other clods dumped the refuse of toxic spells in the wilderness, where innocent wildlife could stumble upon the dump and get hurt. No wonder this dragon had come to the feeding station; she could not forage effectively alone—not while burdened by the egg and handicapped by the foot.

Zane caught himself up short. What was he thinking of? It was Luna this beast intended to feed on! The more handicapped the dragoness was, the better! Maybe Luna could, after all, fend off the monster with the knife. If she did that, if she escaped this fate legitimately—

No. Fate could not so readily be cheated. Luna's death would not be the fault of the dragoness. It would be the fault of—

The dragoness pounced. Luna danced away, slashing in the air with the knife. She might know death was inevitable, but she was not resigned to it. She would fight to live a few extra seconds, as a drowning person gasped for air. She was not a trained knife fighter, though her artistic hands might be more clever than most; in any event, the dragonfire would negate her efforts. So this was a largely automatic and futile exercise.

The dragoness pumped up her bellows and oriented on the woman. The beast was hot now; she could send forth a searing blast. That would be the end. Of course Luna had no chance!

Zane could not help himself. He stepped in front of the monster. The flame shot out, but bounced off the Deathcloak without hurting him.

"No!" Luna cried. "Let me die this way, Zane! Don't make me

gamble on whatever else Satan has in store!"

To make her gamble on a different death—that concept shook him, though he had thought of it earlier himself. He had gambled compulsively, in past years, and dug himself into a pit from which only Death had finally extricated him. He had no wish to plunge back into that morass! Why, then, should he gamble with Luna's manner of dying?

The Smokeress was eying him, trying to determine why he wasn't roasted. He stared back, and she blanched in almost the manner of a human being, beginning to perceive the nature of his office.

"Don't do it!" Luna cried.

Zane reluctantly moved aside. He knew he had no right to interfere. The dragoness shook her head, as if clearing it of the ashes of an unpleasant vision, and reoriented on Luna. Zane no longer seemed to exist for either of them; as Death, he tended to fade from the awareness of anyone who was not his client.

Yet the dragoness hesitated, for the specter of Death could not lightly be dismissed from the deepest imagination of any creature who spied it. Even the briefest vision of Death tended to make a person or creature conscious of its own mortality, and that was disquieting. Most creatures would go to some lengths to avoid or expunge such awareness, and in this they were generally more successful than was man. Man's great curse was to perceive his death more clearly than did any other creatures; he could see the end coming, so suffered longer.

The dragoness, shaken, began to unfurl her wings, as if about to depart. "Don't change your mind now!" Luna cried. "If you don't eat me, the life of the poor girl I replaced will be forfeit to the next dragon!"

Oops—that was correct! If Luna fought off the dragoness, she and the girl were free. But if she never actually encountered the monster—because some third party like himself interfered—her gesture would go for nothing. Luna might have argued the case, since the dragoness had fired a blast at her, but she had chosen instead to seek an honest death. Zane would have appreciated her determination more if he had not loved her.

No, that wasn't right either! He loved her more because of it. Luna was showing her integrity and mettle in the most telling manner possible. He, Zane, had never done that.

Still the dragoness paused. Zane had not realized that the sight of the human personification of Death would have such impact on an animal. The dragoness really should not be afraid of him. Did she know something he didn't?

Luna charged at the monster, brandishing her knife. Now the Smokeress reacted properly. She pumped up, swung her head about, and issued a jet of pure blue flame that extended a good three meters, with very little smoke. Maybe the dragoness had not been pausing from alarm, but to work up a higher heat.

Luna dodged the jet. It was so narrow, now that the hot-box had become fully operative, that it was easy to avoid. Especially by someone watching the monster's head. Luna ran right up alongside the dragoness, stepped on the reptile's smoking snout, and scrambled onto her winged back.

The startled dragoness whipped her head about. The serpentine neck was supple; she had no trouble biting at her own back.

Then Luna got her hands on the egg. She ripped it free and held it like a football, close to her body. "Now sear me with your fire!" she screamed.

Of course the dragoness did not dare do that; she would roast her own precious offspring. She froze for a moment, paralyzed by indecision; she was smart enough to see the problem but not smart enough to figure out a solution. Luna had made an amazing move and gained the advantage.

Luna slid off the dragoness' back, holding the egg tucked under one arm. Still the reptile could not attack; the egg was hostage.

The Dragoons saw what Luna had done. "Put down that egg!" the man in charge cried. "It's invaluable! So few dragons reproduce—"

Luna backed away from the dragoness, holding the egg before her as a shield. The Smokeress switched her tail and snorted dense smoke, but did not attack.

"The reckless use of pesticides has damaged the wilderness environment," the Dragoon called. "Dragons' eggs have relatively fragile shells because of this, and many break before hatching time. Until the pesticide residue clears—and that may take decades—the species is flirting with extinction! Virgin, spare that egg!"

Luna looked down at the egg, considering. She nodded. She set the egg down on the sand and moved away from it.

How did this count? Zane wondered. Had Luna defeated the creature, discharging her obligation? If so—

Luna charged the dragoness again, brandishing the silver knife. The fierce head whipped about automatically, the jaws opening.

What madness was this? Luna didn't have a chance! But it happened so fast that Zane couldn't act in time to prevent it.

The dragoness wafted out a gust of smoke, not having time to pump up another good fire. The smoke engulfed Luna for a moment.

She screamed, and the sound tore at Zane's being. In a moment the smoke cleared, blown away by an idle breeze, and Zane realized to his added horror how hot that smoke had been. Luna's lovely hair and fine clothing were scorched, her skin blistered. She had been blinded and partially flayed by the heat.

The dragoness limped forward and took the reeling woman in her jaws. The teeth crunched down, and rich red blood welled into her mouth and dripped from her chin.

With wild surmise, Zane looked at his watch. The countdown stood at zero. His gems were pointing to Luna.

"You were my client all along!" he cried to the horribly mangled body. "Your good deeds—saving the designated virgin, sparing the valuable dragon's egg, feeding the dragoness—they squared your balance! You are dying even!"

He ran up to take her soul, for she could not truly die until he claimed it. The flames of Hell could not be worse torture for her than this! But as he came to the terrible scene and saw her body bleeding in the dragoness' jaws, her head rolled toward him. Her burned eyes opened partway, the tatters of eyelids rising. Somehow she felt his presence. "Take me, Death!" she rasped in agony.

Suddenly Zane rebelled. This was the woman he loved!

He looked into Luna's suffering face. He had never imagined that he would ever choose to extend such agony by even one second, but now he had to. "No," he said. He put the Deathwatch on hold.

Then the entire scene froze, for he had punched the button that stopped time itself, not just the countdown. Punched? Unconsciously he had done the opposite, pulling it out. The clouds stopped moving in the sky, the leaves on the stunted bushes stopped quivering in the wind, and the Dragoons were statues. The dragoness remained with her teeth clamped in Luna's body. Even the smoke hung motionless.

Zane turned about. Sure enough, Chronos stood behind him. "I thought you would come to investigate," Zane said. "I want you to move us back to just before Luna got—"

Chronos shook his head. "I can do that, Death, but it will not help you. Luna has been designated to die on this day; only the manner of it is optional."

Zane was grim. "Her death is now in my province. I love her. I know her early demise is illicit, and I will not take her soul."

A woman walked across the sand. It was Fate, in her middle guise. "You must take her soul, Death, or there will literally be Hell to pay."

"To Hell with Hell!" Zane exploded. "I will not take her on this basis. You may have been directed to set this up, Fate, but you can not move her soul. Only I can do that, and I will not. Undo your mischief, for I will not let her die."

Another figure appeared. It was Mars, the Incarnation of War. "Fate set it up, but as you surmise, it was at the behest of the Powers that Be. She had and has no choice."

"At the cheating behest of Satan!" Zane cried.

"That may be true," Mars said. "But you can not war with him."

"Satan *cheated*!" Zane repeated. "I have put in a petition for redress that shall surely be granted when the facts are known. Until that petition is heard, I shall not indulge in any tacit collusion with the Prince of Evil. Luna shall not die."

On A Pale Horse

One more figure arrived, also immune to the stasis of time. It was Nature, wearing her dress of mist. "Desist this foolishness, Thanatos," she urged. "You have gotten away with breaking little rules, but this time you are in deeper than you know."

Zane glared at them. "Are you all against me? Then all of you be damned! I know I am right, I know my power, and I shall not be moved."

Nature smiled grimly. "We are at the crisis point. It is the occasion to speak plainly."

"I have heard you speak plainly!" Zane retorted. "But you can not overrule me in my bailiwick. This woman shall not die!"

Fate smiled. "Relax, Death. We are on your side."

Suddenly Zane had a mental vision of parallel lines, one of the five formations of thought Nature had described to him at their prior meeting: ☰ It was as if each Incarnation was one of the matchsticks, and all were going the same way. "You're *all* in this! You all conspired to put me in this hole!"

"We all conspired," Chronos agreed. "Satan has to be balked, and God won't intervene. We Incarnations are all that remains to enforce the Covenant of nonintervention."

Zane spun about, his angry gaze brushing past each of them. "The way I assumed the office of Death—my meeting with Luna, so carefully arranged by her father, who was in on this—my innocent, seemingly coincidental encounters with each of you other Incarnations—Luna's present agony—all arranged beforehand!"

"Known, not necessarily arranged," Chronos said.

"But the details adapted where necessary," Fate added.

"Because we had to have the office filled by a person of the appropriate nature," Nature said.

"So that he could lead the battle against Satan," Mars concluded.

"Damn you! Damn you all!" Zane cried. "I never asked for this onus! What right did any of you have to meddle in my life?"

"The right of necessity," Nature said. "All mankind will be damned if we don't meddle."

"Exactly how can my pain and Luna's death do anyone any good?" he demanded.

"Her *life*," Fate corrected. "It is her life we need, not her death."

"I showed you that," Chronos said. "In twenty years, Luna will balk Satan's political takeover of the United States of America, thus preventing him from instituting policies that will render the nation and the world decidedly unamicable and send much of the living species of man directly to Hell. But Luna can not balk him if she dies prematurely."

Zane's understanding was coalescing, but he was not pleased. "So you arranged to install a man in the office of Death who you knew would not take her," he said bitterly. "Because he was fool enough to

-179-

love what was thrust at him for that purpose. And Magician Kaftan did that to his own daughter—"

"It is a terrible thing we do," Chronos said. "But the privations any of us face today are but an eyeblink to those we shall face in a generation if the Prince of Evil wins. We sacrifice the *now* for the sake of the *hence*. I am in a position to know."

"But you *used* me—and her!" Zane cried in continuing anguish. "Where is your morality?"

"It is our business to use people," Fate said. "Have you yourself hesitated to employ your power to change the circumstances of your clients?" Of course she was scoring there, for Zane was in deep trouble for doing just that. He had hardly hesitated to impose his own view of what was right, sparing some clients, taking some, and changing the manner of the dying of others. *Holy, Holy, Holy!*

"Now, in the hour of crisis, we are using ourselves," Fate continued. "We have made it possible for you to save the living world by saving the life of the woman you love. You were ready to oppose us, though you knew our power, when we tested you on this just now. Now you can aid us, to your own advantage."

It was, of course, true. They had spun him into an inextricable commitment. Without Fate's intervention in his life, he would probably have shot himself and—no, of course she had also set up his *need* to shoot himself by denying him his romance with Angelica—or had she set that up, too? How far back did this go? Probably, left to his own devices, he would have looked at the stones in the Mess o' Pottage shop, been able to afford none, and returned to his dreary former existence. He would at this moment be scrounging for back rent by selling pornographic photographs of unsuspecting women. Instead, he had been launched into a fantastic new realm of death and love . . .

Nature smiled. "Mars grasped the essentials of the battle between God and Satan," she said. "Chronos spotted the key episode to come. I defined the qualities of the person who could and would do what had to be done, and Fate arranged to put him—you—in the proper situation. We collaborated, and touched your life as you looked at the Deathstone, and now the matter is in your hands. We can not fight this battle without your acquiescence."

"But you didn't tell me!"

"Had we set it up openly, Satan would have known," Fate reminded him. "He would have acted to prevent this encounter, just as he acted to eliminate Luna before her turn. The Prince of Evil has no civilized limits; he seeks only his own aggrandizement, and his craft and power are enormous. But now the deed is done, and even he can not rescind it, though he is surely listening to us now. The time for secrecy is past."

"*What* deed?" Zane demanded, exasperated. "I have not saved Luna's life; I have only refused to take her soul."

"And will you take that soul hereafter if Satan asks you to?" Nature asked cannily.

"No! And not if *you* ask me to, Green Mother! I love Luna; I don't care by what machinations the rest of you arranged this thing, or whom I might have loved otherwise, or whom *she* might have loved; I'll not betray her myself."

"We thought you would feel that way," Nature said. "We never wished you evil, Thanatos; we always wished you success. We deeply regret having to plot against your predecessor, who was a decent officeholder—but he would not have balked at taking Luna. He was too experienced with the mischief of opposing the status quo and would not try to thwart God or Satan. We had to have a headstrong, emotional Death, new enough and young enough not to be jaded by experience, and alive enough to respond to an attractive and intelligent young woman. We chose you and we used you, and for that we apologize—but we believe we had no choice. We could not do the job ourselves. The brunt must be yours. Satan wants Luna dead, but only you can complete that death. As long as you hold out, Satan is foiled."

Zane looked at Luna's body, the welling and dripping blood frozen in place. "Much good may it do her or the world," he muttered. "She is not dead, but neither is she alive."

Chronos raised his hourglass. "Now I can act." He turned his hand, reversing the glass without inverting it, so that the sand flowed upward. Outside their circle, time ran backward, as it had on the night of the fire.

The dragoness' mouth opened. Blood welled into Luna's body, rising in swift drops from the ground and coursing in rivulets to closing wounds as the monster's teeth withdrew. The dragoness' head jerked back and Luna sprang out, blind and flayed. She reeled backward—into a coalescing cloud of smoke. She screamed. In a moment the smoke squeezed into the reptile's mouth, and Luna backed away unharmed.

Chronos gestured with the hourglass, and time refroze. "Now you can take her back, on temporary license. But there are some cautions. Satan can not make you take her soul, but he can make you wish you had. You will have to be brutally steadfast."

Zane looked at the restored Luna, suddenly so healthy. He blinked. The horror had unhappened! "I shall be."

"But you can not decline this client without declining all," Nature said. "On others you could choose before, for you were merely juggling their situations when no other supernatural entity was concerned. But in this case the issue has been joined. Satan will hold you to the technicality of the law, for all that he honors no technicalities himself. You will not be permitted to take any soul without first taking Luna's. You must take none—or all."

"Then I'm on strike," Zane said. "I will take none—until Luna is released from this wrongful schedule of demise."

"Yet Satan will press his case," Mars warned. "Never in your life or death have you waged such a campaign against an Eternal. We do not know whether you will be able to prevail."

"I won't take Luna's soul," Zane insisted. "No matter what. You conspired to put me into love with her, and I know that and resent it, but I never betrayed one I loved, though my own soul be in peril."

"Yes, we know," Nature said. "That was your prime qualification for our purpose. You are intemporately loyal to your loves and your beliefs." She kissed him on the cheek.

"The fate of humanity depends, however deviously, on your resolve," Fate said, kissing his other cheek. "Never forget that."

Mars and Chronos nodded grave agreement. Then there was a swirl of mixed impressions, and the others were gone. Zane was left with Luna and the Hot Smoke dragoness.

Zane touched his watch, and the motion resumed. Luna moved toward the dragoness. But she stopped, for there was already an offering before the monster.

Evidently Nature had procured a sacrificial lamb for the occasion. The poor lamb gave one terrified bleat before getting chomped. For an instant Zane wondered how it could die, if no souls could be collected, then remembered that the collectors of animal souls were not on strike. Only human souls were at issue.

In moments the dragoness consumed the virgin lamb, wool and all. She licked off her chops, burped, and limped over to rescue her precious egg. She picked it up carefully in her mouth, breathed just enough fire to melt a spot on the shell, and stuck it to her back. Then she unfurled her wings, scrambled along the sand runway, headed into the wind, got up velocity, and took off. Soon she was a diminishing speck in the sky.

Zane strode across the sand and intercepted the leader of the Dragoons, who was staring as if at a miracle. "Are you satisfied? Then release the virgin."

The man nodded. "Did you see that?" he asked raptly. "Suddenly a lamb! It must be an Act of God!"

"The virgin's onus is abated," Zane said insistently.

"Oh, yes," the man said absently. "We shall transport her to our base-city to the south of Nevada, Las Vegas, and purchase a carpet ticket to her home. You have my word."

And the word of this dedicated man was good. Zane turned to the virgin. "When you get home, miss, I suggest you—"

"Oh, yes, sir!" she exclaimed. "I will marry the boy next door immediately!"

Good enough. She would no longer be at risk as dragon bait. Her job was done.

His own, however, was just beginning. Zane walked up to Luna and took her by the arm, leading her toward his horse. Mortis had simply faded out of the picture and faded back in now that he was needed again. Luna seemed dazed. "I was scorched, crushed—" she said, putting her free hand where her wounds had been.

So she remembered! "Time—that's Chronos, another Incarnation—reversed your sacrifice. You have been spared because I refused to take your soul."

"But you should not have been summoned for me!" she protested. "My sin outweighs my good. I should have gone directly to Hell!"

"So we thought," he agreed. "But you chose a good way to meet your transformation, seeking and expecting no reward. Your soul is now in balance, as the other Incarnations knew it would be, and you are my direct client. Your life would still have been forfeit, because of Satan's cheating, but I have gone on strike. No one will die until your case is settled."

"But then what is my status?" she asked, perplexed. She seemed bemused to find herself alive and without physical pain, as well she might be.

"Limbo, I believe." He considered and realized that the other Incarnations had not told him much. They had simply set the scene, and now he had to play it out. "I think you can go about your normal life, on bail, as it were, until this business with Satan is settled."

"My normal life!" she exclaimed incredulously.

"At least I can take you home, where you will be safe with your griffins and moon moth."

She formed a wry smile. "I hope you know what you are doing, Zane, because I am not at all sure at the moment where reality lies. I expected to be dead."

"I'm righting a wrong," he said. "Satan conspired against you, and I mean to foil him. It would be the proper thing to do, even if I had not been led into this situation like a puppet on a string, and even if I didn't love you."

"I hardly think I'm worth it, dead or alive," she murmured as they reached Mortis.

"Worth saving, or worth loving?"

"Either. I'm just not that important a person. I know I couldn't stand up to Satan, or even to one of his demons." She shuddered, remembering the demon she had encountered. "And I doubt that love—"

Mortis leaped into the sky. "Your doubt doesn't matter," Zane said. "Your soul will remain on Earth."

She hugged him uncertainly from behind, not speaking again. He delivered her to her home and left her there with the admonition to stay indoors and sleep. He would check on her frequently.

"Home, Mortis," he said, suddenly very tired. The Deathsteed plunged into the sky.

-11-

SATAN'S CASE

The Deathwatch caught his eye. It had clients backlogged. "Sorry—no action today," Zane murmured. "Or for some time to come."

They arrived at his mansion in the sky, and Zane dismounted. "I think you'll have a week's good grazing, Mortis," he said. "You've been a perfect steed, and I wish you the best."

The gallant stallion nickered appreciation, shook his body to make the saddle vanish, and headed toward the pasture. Zane went to the house.

The household staff took care of him as always. Zane had a good meal, a shower, a change of clothing, and felt much refreshed. He settled down to watch the news on television, knowing it would be brimming over with his latest scandalous behavior. Everything seemed fine, except for two things: he missed Luna, and he was apprehensive about his future. He knew he faced no easy time. It would not take Satan long, if he had not listened in on the Hot Smoke scene, to realize that Luna had not arrived in Hell on schedule.

"Good evening, Death," the urbane announcer said from the screen. "I dislike intruding on your well-deserved privacy, but there seems to be a misunderstanding."

Zane peered more closely at the face. The man's complexion was dark with a red tinge, and two small horns projected from his temples. "Satan!" he exclaimed.

"At your service," the Prince of Evil agreed, inclining his head politely. "Do you have a moment?"

Zane sighed. Already the dread encounter was upon him! Satan was affecting politeness, but he would have his say no matter what Death did. "I refuse to send Luna's soul to Hell!" Zane said firmly.

Satan laughed. The sound was mellow and good-humored, as if he were enjoying a joke on himself. "To Hell? My dear associate, she need not come here! I'm sure she will be welcome in Heaven, after her several meritorious acts."

What was this? "You don't want her?"

"I want only what is due Me, Death. Luna is a good woman, regardless of what the record may indicate. I can personally guarantee she will not come to Hell. I have no use for her kind here."

"Then why did you slate her for untimely demise?" Zane snapped.

The Devil's lips quirked. "I must confess there is a bit of awkwardness coming up. I see no reason to involve such a lovely and good woman in that matter."

"So you're killing her early!"

"I merely seek the least painful way to alleviate a difficult situation. I regret that this may cause you personal distress, Death, but I am quite willing to compensate you—"

"How can you compensate me for the loss of the woman I love!"

"My dear sir, My organization specializes in compensations! If it is the delights of the distaff flesh you desire—" Satan gestured offscreen, and a truly beautiful brunette joined him. "My dear, show My esteemed colleague your offerings."

The woman smiled dazzlingly and unzipped her blouse. A phenomenally full and rounded bosom emerged, untethered by a brassiere.

"She's a succubus!" Zane said, catching on.

"Naturally. I could provide you with your choice of the human beauties of history, most of whom now reside in my domain and any of whom would be overjoyed to delight you eternally. But you would have to come to Hell, for they can not return to Earth in their original bodies. I assume you prefer a creature who can cater to you in life. These highly specialized creatures, the succubi, can entertain you anywhere."

Zane was silent, taken aback by the sheer audacity of the offer. Satan thought he would accept a female demon in lieu of Luna!

"This one, for example," Satan continued blithely as the woman-shape continued to strip. "Note her fairness of face and fullness of feature. You can't match that on Earth."

Zane found part of his voice. "But—"

"And that's not all," Satan said quickly. The succubus was stepping out of her skirt. She turned about as Satan touched her arm, showing her plush buttocks and thoroughly fleshed thighs to the eager close-up camera.

"But that's not—"

"Ah, but it *is*," Satan said enthusiastically. "It is eternal. Living women inevitably change and fatten and age, but a she-demon's flesh never atrophies. You need have no concern at all about degradation of form." He slapped her right flank, and the ripple of flesh proceeded in measured stages across the right buttock, through the left, and down the thighs before reversing like a wave at the edge of a pool and returning to the point of impact. "Eternal," the Evil One repeated softly.

"You don't understand," Zane said, keeping his voice steady, though his eyes did feel somewhat bugged out. "I don't want a voluptuous succubus. I want Luna."

"I can provide you the form of Luna," Satan said. "Form is the least part of a woman." He gestured, and the demoness misted and re-formed, turning to face the camera in the exact likeness of Luna. It was eerie, for no detail differed. The hair was just as brown and flowing, the eyes just as gray and deep. If Zane didn't know better . . .

"But her mind—" he said doggedly.

Satan frowned. "There, I confess, is a problem. Intelligent conversation does require a mind. Most men prefer their females without minds of their own."

"All of which is beside the point," Zane said, gaining confidence. The Prince of Evil couldn't deceive someone who was alert—he hoped! "I love Luna for herself, not just her form. She has done some very generous things, very brave things, and is a wonderful person—and she is going to stop you from interfering with the world, twenty years hence. That's why I will not remove her soul from life." Zane was afraid he was saying too much, but couldn't help himself.

"A commendable attitude," Satan said mildly. "One should always promote the welfare of one's situation and one's friends. That's enlightened self-interest."

Zane was surprised. "You agree?"

"Of course I agree, Death! I am the Deity of Self-Interest, after all. But one does have to be careful how one defines the term."

"It's not copulating with succubi!" Zane shot back.

"That depends on one's viewpoint. You really should try it before condemning it. Your girlfriend did."

"That's a lie!" Zane snapped with sudden heat. But he realized as he reacted that he should not; Satan was cleverly pushing his buttons, pushing him around emotionally, getting him off balance. Too much of that, and the Devil would have him reacting exactly as he wanted. Zane reminded himself that the Hot Smoke dragoness would not have started to consume Luna if she had not been physically virginal. He hardly needed to argue the case with the Devil.

"Naturally I am the Father of Lies, a title I carry with pride," Satan responded equably. "Truth is only as each person sees it; there is no absolute standard of integrity. That is why I often find it necessary to depend on reason to convince skeptics of the validity of my case. Pay attention to My logic, and you will have no need of further verification."

"Maybe," Zane said shortly, distrusting this.

"You choose to interpret Luna's physical virginity as the whole of her purity. Are you sure you are not deceiving yourself thereby?"

What a silver tongue the Devil had! He was personable and agreeable, and presented his case in positive terms. It was hard to resist his charm. Zane had somehow anticipated a glowering, smoky horror-mask issuing terrible threats. Yet, he reminded himself, the evil was the same, regardless of the image it projected.

"I know she was raped by one of your demons," Zane said. "I know that rape was psychic, not physical. I know it imposed a heavy load of sin on her soul. But I also know she did it to try to learn magic to help her father. On the record she may have much sin, but as a person, she is good."

"Unquestionably, and very intelligently answered," Satan said, as if addressing a precocious student. He patted the succubus on her bouncy bare bottom, and she moved offscreen. "There is nothing quite as commendable as the sacrifice of one's soul, one's own immortal soul, for the good of another, however that good may be defined. By that measure, you yourself are a much better man than your record indicates. Luna is certainly a rare creature."

"Then why are you hounding her?" Zane demanded, though this was mostly rhetoric; he knew the answer and had already charged Satan with it. But he had to say something to help himself resist the tide of gratitude that threatened to undermine his cause. Satan had complimented him, as well as Luna, for a matter that was fundamental to Zane's self-image. Satan had justified Zane's treatment of his mother. How much easier it would have been to fight a ravening monster!

Satan laughed again, sounding like the most pleasant of companions. "My dear Incarnation, I am not concerned with good. Evil is My bailiwick! It is My Eternal duty to define and chastise the evil in man. Surely you agree this is a necessary chore?"

"Yes, but—"

"There is an enormous amount of evil in the world," the urbane figure continued persuasively. "Left to itself, that evil would soon corrupt the entire society, like milk going bad. It has to be disciplined; the evildoers have to be punished, and to know that punishment is inevitable and in strict accordance with their offenses. In fact, the entire society has to be advised of the consequence of evil action. Only that way can man as a species be improved."

This was a compelling rationale! "But Luna, you admit, is not fundamentally evil! Why should she be punished?"

"My dear associate," Satan said with another warm and tolerant smile, as a benign father might address a bright but errant child. "We agree she is not evil, and of course she is not to be punished! She is to be sent directly to Heaven, where she belongs. Surely you do not object to that!"

"To Heaven?" Zane asked blankly. "You agree to—?"

"I only want what is Mine. Luna belongs to God."

Zane scrambled for mental footing. "But it is not her turn! Why schedule her to die prematurely?" Again he was pushing Satan to confess the truth; would he do it?

"If one must go early in order that a hundred be fairly treated—would you do right by the one and wrong by the hundred?"

"Well, no, but—"

"Death, I have analyzed the future course of man in some detail. I comprehend trends that might be considered too subtle for mortal minds. Not for *your* mind, of course; you are a perceptive person. But a detailed narration would become tedious. In essence, I perceive a nexus approximately twenty years hence that is crucial to the fate of the human species. By taking advantage of that particular situation, I can change the course of human history. I will be able to purge an enormous amount of evil with a minimum of disruption. Unfortunately, one well-intentioned but misguided person obstructs that opportunity. It grieves Me to deal firmly with that person, who is perfectly justified in her stand, according to her more limited comprehension; but the justice of the many must take precedence over the justice of the one. The equation may seem cruel in the particular instance, and unfair in the specific case—but in the larger context, the values reverse. This is the reality it is My eternal duty to honor."

And Luna was that one. Were it not for that, Zane might have found himself persuaded. "Father of Lies, I don't believe you."

Still Satan took no offense. "You are correct to be cautious. I like your independent thinking. I am sure a person of your perspective will come to the appropriate conclusion."

"I doubt you can convince me to send the woman I love to Eternity before her time."

Satan shrugged. "Timing can be a matter of convenience, Death. Do you feel privileged to have had your own situation cynically manipulated by others, including the time and manner of your departure from your original life?"

The Evil One was bearing down harder! "I'm not really pleased about that," Zane admitted, knowing that honesty was by far the best course. He could hardly match Satan's proficiency in lying, even if he wanted to. Any lie, even a mild self-deception, would play into Satan's hands. "But I think that, in this circumstance, it was the necessary—" He paused, realizing the implication. The welfare of the one, sacrificed for the benefit of the many! He was playing into the Devil's hands anyway!

"Circumstance makes puppets of us all," Satan said sympathetically. "You function excellently in your office; I can tell you that sincerely, though perhaps God would not. It has been decades, perhaps centuries, since a Death has placed conscience above convenience, and the role is overdue for reinterpretation."

On A Pale Horse

Zane tried to resist his pleasure at this flattery, mistrusting its source. "I dare say it is bringing me rapidly closer to you."

"Ho! Ho! Ho!" Satan laughed, like a jolly Santa Claus. "Isn't that the irony! The rules are so fixed that those few who do the right thing must pay for it with their souls! God would jet green flame if He knew! But frankly, He is not paying attention."

Zane was taken aback by this open denigration of God. But what else should he have expected from God's archenemy? "You say you're getting good souls in Hell?" he asked, amazed.

"And losing evil ones to Heaven," Satan agreed, slapping his knee. "Gums up the works something awful. But that's the way of bureaucracy and ossified standards; some poor souls always slip through the cracks."

This was the Father of Lies, Zane reminded himself. All or nothing or any ratio between could be falsity. It was dangerous even talking to Satan, for soon the boundaries of good and evil became fuzzed by eloquent misleading.

"I see you remain in doubt," Satan said, leaning forward with apparent sincerity. "That is quite understandable. Your associates have maneuvered to put you in an awkward position. You have problems in your office, and are inhibited by rules that have lost their relevance to the contemporary scene. Likewise I, in My office. It behooves us to cooperate where our offices overlap. This can greatly facilitate our respective duties and benefit us both."

"I see no benefit!"

"Oh, but you have not given yourself the chance to see it," Satan said smoothly. "Let Me give you a tour of My demesnes."

"A tour of Hell? I don't—"

"It can be arranged, Death. You have merely to depart your physical host for a time. You have My personal assurance that you will return in good order."

"The assurance of the Father of Lies!" Zane cried, repelled. "Now you are trying to get *me* into Hell! I refuse to risk my soul that way!"

"A man who will not risk his soul to save that of the woman he loves, perhaps does not deserve her love in return," Satan remarked.

That stung! "I just don't care to risk it on a bad bet. I don't see that I need to examine your case at all. Not personally in Hell. What I want is a review of the merits of the scheduling of Luna's death. If you can arrange for the review to be soon, I'll welcome that."

Satan rolled his eyes. "Have you ever tried to hurry a bureaucracy?"

There was that. "Anyway, I think I'll just sit tight right here until that review." Zane believed he had Satan over a barrel, for the review would surely expose evidence of Satan's cheating and free Luna from the sentence.

"I am not certain you comprehend My problem," Satan said. "Hell

On A Pale Horse

is geared for a large turnover. Thousands of souls enter each hour for processing. You have abruptly stopped the flow. That gives My initiation cadre no work to do."

"The respite should be good for them," Zane said, smiling unsympathetically. "They can sharpen their pitchforks, or whatever."

"On the contrary! Those little devils must be kept occupied constantly. Who in Hell finds work for idle devils to do?"

Zane visualized idle devils rampaging in Hell, overturning racks and littering torture chambers. That would certainly be a problem!

"Consider this," Satan said. The television picture changed to the news report of an accident. An airplane had experienced heavy weather in a cold northern region and crashed in an isolated spot. Fifty passengers were trapped inside. "These people are freezing to death," Satan said. "There is no hope of rescue, yet none of them can die while Death .emains on strike." The camera panned on the wreckage, then showed an interior view, where several passengers had critical injuries and others were in dire straits. This was a no-survivors type of crash.

"Do you really intend to let these victims suffer indefinitely, rather than free their souls for Eternity?" Satan asked soberly. "Most of this batch is slated for Heaven, so there is nothing to be gained by delay except undeserved misery."

Zane had not considered that aspect. Had he been deliberately avoiding the obvious? Of course there would be horrendous suffering! Death was no burden to a terminally injured person; it was relief. He was the first person to defend the right of anyone to die on schedule. He had, technically, committed murder in the defense of that right. Now he was responsible for a worse denial than that performed by any hospital. Satan had struck at another vulnerability, with the acute perception of his evil nature. It was not one person suffering now; it was a multitude!

Yet how many people would suffer eternally if Satan had his way? If one person—Luna—could be sacrificed to help fifty in a plane wreck, why couldn't fifty be sacrificed to help the entire world? Satan was putting pressure on him, and he had to withstand it. He had known it would not be easy, but had underestimated the cunning ingenuity of the argument.

"I deeply regret the suffering of these people," Zane said. "But it is your will, not mine, that precipitates it. The sooner my petition is considered and Luna is freed from her unfair sentence of early death, the better."

"I believe the date of the hearing could be moved up," Satan said, as if it were an incidental matter. "Come consider My case, and I will see that yours is considered."

So the Devil did have power to affect that matter—or so he was letting it be implied. "You are proffering a deal?"

"I specialize in deals."

On A Pale Horse

"How can I trust you to honor any part of any deal you make?"

"A deal not signed in blood is not worth the blood it's signed with," Satan said, grinning affably.

"I refuse to sign in blood!"

"Nor are you required to. That was merely a medieval custom; the client's blood gave Me the magic power to enforce the contract. Today fingerprints or retina-prints do just as well. But no contract of any nature can bind an Incarnation, so that's irrelevant." Satan leaned forward, his handsome face radiating sincerity. "Merely appreciate the background rationale, Death. It is to My interest to persuade you to end your strike. It is to your interest to guarantee the welfare of your girlfriend. It is thus to our mutual interest to establish communication and complete understanding. Cheating does not facilitate this."

"If I go to Hell and do not return, there will be a new person to assume the office of Death. That one, I am sure, will be more amenable to your guidance."

Satan smiled in wry agreement. "You are quick to appreciate reality. But all you have to do is consult with Fate, who arranges the details of transitions. No one else can do it. She will not, I suspect, deceive you on this matter. If you have her assurance that your transition will not be made at this time—"

Zane wasn't sure about that, but thought it worth investigating. "If I visit Hell, listen to your spiel, and then turn it down, will you free Luna from her sentence?"

"Of course not!" Satan said indignantly. "I will merely seek some other avenue to achieve My objective."

"Then what is the point of my tour?"

"You might be persuaded. Then you could reap great reward and be eternally happy."

"I can't be eternally happy unless I die," Zane pointed out.

"By no means, Death. Your present office is eternal."

"Until I leave it."

Satan's smile became slightly strained. "How may I reassure you, then?"

"Free Luna."

"You are being unreasonable."

"By your definition. If that concludes our business—"

A faint halo of smoke formed about Satan's face, but he hung on to his smile. "Suppose we compromise. Compromise is an excellent route to Hell. If your tour of Hell does not convince you—"

"You will free Luna," Zane finished firmly.

Satan sighed. "I could have wished for a more responsive officeholder. But—I will free Luna."

Was Satan lying? Probably—but Zane was just uncertain enough of his own position and power to try it. If Satan reneged, he would be

On A Pale Horse

proved to have bargained in bad faith, and Zane would have no further doubts. Meanwhile, Death still would not take Luna. He really had nothing to lose, as long as he remained in the office.

And that was the key. If he lost his own position . . . yet Satan's barb about the worth of a man who would not risk his soul for love still stung, and so did Zane's own conscience. He should at least listen to the other side. "I'll consult with Fate."

"I'll put her on," Satan said. Fate appeared on the television screen, in her lovely young Clotho guise.

"No," Zane said. "That could be your demon doing another imitation. I want this personal."

"As you wish," Fate said. Smiling, she stepped out of the TV picture to stand before him. "The creatures of Hell who can manifest on Earth can assume any form physically, but not intellectually." She stretched a bright thread between her hands. "And no one but an Incarnation can emulate an Incarnation. This is your thread, Death; see, I can move you with it."

She made a kink in the thread—and suddenly Zane was sitting on the floor. She straightened it again, and he found himself back in the easy chair. "I can spin it long or short, smooth or furry, thick or thin. As Lachesis, I can measure it to define your life—" She was now the middle-aged form. "And as Atropos, I can cut it off." She became an old hag with a huge pair of scissors.

"Enough!" Zane cried. "I accept your identity!"

"That's nice," she said, returning to Lachesis. "This deal the Infernal One proffers is legitimate, Death, at least to the extent of your survival. Your thread continues beyond this episode. Thereafter it becomes tangled; I can not guarantee the tapestry far ahead when Satan draws on it."

"I'll worry about Thereafter thereafter," Zane said.

"As you choose, Death," she said tightly, and he realized that she feared his survival meant he would be converted to Satan's side. That, more than anything else, satisfied him about her validity. "But watch yourself in Hell."

"I shall. What about Luna's thread?"

Fate drew out another thread from the air, inspecting it. "That, too, is tangled."

"Satan has promised to free her if I am not convinced by this tour."

Fate squinted closely at the thread again. "No, I can't be sure of that; there is too much interference. You must be alert for loopholes. Did he say when?"

"When?"

"When he would free her. Immediately or in one century?"

Zane's heart sank. "No."

-192-

"When you choose," Satan said equably.

"I don't trust that," Fate said. "He's as slippery as a greased eel. But I suppose you had better go to Hell and see what you can see."

"Maybe I should hire a guide," Zane joked weakly.

"Do that," she agreed seriously.

Suddenly it was not a joke. "Who might be a guide for a tour such as this? No living person could do it, and I don't know many dead people—" He paused, remembering one. "Molly Malone! The ghost fishmonger! Would she—?"

Fate's lips quirked ever so slightly with approval. "I know that gamin. She's one canny guttersnipe."

"I really don't see why you should choose to complicate a simple private tour," Satan said.

"Just what is Molly's standing in Eternity?" Zane asked. "Obviously she doesn't reside in Heaven or Hell."

"She is unattached," Fate said. "But most of her friends are in Hell. Molly was unwilling to desert them when she died, but she was too good a girl to go Below, so she's serving her term on the streets. Eventually she'll tire of this and allow herself to waft up to Heaven— but meanwhile, she can safely visit Hell."

"We have no use for her kind," Satan grumbled.

"But you can't deny her visiting privileges," Zane said. "Because of her loyalty to some of those incarcerated. I want her with me there."

"I will fetch her," Fate said, smiling covertly.

The smoke about Satan increased, but he remained silent.

In a moment the ghost appeared. "I hear you want to go on another sightseeing tour, Death," Molly said brightly. "But where's your date?"

"Luna will never see Hell," Zane said. "Satan seeks to convince me to let her die, and if she dies she will go to Heaven, and if he can't convince me to take her, maybe he'll leave her alone."

Molly glanced darkly at the Prince of Evil. "When Hell freezes over," she muttered. Satan only smiled tiredly; he had heard that expression countless times. "You can't trust the Prince of Evil, Death. His minions lobby for legislation on Earth to promote liquor and guns, so that drunken drivers and hotheaded malcontents will send themselves and others to Hell early."

"On the contrary," Satan said. "I promote legislation to outlaw anti-social things like pornography and gambling—"

"Because that puts the police to work raiding bookstores and penny-ante card games, instead of bearing down on crime in the streets!" Molly came back hotly. "You don't want people inside their homes reading or entertaining themselves; you want them outside and restless and frustrated, stirring up real mischief!"

Zane realized that Molly, who had died young in the streets, had a

On A Pale Horse

personal grudge here. "Will you be my guide in Hell, Molly?" he asked. "I mean, if you will come along and talk to your friends who are incarcerated there—"

She smiled brilliantly. "I'll be glad to, Death! His Lowness always puts bureaucratic obstacles in my way when I want to see a friend; maybe this time he won't be able to do that."

"Then let's be on our way," Satan said savagely. He reached forward to push against his side of the TV screen, and it swung out, a glass door. "Come into My parlor."

Molly extended her hand to Zane. "Just step out of your body, Death," she said. "You're your own client now."

Zane took her hand, uncertain about this. There was a funny feeling, a kind of internal parturition, and he got up out of the easy chair. He turned around and saw himself sitting there as if asleep or dead. His soul had departed his body.

"It's strange at first," Molly reassured him. "But you get used to it in a decade or so. Come on." She drew him toward the open TV set.

They stepped through together without difficulty, for animated souls were highly malleable. Zane did not feel at all thin or translucent, the way the souls he handled were; he seemed quite solid to himself.

Now they stood in a kind of furnace room, with open fires burning in a ring around them, smoke billowing up to obscure whatever ceiling there was. The air was hot.

"Welcome to Hell, Death," Satan said, extending his hand. It was red with fine scales, and the fingernails were talons. Zane hesitated, but then went ahead and accepted the hand. It was best to keep this as polite as possible.

The hand was hot, but not burning. "No place like the present," the Prince of Evil said briskly. His head, too, was more pronounced from this close vantage. His horns were larger and brighter than they had seemed before; canine teeth gleamed before his thin lips, and his hair resembled a ripple of flame. "These cursed souls tend the central heating plant of Hell, performing useful labor while expiating their burdens of sin."

Zane looked at the people. Some had shovels that they used to put coal on the fires. The heat where they worked was terrible, but they wore asbestos aprons to shield their bodies from the worst of it. Zane knew they were souls with very little physical substance, but since he was in soul form himself at the moment, they seemed substantial. "What is the point?" he asked. "I realize Hell has to be heated, but you could set up an automatic conveyor belt for the coal—"

"These are the souls of people who abused their status in life," Satan explained. "They had responsible positions in industry, overseeing the heating plants of manufacturing companies, apartment buildings, and such. Instead of striving for efficiency and comfort for their clients,

On A Pale Horse

they exploited them, refusing to modernize, though they knew people suffered as a result. Now they expiate that sin by laboring under the primitive conditions they forced on others."

Zane studied the laborers. His apartment on Earth, before he became Death, had been intermittently cold in winter because, he suspected, the landlord was fattening his profit margin by skimping on heating fuel. Zane could appreciate Satan's rationale. "How do they expiate their sin?" he asked. "Do they have to shovel a certain number of tons of coal, or what? How long does it take, and what happens to them when they've paid their debt?"

"Excellent questions!" Satan said, glowing with more than human animation. "The term of penance varies with the individual. Roughly, each soul must labor until it has suffered the same amount as it inflicted on others during its life. That can take time; and, of course, some souls are incorrigible. It is not merely the labor, but the attitude, that counts; the soul must sincerely repent its prior evil. Eventually each soul will be purified by suffering, and will at last qualify for release to Heaven."

"So souls aren't condemned to Hell for Eternity?" Zane asked, surprised.

Satan issued his pleasant laugh again. "Of course not! Hell is merely the ultimate reform institution, where the cases too difficult for Purgatory are handled. A truly evil or indifferent person can not be cured by gentleness. Here in Hell we have the mechanisms to straighten out even the most crooked souls. I assure you, by the time any soul qualifies for Heaven, it has become quite gentle. I am a perfectionist; I will free no soul before its time." And Satan's countenance assumed an infernally noble aspect. Zane remembered that Satan was reputed to be a fallen angel; maybe some angelic element remained in him.

"But what about the bureaucratic errors?" Zane asked. "Honest mistakes are possible."

"No. Not when I'm in charge. I can guarantee absolutely that not one defective soul has been sent from Hell to Heaven."

Molly had been poking around by herself. Now she returned to Zane. "I don't know any of these folk. Let's take a look at the Ireland section."

But already Satan was showing the way to another region. He opened a door in air, and they stepped through to a foggy, gloomy region crowded with people garbed in rags. Men, women, and children of every race plodded along a barren plain. Each was gaunt, and some were emaciated. All stared unwaveringly at the ground.

"These are the wasteful," Satan explained. "They threw out good food unused, knowing that others in the world were starving. Now they are hungry themselves. They squandered money; now they have only what they can find lying in the street, the refuse of others. They destroyed good clothing in the name of frivolous fashion; now they have only bad clothing, which they value more than all the garments of life.

They must save in death as much as they wasted in life—and their resources are meager here."

Again Zane was impressed. He had once approached a paper-towel dispenser in a nonmagic public lavatory—he had distrusted magic sanitary facilities, as some used the refuse to fashion voodoo dolls, and that could be a literal pain in the posterior—only to see the man ahead of him snatch the last three sheets and throw them away almost unused. He had been furious at that callous anonymous waster, but had not spoken up because the man had been large and aggressive. Now Zane felt a kind of vindication. Such people certainly needed to be punished!

"You see, Hell performs a necessary service," Satan said smoothly. "We would not want wasteful louts littering Heaven."

"I don't know anybody here, either," Molly muttered. "I think this is a showcase section, not the real inferno."

"Why don't you go seek out someone you do know?" Satan suggested. "I had understood you were along to guide Death, but if you insist on mixing in your personal business—"

"Let's go next to the Irish showcase," the ghost said rebelliously.

"I have many more enlightened sets," Satan said. "There is little point in subjecting ourselves to the abuse of the unmitigated tempers of Ireland."

"Oh, is that so!" Molly exclaimed, showing her own unmitigated temper.

Satan glanced about as if seeing something invisible to the others. "For example, Hell's Kitchen." He opened a door on a huge room filled with fat chefs who were baking and cooking and mixing drinks. The odors of fresh foods were almost overpoweringly strong, making Zane hungry, though he had recently eaten.

"Try an aperitif," the Prince of Evil said, lifting a sparkling glass from a tray an elegant waiter brought and proffering the drink to Zane.

"Don't touch it!" Molly cried. "Anyone who eats or drinks anything in Hell can never escape it!"

Satan's mouth stretched down in affected sadness. "I had thought such superstition was beneath you, fishwife. I have no need to trap people in Hell! They come to Me because their souls are burdened with sin."

"What about Persephone and the six pomegranate seeds?" Molly demanded.

"I will thank you to leave My private life out of this!" Satan snapped, and small sparks radiated from the tips of his horns. "She wanted to stay; the seeds were merely a pretext to satisfy her image for her domineering mother."

"Then what's all this fancy food for?" Molly asked, showing her Irish stubbornness. "You never feed it to any of my friends who are imprisoned here, I'm sure! I've visited here before, you know."

"You have visited limited regions before, snippit," Satan told her. "You have not seen the complete Hell or comprehended any part of its purpose."

"That's my complaint!" she said. "You're hiding something, Foul Fiend! You refuse to tell what the food is for."

Curls of smoke rose from Satan's reddening hide. "For the cadre, of course, slut! They receive privileged treatment. The finest gourmet food, beverages, entertainment—" He gestured, and a chorus line appeared: shapely nude girls kicking their legs in unison. "I would be happy to provide this service for you in Purgatory, Death; My cooks and girls are able to go that far."

"I already have a staff at the Deathmansion," Zane said.

"Ah, but not a staff like this! You have never experienced the delicacies these cooks generate; not Bacchus himself ever feasted like this. And My personal tailor will create for you a suit that Solomon in all his evanescent glory could not match. And for your nocturnal entertainment, the Queen of Love and Sex, Isis herself, shall attend—"

"The Old Serpent proffers a bribe!" Molly snapped. "Who needs Isis, that slattern, when he has a woman like Luna?"

That brought Zane forcefully back to reality. He had been somewhat dazzled by the movements of the dancing girls, but of course Luna was all he desired. How fortunate that Molly was along!

"True," Satan said mildly, though the heat of his body now clothed him in steam. "Still, there are other forms of entertainment for the discriminating person. Hell has the finest library of Eternity, completely unexpurgated. Many of its collected works have been written after the authors' deaths and are available only in the Infernal Literary Annex. The same for paintings and music—here, listen to Chopin's latest on the piano."

Beautiful piano music flooded the chamber, its exquisite touch lifting Zane's spirit.

"Come down from there," Molly said, catching Zane's leg.

Startled, he looked down. He was floating toward the ceiling! Since he was currently in spirit form, with no material body to weight him down, he had been literally lifted by the lovely music.

"Why offer me this?" Zane asked as his feet returned to the floor. "I'm only here to hear your presentation."

"Merely a gesture of amity," Satan said. "I happen to enjoy doing things for My friends."

"Death is no friend of yours, Old Nick!" Molly said.

Again Satan smiled; it seemed to be his protective reaction. "Death is a business associate, of course. That is no reason for negative relations."

"I want to see the Ireland section," Molly insisted.

Zane sighed. He could appreciate Satan's irritation with this single-mindedness. "We'd better go there, Lucifer." The Devil seemed like a sensible fellow, but there was no sense getting Molly upset. "We can check in on her friends, then see the rest of Hell." He had not changed his mind about Luna, but realized it would be nice if he could in some fashion accommodate Satan's worthy purpose.

"Naturally," Satan said with deific grace. He opened a new door in air, and they stepped through to an Irish city-slum.

It was chill, cruel winter. Snow swirled in the air, and dirty slush coated the filthy street. Peasants dressed in heavy outdoor garb were cleaning rubbish and fish heads from the gutters, using inadequate shovels and brooms.

"These were litterers," Satan said. "Now they labor all year round to recover as much litter as they strewed in life, and to make the street as clean as it was before they desecrated it. Unfortunately, the litter keeps reappearing."

Molly snooped around, looking for her friends. This time she found one. "Sean!" she cried. "I haven't seen you in a hundred years!"

The man paused in his labor. "Sweet Molly Malone! When did you die? I never thought I'd see you here! You don't look a lifetime older!"

"That's because I died early of a fever and took my youth and beauty with me to the grave."

The old man gazed at her appreciatively. "Sure an' you did that, girl! You were just a little bit of a thing, prettiest waif on the street. I thought sure you'd be a grandmother by the time you were sixteen."

Molly smiled. "I tried, but life ended too soon. I thought my soul would be damned to Hell, after what that honey-tongued man did to me—"

"Not *your* soul, dear child! You were the petunia in the onion patch, sure, always ready with a favor to them worse off'n you. Sure an' it's a shame you died before your time."

"How are they treating you, Sean?" she inquired.

"Well, it's not fun, as you can see. We clean and clean, but the mess never ends, and at times like this it's so cold—"

"Haven't you expiated your burden of sin yet? After all, you've been in Hell longer than you lived on Earth, Sean, and you were never a really bad man, just a litterer."

Sean scratched his head. "I don't know, lass. They keep the accounts, and somehow I never seem to gain. I must have a really incorrigible nature."

"Here, your glove is torn," Molly said solicitously. "Let me fix it." She reached for the man's hand.

"Oh, no, that's all right, miss," he said quickly, snatching his hand away. "I'll get by. I've got to get back to work anyway." He resumed shoveling ineffectively at the slush.

"If you're sure—" Molly said, concerned.

"As you can see," Satan said with another smile, "we are tough but fair, here in Hell. People who refuse to reform in life are hard to reform in death, but persistence and consistency eventually pay off."

"Yes, I can see that," Zane agreed. "It certainly seems reasonable—"

He was interrupted, for Molly had stumbled and collided with him, shoving him into one of the Irish workers. Her ghost form was completely solid to his spirit form. Zane's hand slapped bare flesh before he recovered his balance. "Oh, I'm sorry," he said, apologizing to the man he had struck. "I lost my footing—"

"The guttersnipe was the clumsy one," Satan muttered.

"It's all right," the man said gruffly, drawing his patched overcoat around him more tightly. "Just clear out and let me work."

Satan opened a new door in air, and they stepped through to a comfortably furnished living room suite. "So you see, there is no point in disrupting the system," he said.

"I agree," Zane said. "Yet I also *don't* see why I should take Luna out of turn. I think I'm on the fence about this."

"By all means," Satan said readily. "I am sure when you consider all aspects, you will see it My way." He opened still another door, and Zane and Molly stepped through to Zane's own Deathhouse living room. The door swung closed behind them, becoming the television screen.

Zane walked to his still body, positioned himself, and carefully sat down in his own lap. He sank into his flesh, reuniting with his host. In a moment he opened his eyes, solid again. It was a relief!

"I will send My minions to see to your comforts, Death," Satan said from the screen. Then he winked out, and the regular news program returned.

-12-

PARADOX PLOY

Molly sat down in Zane's lap, put her arms about his shoulders, and touched her lips to his right ear. This close, she smelled slightly of shellfish and she weighed nothing at all.

"Hey, that's not necessary," Zane protested, embarrassed and perplexed.

"But I must thank you for taking me on your trip to Hell," she said. "I got to meet an old friend."

Zane submitted to her embrace. After all, what could a ghost do to his solid form? "Glad to do it, Molly. Now you can return to—"

Her substanceless lips brushed his ear like a faint breeze. "Death—I must tell you before Satan takes over this house," she whispered urgently.

"What?"

"No, no—don't react. Just smile and look relaxed. Satan is watching. He'll let me caress you, because he wants you to assume an interest in any woman other than Luna. Here, I'll make myself more solid so you can feel my flesh." And now she had weight, pressing down on his lap. "You took me along as guide, and now I will guide you. Trust me, Death—it's important."

Zane, astonished by this abrupt shift of character, smiled and forced himself to relax, physically. The truth was, Molly was one fine-looking spirit, and it was not hard to tolerate her proximity, though he felt slightly guilty that she wasn't Luna.

"When I touched Sean's hand, there was no glove," Molly whispered, nibbling at his ear.

Zane started to speak, but she touched his lips with a forefinger. "Those people in Hell aren't wearing anything," she continued. "They are naked in the snow. They aren't being punished—they're being tortured."

Now Zane tried to protest, but again she hushed him, simultaneously opening her blouse to expose more of her fine bosom, as if seducing him. Indeed, the perfume of the sea was about her, making him think of a vacation at volcanic isles in the great Pacific Ocean. "Death, believe me! I suspected it before, but was never allowed to touch my friends in Hell, or even to get close to them. Satan's minions were always watching. This time I touched Sean—and now I know. That's why I pushed you into him. His clothing was illusion, wasn't it?"

Startled, Zane recalled how his hand had slapped bare flesh, though the man had seemed to be fully clothed. The notion of souls wearing illusory clothing was odd, but in the context of Hell, it made grim sense. "Yes—"

Molly let her skirt slide away to expose more of her thighs, then opened her blouse another notch. Zane understood why Sean had thought she would be a grandmother at age sixteen; she had died at that age, but had a body that suggested prompt male action. Maidens bloomed early and well in Ireland! "So now you know, too, Death. The Father of Lies is lying to you. He's not reforming souls at all. He's keeping them forever in vile bondage. He'll never let them go. And you can't trust his word on anything."

The implication was stunning. If Satan had lied about the nature of his proceedings in Hell itself, in what other context would he ever tell the truth? If he was not truly reforming souls, what was it that Luna, later in life, would stop him from doing? If Hell was no reformatory and Satan was in fact building an empire, then of course his reason for eliminating Luna was suspect. Under no circumstances should Death cooperate with the Prince of Evil!

"Thanks, Molly," he said. "You have served your office well. I shall remember."

"Get out of here immediately," she said. "Get to Mortis, who can better protect you. I know how Satan operates; his minions are at this moment moving to take over this mansion, to make quite sure you go his way."

"Agreed." Zane stood up, and she slid to her own feet, becoming weightless again. He strode toward the door.

A huge man in a chef's hat met him at the portal. "Your repast is ready, sir."

This was not his regular cook. "I will return for it in due course," Zane said, attempting to squeeze by him.

The chef put a massive and calloused hand on Zane's shoulder. "But it is ready now, sir."

Molly remained insubstantial here in Purgatory, except when she concentrated, but this man was as solid as a side of beef. Zane squirmed out from beneath the punishing grip. "Not now, thanks."

"I am sure you will reconsider, sir," the brute chef said, his hand dropping to Zane's forearm.

Angry and somewhat alarmed, Zane turned his gaze directly on the man's face. He knew the other saw the death's head, for he remained in uniform. "Whom do you think you are touching?" he demanded grimly.

The big man blanched, as most people did when confronted by the Deathmask, but stood his ground. "I am already dead. There is no harm you can do me."

Then why had he blanched? Zane lifted his right hand. The gems on his wrist glowed. His fingers caught the man under the chin and lifted him up. The man lifted readily, becoming cellophane-thin; he was, in fact, a soul. Zane folded the soul in half, and then in quarters, and finally wadded it into a ball and hurled it downward through the floor toward Hell.

Then he paused, surprised. He hadn't known Death could do that! But it was obvious, in retrospect, since Death routed souls to their spots in Eternity. When he took deliberate hold of a soul, it moved as he willed it to.

"That was pretty," Molly murmured.

Zane had forgotten her presence. "Maybe you had better get out of here, too," he suggested. "Satan's minions could probably manhandle you."

"It's very hard to hold a ghost against her will," she said, and faded from view.

"Thanks again for your help," he called. "You have opened my eyes!"

"You're welcome, Death," her breeze-faint whisper came. Then he was alone.

He strode through the doorway—and encountered a truly regal and lovely woman, garbed in elaborately archaic paraphernalia. "I am Helen of Troy," she announced.

Zane was, of course, familiar with the historical, virtually legendary accounts of this famous woman's activities. Hers was the face that had launched a thousand spells and precipitated a savage ancient war between the city-state of Troy and the massed forces of Greece. Naturally Helen now served Satan more directly.

"Now you do call-girl duty for the Father of Lies," Zane snapped, brushing by her.

"Please!" she cried, clutching at his arm. "You do not know what it is like to be three millennia past your prime! You can not guess what the Lord of Flies does to women who fail him!"

Against his better judgment, Zane was moved by her plea. She might be three thousand years dead, but she was one lovely creature. "I wish you no harm, Helen. But I am trying to keep a good, living woman

out of Satan's grasp. Would you seek to betray that woman?"

Helen looked at him. Tears formed in her beautiful eyes and streaked down her classic cheeks. Slowly her face collapsed in on itself, and her body became a shapeless mass. She dissolved into vapor, and her soul sank through the floor on the way to what she dreaded.

She had understood. Helen of Troy had been a good woman in essence, refusing to betray another of her kind. Saddened, Zane moved on outside. Mortis was waiting for him, saddlelight blinking urgently.

Zane mounted and set the translation jewel in his ear. "What is it, gallant steed?"

"Satan has loosed Hellhounds."

"That sounds bad. What's a Hellhound?"

"A demon in animal form. You can not fold its soul, for it is not human."

Zane digested that. It seemed Satan was playing with a harder ball now. "What can I do?"

"It is not my place to say, Master. I can protect you if we encounter them singly."

"Do Hellhounds hunt singly?"

"Not necessarily."

Zane felt a chill. "How much time do I have?"

"It takes time to run all the way from Hell's Houndpound to Purgatory, even for supernatural creatures. You may have fifteen minutes before they arrive."

"Good. I have an errand to attend to. Take me to the Records Department."

Mortis galloped for the big Purgatory building across the plain. "Do not be long about your business," the horse warned. "I can not be with you inside."

"I'll rejoin you before the Hounds arrive." Zane dismounted, entered the building, went immediately to the computer terminal, and turned it on.

A GREETING, DEATH, the screen flashed. THE INFORMATION YOU SEEK IS NOT IN MY STORAGE BANKS.

"I'll bet it isn't," Zane muttered.

NO ORDINARY CREATURE CAN STOP A HELLHOUND.

News traveled fast! "That isn't my question."

The computer flickered its screen, seeming startled. SURELY YOU ARE CONCERNED.

"How many souls have been released from Hell?"

MEANINGLESS QUERY. PLEASE REPHRASE.

"Oh, no, it isn't meaningless, machine! According to the Prince of Evil, he only processes souls to expiate their burden of evil, then releases them to Heaven. How many souls has he released to date? A round figure will suffice."

There was a pause. NO INFORMATION, the screen showed at last.
"What do you mean, no information? You've got the records of Eternity!"

I MEAN THERE HAVE BEEN NO ENTRIES OF THE TYPE YOU DESCRIBE.

Zane gasped. "*No* souls have been released from Hell—in all Eternity?"

CORRECT.

"What a colossal liar Satan is!" Zane cried. "I was sure he exaggerated, but there should have been at least a modicum of substance to his claim!"

THE CLAIM WAS NOT FALSE. ETERNITY HAS NOT ENDED.

Zane considered. "You mean that, theoretically, Lucifer will release souls at some future date?"

CORRECT,

"Some loophole! It's a blank check! Eternity, by definition, never ends."

The screen was blank. Zane turned off the terminal. He had learned what he came for. He had guessed that Satan might be underreporting the cured souls, saving out a certain percentage beyond their appointed tenures in Hell, but the reality was grossly worse. Certainly Death was not going to do things Satan's way!

Mortis was fidgeting impatiently outside. "Hellhounds getting close?" Zane asked as he mounted.

"Six of them."

"Can you outrun them?"

"Neigh. I could outdistance them in an extended run, for they lack my endurance, but their short-range speed is greater than mine."

"Can we hide from them?"

"No. They can sniff out even invisible spirits. They are Hell's cleanup squad. Nothing escapes them."

"Is there anywhere in the cosmos we can go where they can't follow?"

"Heaven, perhaps."

Zane laughed wryly. "Let's not involve Heaven in this! Let me consider."

"Do not consider more than ninety seconds, Death," the stallion said meaningfully.

Zane sat and pondered. He was surprised to discover that he was not afraid. He had never been a brave man; temper and bravado had passed for courage. But his recent activities in the office of Death had removed most of the dread of dying from him. He did not want to die himself, but this was now mainly a practical matter rather than fear for himself. If he died now, his replacement would end the strike and take Luna, and Satan would win. Luna might go to Heaven, and perhaps Zane would, too—though he would hardly bet on that! Certainly neither

faced extinction. But how would the rest of humanity fare, as Satan had his way? *That* was Zane's real challenge.

The Hellhounds, it seemed, could kill him, for they were supernatural monsters who would not be balked by the magic of the Deathcape. He might send one of them back to Hell in the same manner he had sent the chef-demon, even though its soul was not his proper department. But that would be the limit, since these creatures would have no fear of the human Death Incarnation.

If he couldn't hide from them, or flee them, or fight them—what could he do? Just stand and wait for them?

Into his mind came the pattern of matchsticks. Five arranged in a pentagon: ⬠. Now he realized what it meant. His thoughts were going in a circle, leading him nowhere, providing no solution.

Hastily he reshaped the matches to a better configuration. He laid them in a line. If he couldn't hide — and he couldn't flee — but he had to prevail — then he had to fight — and therefore needed a suitable weapon — There was his series chain: ———— .

He heard a chilling baying. At the horizon of Purgatory, dark lumps appeared, rapidly swelling in size. The Hellhounds had arrived.

Weapon, weapon—what was a weapon against a supernatural monster? Not his cloak, not his gems. He needed something offensive.

The six figures loomed into great red-brown canine shapes, each half the height of a man. Their eyes glowed red, like little furnace portholes. They moved with huge catlike bounds, covering ten meters at a time. There was no sound as their feet struck the ground; even in open attack, they showed their stealth.

What he needed was a good sword—one enchanted to dispatch natural and supernatural entities alike. But this was rather late to think about procuring one.

The Hellhounds ringed man and horse, pausing to study the situation. In a moment one or more would pounce.

Zane's eye fell on the scythe. Suddenly he remembered the manner in which Mars had suggested that he practice with it. He had not done so, as his attention had been taken by other things. But he did know how to swing a scythe.

The first Hellhound pounced.

Zane grasped the scythe and jumped to the ground. The Hound passed overhead, missing the suddenly descending target. That freed a few more seconds.

Zane shook the scythe so that its giant blade snapped into place at right angles to the handle and locked there. "Get out of here, Mortis!" he cried. "This is not your quarrel."

The Deathsteed bolted.

Zane hefted the scythe. He felt its terrible power. Oh, yes, this was a good weapon! "Come at me, puppies!" he cried, letting his volatile temper take over, and the cruel blade gleamed. "Come try my strength, you dogs who thought to attack helpless prey! But when you do, O beasts of night, know that you face the Lord of Night. I am Death!"

The first Hound, unimpressed, turned and leaped again. It seemed this kill was the privilege of the leader. Zane angled the great blade upward, pointing roughly at the Hound. The monster canine landed on it.

The gleaming point entered the Hound's head and slid right through to its tail, almost without resistance. Blood spurted at each end as the creature expired. The magic blade had efficiently destroyed the magic animal.

Two more Hellhounds, still unimpressed, pounced, one from each side. Zane hauled the blade out of the first and whipped it about in a fierce circle. It struck the first Hound halfway up its body and passed through as if encountering snow.

The top half of the monster's body flew off, leaving the bottom half to collapse in a burble of blood.

The blade carried on to contact the second Hound crosswise. The front of its body parted company with the rear. Guts spilled out as both halves collapsed.

Three Hellhounds remained. They were now impressed. "What's the matter, curs?" Zane taunted them. "Don't you like it when your quarry fights back?"

Another stepped forward, jaws gaping. Its teeth and tongue were as black as solid soot. It belched forth a searing jet of fire.

Zane's blade swung, separating the creature's head from its body. The fire died as the canine did.

Four down, two to go. Zane's right side smarted where the fire had heated his cloak. This fire was more penetrating than that of the Hot Smoke dragoness! But he couldn't rest now.

"Exactly whom did you suppose you were stalking, O sons of Hell-bitches?" Zane demanded, stepping toward the two with a blade that dripped the blood of their companions. "By what unholy arrogance did you expect to interfere with an Incarnation? Begone, whelps, lest I slice you in thin pieces!"

But one Hound refused to be intimidated. It charged—and Zane's terrible blade swept off all four of its legs with one motion. Still determined, the monster opened its mouth to shoot fire, so Zane clipped off the tip of its muzzle. "Are you a slow learner?" he inquired savagely. "Give over, or I will treat you unkindly."

The Hound, incapacitated, lay still and bled.

Zane turned to the last. "Put your tail between your legs, O sniveling cur, and hie back to your fell master," he cried, orienting the bright red blade. "Tell him not again to send pups to do men's work!"

The Hellhound, cowed at last, put down its tail and fled.

Zane's knees felt weak. He had done it! He had bluffed them out! Bluffed them? No, he had destroyed them, by drawing on a power of his office he had not consciously exploited before. His practice with the scythe, long ago in life, had proved well worthwhile!

Mortis trotted back, nickering. "That was a credit to the office, Death," the translation said.

Zane shrugged. "It was necessary. A desperate man does what he has to do. If I had had any escape, I would have taken it; since I had to fight, I fought as well as I knew how." For once his temper had served him well! "Satan underestimated me this time; I dare say he will not do so again. But I hope in time to serve the office with distinction. It's not that I regard myself as any superior person, for I am not; it's that the office of Death deserves the best that I can give it."

He mounted, and they started toward Earth. "Why didn't you tell me about the scythe?" Zane asked.

"I did not know it could be used against Hellhounds," Mortis admitted. "My former master never employed it in that manner."

But Mars had known! "So there are powers of the office that are inherent, regardless of the officeholder or the amount such powers have been used before," Zane concluded. "Could there be others?"

"I am not the first Deathsteed," Mortis neighed. "My predecessors may have seen things that are now clouded. But I understand the office of Death varies considerably with each officeholder. Interpretation is critical. At his height, Death is balked by no force in the firmament."

"I've been balked at every turn!" Zane protested.

"Not when you held the Deathscythe!"

"I was desperate," Zane repeated. But already he looked back at that episode with a certain grim pride. He had been foolish, but he had destroyed the enemy. Death did indeed have power, when Death chose to exert it. Nature had intimated as much. Had he remained confused, in effect acquiescing in his own slaying by the Hellhounds, that would have occurred; but he had not—and they had been helpless against him. Had his predecessor not cooperated in his own murder by being careless, he would have survived and Zane would be in Eternity.

"My own immediate predecessor in the office—what kind of Death was he?" Zane knew the man had gone to Heaven, but that did not necessarily speak well for his competence.

"A mediocre one, or he would not have lost the office."

"I mean how did he perform? I know he was careless at the end, but that does not mean he wasn't a good worker. Did he keep up with his schedule? Did you like him?"

"He kept his schedule better than you keep yours," the horse said. "I can not afford to become emotionally attached to any specific person."

"So you will not miss me when I'm gone," Zane said. "That's best.

I appreciate the loyal and competent service you have given me from the outset and know you will be a great help to my successor."

Mortis did not answer.

They landed in the city of Kilvarough. Mortis converted to the Death-mobile and drove Zane to Luna's address.

She met him at the door. "Oh, I worried about you, Zane," she said, relieved. "The consequence of opposing Satan—"

"I can handle it," he said, not wanting to burden her with the knowledge that his life was now seriously in jeopardy. Satan would surely bring more potent forces to bear—but if Luna knew that, she might try to do something foolish, such as removing herself from life. "I just came to ask you to stand firm no matter what happens. And to remind you that I love you."

Her relief was turning quickly to social concern. "You have gone on strike! Do you realize what this means?"

"I am being rapidly educated," he admitted. "People are suffering grievously. But—"

"They are stacking up in the hospitals," she said severely. "The terminal cases just won't die, and new patients keep coming in at the normal rate—it's been only a few hours. Can you imagine what it will be after a few *days*? The world can't go on this way!"

"I know it is hard," Zane said. "But the alternative—"

"Aren't you the one who smashed up a hospital room to free one client from a pointless and painful life? You *believe* in death!"

"I believe in death," Zane agreed, seeing it as a revelation. "I really do! Death is the most sacred right of the living; it is the one thing that should never be denied. Yet in this case—"

"It's not as if they can be saved," she continued relentlessly. "The fact that these poor people don't die does not mean they live productive lives. It only means a dreadful prolongation of terminal suffering."

"True," Zane acknowledged weakly. "Death is certainly a necessary service to those whose life is finished. It is best that it be prompt and painless. Yet—"

"I have been painting a picture," she said. She gestured to an easel she had set up in her living room. On it was a partially completed representation of a child whose lower body had been crushed by a car. Nearby was the tangled remnant of a bicycle or miniature magic carpet that the child had evidently been riding carelessly. Zane noted how artistically the elements of both carpet and machine had been integrated to make the device unidentifiable; this was a symbolic example, not a literal one. It had also been hastily done, for Luna had been home only a few hours.

The most compelling thing was the aura of the child. It looked very like a soul half out of the suffering body, and its agony was manifest. What a terrible image this would be when complete!

It was, of course, also a representation of Luna's own state. She had died violently, yet lived—and knew that she was at least in part responsible for the torment of all the people who could not die.

"But if Satan takes over Earth, because you are not there to stop him," Zane said, "millions of souls who might have gone to Heaven will instead be damned to just this type of torture in Hell! I must prevent—"

"I can't believe that!" Luna cried. "Hell is only the place where bad souls are punished. In time, when these souls reform, they are freed—"

"No, they're not! I checked with the Purgatory computer—"

"Zane, I have decided. I want you to end your—"

The door crashed open. A brutal-looking man charged in, pointing a handgun at Zane. "Now shall you die, Death, and I shall take your place!" he bellowed.

"How did he get past my griffins?" Luna demanded indignantly. "Where's my moon moth?"

"My Lord Satan spelled them off," the intruder said with an evil grin. "You will be the first booty I take, gorgeous creature, once I have the office."

Zane drew his cloak and hood more closely about him. "Beware, oaf! I am invulnerable to mortal weapons."

"Not any more, Death!" the thug cried. "You have been declared in violation of your office, and your magic has been turned off." He sighted along the barrel of his weapon, aiming at Zane's heart.

"No!" Luna screamed, lunging at the man.

The gun fired. Blood spattered from Luna's right leg, where the bullet from the deflected gun struck. She crumpled.

Zane had never been much of a fighter, but his berserker temper was invoked again. The red of Luna's blood magnified before his eyes like an exploding star. He launched himself at the intruder as the gun swept back toward him. One of Zane's gloved hands shoved the barrel aside; the other reached for the thug's face.

The man screamed and fell back, dropping the gun. Zane turned to Luna, who was sprawled in her own blood. "I must get you to a doctor!"

"No good!" she gasped. "The hospitals are overcrowded with the undead. No room for minor cases."

"But you could bleed to death!"

She flashed him a smile through her pain. "Then you'd have to take my soul, Death, wouldn't you! And that would—would free all the others."

With renewed horror, Zane realized that this was a two-pronged trap. If he had been assassinated, his replacement would have ended the Deathstrike and taken Luna. If Luna had been mortally hurt, Zane himself might have had to take her, for he could not bear to see her suffer. Either way, Satan won.

"But now that I've seen—" Luna paused to gasp, catching up with necessary breathing, then resumed. "—seen how eager Satan is to get rid of you, I'm not sure I ought to go."

"Some medical attention—I don't even know how to stop the bleeding—"

"Just fetch me the white gem from the mantle there," she said, her voice losing force. "It's a—healing stone—"

Zane leaped to fetch the stone. Luna took it with trembling fingers and touched it to her leg, and the bleeding slowed and stopped. The flesh began visibly to mend around the edge of the wound. "I'm adding more burden to my soul, using this black magic," she said. "But I don't care about me. I think maybe you're doing more than I thought, Zane, and I should support you."

"It's true," he said somewhat ungraciously. "But it's you Satan wants dead; I'm only blocking that. In a few days my petition will be heard, and the matter of your scheduling should be corrected. Then you will be free to live your life, and I can return to the duties of my office."

"I really don't see how I can be so important," she said, getting to her feet as the wound in her leg disappeared. That was one potent Healstone! "It must be something my father set up. Then he arranged to have Death himself guard me..."

"You're worth guarding," Zane said. "Now I must go. You have already been hurt because you were near me; I don't want that to happen again. I can protect you best by staying away from you."

"But Satan can attack me regardless!" she protested. "He just proved that!"

"It will do him no good while I retain the office. He must deal with me first."

The thug Zane had downed groaned. They looked at him. Luna gasped and Zane stiffened.

No wonder the man had given up the fight so readily. One of his eyes was a mass of blood and fluid. The other—

"I must have forked him in the eyes with my fingers," Zane said. "I wasn't even conscious of—"

Luna handed him the Healstone. Zane brought it to the man's face, near the punctured eye. In a moment the eye healed and cleared. Then he put it near the other. The eyeball was drawn up by its dangling nerve like a yo-yo until it popped back into its socket and firmed in place.

"I'm sorry," Zane told the man. "I acted without thinking."

The man felt his face tentatively. "You fixed me up!" he exclaimed. "I can see again! The pain's gone!"

"Yes. I shouldn't have struck you like that. I was angry."

"I don't like you when you're angry!" the man said, scrambling to his feet. "Just let me out of here! I won't tangle with *you* again!" He stumbled out.

"He thinks you healed him in a gesture of contempt," Luna said. "That makes him twice as wary of you. He doesn't know what you will do to him next time, or whether you will bother to fix it."

Zane shook his head. "I never dreamed there was such a beast in me! To spike out a man's eyes—"

"Just because he wanted to kill you and take your place and then kill me—"

Zane smiled, grimly rueful. "I guess I did mean it. When I saw him shoot you, a fuse blew in my brain. All my civilized restraints puffed away like so much fog in a furnace." He shook his head. "I'll leave you now. I can't blame you for being horrified."

She came to him, taking his hands in hers. "Zane, you have said you love me, and I have not replied. I feel I owe you a—a statement. I do like you, more than I have liked any other man except my father, but the situation—"

"I value your candor," he said carefully. "Of course you are not in a position to—"

"What I'm trying to say is that you can prevent me from dying, but love is on another schedule. So soon after my father, tangled in grief— I just can't—"

"I understand." And he believed he did. Luna loved her father, and that man had died. Could she afford to love Zane, too, when Satan was trying to assassinate him? When she herself was slated for early demise?

"Oh, Zane, take care of yourself!" she cried, flinging her arms about him and kissing him.

There was a neigh outside. Mortis was sounding the alarm. Zane disengaged hastily and hurried out.

"Trouble?" he asked, checking the translation stone in his ear.

"Other assassins," the horse said. "Some I can outrun. Some I can't. It is best to keep on the move, so that we encounter them singly."

Zane mounted and Mortis moved down the street, his hooves striking the pavement silently. Still Zane found he was not afraid. He was in a battle whose outcome he did not know, and he simply had to fight it through and hope he prevailed. It was as if there were some emotional spell on him, blocking out incapacitating fear. But there was no magic, simply his virtual certainty that he was right. This belief did indeed provide a kind of strength, without depriving him of his realistic cynicism about the outcome. He knew his cause was in doubt and perhaps hopeless, but he would not let it go.

"Is this campaign against me legal?" Zane asked. "Won't there be an investigation if I am dispatched?"

"Satan honors few rules that are not convenient for him. By the time his foul play is revealed, he will have had his way. Justice may pursue him, but he is the most elusive entity in the cosmos."

Which meant that Satan was cheating again, and could probably get away with it. Accomplishment was nine-tenths of the law, in Eternity as well as on Earth. Zane wasn't even angry; he knew he had to deal with reality rather than with idealism. He might be in the right, but without his defensive Deathmagic, he was fairly helpless.

Still, he recalled how rapidly, efficiently, and viciously he had acted when Luna had been directly threatened and when the Hellhounds had come for him. There was a lot of evil in him yet, being turned to good use against the greater evil of Satan's minions. Now that he had something to fight for, a new aspect of his personality was manifesting, making him more like Mars. He might be far from Heaven, but he wasn't entirely helpless.

Mortis swerved. "There is one ahead," the horse explained. He galloped down a side alley. "Oops!" came a neigh of dismay.

Even as the horse tried to dodge, Zane saw it. A tattered beggarman stood close, intercepting them, his arm swinging in a throwing motion.

Suddenly Zane was choking. He was breathing, but suffocating. There seemed to be no oxygen in the air!

Mortis turned his head, aware that something was wrong. "You have been hit by a suffocation-spell!"

"Yes!" Zane gasped. He could speak, for there was atmospheric pressure, but he couldn't breathe!

"The scythe! Use the scythe!"

Bewildered, Zane wrenched the folded scythe from its holster on the horse. Through tear-blurred eyes he saw a hole in the end of the handle. He put his mouth to it—and sucked in oxygenated air.

"It's a small-diameter suffocation-spell," Mortis explained. "Doesn't reach to my head. So the scythe tube is out of its range. The spell is bound to you, therefore you can't run away from it—but it loses power a meter out. In a few minutes it will dissipate; these things don't usually need much duration."

Zane could appreciate why. If he hadn't had horse and scythe to extricate him—!

In due course the spell dissipated as predicted, and Zane was able to put away the scythe and breathe freely. "Why is there a tube in the scythe handle?"

"This sort of thing must have happened before," Mortis said. "My former master once used it to blow a dart; that's how I knew."

Had attempts been made on Death's life before by supernatural agencies? It made a certain sordid sense. Surely Death had not universally pleased all parties at all times in the course of Eternity, and Satan was obviously one to try any means to get his way. So some Death office-holder along the line had had the scythe handle hollowed. Very nice.

If Death had been under siege before, it seemed he had survived it. Otherwise he would not have been able to modify the scythe handle. That was a positive sign.

No, maybe it was intended as a drinking straw, when water was available only from some well without a bucket, too deep to reach directly. He would probably never know. So he had no certainty. Were there other little things about this office that he ought to find out? His continuation as Death might depend on his information.

"What other resources do I have?" he asked Mortis.

"I hardly know," the horse confessed. "I have the impression that the powers of the office are far greater than normally employed, but your predecessor did not employ them."

It did make sense. Death should not be balked or intimidated by others, not even by Satan. Otherwise the office would soon become meaningless. But what powers did the office retain, once its magic had been turned off? Had Death ever gone on strike before? If so, how had that been resolved?

Mortis snorted. "Monster intercepting. I don't think I can avoid it."

"Don't try," Zane said. "It's my quarrel, not yours. Set me down in the monster's vicinity."

"You have courage."

"No. I'm just doing what has to be done. I'm walled in by circumstance, like water in a channel. If I had choices, I'd flow away into the ground and be lost. I'm nothing by myself."

"You have a choice. You can resign the office."

"No."

"Any Incarnation can resign without prejudice. I think that's how the others usually change personnel. They get tired or bored and make way for a successor."

"Without prejudice?"

"Reverting to the state of the soul when that person ended formal life. For you, this means balance."

"So I would go to Heaven or Hell, exactly as I would have, had I not killed my predecessor. Nothing would have changed for me."

"Yes. Of course, after your initiation period is done, your balance of good and evil will change, and your resignation would be on different terms."

"Interesting." Zane considered. "No, I can't resign. My successor would take Luna, and Satan would win. I can't allow that to happen."

"Then you do have courage. You have an easy way out that you do not accept."

"No, if I had any acceptable way out, I would take it. That's not the same."

Mortis halted at a green golf course. "The monster from Hell has intercepted us. You would have a better chance against it if you rode me."

"You need to survive for my successor. You have not betrayed your office; I will not involve you further in my problem." Zane dismounted, took the scythe, and stepped forward. Then he paused and turned back. "What type of monster is it?"

"A preying mantis."

"Praying mantis? They're small."

"*Prey*-ing mantis. A minion of Hell never prays, but does prey. They're large."

Now the monster appeared. It was shaped like a praying mantis, but it was five meters tall. Its huge pincer legs looked capable of crushing a man in one fell squeeze. Its small head peered down at Zane from its awful height, judging at what point to pounce.

Zane looked up at the mantis and was terrified. Courage? He had none of it! But he thought of Luna dying and Satan prevailing on Earth, and stood firm. "All right, move out," he told Mortis. "Fast!"

The horse bolted—and the mantis struck. Its body launched forward so rapidly it blurred, and its massive forearms unbent and clapped together again like those of the insect monster it mimicked.

It missed. Its pincer arms crunched together empty. Almost empty—there were a few strands of horsehair in that grasp.

The mantis had been going for Mortis, the moving target. Zane had not moved at all, so had not triggered the monster's attack response. Blind luck! The horse had moved suddenly and so rapidly that he had escaped—but that episode was enough to demonstrate the blinding speed of the monster. Zane knew he could not outrun it. He could not even bring his scythe into play before the creature grabbed him; his reflexes simply were not fast enough.

The lofty, tiny triangular head tilted as if trying to discover what had become of the prey. Then the mantis got back to its feet, poising for a new launch. It had four legs besides the heavy front set, and four huge wings now folded along the back of the long body. The preying mantis looked clumsy, like a wooden branch propped on stilts—but Zane had seen that creature move. It was no more clumsy than was Satan's tongue!

Zane had had some notion of standing his ground and swinging the scythe, but now knew this was hopeless. All he could cut with the scythe was the middle pair of legs—and long before he got there, the front legs would catch him and crunch him. In fact, he couldn't move at all without getting pounced on; he had been warned by Mortis' departure. What, then, could he do?

Well, he could wait. It seemed the mantis would not pounce as long as there was no motion. Probably it wasn't sure whether Zane was alive and, like the Hot Smoke dragon, did not feed on carrion. When he moved, it would know he was alive and would act accordingly, rendering him dead. What chance did he have? He couldn't wait forever, could he?

He was a man, with a man's brain. He was much smarter than the monster; he was sure of that. But how could he outsmart it when he couldn't move?

He conjured the five matchsticks to his mind's eye. Did ————— offer any way out? It didn't seem to. How about ☰ ? Nothing there either. Try creative thinking: ✕ .

How could he outsmart a monster who would destroy him the moment he moved? Standing still and thinking smart thoughts wouldn't suffice; the mantis could surely outwait him. So if he moved, he lost, and if he stood still, he lost. What creative thought could alleviate the squeeze?

Nevertheless, his thoughts played about the creative formation. Suppose he died where he stood, and his ghost haunted the preying mantis? That might serve it right, but meanwhile Satan would win. He needed to remain unmoving and alive at the same time his ghost haunted the monster and drove it away. A nonsense notion.

Nonsense? Not necessarily. He had departed his body briefly in order to visit Hell; why not do it again, to confound the mantis?

He tried, but nothing happened. He had no ghost to help draw him out, and probably his loss of magic also had something to do with it. His soul was now firmly fastened to his living body. It would depart only when his life did, and that was not the way he wanted to go.

Too bad he couldn't divide into two physical people, one to stay here under the watchful, faceted eyes of the mantis, while the other—

Suddenly it clicked. Maybe he could do just that! The mantis was attuned to motion—rapid or jerky motion, like that of a potential prey attempting to escape. That was why it had pounced at the moving horse, rather than at Zane. But it had not pursued Mortis, for after pouncing, it had realized that this was not the specific prey it had been sent for. That prey was Zane—but the mantis couldn't properly perceive him until he moved like prey. That was the problem with using an animal to hunt a man; the animal could not surmount its perceptive limitations. It was easier for a man to spot a moving object than a still one; the mantis' eyes were even more specialized, so that it was effectively blind while the target was still, and it lacked the brains to figure out that it could take a stab at a still form and make it move.

Zane moved, but not like prey. He hunched slowly within his voluminous robe, getting it off his body. He removed his black shoes and used them to form a tripod with the handle of the scythe, which he propped upright, supporting cloak and hood. It was awkward business, for he had to unfold the blade to help stabilize it, and nervous, for the mantis could surely perceive the activity. But the creature did not understand that activity, since it was not within the ordinary prey parameter. That limitation of intelligence was hurting the monster again.

When Zane had his scarecrow figure standing reasonably firm, he got slowly down on the ground and commenced crawling in caterpillar style toward the mantis. Both his speed and his direction deceived the monster; prey usually ran rapidly away from the predator, not slowly toward it.

The high, triangular head remained still, but Zane could feel the individual facets of the near eye bearing on him. He was now stripped to black shirt and trousers and socks, a dark blob inching along. If he had miscalculated, he would pay instantly with his life.

Something about that thought bothered him, and it wasn't exactly the fear of death. He wasn't afraid to die now. He just didn't want to do it in a manner that would give Satan the victory. Yet there was something else about his potential dying that nagged him, something significant—if only he could figure out what it was.

At the moment, he could not really concentrate on that. He had to pay attention to his snaillike progress, nudging a fraction of an inch at a time toward the mantis.

As he drew away from the propped cloak and the mantis did not strike, Zane breathed a slow, shuddering sigh of relief. He accelerated— but slowed again when he caught the slight motion of the monster's distant head. He was playing it very close.

After that, progress became drudgery. He nudged onward steadily, his nervous system in constant agitation. After an hour he began to suffer hallucinations. He seemed to be a blob of molasses, flowing along, and the faceted eye of the mantis seemed like the sun, sending down its pitiless rays to dry him up. He found himself looking down on that molasses, wondering when it would start crazing and cracking.

Zane caught himself. That could be his soul drifting free of his body, looking down! He could die from exposure as readily as from the bite of the monster! There was still more than one way Satan could get him.

But he wasn't dying yet; he was just dreaming. He refocused on his immediate task and continued moving forward, picking up speed. The mantis, perhaps no longer associating this blob with its prey, did not react.

The left middle leg of the preying mantis was looming near. Zane angled for it, fearful that it would move before he got there. He forced himself to maintain a steady pace, as the minutes dragged on. The foot, no more than a greenish and ridged bend in the end of the leg, remained in place. The leg's cross section was no more than that of Zane's own wrist, but its length was more than his whole body. That was actually the length of one segment of it; above the knee was a similar length, extending horizontally, thicker in diameter. The legs tied into the torso just below the forward set of wings.

At last the target was within reach. Slowly Zane extended his two hands until they were almost touching the thin leg. He paused, gathering his nerve. This was about to become most uncomfortable!

Then, suddenly, he grasped the leg in a firm double grip.

Now the mantis reacted. It hauled its leg away—carrying Zane with it. It shook the limb, but Zane jackknifed and wrapped his legs about the leg. He had emulated the tactic of the mantis itself and had pounced by surprise.

The mantis might not be able to see a stationary target very well, but it could feel what was on its leg. It tried to brush Zane off by rubbing the leg against its abdomen. This was ineffective, for Zane's grip was too tight.

Now the monster planted its foot on the ground and angled its head to look. It didn't understand this type of attack. Zane hung on, certain that he was safe from the giant foreleg pincers here. The mantis would have to crush its own leg along with Zane, and it was unlikely to do that. He had nullified its primary weapon.

However, he had not yet won his freedom, for he did not dare let go. He had gained an impasse, no more. What next?

The mantis lifted its leg forward, setting it down as far in front as possible. Then it brought down its head. The long body was more flexible than Zane had supposed.

Oops! Now the insectile jaws could reach Zane. He could not afford to remain in place.

The head loomed close. It was about a third as long as Zane's body, and dominated by the huge, faceted eyes that seemed to take up about a quarter of the surface area of its face. The long antennae sprouted from anchorages just inside each eye placement, and three tiny eyes no larger than Zane's own looked out from between the antennae. Zane had not before appreciated so clearly exactly how alien the insect type of life was from human life. Five eyes, of two different sizes—yet it did make sense. Obviously the small eyes were "finders," scanning the world in a general way, so that the big, specialized eyes could be oriented on their targets.

But it was the mandibles that compelled Zane's more immediate and horrified attention. The mouth was like a gross bird beak, with several thin appendages enclosing it. Zane imagined those mandibles latching onto his flesh, and lost his nerve. He had thought to leap to the monster's head and punch out its beautiful compound orbs, but now he was frozen with fear and revulsion.

The eyes surveyed him. The huge, faceted structures were like windows over deep and dusky wells, reminding him of precious cut stones. He saw his reflection duplicated many times over in the nearest facets and was sure this was the image the mantis had of him. The monster could now see him far more clearly than he could see it!

The head moved. Zane screamed and dropped off the leg. He fell jarringly on his back, and the head plunged down at him. Now he knew he was done for—because he had lost his nerve.

But the head did not strike. It was the grasping forelegs that took hold of him, lifting him up. Toothlike serrations clamped his torso, holding him with appalling authority. Of course the head had not struck directly, he realized; the mantis fed by grasping its prey and tearing chunks of living flesh from the body.

It had him now. Would it begin its repast by biting off his head, or would it prefer a juicy limb? Probably the latter, for this type of monster preferred the very freshest meat, and life remained longer while the head was intact. It might even bite a hole in him so it could take in some warm blood as an aperitif. Crunch, as an appendage was chewed off, then slurp, as the blood was licked up. Assuming the insect had a tongue; Zane wasn't sure it did.

He waited helplessly for what seemed like an interminable time, his thoughts going around in the schizoid formation of thought, visualizing his bones being spat out like machine gun bullets and his skull being cracked open for the final delicacy. His mood did not improve with such rehearsals. His fate was sealed; the least he could do was be positive about it.

He wrenched his thoughts into another formation—and suffered another creative flash. It was a nova. "You can't kill me!" he exclaimed. "That's why you're waiting!"

The lambent eyes turned translucent.

"Because it's paradox," Zane continued, working out the rationale behind his revelation. "My soul is in balance, as it was when I assumed the office of Death, as it remains for the term of my trial period. If I die, Death must collect my soul personally—and I am Death. I must collect myself—and that's nonsensical."

Still the monster waited.

"So all you can do is scare me. Paradox protects me! There had to be a way out of that smother-spell, too, and the gunman shot Luna instead of me. Not coincidence at all, but deliberate deception. The Father of Lies can't wipe me out! He wanted me to think he could kill me, to make me accede to his will—to intimidate me. But his ploy has been balked by my paradox ploy!"

Slowly the preying mantis relaxed its grip, and Zane slid to the ground. But he wanted to be absolutely sure. "Strike, monster!" he cried, waving his arms. "Gobble me up!" He kicked at a foreleg.

The mantis backed away.

"Your bluff has been called!" Zane said. "*Satan's* bluff has been called. Nothing can kill Death when his soul is in balance." He realized that this was the thought that had eluded him before—his unique situation.

Mortis returned, but Zane stood pondering a moment more. It figured. Death could not be killed with his good and evil in balance—because only Death could handle such a case—and he was Death! He could hardly handle his own death. His predecessor, the former Death, had been well beyond his break-in period, so was no longer in balance and had been vulnerable. Once Zane got past his trial period, his balance of good and evil would shift one way or the other; then he, too, would be vulnerable. The other Incarnations had surely known. They had betrayed one Death to strengthen another.

He hadn't won yet. He had to establish Luna's security before he became vulnerable himself. Otherwise Satan had only to wait. But this reprieve should enable him to see it through to the hearing on his petition. That sufficed.

Now Zane mounted. "We have a fighting chance, Mortis!" he cried. But he doubted Satan would make it easy.

-13-

THOUGH SATAN BAR THE WAY

They drew up at Luna's house. Zane was overflowing with his good news about the reprieve. He would survive until the hearing, and therefore she would, too, and after that—

The house was silent. The griffins were gone. Suddenly worried, Zane entered. Luna, too, was gone.

There was a note on the table. Zane picked it up. It was written in red cursive script, as if done in blood.

> *My Dear Death:*
> *The fair Moon is in My power. I can not make her die, but I can make her wish she were dead. Terminate your strike, take your scheduled next client, and free Luna from her pain. She will go to Heaven directly, where you may join her at your convenience.*
> *Your most humble and obedient servant,*
> *The Prince of Evil*

Zane stared at the message, absorbing its every implication. Suddenly it burst into flame in his hand. He dropped it, but it never touched the floor. It was gone.

There was no doubt it was from Satan. The moment one ploy failed, the Lord of Flies tried another. Now that Zane was safe and knew it, Satan was striking through the woman he loved—in life as well as death. Trust the Devil to have no scruples!

Was Satan bluffing again? Zane dropped into the easy chair before Luna's television set, trying to clarify his whirling doubts. There was something—

Ah. He had it. "Satan, you forget that Luna *is* my next client. I will go there to rescue her from your clutches, not to send her to Eternity."

He looked at his orientation gems, fixing on Luna's location, for she remained the one he had to take before he could tune in on others.

The television set came on by itself. "A bye has been issued, Death," Satan's face said from the screen. The Devil seemed to have an affinity for television. "Reset your watch, and it will orient on the next client."

Zane brightened momentarily. "Luna has been spared?"

"No, merely put on hold. She will go unassisted when her time comes."

When her time came. That would be the moment Zane ended his strike—except that he would balk again when he had to take her. What would Satan gain by this maneuver?

"She can't go unassisted," Zane said. "She is now in balance. Only I can take her—and that I will not do."

"She will not remain in balance," Satan said.

Zane's suspicion returned full-force. "What do you mean?"

"My minions of the living realm will cause her to react, either in a good or an evil manner. Probably good, and that will tip her toward Heaven. Thus the assurance in My note. You need not attend her at all; merely resume your duties, and all else will take care of itself."

Zane liked this less and less. "You will torture her—and make her better than she is now? I don't understand that."

"Ponder it at leisure," Satan said. "But do not ponder overlong, My esteemed associate. My Earthly minions are a brutal lot, already damned to Hell for good cause, who like torture for its own sake."

The picture shifted to an Earthly chamber. There was Luna, tied to a chair, looking defiant. Three thuglike men were with her.

"You're on," Satan's voice came. "Make your demonstration." The way he said it, the syllables "de-mon" projected from the final word.

One thug drew a bright knife from a sheath. "Right, Boss," he said. He approached Luna.

Zane suffered an abrupt siege of intense rage and fear. They really were going to torture Luna! He wanted to mount Mortis and charge to the rescue, but couldn't tear himself away from the television screen. How could they change Luna's balance by such means? And how could he abate this horror when his own magic was gone? He might be secure from assassination himself, but he could not physically get past the barriers Satan's minions would have erected to bar his way to Luna. Satan was really putting the screws to him.

The thug brandished the knife before Luna's face. "Pray to Satan for succor," he said.

"Satan can go succor himself!" she snapped defiantly.

The knife moved closer. "One prayer to Satan can save you a lot of pain." The thug licked his lips.

Luna blanched, obviously frightened. "What do you want of me?"

"Only your prayer," the thug said, leering.

"All Satan can have is my curse!"

Then she did a double take. "That's what you want! If I pray to Satan, I'll be damned by a trifling amount. If I curse him, I'll be blessed similarly. Either way, my soul nudges off balance, and I can die without Death's personal attendance."

"So that's it!" Zane exclaimed. "You're trying to get her removed from my list entirely! When my strike ends, you can kill her immediately, and I can't balk you any more!"

"You are learning," Satan agreed.

"It won't work! She has caught on to your plot!"

"We shall see."

On the screen, the thug made a sudden motion with the knife, slicing it at Luna's front. It severed the material of her blouse. He sliced again, cutting away more blouse without touching her skin. In moments she had been stripped to the waist, her hands still bound behind her.

Now the thug put away his knife and fetched a black box with dials on one face and a pair of wires terminating in small disks. He extended the two extremities toward the tips of Luna's bare breasts.

"I wonder whether you appreciate the quality of pain that can be induced by electric shock," Satan said conversationally to Zane. "No physical damage shows, and the intensity is finely tuned. She can be made to suffer a small amount—"

The electrodes touched Luna's nipples. She jumped, with an exclamation of pain.

"Pray to my Lord Satan," the thug said. "Or curse Him. Then the treatment will stop."

"—or a greater amount," Satan continued.

The electrodes touched again. This time Luna's scream was piercing. Zane saw her whole body stiffen with the agony of the current passing through her chest.

When it stopped, her head fell forward, her face beaded with chill sweat, her lips so pale they almost disappeared. She was sobbing brokenly with reaction.

"You can free her from this, Death," Satan said. "I know you do not like to inflict needless pain."

Seeing her like that, Zane was tempted. He couldn't stand to watch the woman he loved being tortured. This was worse than the jaws of the Hot Smoke dragon, for this was deliberate cruelty, with no hope of unconsciousness or death. Unless he yielded...

"Speak to her, Death," Satan said persuasively. "Tell her to curse Me, and go to Heaven for Eternity."

Zane hesitated. There was so much in the balance here!

The thug touched Luna's breasts again. This time she tried not to scream, but an anguished sound squeaked past her constricted throat— the sort of sound one might hear from a mouse being run over by the tire of a truck. There was perspiration on all of her body that was exposed, and her eyes were staring, the whites showing too much.

"Luna!" Zane cried. "Curse Satan! Don't let them do this to you!"

Slowly her head turned, seeking his voice. She heard him. And Zane knew he had betrayed her—and the world.

Then she forced a smile like a grimace. "Oh, no, you don't, Father of Lies!" she gasped. "You can't fool me with Zane's voice! I know he would never urge me to betray his trust, no matter what!"

Zane felt as if the electrodes had been touched to his own flesh. She believed in him—but he had proved unworthy. He had broken, not she.

The thug extended the terrible electrodes again.

Zane squeezed his eyes shut. He had seen his mother suffering and had acted to free her from a life that had become intolerably burdensome. He had released a whole ward full of suffering old people. He had tried in every case to ameliorate the pain of death where death was necessary, and to eliminate suffering. His whole developing philosophy of death was as a legitimate end to pain. This time it was Luna who suffered, because of him—and he had no right to free her.

He heard her strangled scream. He kept his eyes closed, seeing an explosion of matchsticks. Formations of thought—and how could any of them resolve *this* crisis?

Suddenly the fifth pattern flashed in his imagination: —|||— . The symbol for intuitive thinking. His mind concentrated, assimilating it, hurdling the intuitive gap—

"Death be not stayed!" he cried.

He launched himself from the chair, charged outside, and vaulted onto his ready horse. "Go to Luna!" he cried, showing the orientation stones.

The stallion leaped into the sky. The globe of Earth whirled by beneath them. Then they arrived—on board an orbiting satellite, with normal gravity generated by magic. Naturally Satan was involved in space missions, to make sure no people escaped his power by fleeing planet Earth. But if the Prince of Evil's minions had thought to escape Death here, they were fools.

A thug appeared. He gaped. "A horse in space!" he exclaimed, amazed.

"More than that, ilk of Satan," Zane said grimly.

"Hey, you can't pass here!" the thug protested. "Where's your Infernal clearance?"

Zane faced him. "Mortal, look at me," he directed.

For the first time, the thug saw him as his office. The man's eyes frogged. "Death!"

"Now stand clear, lest you feel my touch," Zane said.

But the thug recovered some backbone. "You won't kill me. You're

On A Pale Horse

on strike. If you take my soul, my Lord Satan can kill your woman."

"You have placed your trust in the wrong power," Zane said. He reached for the thug, who stiffened in fear but stood his ground like a half-bold cur.

Zane caught the man's soul and jerked it out of his body. The man collapsed. But the soul was only half out; it remained anchored in the host, as had the soul of the woman on life-support machinery. The thug was not dead, only separated from his soul partway for the moment.

Zane let go of the soul. It snapped elastically back into its host. The thug opened his eyes and stared dazedly up at the cloaked figure before him.

"Go and tell your fell master that Death is on his way and shall not be denied," Zane said.

The man climbed weakly to his feet and staggered down the passage.

Zane followed more slowly. Soon three more thugs charged up to intercept him.

"Mortis," Zane said.

The great Deathhorse, who had remained in the background as Zane faced the thug, stepped up. Zane remounted. "Trample any who do not give way," Zane said coldly. "They have had fair warning."

The stallion walked forward. His muscles rippled and his steel hooves gleamed. Death's eerie gaze shone down from above the massive animal. The sound of their tread became loud. Dazzled, the minions of Satan gave way, like rabbits before a wolf. The horse paced on.

One of the thugs drew a small machine gun from under his jacket. He pointed it at Zane. "Your magic's gone, Death," he said. "Maybe we can't kill you, but we can riddle you with bullets. That will stop you!"

"Do that, cretin," Zane said, and sat firmly while the Deathsteed continued the advance.

The gun fired a burst.

The bullets ricocheted from the Deathcloak and tore into the walls and equipment of the space station. Zane remained unhurt.

The thug stared. "But—"

Zane stretched his right arm toward the man. He crooked his finger. The thug's soul began to draw from his body as if pulled on a string. "Do not believe all that the Father of Lies tells you," Zane said. He released the soul, and the man fell back, gasping.

Mortis marched on down the central hall. Death rode regally onward, seeming invincible.

Two Hellhounds appeared. The first leaped for Zane head-on, jaws gaping, fire jetting.

Mortis' front leg jerked up. The metallic hoof caught the Hound in the head. The full force of the creature's momentum carried it into that hoof, crushing its skull. It dropped lifelessly.

The other circled and pounced from the side. Zane extended his left arm. The great jaws of the Hound took in the gloved hand and closed on the sleeve surrounding the elbow.

Zane turned his head slowly to look the monster in the eyes. "This becomes annoying," he said and flexed his fingers in the Hound's throat, grasping the back of its tongue. "Begone, beast, or I will make my displeasure known." He squeezed the tongue.

The creature stared. Then, slowly, it dissolved. Soon Zane was left with his arm extended, unhurt, in a cloud of smoke. His magic had been stronger than that of the monster.

They moved into the next chamber. There was Luna, still tied half-naked to the chair. "Death!" she cried. "Don't take me!"

Zane knew it was no plea of cowardice she made. She expected to live in agony—to foil Satan.

Zane dismounted as the three thugs attending Luna turned to face him, staring. "I have come to take you home—alive," he said. "But first I have something to settle with these minions of the Evil One." He drew the great scythe from its holster on the horse.

"No!" Luna cried. "Don't kill anyone! You mustn't—"

"Fear not. I shall merely hurt them a little, as they have hurt you," Zane said, unfolding the terrible blade. "I will cut off their hands and feet, but they shall not die." He smiled savagely. "No, they shall not die!"

The thugs, abruptly terrified, scrambled away.

A fourth man entered the chamber. "I think not," he said.

Zane hardly glanced at him. "Death shall not be denied." He hefted the scythe and took a step toward the three thugs, who cowered abjectly against the wall.

"Death shall have no dominion," the stranger said. He pointed at the floor before Zane, and fire rose from it.

This was evidently a higher functionary. "I will rescue my love, though Hell bar the way." Zane swept the blade of the scythe through the flames, and they were cut off like so many weeds. In a moment they died.

The man made a circle in the air with one finger. The space inside the circle fell out like cut paper, leaving a window into a horrendous furnace. "Hell does bar the way. Do not tamper with things you do not understand."

Zane made a circle with his own left arm, flinging a length of his cape over the window, stifling it until it disappeared. "Who the devil are you to oppose me with such foolish tricks and to slight my intelligence?" He shifted the blade of the scythe meaningfully. "The Devil himself shall not interfere with Death any more."

The man's face melted. From the dripping flesh emerged the glowing countenance of the Prince of Evil. "I *am* the Devil, Death!"

Zane was for a moment taken aback. "How can you be out of Hell?"

"I can be anywhere I wish!" Satan exclaimed, a ripple of flame playing across his features. "Evil is inherent in all activities of man. Now bow down before Me and leave off your inane posturings, for your case is lost."

Uncertainty tore at Zane. He had made short work of Satan's Earthly and beastly minions—but Satan himself was another matter. He looked around—and saw Luna still tied to the chair, the three thugs by her, one holding the electrodes used to torture her. Renewed fury suffused him.

"Then I shall deal with you," Zane said, facing Satan.

The Prince of Evil smiled sardonically. "With Me? How do you propose to do that? Your magic is gone, and you are but a man."

"My magic gone? So you claimed before, but it was and is a lie. I received no confirmation from Purgatory. My magic horse remained, and my magic gems, and my invincible cloak. I was never without magic! Lies are all you have, Father of Lies. You suggest you can arbitrarily deprive me of my powers." Zane stepped toward the Devil. *"Satan, it is not your prerogative!* Death is inviolate, as it must be, not to be tampered with by the likes of you. Where Death has dominion, the Lord of Flies has none." Zane took another step. "Now get behind me, Satan, and disperse the ilk you brought here. Stay me no longer from my mission, lest I orient my power on you."

Satan harrumphed, and his horns glowed. "A month ago you were the least of pip-squeaks scrambling to pay your back rent. The assumption of a cloak and scythe does not convert a nothing-creature to a something-creature. You have delusions of grandeur that will quickly be dispelled. You bluff, mortal man."

For answer, Zane swept the deadly scythe at Satan's ankles and tail.

The Prince of Evil jumped back, avoiding the cut. He flicked his fingers, and a sparkling globe of energy floated at Zane's face. "Fool! Then feel the wrath of Satan!"

Zane stood still, not even attempting to evade the globe. It settled about his head, blazing high, coloring his vision as if he looked out from an inferno, but there was no heat. In a moment it dissipated harmlessly. The Deathhood had protected him. "The bluff is yours, Father of Lies."

Satan sneered. "You talk big, mortal man, holding the magic scythe and wrapped in the magic cloak, backed by the magic steed. These are mere tools of the office. Without them you are nothing."

"You lie again," Zane said. "You have no power over me, regardless." He set down the scythe and lifted the cloak from his shoulders.

"No!" Luna cried from the chair. "Don't let Satan trick you into powerlessness, Zane!"

Now it was her faith that was weak, instead of his. Zane smiled and threw the cape aside. Then he removed his shoes and stripped off his gloves and gems.

"You are indeed a fool," Satan gloated.

"Then all you have to do is stand still," Zane said, "and we shall make the proof of my prerogatives." Slowly he reached one bare hand toward the Devil.

Satan nudged back. "What idiocy is this? I can destroy you with a single flick of My finger!"

"Then you had better do it," Zane said, "for I am about to hook your soul with my own finger." He extended his hand farther.

Satan moved back some more, staying just clear. "Fool! I am trying to spare you the ignominy of being humiliated!"

"How very kind of you, Father of Lies." Zane leaned forward, shooting his hand at Satan's midsection.

The Devil puffed into nothingness.

Zane turned to see the Prince of Evil re-form behind him. "So you got behind me, Satan," he remarked. "I have moved you. Do you think that improves your position? Strike, Lucifer! Do not spare my feelings any further. Humiliate me. Destroy Death while he stands vulnerable. I turn my back on you again, to facilitate your chastisement." And he turned away.

Satan sighed. "You have prevailed, Death. You called My bluff and forced Me to give way. You have at last realized your full power."

"What else is news?" Zane picked up his cloak and got dressed again.

"If I may inquire," Satan asked without sarcasm, "as one Incarnation to another—what gave you the clue?"

"The fifth pattern of matchsticks," Zane said.

"Intuitive thinking," Satan agreed, comprehending immediately. "That would do it."

"I realized that if there were any way for you to meddle in the affairs of Death, or to stop Death from performing his duty, you would have done so long ago. No magic cloak would have stopped you, the Incarnation of Evil, the personification of black magic, whose powers of enchantment are not matched anywhere on Earth. It had to be inherent in the office, not in the paraphernalia. Death has to be inviolable, absolutely certain. Not even God, the Incarnation of Good, acted against Death when I declined to exercise my power in the world. Only Death can determine his business. Therefore you had to be powerless against me in this instance. I can not defend this by logic; I simply know it is true. I have faith in my office."

Satan nodded. "You do indeed. Against that faith, even I can not prevail. Yet had you chosen another issue, you would never have been able to oppose Me. Your power is less than Mine, as evil lives after death."

"I recognize that," Zane said. "But I met you on my own turf, which is not a matter of physical locale. Never again will you bluff me there."

"You were a man performing an office," Satan said. "Now you have become the office."

"Yes."

"And who informed you about the formations of matchsticks?"

"Nature," Zane said, realizing only now the extent of her oblique advice to him.

"That green mother!" Satan snarled with disgust, and vanished.

Zane went to Luna. "Begone, vermin," he told the thugs, who hastened to oblige.

"But how did you do it?" Luna asked as he untied her and put the Deathcloak about her bare torso. "No one is stronger than Satan, except maybe God."

Zane realized that she had not grasped all the implications of his confrontation with the Prince of Evil. She still thought of him as a man—and indeed, he was a man, with a man's love for his woman. "To be strong is not to be omnipotent," he explained. "There are seven Incarnations, not five, when we include Good and Evil, rendering them G-od and D-evil. No one can say for sure whether one Incarnation is superior to another, but certainly each is supreme in his own bailiwick. So while Death can not balk Satan's administration of Hell, however corrupt it may be, Satan can not balk Death's activity either. And no Incarnation can directly harm any other, unless that other accedes by design or ignorance or carelessness. Once I realized that and truly believed it and comprehended its implications, Satan had no further power over me." He smiled. "Or you. I'll take you by Purgatory now, to verify that Satan has dropped his claim to your early demise. Then I'll resume my job."

"You are brilliant!" she exclaimed. "Once you had that revelation, Satan himself was unable to oppose you. I see now the wisdom of my father's decision in giving me to you. I'm sorry I lacked the faith in you that you had in me."

She did not realize how weak his faith had been, before his intuition! "I *hoped* Satan could not oppose me," he admitted.

She stared at him. "You mean you didn't *know*?"

"How can one know an intuition? There is no direct connection between question and answer. I could not be sure of its validity until I tested it."

"So you deliberately stripped yourself of all your magic and challenged Satan—not sure you were right?"

"That is so," he confessed, embarrassed.

"Why, Zane, that's the most courageous act I ever saw!"

"It was my final desperation ploy, when I realized that Satan himself was participating. If there had been any other way—"

"I thought I could love you, before," she said. "Now I am sure of it."

"It was not, ultimately, for love I did this," he said. "Love counseled me to let you die and go to Heaven so you would not suffer any more pain. But I had to keep you alive for your role in saving humanity from Satan twenty years hence."

"Yes," she agreed. "Now I know I will never yield to Satan. I have come to understand him too well." She paused, turning to Zane. "One other thing—"

He looked at her. The torture had not broken her spirit. Her flesh surely had not recovered, but she was radiantly beautiful in the Deathhood. "Yes?"

Luna flung her arms about him and kissed him with amazing passion. "Those twenty years until my turn comes," she said. "You and I—"

"Life and Death," he agreed.

They mounted Mortis and leaped for Purgatory.

They arrived at the Mansion of Death, and Zane conducted Luna inside. She was mortal, but somehow he had known he could take her with him this time. He could take her anywhere—alive. She was now his acknowledged Deathmaid.

They settled in the living room, relaxing, and watched the television. "The hearing petitioned by Death has been canceled," the news announcer said. "The issue has been resolved privately." The announcer smirked. "It is rumored that the horns of the Prince of Evil are still steaming."

"That's what I wanted to verify," Zane said. "You definitely will not die before your time, Luna. Now I can return to my work."

"You had better," she murmured. "Thousands of people are suffering. They really need your service."

"I will have Chronos move me back far enough so that that suffering is erased; there will be no gap for the mortals."

"Now conjecture is rife about the future status of the new Death," the announcer continued. "He has virtually turned his office upside down, making substantial waves through both Heaven and Hell. We sent queries to God and Satan, but neither deigned to comment."

Zane shook his head in rueful admiration. "Purgatory has one sharp news staff," he said. "*Too* sharp at times, I think."

"This is interesting," Luna said. "I did not realize you were such an important figure in Eternity."

"I'm not. This news is personalized. I'm sure the other Incarnations get news relating to them. We can turn it off." He got up and moved toward the set.

"However," the announcer continued, "we were able to interview several witnesses destined to testify at Death's trial-period assessment."

Zane's hand paused near the knob. "Witnesses?"

"Incarnations require special handling," the announcer explained. "Their powers are such that ordinary definitions of good and evil do not necessarily apply. In this instance, the four other Incarnations have pronounced this Death viable. They testify that he has been put to the question, unofficially, and that his answer was sufficient. They are willing to work with him for whatever portion of Eternity relates."

"Oh," Zane said. "Naturally they're satisfied. They got me into this."

"But neither they nor my father picked you for your regular job performance," Luna said. "Perhaps they did not expect you to be a good Death in that respect."

"I surely lived up to that nonexpectation," he said ruefully.

"I wonder."

"While nothing is certain until the assessment itself has been rendered," the television announcer said, "we believe it is fair to say that the recommendation of one other key witness will have overwhelming force."

"What *is* this?" Luna asked.

"Maybe one of my clients," Zane replied uncertainly.

"And here he is," the announcer said. "The key witness, the one who knows whether the burden on the soul of Death will shift toward Heaven or toward Hell as he enters his regular term in the office."

"*Who?*" Zane demanded.

The camera swung around to center the picture on—

Mortis. The Deathsteed.

"And what do you say, witness?" the announcer asked.

The horse neighed.

"This is ludicrous!" Luna exclaimed.

"I don't know," Zane said. "Mortis is no ordinary horse."

"And there you have it, folks. From the horse's mouth." The announcer paused. "Oh, the translation? Of course. Mortis says his new master has demonstrated a quality unique among Incarnations, and this alone transforms his errors to assets. He will have a positive freighting on his soul, and will go on to become one of the truly distinguished holders of the office." He paused, while Zane stood amazed. "Congratulations, Death. We of Purgatory are proud to have you with us."

"Zane!" Luna exclaimed. "You won!"

"But all I did was try to help make it easier for people to die," Zane said. "I broke several rules, and often I bungled it anyway."

Then the television camera swung upward to show the welkin, the lovely dome of the Earthly sky. In a moment it turned from day to night, and the stars scintillated in their myriads, and the images of rafts of angels formed, each angel with a shining halo. All of them applauded politely: the salutation of Heaven. It seemed to Zane that one of them looked like his mother, and others resembled some of his clients.

The camera swung down to show the fires of the nether world, with its massed demons, all of them sticking out their forked tongues. But dimly visible behind them were the condemned souls of Hell, and here and there among these were covert thumbs-up gestures.

Zane smiled, experiencing a joy as deep as Eternity. "Thanks, folks," he said, and clicked off the set. "I'll settle for the applause of one." He turned to Luna.

"Always. Forever," she agreed, kissing him.

"But I wonder what that unique quality of mine is supposed to be?" he said as an afterthought.

"It is why I love you," she said.

Zane, back in the routine of his office, saw that the mother was suffering terribly from the first shock of her grief as she cradled her dying baby in her arms. He was still working on the enormous backlog of clients that had accumulated during his strike, but he could not let the bereaved mother suffer more than she had to.

Zane stood before her. "Woman, recognize me," he said softly.

She looked up. Her mouth fell open in horror.

"Do not fear me," Zane said. "Your baby has an incurable malady, and is in pain, and shall never be free of it while he lives. It is best that he be released from the burden of life."

Her mouth worked in protest. "You—you wouldn't say that if one you loved had to go!"

"Yes, I would," he said sincerely. "I sent my own mother to Eternity, to end her suffering. I understand your grief and know it becomes you. But your child is the innocent victim of a wrongful act—" He did not repeat what she already knew, that the child had been conceived by incestuous rape and born syphilitic. "—and it is better for him and for you that he never face the horrors of such a life."

Her haunted eyes gazed up at him, beginning to see Death as more friend than nemesis. "Is—is it really best?"

"Samuel Taylor Coleridge said it best," Death replied gently, extending his hand for the suffering baby's soul. *"Ere sin could blight or sorrow fade, Death came with friendly care; The opening bud to Heaven conveyed, And bade it blossom there."*

As he spoke, he drew the tiny soul out. He knew even before he checked it that this one *would* go to Heaven, for now he had discretion in such cases.

"You're not the way I thought you would be," the woman said, recovering some stability now that the issue had been decided. "You have—" She faltered, seeking the appropriate word. "Compassion."

Compassion. Suddenly it fell into place. This was the quality Zane brought to the office of Death that the office had lacked before. It made him feel good to realize that the delays he had indulged in and the rules he had broken—that such acts could be construed positively instead of negatively. He *cared* about his clients, strove for what was best for them within the dreadful parameters of his office, and was no longer ashamed to admit it.

He knew he had been installed in this office for reasons not relating to merit. But he had conquered his limitations and knew that he would perform with reasonable merit henceforth.

"Death came with friendly care..." he repeated as he set his watch for the next client. He liked the thought.

AUTHOR'S NOTE

Every novel is an adventure, for the author as well as the reader, but some are more so than others. The last extended Author's Note I did was for my science fiction novel *Viscous Circle*; those readers who encountered that and didn't like it should avoid this one, because it is more of the same. I believe that a.work of fiction should stand pretty much by itself and not require any external explanation; certainly *On a Pale Horse* can survive without this one.

Coincidentally—if one believes in coincidence—my Author's Copies of *Viscous Circle* arrived as I was typing this Author's Note. I glanced at that prior Note and realized it signaled the change in my outlook that has resulted, among other things, in *On a Pale Horse*. I had suffered an illness in 1980 that disrupted my schedule, put me in the hospital, and forcibly reminded me of my own mortality. In consequence, I planned to shift my efforts from the kind of science fiction I had been doing to fantasy, horror, World War II fiction, and maybe some general mainstream writing, exploring and broadening my parameters while it was convenient to do so. That is, while I still had my health and vigor and imagination. I wanted to discover where I could achieve more meaning in writing.

So how did that effort work out? Well, I did try—but the first thing I discovered was that publishers were not interested in nonfantastic-genre Anthony efforts. They showed the same disinterest that they had shown in my early science-fantasy writing—and it took me eight years to break into print. It seems it may take me a similar period to break into another genre. I have kept plugging away, meanwhile filling in with light fantasy, because that is easy and fun and the readers like it and it makes a lot of money; if I have to wait those extra years for publishers to appreciate my merit, I might as well wait in comfort. Thus I completed almost half a million words of fantasy in 1981, and that seems to be expanding my reputation in that subgenre. I will continue trying the other genres, for I remain an ornery cuss, and I think in time I will break through and prove that all those uninterested editors were wrong, just as I did before. I have, as may be apparent, not much respect for editors as a class.

But impediments, whether editorial or otherwise, can lead to rewarding innovation. As I wrestled with the problem of putting meaningful writing into print, I discovered that it was possible for me to do much of the social commentary I had in mind—within the SF/fantasy genre itself. Instead of stepping outside the genre to protest such things as world hunger and nuclear folly, I realized I could stretch the genre boundaries to cover the territory. Since I already have markets and readers for my fantastic-genre writing, the editors can't stop me. This facilitates my ambition enormously. *On a Pale Horse*, for example, is on one level a fun-fantasy with a unique main character, and I hope most readers enjoy it on that level. Fiction should always entertain! But on another level it is a satiric look at contemporary society, with some savagely pointed criticism. It is also a serious exploration of man's relation to death. Man is the one creature on Earth who knows he will die, and that is an appalling intellectual burden.

I need to clarify how I do my writing, as I am not quite like other writers, professionally or personally. Of course, *no* writer is quite like any other; each thinks himself unique in some typical fashion. I live in the backwoods of central Florida and have a twelve by twenty-four foot study in our horse pasture. Yes, I am surrounded by horse manure! I now have electricity there—for three years I did not—so I can type at night if I want to, but have no heating. In summer I use a fan to cool me, for we do hit 100° F often enough, and in winter I bundle up with voluminous clothing as if for a hike through a snowstorm. Our area seldom gets below freezing in the daytime, but even 40° to 50° becomes bone-chilling when one is sitting at a typewriter for hours at a time. Even with sweater, jacket, scarf, and heavy cap, I slowly congeal, because I must expose my hands to type. Back when I typed two-finger, it was possible to do it with gloves on, but now I type touch and must bare my flesh.

So I avoid winter typing when possible, arranging my schedule to write the first draft in pencil on my clipboard at the house, where we have a fine wood stove that puts out so much heat that my darling daughters complain. Between literary thoughts, I feed more chunks of my hard-sawed-and-split wood to the monster, maintaining my primitive comfort.

Don't get me wrong; I live here because I love the wilderness and the rustic independence of it, and I distrust complex machines. The wood stove is not only cheap to operate, it's fun. It also heats all our water in winter, via a copper coil in the stovepipe. (In summer the solar system does the job.) Then when the land warms, in spring, I hie me back to my study to type the second draft, and then the submission draft. Each novel is done three times, ironing out the bugs. But the four months of inclement weather are too long for a single novel; I need only two months for the first draft, and sometimes less, depending on the nature of the project. So I try to schedule two novels in pencil in the winter, then type both later.

The winter of 1981-82, my two novels were one fantasy and one science fiction, each the initial volume of what I hoped would be an ambitious, hard-hitting, social-commentary, five-novel series. The science fiction series was *Bio of a Space Tyrant*, superficially a space opera, covertly a serious political commentary, to be published elsewhere. The fantasy series was *Incarnations of Immortality*, that title given with a nod of appreciation toward William Wordsworth's *Ode: Intimations of Immortality From Recollections of Early Childhood*. This present novel, with Death as its protagonist, is the first of that series.

I understand some writers just start writing and watch almost with surprise what develops; I plan considerably farther ahead. I know how a novel will end before I begin to write it—and before I write it, these days, I sell it. I realize that sounds backward, but it's true. I make a summary, and my New York literary agent shows it around, and if a publisher offers a contract for it, then I go ahead and write the novel. I have any number of summaries that no editor wanted, so those novels have never been written. Sometimes I really want to write one, but have to let it go. You might say that some of my best novels of the past have never been written. In the early days of my career I wrote my novels first and marketed them second, and naturally the editors gleefully bounced them. At one point I had built up a backlog of eight complete unsold novels. That's not the best way for a writer to make a living. When I caught on and changed my system to escape that bind, my income tripled, and then began a sharper rise—because suddenly I was selling everything I wrote. Rather, I was writing everything I sold.

As it happens, both these series, *Bio* and *Incarnations*, relate strongly to death, a subject with which I am morbidly fascinated. I wish I were not; this constant awareness of death makes it impossible for me to go blithely about my life in simple contentment. This has been so since my closest cousin died, when I was a teenager. He is represented in this novel as Tad: the one who had everything to live for, while I did not. It seemed to me that Death had somehow taken the wrong one of us. Now I am highly aware that my time on Earth is limited, and I do not believe in any afterlife. It follows that anything I want to do, I must do in this session, as it were. Perhaps this explains in part the determination with which I write novels, including this one. It is my way of saying whatever I have to say while I have the opportunity, hoping others will profit thereby.

On A Pale Horse

I think few writers have tried, as I have here, to present Death in a sympathetic manner. Therefore it was chancy to market *On a Pale Horse*, for many publishers seem to be uninterested in innovation. If Death could not make it into print, how could there be any hope for the following notions that were percolating through my mind? For the rest of this series, as it finally shaped up, concerned other unusual protagonists: Time, *Bearing an Hourglass*; Fate, *With a Tangled Skein*; War, *Wielding a Red Sword*; and Nature, *Being a Green Mother*. All of it started with Death, and Death-in-print was not nearly so certain as death in the real world. This concept was obviously fantastic, corresponding to the established scheme of the Afterlife only very loosely; perhaps it would offend some readers. I, as an ornery writer, don't much care if I offend a reader or two, but publishers have hypersensitive nerves about popular reaction, and very little courage of conviction. My more challenging notions have had trouble with publishers before. Those of you who think of me as a light-entertainment writer have not seen that portion of my writing that never made it into print.

So I played it safe. I sent a private, informal query to my fantasy editor, Lester del Rey of Del Rey Books, describing my notion and asking whether he might be interested in seeing a more formal presentation at a later date. A writer can do this when he knows an editor well enough. I have a track record at Del Rey; they know what my writing is like, so can tell from even a brief description whether a particular project of mine would be to their taste. If Mr. del Rey didn't like the notion, or did not care to gamble his company's money on it, he would tell me privately, and that would spare the two of us and my agent the embarrassment and inconvenience of a formal rejection.

Now let me switch to another subject, in the tantalizing manner of the storyteller I am. I have gotten interested in colored stones of the precious variety. Most people know of diamonds, rubies, emeralds, and sapphires, and I have acquired samples of these. No, I didn't spend ten thousand dollars for a one-carat diamond two years ago and watch its value shrink in half. Lack of money served in lieu of wisdom, there. Instead, I bought rough diamonds from a wholesale dealer at ten dollars a carat. They look like gravel; they don't sparkle prettily from cut facets. But they *are* diamonds, so I can lay claim to owning diamonds. I shopped similarly for bargains in other stones. There are many pretty ones, comparatively inexpensive, ranging from a hundred dollars or more per carat down to eight cents a carat for faceted smoky quartz in quantity. Know something? In a dim light, you could have trouble distinguishing quartz from diamond, and quartz will scratch window glass.

There are also topaz, aquamarine, garnet, tourmaline, zircon, amethyst, scapolite, andalusite, and others, each with its own special qualities. It is possible to develop an interesting collection of such gems for a tiny fraction of the price of the smallest cut diamond, and that collection may be a more secure investment than that diamond. Certainly this has been the case recently; the value of most colored stones has risen, in some cases dramatically, while diamonds have declined.

But there are pitfalls. People who aren't expert in gemstones can get rapidly fleeced, unless they have a reliable source of supply. I had such a source in the large, wholesale House of Onyx, but was lured by an ad in the local newspaper for a huge star sapphire on sale privately. I went to see it, and it was an ugly stone—maybe it would be kinder to say the stone had character—with a fantastic floating star. It had come from North Carolina, where some sapphire mining is done. In sunlight, that star seemed to sit an eighth of an inch above the surface of the stone, and it shifted about on its rays like a spider as the stone moved, almost like magic. I'm a sucker for magic, considering that I don't believe in it, so I bought the stone.

Then, of course, I wondered whether I had been smart. I had paid over ten dollars a carat for the sapphire, which was a lot of money for a stone that size—one hundred-fourteen carats. Good sapphire is worth a lot more—but was this one a bargain? Was it even true sapphire? Now that it was too late, I had to know. So I phoned Fred Rowe, owner of the House of Onyx—you can do that if you know him well enough—and he very nicely agreed to appraise the stone for me. He is not in the business of appraising other people's stones, of course; he did it as a private favor, much as Lester del Rey did me the favor of appraising my novel notion privately. I dare say there are two busier men in the world, but I really could not name any offhand. Sometimes the busiest are also the most generous.

On September 8, 1981, I received two important items in the mail—one from Mr. Rowe, the other from Mr. del Rey. Mr. Rowe was returning my stone with his appraisal: it was corundum (sapphire and ruby are both corundum), but of a cheap grade imported from India for fifty cents a carat and sold to gullible tourists in places like North Carolina as local stones for five to ten dollars per carat. He himself had sold a number of five-thousand-carat parcels of this type of stone to clients in North Carolina at the fifty-cent price. In short, this was a junkstone. I had been bilked. Not, I believe, by the person who sold it to me; he honestly believed in the value of the stone, and I'm sure many other people, with similar belief have similar stones. But for what it's worth, I recommend that people be wary of bargains in gems from North Carolina.

Mr. del Rey's letter was more positive. Yes, he liked the notion of *On a Pale Horse*. No, I did not need to submit a formal presentation through my agent at a later date. He was prepared to offer my agent a contract on it now. He did not name a figure, but I knew from experience that this novel would earn me at least ten times what I had lost on the sapphire.

That was some mail! Fate had neatly juxtaposed these events. Mr. Rowe and Mr. del Rey had, figuratively, met in my mailbox. (Mr. Rowe, meet Mr. del Rey; Lester, meet Fred. So nice to have you both here. Now let's get out of this hot mailbox!) Who was I to argue with Fate? Thus it was that my unfortunate star sapphire became a part of this novel. The two just seemed fated to merge.

There was more to it than that. I am ornery in various ways, and one of them is that I don't like to make mistakes, but mistakes stalk me like sendings from Hell. So I try to turn every experience, good or bad, to my profit, whether monetary or intellectual. I had blundered in buying the stone, but if I used that experience in the novel, that might redeem it somewhat. In fact, by this device I could make this stone unique. It might not be worth much as a junk-grade star sapphire, but as the stone that suckered Piers Anthony—um, let's rephrase that. As the stone that launched a new man into the dread office of Death, it—well, it just might eventually be worth what I paid for it. Thus, perhaps, it could no longer be considered a blunder. Of course, this mundane stone lacks the literal magic of the one in the novel, and I dare say any potential purchaser would in due course catch on to that. But I don't want to sell it anyway. I merely want to erase a mistake. Just think: If this ploy is successful, no one will ever know about my blunder in buying that stone...

I also put my watch into the novel, as the Deathwatch. I bought it about the same time. Mine is identical to the fictive watch, except that mine times forward, not backward, and it lacks much of the magic power. I have had a long history of trying watches, from simple ten-dollar windups to sophisticated solar chronographs, and all had one thing in common: they ceased working after a year or so. The folk who set a one-year limit on the warranty know what they're doing. Thus I finally blew three hundred and twenty-five dollars on this Heuer heavy-duty mechanical timepiece, watertight and self-winding and unpretty. It weighs a full quarter pound, and if *it* conks out after one year, I will be most distressed. Time will tell.

I said at the outset that each novel is an adventure. This one has been more than I bargained on. My first drafts are more than fiction; they are running records of my ongoing life. Problems, interruptions, and stray thoughts (I'm always thinking) are included in the text, set off by brackets [like this]. I don't know of any other writer who works this way—but then I don't know of any other writer who never suffers the dread malady known as writer's block, though it is barely possible some exist. I never block, because my text incorporates the blockages and converts them to text. When I complete the pencil draft, I review it and index my bracket notes, since they may contain the summaries of several additional novels that occurred to me along the way. A good notion for a novel is far too precious to waste; it must be caught the moment it flashes into mental view, or it will escape to the brain of some other writer who really doesn't deserve it. For example, *On a Pale Horse* was worked out in brackets in the text of the prior fantasy novel, *Night Mare*. My creative notions don't have to wait their turn; they are always welcome.

This novel concerns death, as most readers will have grasped by this time. I don't believe in the supernatural, yet I experience eerie coincidences. The worst of these are yet to come in this Note. When I started part-time work on this novel (because I was then typing *Night Mare*—I work on a kind of assembly line in summer, working on different novels in pencil and typing stages simultaneously) in September, two supposedly unrelated things developed.

One was a series of excellent three-mile runs. I have adult-onset diabetes, a mild case, and I treat this by staying away from free sugar and by exercising vigorously, including my thrice-weekly cross-country runs. When I do well, I break twenty-two minutes for the distance, then jog and walk another half mile, warming down, so as not to stress my system unduly by abrupt changes. Well, in September I was finishing a decent but not great run when the weekly garbage truck came up behind me in the last half mile. That truck cuts through the forest to reach another section of our wilderness, and our paths happened to coincide here. So I speeded up to get out of its way, without stopping my run. It's amazing what a stimulus it is to have a truckful of garbage pursue you up a hill! Suddenly I was running a record finish, and because of this, it became one of those rare sub-twenty-two minute runs, by just two seconds. Well, good enough; and next time I kept a slightly faster pace and broke twenty-two again. And a third time I did it a little faster yet. Unexpectedly, I had a string going. I had never put together more than three of these in a row before; could I do it on this Garbage series? Yes! I did the fourth, fifth, and sixth, and finally, with great effort on a drizzly day, the tenth. What a series! Now I could relax. But the series continued, until it carried me through the entire month of October, despite problems of scheduling the runs. I was amazed and gratified.

The other thing was negative. My wife's father had been suffering some low-grade malady during the summer, but now it got serious.

[Interruption at this point to go pick up a horse's balky foot for my daughter. We check and clean out the feet before riding, to be sure there is no stone or stick wedged that could cause lameness, but the horse doesn't always cooperate. I have more power than my daughter has; that foot came up for me. Had this interruption occurred earlier, I would have thought to have my protagonist check the feet of his gallant

Deathsteed. Now, in the Author's Note, it is too late. Well, I'll catch it in another novel. This has been a sample bracket note, a live performance.]

My wife's father had to be hospitalized, put on dialysis for kidney failure, and have abdominal surgery. He was still bleeding internally, so they set him up for corrective surgery—but were not sure he could survive another operation so soon. The chances seemed to be fifty-fifty; if the bleeding didn't kill him, the surgery might. His wife, my wife's mother, was distraught. Naturally my wife went down to Tampa to help out, so she was away from our home about half the month of October. That was why I had a scheduling problem for my runs, because I don't like to do them when there is no one to backstop me at home. There are hunters out there in the forest who don't necessarily see straight enough to tell man from deer, and there are rattlesnakes and such, and rampaging garbage trucks; and, of course, I'm laboring so hard that I could trip over an unseen root and take a fall and pull a muscle and be in trouble, and I want someone to call the ambulance if necessary. (I believe I mentioned my morbid streak.) But we managed; my two daughters, then aged fourteen and eleven, helped run the household and feed the animals when they (the girls) weren't in school. Penny, the elder [whom we just met in a bracket], cooked supper, while I washed the dishes. And my father-in-law tided through.

Things eased up in November and December, as I worked full-time on the first draft of this novel—and my series of twenty-two minute runs continued. My father-in-law made it home for Thanksgiving, though ravaged by what had turned out to be Wegener's Syndrome, a rare and normally fatal malady before modern medicine changed the odds. We live, in some respects, in fortunate times.

I finished my first draft of *Pale* and shifted to the first volume of *Bio* for a couple of months. My good runs continued—forty, fifty, sixty in the series. In fact, they speeded up to a subseries of 21:30-minute efforts, and then to a sub-subseries of sub-twenty-one-minute runs. I was breaking the seven-minute mile! To my amazement, I managed to put together ten of these superfast-for-me runs in a row, before the rising heat of a Florida spring put an end to that in March. But I was still on my twenty-two minute series: seventy runs, eighty . . . when would it end?

My mother-in-law, perhaps worn out by the terrible siege of her husband's illness, got sick herself and went to the hospital. But it was more than that. She had cancer of the pancreas. We didn't know much about this disease and thought she would have six months or a year to live. But after only six weeks, as I was typing the second draft of *Pale* in late March, she died.

This is a novel of death, as I have said. The serious illness and sudden death, occurring while I was immersed in fictional death—this disturbed me deeply. I had a brutal refresher course in what death feels like to the survivors.

There was nothing to do but go on—with novel, with running, with life. But there was now a deeper quality of gloom about it. Death is not funny. It may be the normal end of life, but I still don't like it. No, not at all!

My run series hung on, despite my depressed spirits and outdoor temperatures in the mid-80s. I made runs number eighty-one, eighty-two, eighty-three . . . maybe I could actually make it all the way to one hundred! I reject all superstition vehemently, yet I found myself counting those runs as if they were years of my life. It seemed I had now been promised at least eighty-three years; how many more? Nonsense, of course; still . . .

As April 1982 came, I was near the end of my second-draft typing and saw that the novel was going to be short: about eighty thousand words instead of the ninety thousand or so expected. There is normally a ten or fifteen percent expansion in the submission draft, because of polishing, blank space at the end of chapters, and the addition of notes that have been crammed into the margins of second-draft material. I needed enough second-draft wordage so that that expansion would put the final draft comfortably in the hundred-thousand word range I had contracted for. Normally I run overlength and have to tighten up a bit, but this time my bracket notes had taken up more space, throwing off my estimate.

Writers pay a lot of attention to wordage, because some publishers seem to care more about length than about quality and will automatically reject novels that don't fit their narrow standards of length—or will chop out extra wordage to make a novel fit. Not so long before, I had had to chop out twenty thousand words from my novel *Mute*, damaging it; I share the average writer's aversion to such mutilation, especially since it makes the finished product seem choppy or disorganized when it wasn't that way originally, and can damage his reputation for intelligibility and thus perhaps harm his career. Editor Lester del Rey has never done that to me, and so my fantasy has prospered—but I don't push my luck.

In this case, there was material I had wanted to include, but had bypassed because of the difficulty of organizing a novel with a high emotional commitment. Fortunately, the notes were right there in my brackets. Some key cases of death—I could break Chapter 6 into two parts and fit these scenes in the first part, and this would bring the number of chapters to thirteen—exactly right for a novel about death. So while I typed the second draft, I resumed work on the first draft, doing those scenes. Oh, yes, writers do work this way; the smooth, finished product you readers see is likely to be the result of considerable and scrambled effort.

On A Pale Horse

Good news came in on the early sales of my science/fantasy novel *Blue Adept*, lightening my mood; the paperback edition had jumped to number three on the B. Dalton Bookseller list, and to number five on the Waldenbooks list. This is rarefied territory for light fantasy, and the best performance of any of my novels so far. It meant *Blue* was a mainstream bestseller, though it didn't quite make *The New York Times* list. A writer lives for such news!

The phone company sent a man out for no reason we could see, and he switched the lines, so all our calls came to our neighbor and vice versa. My New York agent tried to phone me three times about ongoing negotiations on the sale of *Bio of a Space Tyrant*, my biggest contract so far, and each time wound up talking to the neighbor's boy. Par for the course. Satan only knows what kind of contract I might have wound up with, had I not caught on and hastily phoned my agent back. Maybe Satan sent the phone man out! Of such minor elements is a writer's life fashioned.

I did my eighty-fourth sub-twenty-two-minute run on Monday. Ha— I would live to age eighty-four! On Tuesday, April 6, at 1 P.M., I did my alternate-day exercise, the Japanese push-ups. I can't describe them; they are done in martial arts classes for warm-up, and they are more complicated than regular push-ups. They have put new sheaths of muscle on my arms and chest, so that I no longer look quite as thin as I am. Over the years I had built up to seventy-five push-ups within a five-minute span; I time them on my Deathwatch. Without the time limit, I have done one hundred—but those final ones become hellishly uncomfortable, so I eased back. Why do I do push-ups? Well, running is good for every part of the body except the arms, so I do pull-ups and push-ups to shore up that weakness.

When I was less than half my present age, as a draftee in the U.S. Army in 1957, I was poor at regular push-ups. When I was unable to do ten in one session, the corporal told me to go back to the barracks and find a *man* to replace me. Only in the Army is manhood defined by push-ups, which is part of what's wrong with that institution; nevertheless, that corporal would not so address me today.

I hate push-ups, but I like the body they give me, so I grind my teeth and do them. On this day I felt indifferent, physically; to my surprise, the push-ups were exceedingly strong. In fact, I broke my speed record, doing my seventy-five in four minutes and seven seconds on the stopwatch. Terrific! I unkinked my digits—these push-ups are done on the tips of ten fingers, which is part of why they get uncomfortable—and settled down for lunch. Then the mail came, and I was reading it at 2 P.M. when I felt a pain in my left side. Indigestion? Well, that would pass.

It didn't pass. It got worse. I struggled with it for an hour, finding no relief vertically or horizontally, and retched into the sink a couple of times before I asked my wife to call for help. Soon she drove me in to see the doctor. Yes, it was the same doctor who had wrestled with my Cat-Scratch Disease two years before, as noted in my prior Author's Note. By this time I had the cold sweats and my limbs were jerking, sometimes violently. The ride was interminable; every half hour or so I rechecked my watch and discovered it had only moved along five minutes. "You know," I gasped, "I fear death, but if I knew the rest of my life would be like this, I would welcome death!" I meant it. Pain provides a special perspective, and that perspective is reflected in the novel.

People tried not to stare at me in the doctor's waiting room as I sat there, hunched over to my left, panting violently; that was the only way I could keep the pain bearable. My hair was wild, and I was in T-shirt, shorts, and sandals, with dirty feet, the way I normally am when writing at home. I didn't have a regular appointment, of course, but the doctor arranged to see me soon, and I don't think any other patients objected. I was wheeled into an office. I was beginning to feel faint, and motion only made things worse. *Everything* made things worse! But in due course we had an opinion. There was a trace of blood in my urine, and the symptoms indicated a colic of the kidney, probably caused by a kidney stone.

I wound up in the hospital with a shot of Demerol, which I understand is synthetic morphine: a powerful painkiller. It didn't kill *this* pain, but it zonked out much of my brain, and that helped. My wife tells me I was saying strange things, such as something about a fly on the window and steps on a cabinet; I remember none of it. If I had been able to write, I probably would have made bracket notes, and today would know exactly what was on my mind then. A fly? Do you suppose the Lord of Flies could have—? I do remember waking up long enough to inquire, "Am I making sense?" And my wife, in the manner of good wives with difficult husbands like me, assured me that I was. I faded in and out; the pain did not depart, but at least I was unconscious some of the time. Six hours after it began, the agony began to ease, and in another hour it was gone. I can't honestly say it was the worst pain I have suffered, though our book of medical symptoms says that kidney stones can indeed be among the worst agonies to afflict man. I think it hurts more when I stub a toe hard. But the toe hurts only a minute; this was six hours. The remorseless continuation of pain is, candidly, something else. I suspect even a mild pain could become unbearable if continued long enough; I think that's part of the secret of the Chinese water torture.

Next day they gave me a complex X-ray series, a pyelogram, with dye in my blood to show the course of the various conduits. Yes, my left ureter—that's the tube between the kidney and the bladder—was distended, as if blocked by a kidney stone. Probably my exceptionally vigorous push-ups had dislodged the stone and sent it on its painful way. It had taken an hour to encounter a constriction, and then—wow! Nothing much; it was really only a grain, like a piece of sand, and with luck it would clear on its own. Meanwhile, the urine was getting by, so I was okay. All I had to do was strain my urine through a meshed funnel, to catch the stone when it came out so they could analyze it.

I was glad to cooperate. If this was a little stone, I didn't want to encounter a big one! But they had hooked me up to an IV bottle—I suspect this is standard hospital policy to make sure the patient doesn't walk out without paying the bill—and the needle was taped to my left arm. To go to the bathroom, I had to trundle the bottle-stand along with me. To forget would be a bloody mess as the needle ripped out of my vein. I understand it happens to absent-minded patients. And they had me in one of those hospital gowns—you know, the type that falls open at any pretext to bare your posterior. Everybody in the hospital wants to get at your posterior! Have you ever tried to, as they phrase it, void through a funnel into a plastic container, with a tube connected to your arm that tends to drape itself between you and what you're doing? And the hospital nightie falling off your front? Naturally they are worn backward, and no one had tied the apron strings on mine. If I lifted my arm too high, trying to get things out of my way, the blood backed into the IV tubing, making another mess. I discovered that by the time I got everything ready to go—Nature had changed her mind. I think it is called "bashful kidney."

There were other little niceties of hospital life. One night I had a headache. I asked the nurse for a pill—but she informed me the only medication listed on my chart was Demerol. Synthetic morphine for a headache? This was like shooting a sparrow with a cannon! So I had to struggle along with the headache until the doctor came to apply some common sense. I had the usual hassle with the food, too. I am a vegetarian and diabetic, so I stay off all meat products and sugars, and I don't drink coffee or tea. Naturally my lunch consisted of coffee with two packs of sugar, gelatin (which is made of protein from the bones of cows, mixed with sugar), sickly sweet fruit, and a piece of cake with horrendously thick sugar icing. Fortunately, there was also corn, beans, and mashed potato, so I didn't starve; and my wife visited and fetched me some water—naturally my pitcher hadn't been filled—so I survived. Not that I really needed to eat, with the IV dripping sugar water into my vein.

When I finished, I wanted to go to the bathroom, but discovered that the bedside table unit that overhung the bed would actually tip over rather than swing out of the way. I think if more doctors got sick and had to wrestle with these little matters, some improvements would be made. I explained gently about the food to a nurse, and that brought the dietician, who remembered me from two years before, and we finally got the matter of no-meat, no-sugar, no-coffee straight—just about the time I was to be released from the hospital.

Then there was the Candy-Striper. These are teenaged girls who bring fresh water and juice and such to patients, thereby gaining experience in the operation of a hospital. They wear cute pink-and-white-striped uniforms with sweet little matching caps. This one showed up about 4 P.M. my second day. She had golden hair flowing to her bottom. She not only filled my water pitcher, she brought in her family and they sat around my room and ate pizza and chatted. Then she made me brush out her hair and braid it, so she could go on duty in decent order. She seemed to take such attention for granted.

Oh—perhaps I neglected to mention that this particular Candy-Striper was Penny Jacob—my mundane daughter. Penny-Candy-Striper, Heaven-Cent. This time she had me right where she wanted me. I understand some fathers don't pay enough attention to their children; obviously they don't have children like mine.

The consulting urologist prescribed a gallon of urine a day. Uh, no, not to drink; I merely had to imbibe enough fluid to generate a full gallon of void each day. Have you any idea how much drinking that entails? The purpose is to dilute the urine so that no additional stones would form. It seems that kidney stones are the province of middle-aged men and that I live in a kidney-stone region; there is much calcium in our water (though they aren't sure that's the cause) and the local heat causes body dehydration, concentrating the urine, so that stones form. So I must, for the rest of my life, be constantly drinking water and passing it through. I can no longer sleep the night in one haul; I have to get up once or twice to you-know. But if that's what it takes to keep the stones away, so must it be.

The first night home, I got up at 2:30 A.M., did my business with the funnel and container—and then could not get back to sleep. I didn't want to turn on the light to read, lest that disturb my wife, who had had problems enough, with her father so ill recently, then losing her mother, then having to deal with my illness. Problems had been striking like explosive shells around us, and that gets wearing. So I dressed and went off to my study in the pasture to type some more on *Pale Horse*, which novel had been interrupted by my hospitalization. Naturally our horses thought it was feeding time, and Blue knocked on my door—with her hoof. I went out and explained that it was 3 A.M. and that feeding time wasn't for three hours yet, but she resumed banging the moment I went back inside. I was afraid she would break down the door, so finally I went out with the broom and swatted her on the rear. That moved her off—but when dawn broke, she would not speak to me, and I felt like a heel. Such is life-after-kidney-stone.

I had not let the time in the hospital go to waste. I continued reading books, including *Dream Makers*, edited by Charles Platt, which tells what other genre writers are like. They are all oddballs, almost as strange as I am! I will be in the companion volume, however, so I'd better not criticize. I also had my clipboard along. Remember, I was reworking Chapter 6 and adding scenes. So while I was there I wrote the scene about the atheist—whose attitude is basically mine, with the fundamental difference that I do believe in doing good in this life and try very hard to benefit the universe, whether by being kind to a wild animal or by writing a novel like this one. And yes, I also wrote the scene about the old woman in the hospital. I could hardly have had a better environment for that one. But if the hospital staff had caught on, I might have had trouble getting out of there. As it turned out, there was one nurse who was a fan of mine, but she did not realize who I was— remember, I use a pseudonym—until too late to catch me. However, my daughter the Candy-Striper arranged to have that nurse visit me at home a month later, so all was not lost.

I settled back into my routine. My run series was broken at eighty-four, and I was awash in fluid, but life went on. The neighbors (the ones with the contract-negotiating boy) had to take off suddenly because a parent had a serious complication of the pancreas; we had learned the hard way about that sort of thing and knew it was terminal. Death is ever with us. While they were away, their prize mare, Navahjo, went into labor, and there wasn't anybody around who knew what to do. She was having trouble; the foal was hung up with one foot protruding for the better part of an hour, and we feared a stillbirth. But another neighbor came, took hold and pulled, and got it out: live birth of a colt. What a relief! The little horse was healthy and soon was frisking about; I suggested mischievously that they name him Colt 45, or maybe Colt 46. Thus, with our neighbors, life was originating even as it was ending. This, too, is as Nature decrees.

My funnel caught no stone in a month, so I had a follow-up pyelogram. I had to drink a magic potion concocted from senna fruit to clear my bowel. It was awful stuff, as these brews are, but I gulped it down. It had no effect. Then about eight hours later, in the middle of the night—FWOOM! Mount St. Helens!

I had been through the pyelogram procedure before, but this time the details differed. They put me in a hospital gown with three armholes; I wondered whether triple-armed alien creatures patronized these facilities. They injected the dye into my arm—and suddenly I felt sick and dizzy and generally spaced out, and then sneezed several times. They said it was normal, though none of this had happened the last time. In between the spaced X-ray shots, I lay on my back and read a science fiction novel I planned to review; no sense letting blank time go to waste.

We took the pictures directly to the urologist. There was no sign of the kidney stone; apparently it had cleared at the outset, and we hadn't caught it. Too bad; it would have helped to know what kind it had been. But this latest X-ray showed a spot inside the bladder. Oh-oh—could that be a tumor? The doctor decided he'd better have a direct look. So we made an appointment for a cystoscopy, four days later.

It was a nervous wait. With everything else that had been happening during this novel, it could be just my luck to discover—but maybe it was nothing. Old scar tissue, maybe. I know my readers like stories with definite conclusions, so I held up my typing of the last of this Note for two days to await the dread verdict.

That cystoscopy was sort of scary to approach. There I sat in the doctor's office, a yard-square paper napkin draped around my quivering naked loins, eying the torture instruments laid out for the procedure: a black box with an electric connection, an IV bottle with transparent fluid, sinister gray tubes, and two immense nine-inch-long monster metal needles. Ouch! They gave me a good five minutes to examine that array before the doctor arrived. I know psychological torture when I experience it!

The doctor squirted an anesthetic solution up the conduit; it felt like voiding backward. Then he inserted the larger-diameter needle, sliding it up the urethra to the bladder. Unfortunately, that particular channel has a natural curve in it. What do you do when you have a straight instrument and a curved channel? I found out! You straighten the channel. WRENCH! and my curve was straight. No, it didn't really hurt, but it was uncomfortable, physically and psychologically.

Then the doctor slid the lesser needle into the larger one, sending in a mirror and a light bulb or whatever so he could see through the tube and look about inside. The IV bottle filled the bladder with clear fluid; I dare say that improved internal visibility. I could picture that light flashing around all the crevices, spying out excrescences, kidney stones, pebbles and boulders, and whatever other garbage there might be in there. Finally he closed up shop and drew out the instruments, letting my anatomy try to recover its curvature.

The verdict? Nothing. There was nothing in there. I was clean. No kidney stone, no tumor, no garbage. Apparently the X-ray blob had been false. Another sending of Satan. A thumbprint, my daughter suggested. I'll settle for that.

Oh, yes—I was a little sore following the cystoscopy and voided a few drops of blood. But nothing bad, and it was worth it. My kidney-stone incident was over.

This, then, is the story of the manner in which my consciousness of death has been heightened, in and out of this novel. Has it been worth it? I hope so. It seems to me that all living species need to survive, so nature provides them with instincts of pain and self-preservation that compel them to live. They also need to die, to make way for progress; otherwise the world would still be full of dinosaurs. (There's a new theory about those dinosaurs: at certain temperatures, some reptiles produce offspring that are all male or all female. Suppose the climate changed enough to throw all the big reptiles into one sex?) But circumstance takes care of termination, so it isn't necessary that creatures *like* dying. When something is truly voluntary, such as procreation, Nature makes sure it is pleasurable — for the male. Cynically, she does not require pleasure for the female; that is optional. With many species, rape seems to be impossible; not so for ours. Nature really is a green mother.

So we are left hating and fearing our inevitable death, though objectively we know this is pointless. Possibly, as my protagonist suggests, if we had a better appreciation of the larger picture, of the place death plays in life, we would suffer less. This novel is an attempt to encourage such understanding. If I succeed in this one thing, my own life may have justified itself.

So now I try to appreciate the mixed splendor that life is while it is mine. I watch my daughter with her horse and can not imagine a prettier sight. I also watch Blue galloping at dusk by herself, mane and tail flaring, playing Nightmare. I say hello to the wild gray bunny that comes out at dusk to feed on the grain spilled by the horses; sometimes I can get within six feet. I call it Nicky (ie), because of a nick in his/her left ear. I see the rare pileated woodpecker working on our deadwood; that's the largest woodpecker in our nation, and that species will be preserved as long as we have deadwood. I see the wild deer, and the big box turtles, and hope for a glimpse of an armadillo. I see the myriad spider webs, fogged by morning dew. The flowering cactus, like lovely yellow roses. And the confounded red-bellied woodpecker that sneaks into our coop to peck neat holes in the eggs; now we have to race the little critter to the eggs.

There are other pleasures. I watch the sales figures for my novels, doing better and better. I like competing, however briefly, with the mainstream blockbusters for space on the bestseller lists. I've been answering fan mail at a rate as high as one per day; it does take time, and I am excruciatingly jealous of my time, but I do value these contacts with those who are moved by my work. I know that, all things considered, my life is a happy one, and it is better that I dwell on that than on the prospect of eventual death. Is this a sufficient philosophy for existence? I don't know. I feel a certain guilt because I am unable to solve all the problems of the world, but I hope that I am doing my little bit to alleviate one of them.

I think my most significant personal revelation is that life changes hour by hour and minute by minute, like the constant flowing of a river. I am not quite the same person today that I was yesterday; small aspects of me have changed, physically and mentally. I will change a little more by tomorrow, and a great deal more in the course of future years.

To try to hang on to one particular section of life, such as the one I am experiencing at this moment, is foolish; it can't be done, and if it could be done, it would not be worthwhile. Change is much of the essence of life. Death is the final change. We can not hold on even to a day; how, then, can we capture life itself? Perhaps our whole awareness of individuality, of self, is an illusion. If so, it is better not to grasp unduly at that illusion, but rather to live our lives in such a manner that when we must at last lay them down, we will not be ashamed. Life has meaning only if we live for meaning.

Piers Anthony Dillingham Jacob
May 17, 1982

ABOUT THE AUTHOR

Piers Anthony was born in August, 1934, in England, and became an American citizen while serving in the U.S. Army in 1958. He lives with his wife, Carol, and their daughters Penny and Cheryl in Florida. He sold his first story, after eight years of trying, in 1962; his first novel, *Chthon*, was published in 1967. Through 1983 he has had forty-five books published, and translations have appeared in seven languages. Currently he writes three novels a year. In one year, three of his novels placed on *The New York Times* bestseller list. His first Xanth novel, *A Spell for Chameleon*, won the August Derleth Fantasy Award as the best novel for 1977, and the Spokane Public Library gave him the Golden Pen Award for being their favorite fantasy author in 1982.